IT STARTED WITH A KISS

Miranda Dickinson has always had a head full of stories. From an early age she dreamed of writing a book that would make the heady heights of Kingswinford Library. Following a Performance Art degree, she began to write in earnest when a friend gave her The World's Slowest PC. She is also a singer-songwriter. Her first novel, *Fairytale of New York*, was a *Sunday Times* top ten international bestseller. *It Started with a Kiss* is her third novel.

To find out more about Miranda visit www.miranda-dickinson.com. If you want to know just what goes into the making of Miranda's novels, including exclusive book extras, deleted scenes and details about Miranda's newsletters, her blog is the place to visit. Coffee and Roses is also the home of Miranda's popular blog, *It Started with a Kiss* – a video diary that follows the progress of her novel and gives you a unique insight into the life of a writer. Visit Coffee and Roses at www.coffeeandroses.blogspot.com

Merry Christmas Rebecca!
Lots of love
mum & dad
xxx

By the same author

Fairytale of New York
Welcome to my World

MIRANDA DICKINSON

It Started with a Kiss

AVON

AVON

A division of HarperCollins*Publishers*
77–85 Fulham Palace Road,
London W6 8JB

www.harpercollins.co.uk

A Paperback Original 2011

3

A catalogue record for this book is
available from the British Library

ISBN-13: 978-1-84756-167-1

Set in Sabon LT Std by Palimpsest Book Production Limited,
Falkirk, Stirlingshire

Printed and bound in Great Britain by
Clays Ltd, St Ives plc

MIX
Paper from
responsible sources
FSC™ C007454

I'm a big believer in following your heart – and that's so much easier to do when you have wonderful people believing in you. While writing and editing this book, I have been joined a merry band of lovelies who have watched my vlogs, tweeted with me and offered me so much enthusiasm and love. I hope this book is worth the wait for you!

Three books in, and I'm still blown away by everyone's support. Big thanks to my family and friends for their constant love, Julie Cohen for wise words and woops, Ritzi Cortez, Ella, Barry and Sue for help with narrowboat questions, Joanne Harris for the signal box wedding pictures and Serena at Combermere Abbey (www.combermereabbey.co.uk) for sharing your wonderful wedding venue with me. Thanks also to Vickie Pritchett (Mrs Bou) from The Boutique Baking Company (www.boutique-baking.co.uk) for providing magical cake inspiration for Auntie Mags. And, as ever, huge thanks to Kim Curran (Next Big Thing) for reading every draft, giving awesome advice and being a fab friend.

Massive thanks as always to my lovely editor Sammia

Rafique for her constant belief in me (and long phone chats!), and to the fabulous team at Avon, especially Claire Bord, Caroline Ridding and Charlotte Allen. Big thanks also to Rhian McKay and Anne Rieley.

Inspiration for my characters comes from everywhere, but this time several real-life lovelies have inspired characters in my story. Big love to Phil White (father-in-law-to-be and the inspiration for Uncle Dudley), Wayne McDonald (top bloke and the inspiration for D'Wayne) and my wonderful chums in The Peppermints wedding band (www.peppermintmusic.co.uk) for inspiring The Pinstripes (we're available for weddings, birthdays, events . . .!).

And last, but not least, thanks to my lovely fiancé, Bob – for putting up with tons of wedding research, being my constant cheerleader and making me smile. I can't wait to marry you next year!

This book is about following your heart. I hope it inspires you to follow yours. xx

For the Peppermints:
Andi, Clarko, Dan, Ed, Phil and Susanna.
The best friends ever.

'I dwell in possibility.'
Emily Dickinson

Set List

CHAPTER ONE

The most wonderful time of the year

When it comes to telling your best friend that you love him, there are generally two schools of thought. One strongly advises against it, warning that you could lose a friend if they don't feel the same way. The other urges action because, unless you say something, you might miss out on the love of your life.

Unfortunately for me, I listened to the latter.

The look in Charlie's midnight blue eyes said it all: I had just made the biggest mistake of my life . . .

'*Sorry?*'

Perhaps he hadn't heard me the first time. Maybe I should say it again?

'I said I love you, Charlie.'

He blinked. 'You're not serious, are you?'

'Yes.' I could feel a deathly dragging sensation pulling my hope to oblivion.

Gone was the trademark Charlie grin that had been so firmly in place only moments before. In its place was a look I didn't recognise, but I knew it wasn't a good alternative.

'H-how long have you . . .?'

I dropped my gaze to the potted plant beside our table. 'Um – a long time, actually.' Maybe I should have worn something a bit more 'potential girlfriend material' today? But then this morning when I pulled on my trusty jeans and purple sweater dress I wasn't expecting to have this conversation. And judging by the look of sheer horror on Charlie's face, it wouldn't have made a difference if I had been sitting opposite him in a designer gown and diamonds. This was *such* a mistake . . .

'But . . . we're *mates*, Rom.'

'Yeah, of course we are. Look, forget I said anything, OK?'

He was staring at his latte like it had just insulted him. 'I don't know how you expect me to do that. You've *said it* now, haven't you? I mean it's – it's *out there*.'

I looked around the busy coffee shop. It was overcrowded with disgruntled Christmas shoppers huddled ungratefully around too-small tables on chairs greedily snatched from unsuspecting single customers. 'I think it's safe to assume that none of that lot heard anything.'

As attempts at humour go, it wasn't my finest. I took a large gulp of coffee and wished myself dead.

Charlie shook his head. 'That doesn't matter. *I* heard it. Oh, Rom – why did you say that? Why couldn't you just have . . .?'

I stared at him. 'Just have what?'

'Just *not said anything*? I mean, why me? Why put this on me now?'

I hated the look of sheer panic in his eyes. He'd never looked at me that way before . . . In my perennial daydream about this moment it had been so very different:

Oh Romily – I've loved you forever, too. If you hadn't told me we could have missed each other completely . . .

2

'We're fine as we are, aren't we? I mean, if it's good then why change it? I can't believe you actually thought this would be a good idea.'

Well, *excuse me*, but I did. Somewhere between my ridiculous, obviously deluded heart and my big stupid mouth, my brain got pushed out of the picture and I – crazy, deranged *loon* that I am – found myself persuaded that I might be the answer to his dreams. That maybe the reason for the many hours we'd spent together – cheeky laughter-filled days and late night heart-to-hearts – was that we were destined to be more than friends. Everyone else noticed it: it had been a running joke among our friends that Charlie and I were like an old married couple. The 'Old Folks' – that's what they called us. We'd lost count of the number of times complete strangers mistook us for partners. So if it was this blindingly obvious to the world, how come Charlie couldn't see it?

Of course, I couldn't say any of this to him. Sheer embarrassment stole the clever arguments from my mind so that then and there, in the crowded café packed with people who couldn't care less about what I was saying, I found that all I could say was:

'I'm sorry.'

Charlie shook his head. 'I did *not* see this coming. I thought we were friends, that's all. But this – this is just *weird* . . .'

'Thanks for the vote of confidence, Charlie.'

He stared at me, confusion claiming his eyes. 'I-I didn't mean . . . Heck, Rom, I'm sorry – you've just got to give me a moment to get my head round this.'

I looked away and focused on a particularly harassed-looking couple talking heatedly at the next table over enormous mugs of cream-topped festive coffees. 'You don't appreciate me,' the woman was saying. Right now, I knew exactly how she felt.

'The thing is,' Charlie said, 'you've always been just *Rom* – one of the guys, you know? You're a laugh, someone I can hang out with. But now . . .' He was digging an impossible hole for himself and he knew it. He gave a massive sigh. 'I'm sorry. I'm really not sure how to deal with this.'

This was awful – I'd heard enough. I rose to my feet, intense pain and crushing embarrassment pushing my body up off the chair. I opened my mouth to deal a devastating parting shot, but nothing appeared. Instead, I turned and fled, stubbing my toe on a neighbouring customer's chair and tripping over various overstuffed shopping bags, almost taking a packed pushchair with me as I beat an ungraceful retreat from the coffee shop and out into the bustling street beyond.

Outside, Birmingham's famous Christmas Market was in full flow, packed with shoppers grabbing last-minute Christmas shopping and crowding around the wooden beer stalls. The coloured lights strung overhead glowed brightly against the greyness of the December afternoon sky and Christmas music blared relentlessly from speakers along the length of New Street.

'Rom! Where are you going? I'm sorry – please come back! *Rom!*' Behind me, Charlie's shouts blended into the blur of crowd noise and Christmas hits of yesteryear. I picked up my pace, making my way blindly against the tidal flow of bodies, their countless faces looming up before me, unsmiling and uncaring. I had humiliated myself enough already: the last thing I needed was for Charlie to come back for Round Two . . .

As I passed each shop front the sale signs began morphing

into condemnatory judgements of my actions, screaming at me from every lit window:

Insane!
Stupid idiot!
What were you thinking?

As the jostling crowd propelled me involuntarily towards the marble pillars of the Town Hall, Paul McCartney was singing 'Wonderful Christmastime' like it should have an ironic question mark at the end. Unable to wriggle free, I found myself moving along with the throng. But I felt nothing; my senses were numbed by the faceless bodies hemming me in, and my heart too beset by ceaseless echoes of Charlie's words to care any more. At a loss to make sense of the total catastrophe I'd just caused, I surrendered to the irresistible force of the crowd and, quite literally, went with the flow.

What was I *thinking* telling my best friend in the whole world that I loved him? I hadn't even planned to say it at all – and now I couldn't quite believe I had blurted out my biggest secret seemingly on a whim. One minute we were laughing about last week's gig, his smile so warm and his eyes lit up in the way they always do when he's talking about music; the next I was confessing the feelings for him I've been carrying for three years. What on earth made me think that was a good idea?

Maybe it was the impending arrival of the 'Most Wonderful Time of the Year' (thanks for nothing, Andy Williams) or the deliciously festive atmosphere filling the city today that had caused me to reveal my feelings to Charlie like that. Perhaps it was the influence of watching too many chick-flick Christmas scenes that had tipped my sanity over the edge and made the whole thing seem like such a great idea (Richard Curtis, Nora Ephron, guilty as charged).

Dumped unceremoniously by the crowd at the base of the grand stone staircase in Victoria Square, I managed to squeeze through a gap in the tightly-packed, slow-moving shoppers and emerged breathless into a small pocket of pine-scented air by the barriers around the base of the huge Swedish Christmas tree. Tears stung my eyes and I swallowed angrily in a vain attempt to keep them at bay. *What was the matter with me? How did I get it so devastatingly wrong?*

All the signs had been there, or so I had thought: hugs that lingered a moment too long; snatched glances and shy smiles during nights out with our friends; moments of unspoken understanding during conversations begun in the early evening and ending as birdsong heralded a new day. Then there were his unexplained silences – times when I felt he had something more to say, when unresolved question marks sparkled magnificently in the air between us and the room held its breath – ultimately in vain. There had been more of these lately, peppering almost every occasion we spent together with an irresistible spice of intrigue. If they didn't mean what I thought they meant, then what on earth were they all about?

My mobile phone rang in my bag, but I couldn't face answering the call, so Stevie Wonder continued his tinny rendition of 'Sir Duke' unhindered by my usual intervention. Reaching into the crummy depths of my coat pocket, I retrieved a crumpled shopping list and read down the list of scribbled names: my 'To-Do' list for the afternoon. It was the last Saturday before Christmas and my final chance to buy everyone's presents. Christmas shopping waited for no one, it seemed – not even thoroughly embarrassed owners of newly-shattered hearts.

Mum & Dad
Wren
Jack & Soph
Uncle Dudley and Auntie Mags
Tom & Anya
Charlie

Charlie. My breath caught in the back of my throat as my eye fell on the last name. *No need for that one to be there now*, I hissed under my breath. *I think he's had quite enough surprise gifts from me this year.* I stuffed the list back into my pocket and prepared to dive back into the undulating ocean of people.

'Rom!'

My head snapped upright in horror to see Charlie pushing his way through the crowd, further back down the street. *No*, this was *absolutely not* going to happen now. I couldn't face it – the lead-heavy mortification gripping my insides was already too much to bear. Turning on my heels, I pushed back into the crowd and ran on again.

'Oh come on, Rom! Just stop!' Charlie called behind me, closer this time.

Looking over my shoulder, I shouted back. 'Go home, Charlie!'

I saw him stop, throw his hands up in the air and turn back into the horde of shoppers behind him. Furious with myself for creating this awful situation, I wanted to put as much distance between me and the scene of my worst ever decision. Tears filled my eyes as I put on another sprint, rushing through the swarming mass of bodies. Part of me wanted Charlie to be following me, to catch me and say that he'd overreacted, that I hadn't been mistaken, but I knew that wasn't going to happen and I hated myself for wanting the impossible. Angrily, I wiped the tears from my eyes – just in time to see the gaudy wooden stall laden with soft toys appear directly in front of me a split second before my body slammed headlong into it.

A collective gasp rose from the crowd of shoppers as I tumbled, helpless limbs flailing, in an ungracious slow-motion sprawl. Bears, rabbits and reindeer spun in the air around me like a shower of oversized plush snowflakes and, for a moment, it was as if all noise ceased as I descended. The clamour of the crowd and the Christmas music receded and my senses were now aware only of the sensation of moving through the air. This feeling was short-lived, however, followed as it was by the inevitable gut-wrenching crack as my body hit the unforgiving block-paved ground and I skidded to a halt amid a sea of stuffed animals on the frosted pavement.

It took a moment for me to catch my breath, my ears buzzing from my head's heavy meeting with the floor, but then it was as if someone flicked a switch and all the light, noise and music of the Christmas Market roared back into life – along with the shock of an intense flood of pain along my back and the appearance of one very angry stallholder.

His beetroot-red round face appeared directly over me as I lay there, but instead of helping me up he launched into a tirade of thick German-accented abuse.

'Crazy woman! Look at this mess! It is ruined, ruined!'

Thoroughly embarrassed, I scrambled to my feet, wincing as my bruised limbs creaked and groaned back into an upright position.

'I'm sorry, I'm so sorry,' I mumbled, grabbing armfuls of toys and wishing I could disappear.

In true British fashion, the crowd around me didn't offer to help – the spectacle of the woman who trashed the toy stall frantically trying to reconstruct it far too much fun for them to intervene. The disgruntled stallholder didn't help either, standing by the remains of his stall with pudgy arms folded tight across his squat body as he watched me. As if I wasn't morbidly mortified enough already, I was vaguely aware that some of the onlookers had produced mobile phones and were now happily filming the scene. *Great.* All I needed after the events of today was to become the unwitting star of the latest YouTube viral sensation. I was cold, aching, unspeakably embarrassed and all I wanted was to get home as quickly as possible. Christmas was ruined now anyway: Charlie wouldn't want to see me and when the rest of the band found out what had happened, everything would be awkward there, too. Only Wren would understand – and no doubt even she would have a strong opinion on it.

I bit back tears as I reached out to scoop more of the fallen bears from the pavement . . .

. . . and that's when I saw him.

As my fingers closed around a toy penguin, I was suddenly aware of a gloved hand reaching out for a polar bear hand puppet next to it. Lifting my eyes I came face to face with quite the most gorgeous man I had ever seen. His hazel eyes caught the light from coloured Christmas lights above, while wavy strands of his russet-brown hair picked up the twinkling blue light from the fairy lights that framed the toy stall roof. A slight shadow of stubble edged his jawline and I noticed that his cheekbones were quite defined.

'Hi,' he said, his warm smile and kind eyes momentarily numbing the sting of my bruises. 'Need some help?'

I smiled back. 'Please.'

We slowly moved around each other, gathering up the

scattered stock. As we did so I was aware that he was watching me, his shy smile appearing whenever our eyes met. And I can't explain why, but the sudden arrival of this kind stranger after the utter awfulness of the afternoon felt like a blissful reprieve – as if everything I had experienced was merely instrumental in bringing me to this moment, this meeting.

Once we had retrieved all of the toys from the wide circle they had been flung to, I turned to the stallholder and apologised again.

'Whatever,' he shrugged, disappearing inside his wooden stall and slamming the door.

Spectacle over, the onlookers dispersed back into the crowd and the stranger and I were left alone by the stall.

'Thank you,' I said.

'You're welcome,' he replied, pushing his hands into his coat pockets. I noticed tiny crinkles appearing at the corners of his eyes when he smiled.

For a moment, we stood in silence, our breath rising in puffs of Christmas-light-washed steam. It was clear that neither of us knew what to say and the awkwardness of the silence brought my earlier humiliation flooding back.

He's obviously just being polite, I reasoned, my heart sinking, *and now he's looking for an excuse to leave.*

'Well, I'd better . . .' I nodded in the direction of the Town Hall behind us, as though this would be some universal indicator of the Christmas shopping I still had to do before I could go home. Thankfully, he seemed to under-stand, nodding and looking down at his feet.

'Of course.'

'Thanks again.'

He raised his lovely eyes once again to mine. 'No problem. Merry Christmas.'

As I hurried away, I felt like screaming. Not content with

merely ruining my friendship with Charlie and making a complete idiot of myself in full view of a large section of city shoppers, I had now embarrassed myself in front of a really good-looking bloke. Nice work, Romily.

My shoulder was complaining vociferously as I reached into my coat pocket again for the list. At times like this, practicality was the only way forward. I headed towards the white lights of the craft market section. My aunt loves hand-painted glass and I vaguely remembered seeing a glass ornament stall earlier that day. Forcing my conflicting thoughts to the back of my mind, I wove my way through the dawdling shoppers until I found it.

Two middle-aged ladies wrapped up against the bitter December air were chatting animatedly behind the stall, oblivious to everything else. The voice of Nat King Cole was crooning from the speakers of a small CD player on the counter.

'Gotta love a bit of old Nat, eh?' the taller of the two was saying.

'Tell me about it. Our Eth won't listen to anything else at Christmas.'

'Not even Bing or Frank?'

'Nope. It's Nat or nothing. Him and his chestnuts roasting on an open fire.'

'Always thought that sounded a bit painful myself,' the taller lady sniggered as the shorter one giggled.

I relaxed a little as their jovial banter continued, casting my gaze across the glass baubles of all shapes and sizes, suspended on delicate silver thread from white-painted twigs set in plant pots. A gentle breeze had sprung up, making the hanging glass shapes shiver and spin slowly, so that they caught the light from the white fairy lights woven around the stall edge and the coloured strings of Christmas lights swinging high over the market. One particular bauble near the front of the display immediately caught my eye: a large, teardrop-shaped ornament adorned with tiny painted silver stars – delicate brushstrokes that sparkled from the glass surface. It was beautiful, a real work of craftsmanship, and I knew my aunt would adore it. I reached out and felt the icy coolness of the glass against my fingers.

'It's beautiful, isn't it?' a deep voice said behind my right ear, making me jump and only just manage to save the bauble from falling from its twig. Leaving it safely spinning, I turned, my eyes first meeting a green, brown and cream striped scarf and then heading north to reach the shy smile of the stranger who had helped me. My breath caught in the back of my throat and I nodded dumbly at him.

'I'm sorry to . . . er . . . I just wanted to check you were OK?'

'I'm fine. Thanks again for helping me.'

'You're welcome. I couldn't believe all those people were just watching.'

I smiled, despite the blush I knew was glowing from my cheeks. 'I think they thought I was part of the entertainment.'

'Some entertainment,' he laughed, almost immediately hiding his amusement when he saw my expression. 'So – you're OK? I mean, you aren't hurt or anything?'

His concern was touching but bearing in mind the afternoon I'd had, the last thing I needed was the pity of a gorgeous man. 'All good. Nothing broken.'

'Good.' He stared at me and this time there was something more in his eyes than concern. 'Look, this is going to sound mental, so I'm just going to say it. I couldn't let you go without telling you that you're beautiful. That's why I followed you here. Please don't think I'm a psycho or that

12

I do this a lot: I don't. But you're beautiful and I think you should know that.'

Stunned, I opened my mouth to reply, but just then a shout from behind us caused him to turn.

'Mate, we've got to go . . . *Now!*'

What happened next was so fast that even now the details remain frustratingly sparse in my mind. But here's what I know.

When he turned back to face me, the way he looked at me took my breath away. It was the kind of look you see in movies when a bridegroom turns to see his bride walking towards him for the first time: a heady, overpowering mix of shock, surprise and all-encompassing, heart-stopping love. It was the look that Charlie *should have* given me when I told him I loved him. But this wasn't Charlie; and that, in itself, was part of the problem. Because – apart from *not* being the man to whom I had publicly expressed my undying love not half an hour beforehand – *this* person was almost perfect: from his wide, honest eyes and shy smile, to the woody scent of his cologne now surrounding me.

But most of all because of what happened next . . .

He took a step back and I could see a battle raging in his eyes as the voice behind him called again, more insistent this time.

'We have to go – come on!'

'One minute,' he called back, just as a hurrying shopper crashed into his shoulder, momentarily throwing him off balance – and straight into my arms.

In utter surprise, I held on to him and his strong arms reached round to cradle my back. The shock of it blew all thoughts of Charlie instantly from my mind. Heart racing, I gazed up into his eyes.

'I'm so sorry, I have to go,' he whispered, his lips inches from mine. 'But you're beautiful.'

And then, he kissed me.

Although our lips touched for the smallest of moments, it was unlike anything else I've experienced. It was the type of kiss you only expect to see in Hollywood films, finally uniting the two leads as the credits start to roll over the delicious tones of Nat King Cole. In fact, even the soundtrack was perfect because at that very moment Mr Cole himself began crooning 'Have Yourself a Merry Little Christmas' via the muffled speakers of the bauble stall's CD player. All thoughts of Christmas shopping dissolved from my mind as I closed my eyes and gave in to the unexpected gift of the stranger's lips on mine.

It was almost perfect. *Almost*. But not quite. Because, as suddenly as he had appeared, he was gone: swallowed up by the heaving, unyielding mass of shoppers. I remained frozen to the spot for what felt like an age, dazed yet elated, my heart beating wildly.

And then, from somewhere deep in the recesses of my consciousness, a thought began to push urgently through the swirling mass of emotions.

Go after him!

'Wait! Come back!'

I looked in the direction I thought he had gone, but there was no sign of him. Nevertheless, I began to shove my way through the crowds, rising on tiptoes to scan across the sea of bobbing bodies for a glimpse of his hair or his scarf as I ran. Shoppers tutted as I pushed past, but I was a woman on a mission and oblivious to their disapproving glances.

As I neared the end of the line of wooden stalls, I suddenly caught a glimpse of russet-brown hair, hurrying ahead of me. Heart thumping hard against my chest, I pressed on, gaining on him. Soon, I was within touching distance, so I reached out my hand and tapped his shoulder.

'Hey, you can't just kiss me and then leave without giving me your name,' I said. He turned to face me . . . and my heart plummeted.

'That's one hell of a chat-up line, love,' the older man grinned. His yellowing teeth and pockmarked skin were anything but kissable. 'Now I don't know about any kiss but I'm happy to oblige if you want.'

I recoiled, dropping my gaze as I backed away. 'I'm sorry. I thought you were someone else.'

'Story of my life, chick,' he laughed as I hurried back towards the safety of the Christmas Market stalls. Utterly deflated, I stopped and looked up at the darkening sky, heavy with snow-laden clouds. I had lost him.

How was it possible for something so amazing to happen and then disappear as quickly as it had arrived? And how *stupid* was I for not asking his name? At least then I would know something tangible about him. My scarf still retained traces of his cologne and my lips were tingling from our brief kiss, but that was all I had to show for an event so significant it might just have changed everything.

All I knew about him was what I could remember. To all intents and purposes, he was just another stranger existing in a sprawling metropolis – another life lived in parallel to mine, with little chance of meeting again. But when he looked into my eyes and kissed me, I felt like I had known him all my life. More than an attraction, there was a connection that resonated deeper within me than any other. That one single meeting in a lifetime of acquaintance was enough to alter my life irrevocably.

And that's why I had to find him.

CHAPTER TWO

Dream a little dream of me

'He's a *psycho*.'

'He is *not*.'

'Or some kind of twisted stalker . . .'

'Wren, he wasn't like that.'

'How do you know? He could have been walking round kissing random female shoppers all day! He could get his sick, evil kicks out of doing that . . .' Wren's cocoa brown eyes opened wide. '*Maybe* he kisses the women he's about to murder in cold blood . . . Oh-my-giddy-*life*, you've just had a *Judas* kiss!'

I let out a long sigh as I sank into Wren's oversized sofa in her chic city-centre apartment. 'I wish I hadn't told you about it now.'

Wren placed a concerned hand on my arm. 'No, Rom, you were absolutely right to tell me. If only so I could stop you making a *terrible* mistake!'

Sometimes I wonder how I came to have a friend quite as theatrical as Wren. But then, being a drama teacher, I suppose it's something of an occupational hazard for her.

I wasn't sure I wanted to hear this now, but I was still

reeling from the events of the day before. In a daze, following the stranger's hasty departure, I had stumbled to the train station in a fog of emotion and shock. Slumped in my seat, mind numb, I had called the only person who would understand. Wren has been my closest friend since primary school and she's known Charlie almost as long as I have. Initially, she insisted that I catch a train back into the city and head straight for her home, but all I really wanted to do was to sleep. So instead she made me promise to visit her the next day.

After a restless night with images of Charlie and the gorgeous stranger interchanging in my mind, I arrived at Wren's chic canalside apartment, just along from the elegant bars and restaurants of Brindley Place.

Eyes wide with concern, Wren had listened quietly as I relayed the events of the previous day; but as soon as I finished she launched into an impassioned commentary.

'The way I see it, this bloke is just a diversion from the real issue – you and Charlie. I mean, come on, Rom, one minute you're telling Charlie you love him and then you "just happen" to meet the love of your life?'

'It doesn't make sense, I know. But honestly, Wren, it was the most intense, amazing moment. He took my breath away . . .'

'And your mind off Charlie.'

This was useless. 'Forget I mentioned it, OK?'

Wren gave me her best impression of a serious look (which, in truth, is about as serious as engaging in a staring contest with a fluffy kitten . . .). 'Oh, Rom, I'm sorry. It's just that you have to admit it's a bit odd. Someone you've never met appears out of nowhere, does the knight-in-shining-armour bit and then *kisses* you. What kind of crazed, maniacal freak does things like that?

And if he thinks you're so amazing, how come he didn't stick around?'

I had been asking myself that very question ever since it happened. 'I don't know.' The events of our encounter remained imprisoned behind a frustrating haze. Whatever – or whoever – had called him away had seemed important; but then I'd hardly had sufficient time to know anything about him, so how could I really know what was important to him? 'That's the problem: I have no answers. All I can say is that it was the most amazing moment I've ever experienced. He was . . . perfect.'

'He was a *nutter*. Believe me, hun, you're better off not knowing who he was. I've chased handsome princes before and they've always turned into proper fairytales.'

'Isn't that a good thing?'

'No – I mean *Grimm*.' Seeing my face she quickly hid her mirth. 'Sorry, bad joke.'

I shook my head. 'I know it's crazy. But I can't stop thinking about him.'

'Thank *heaven* you had the good sense to come here, then! Are you feeling OK now? Do you need anything?'

'I'm fine . . .'

Wren snapped her fingers. 'Tea! That's what you need – hot, strong, sweet tea!' She jumped up and dashed into her smart-yet-bijou kitchen before I had a chance to protest. Cupboard doors banged, crockery clanked and spoons jangled in mugs as the one-woman whirlwind noisily prepared my unwanted beverage. 'Tea is the best thing for shock, trust me. Or is that brandy? I can never remember . . .'

'Tea will be fine, thanks,' I called back quickly. The last thing I needed was Wren's idea of a 'shot' of brandy (to everyone else, that's about a quarter of a bottle).

Despite her diminutive stature, Wren can drink more alcohol than me, Charlie and all our friends put together.

Ugh, Charlie. In the craziness of the past hour, I had almost forgotten the gut-churningly awful reality of his reaction, but now it made its horrific return to my innards.

'How did you leave things with Charlie?' Wren asked, once she had thrust a scalding hot, impossibly sweet cup of tea into my hands.

I shuddered as embarrassment launched another crushing onslaught on my guts. 'I didn't. I just legged it. I was *so* mortified, Wren. I mean, what on earth was I thinking, telling him how I felt?'

Wren grimaced. 'I bet you felt a right prat.' Seeing my expression, she raised her hands to her mouth. 'Oh, Rom, I'm sorry! That came out wrong.'

'Don't worry. It's accurate. I just don't understand how I got it so wrong.'

'I don't think you did – at least, that's what all of us thought would happen, sooner or later. But you know Charlie. He's a typical bloke, head goes straight in the sand the moment he's challenged on anything. You know that.'

Without thinking, I drank some tea, recoiling in horror as the high sugar content grated against my teeth. Wren completely misread my reaction and grinned with pride.

'See, I *told* you tea was the answer.'

Not wanting to hurt her feelings, I swallowed, even though every fibre of my being was screaming at me not to. 'Thanks.'

'You're welcome. So did you get the bloke's name?'

I shook my head. 'I just wish you could have been there. He was amazing – just calmly helped me while everyone else stared.' I stood and walked over to the window to gaze out at the tiny slice of the cosmopolitan city heart outside. The afternoon light was fading as Christmas lights from the surrounding apartments, restaurants and bars were reflected in the canal four storeys below. Festive city revellers hurried by on the frozen towpath, muffled up against the arctic weather. 'And he's out there, somewhere, right now . . .'

Wren appeared by my side, watching me carefully. 'He's really got to you, hasn't he?'

I nodded, the memory of his lips brushing mine suddenly bright in my mind. 'I'm honestly not using this as a diversion. I want to find him again.'

'Right. Come with me.' Wren grabbed my hand and yanked me towards the front door.

'Where are we going?'

'To find him, of course!'

'What? Wait . . .'

'We *can't* wait, Rom! We need to find him *now*!'

'But we also need coats?'

Wren looked down at her thin jumper, jeans and large pink fluffy slippers. 'Ah. Absolutely. And *then* we're going!'

One of the things I love the most about Wren is her ability to get things done. Although the lightning-fast change in her attitude to my handsome stranger was a bit of a curveball, there was no doubting the fact that when Wren Malloy puts her mind to something, nothing can shake her from her chosen course of action.

'Wren, it happened yesterday. He won't be there,' I protested as we flew along the canalside and across the bridge to the city centre.

'I know. But there might still be some people around who remember him,' Wren called back, dodging shoppers

20

laden with last-minute Christmas shopping. 'And you need to keep his image fresh in your mind.'

When the small wooden stalls came into view, I pulled up to a halt. 'Wren, stop.'

She stared at me, wild auburn curls blowing about her face. 'What now?'

'Why are you doing this?'

'Eh?'

'Five minutes ago you thought he was a twisted psycho stalker. And then you drag me out here like your life depends on it. I don't understand . . .'

She took a breath and smiled at me. 'You're my best friend. So I'm here to support you.'

Genuinely touched by this, I smiled back. 'Thank you.'

'And anyway, maybe if we go down this route you'll get it out of your system.'

'Ah.'

Wren looked around. 'So, where did you meet him?'

I looked around. With the arrival of a new day the whole Christmas Market had taken on a magical appearance, the brightly coloured lights that framed each stall reflecting in the damp pavements, while the blazing glow from the whirling carousel illuminated the windows of the surrounding buildings. The air temperature had dropped considerably and tiny white flakes of snow swirled in the air above the bustling market stalls. For a moment it was hard to get my bearings.

'I think it was near the beginning of the craft market,' I answered, 'or at least, that's where he kissed me. The stall I demolished was further down New Street because we walked a little afterwards. But it's all a bit of a blur to be honest.'

'Well, let's start at the kiss and work backwards,' Wren suggested, hugging my arm. 'Where did that happen?'

'By a stall with hand-painted glass tree baubles.'

We followed the line of craft stalls, passing displays of garish felt hats, jewellery, delicate silk scarves and hand-dipped candles until Wren let out a squeal and tugged at my arm. 'There!'

My heart began racing as we approached the stall, memories of the stranger's concerned questions, his breath on my face and *that* kiss suddenly bombarding my mind. The large, teardrop-shaped bauble was still hanging from its silver-painted twig in the mottled gold pot at the front of the stall, exactly as it had been when he caught up with me. Shivers chased each other up my spine as my fingers brushed its lustrous surface.

'I was here – looking at this – when he reached me.' I closed my eyes and remembered the warmth of his gentle voice behind my ear, the light touch of his hand on my shoulder.

Wren was already summoning the attention of the stallholder. 'Excuse me?'

'Yes, love?'

'This might sound a bit weird, but we're looking for a man.'

The lady behind the counter let out a cracked, throaty laugh that could only have been created by a serious nicotine intake over many years. 'Aren't we all, dearie! That's what I want for Christmas, eh, Sylv?'

'Ooh too right, Aud,' laughed the short woman beside her who was swathed in so many woollen layers she resembled a forty-something rainbow-hued sheep.

'No, I don't think you understand,' Wren pressed on, undaunted. 'You see, it's a particular man we're looking for . . .'

'That's the beauty of youth,' Sylvia grinned back. 'When

you get to our age, chick, the ones that *aren't that* particular are the only ones we're likely to get!' The two ladies launched into cackles again and Wren shrugged helplessly at me.

'It was yesterday,' I explained. 'I was looking at this bauble and then a guy joined me. He was about six feet tall, with russet-brown hair and a green, brown and cream striped scarf?'

The stallholders' laughter ebbed and Audrey leaned towards me across the fragile glass ornaments. 'What time was this?'

I made a mental calculation. 'Just after two o'clock, I think.'

Audrey made a loud sucking noise of air through her teeth, not unlike the sound my father makes whenever I mention the band I sing with. 'Trouble is, kid, there's been a fair old bunch of good-looking young men past this stall the last few days. All panicking over presents for their mums, bless 'em.'

'He kissed her,' Wren offered. 'And then he disappeared.'

'Ooh, now hold on a tick,' Sylvia replied, her frost-flushed cheeks reddening further with the mental effort. 'Come to think of it, there was a young man we noticed kissing a girl.' Gesturing enthusiastically at me, she added, 'Turn around, chick!'

I obeyed and the two women engaged in some excited muttering until Sylvia instructed me to turn back.

'Now, it's only vague, love, but I do remember something like that happening.'

'Really? Can you remember anything else? About his face, or whether he gave a name?'

Audrey laughed. 'Well, you should know, love. You were a lot closer to him than we were.'

It was clear that this was as far as the conversation could go. 'Well, thank you anyway,' I replied. Wren was still chatting with Audrey and Sylvia as I began to walk slowly away. I was slightly disappointed by their lack of memory but encouraged by the fact that I obviously hadn't dreamt the whole thing. Tracing my steps back past the Town Hall and down towards the start of New Street, I tried to piece together my flight from the toy stall.

Footsteps behind me heralded Wren's arrival and she reached my side, panting slightly, stuffing her hands into her pockets. 'So, that's a start, right?'

I smiled. 'Absolutely. Look, you don't have to do this, you know.'

'I know. But now I know you weren't hallucinating, I'm actually quite excited about the whole thing.' She nudged me with her shoulder. 'It's like something out of a chick-flick, isn't it? The handsome stranger, the sudden meeting, the kiss that should be accompanied by a Randy Newman score . . .'

'Apart from the fact that we have no idea where the leading man is,' I reminded her, thrilled by the analogy nevertheless.

'Pah, *details*. So where next?'

I gazed down the slope of stalls towards a beer bar with strange rotating wooden slats and large polar bear on top. 'There was a toy stall down that way – that's what I collided with.'

'Excellent. And seeing as you more or less demolished the stall, you should be easy to remember.'

Wren has *such* a way with words sometimes . . .

I could feel a cold sweat beading around my neck under my scarf as we headed towards the site of yesterday's second-most mortifying moment. My right arm and shoulder still burned from their sudden meeting with the wooden stall frontage and my cheeks were burning now, too. How had I managed to lose my carefully constructed sense of self-dignity *twice* in one day, in such spectacular fashion? Inevitably, my thoughts strayed to the first such instance and I felt my heart plummet as the memory of Charlie's horrified expression returned. If Wren was correct in her assertion that my preoccupation with the handsome stranger was a diversionary tactic to stop me thinking about Charlie, then it wasn't working very well. Angrily, I shook his face from my mind and turned my attention to the task at hand.

The toy stall was further down New Street than I remembered and I was surprised to see how far the stranger had walked to reach me in the craft market. He must have really wanted to find me. This thought thrilled me. Surely it proved that he was somebody special, that he saw something in me worth chasing after?

When the jumbled pile of plush toys and hand puppets came into view, I braced myself for the abuse bound to flow from the portly male stallholder, but was surprised to see a lanky, bespectacled youth manning the stall instead.

'I can help you, yes?' he asked in a broad German accent, his adolescent eyes drinking in every detail of my best friend as she flashed him her brightest smile.

'I hope so,' she purred, all wide eyes and batting lashes. Even wrapped up in her multicoloured patchwork coat and long black pashmina scarf with its glinting silver sequins, the effect this had on her quarry was considerable. I resisted the urge to laugh, marvelling at Wren's impressive attention-commanding skills. 'I wonder if you remember my friend?'

25

The lanky boy's greasy brows lifted as he surveyed me, clearly congratulating himself at his obvious irresistibility to English women. 'For sure I would *like* to remember you,' he replied, giving me what he judged to be a devastating look.

'No, you don't understand. My friend knocked over your toys yesterday.' Wren pointed animatedly at the drop-down display area.

'Oh, I heard that, *ja*. But I was not here then: it was my brother. He said toys were everywhere.'

Wren clapped her hands as I tried my best to ignore the creeping warmth flushing my face. 'Brilliant! So did your brother tell you about the man who helped my friend to pick up the toys?'

The teenager's expression muddied and then he nodded. 'For sure. There was a guy who was the only one to help.'

Instantly, I forgot my embarrassment. 'That's it! Did he say what the man looked like?'

'I dunno.' He shrugged. 'He just said a young man. That's all I know.'

Wren nodded at me. 'Right, I see. And when will your brother be back on the stall?'

'Oh, he doesn't work this stall. He's one of the organisers here. He was just looking after it for the day.' He winked at Wren and went in for the kill. 'So, you want a beer with me after we close tonight? Birmingham is a beautiful city but a little lonely . . .'

'It's tempting, but I can't, I'm afraid. Have to get my Christmas shopping done, you know how it is . . .' She linked her arm through mine and we walked away, leaving the gawping German youth behind us. 'OK, after that thrilling encounter I need a coffee.'

We made our way slowly through the crowds, pushing

through the flow of people to the very coffee shop where I had made my devastating confession to Charlie. I was thankful that the large leather sofa at the back of the coffee shop was available so I didn't have to sit by the window where everything had changed.

Wren arrived with two enormous cups of frothy cappuccino and two slabs of sticky chocolate cake. 'Caffeine and sugar – just what you need!' she announced, unwinding her long black scarf and removing her coat before sitting beside me. 'So, he's real, then.'

'I told you he was real. At least now you believe me.'

'I do. Actually, I'm starting to think that maybe he might not be a psycho after all.'

'Well, thank you. What changed your mind?'

Wren leaned back, her elfin frame almost disappearing into the sofa altogether. 'I was thinking about it as we were retracing your steps: he was the only one to help you put the toy display back together and even when you said you were fine he still followed you to make sure. If he was some idiot after a cheap thrill, I doubt he'd have been so committed. And he was obviously memorable enough for the ladies at the bauble stall to remember him – albeit vaguely. I just can't work out why he didn't stick around.'

'I told you, he was called away.'

'Yes, but who by? Can you remember whether the voice was male or female?'

'Male.'

'Right. So, best case scenario: mate. Worst case scenario: *boyfriend*.'

I spluttered into my cappuccino. 'Come off it, Wren, he wasn't gay.'

'How do you know? I mean, good looking, well dressed,

27

tidy . . . He might have been kissing you for a bet or having a quick "swing the other way" . . . OK, OK, I'm joking. But he could have a girlfriend or, worse, a *wife*.'

I twisted to face her. 'Then why did whoever called him away let him kiss me?'

She shrugged and speared a large chunk of chocolate cake with her fork. 'Maybe that's *why* he was calling him away . . .'

I didn't want to consider the possibility, yet I found myself trying to recall whether I had seen a ring on his left hand as he helped me retrieve the scattered stock from the damp pavement. Frustratingly, I couldn't. But he *couldn't* be married, could he? The way he looked at me, the way he kissed me – it was as if he was seeing a woman he wanted to be with for the first time. I felt . . . *cherished*, strange as that sounds; it was as if he were cradling a precious jewel he had no intention of letting go.

But he had let me go, hadn't he?

Wren pushed her curls behind her ears. 'Anyway, forget all that. Tell me about the *kiss*.'

So I told her, replaying the detail of our brief encounter that had been on ceaseless repeat in my mind all night and throughout today: how I felt so utterly safe in his embrace, how soft and warm his lips were on mine; how the whole city seemed suspended in time around us; and how I never for a moment questioned what was happening because it felt so right . . .

'Like you were coming home, eh?' Wren finished my sentence with a wistful look in her eyes.

I nodded. 'That's exactly how it felt. And I know it sounds cheesy but it didn't feel contrived or cheap at all. I was just sharing this amazing moment with someone my heart knew. Does any of this make sense?'

She smiled. 'Absolutely, hun. Although personally I wouldn't have let him leave after a kiss like that.'

I felt my shoulders drop as I took a slurp of frothy coffee. 'I know. I've gone over and over it in my mind and I still can't work out why I didn't just hang on to him until he gave me his number. Or at least his name. But I couldn't move for a moment – I think I might have been in shock – so by the time I realised I had to go after him he'd disappeared. And now I have nothing to remind me of him other than my memory.'

Wren patted my hand. 'Well, not exactly,' she said, reaching into her coat pocket, producing a pink and white striped paper bag and handing it to me. 'I thought this could serve as a memento of a momentous experience.'

Surprised, I opened the crumpled paper and slowly unwrapped the yellow tissue-papered object inside. To my utter amazement, I gazed down to see the beautiful teardrop-shaped bauble from the glass ornament stall, its tiny silver painted stars sparkling in the coffee shop lights.

'Oh Wren, *thank you*!'

Wren put an arm around me and squeezed my shoulders. 'You deserve it, sweets. Let this remind you that there is at least one amazing bloke in the city who thinks you're beautiful – although with those sea green eyes of yours and gorgeous smile I'd hazard a guess that he's not alone.'

I laughed at this. For as long as I've known her, Wren has been obsessed with the colour of my eyes, despite being one of the most amazing-looking women I know. Her own cocoa brown eyes and fiery red ringlets are stunning, but she's always said how she'd love eyes 'the colour of the sea in summer', which is how she describes mine. We're quite different in our style – Wren is every bit as flamboyant in her clothes as she is in everything else she does. Yet somehow her crazy, unique way of pairing colours together always works. If I tried to carry off some of her looks, I'd look like some kind of strange hippy, but Wren makes it look arty and gorgeous. We work well together, each a visual foil to the other. My shoulder-length hair has been several colours over the years (blonde, red and even black in my teens) but the dark blonde I've settled on now works best, I think. While Wren spends hours internet shopping for kooky, one-off fashions, I love my high street shops – and I know that we love each other's style. But it's funny how we're never satisfied with what we've been given looks-wise. 'You're good for my ego, Wren.'

'And you're good for mine. That's why you need my help to find this chap of yours.'

'And how exactly are we going to do that?'

'I don't know. But we'll think of something. Now, gorgeous kissing strangers aside, what are you going to do about Charlie?'

I shuddered as a cold shower of reality hit me. 'I have no idea.'

'He hasn't called you?'

'I haven't answered.'

Truth be told, Charlie had been calling and texting me almost constantly since my ill-fated confession, but I just couldn't face talking to him – not yet. Right on cue, my mobile buzzed as a text message arrived.

PLEASE talk to me Rom. Cx

'Maybe you should call him.'

'What would I say? I made such a fool of myself, Wren.

I still can't work out how I ever thought that saying I loved him was a good idea.'

Wren let out a groan. 'Rom, we *all* thought you and Charlie would get it together one day. Everyone notices how close you two have become – I mean, even my *mother* and, let's be honest, everyone knows she isn't the brightest button in the box. So he panicked when you told him. So what? It's understandable. After all, you did kind of spring it on him. But I'll tell you one thing: he's an idiot if he can't see how perfect you are for each other. You guys have always been the Old Folks – the whole band says so.'

'That doesn't matter now. The Old Folks thing is officially dead.'

'Well, it blatantly isn't, if he's trying to talk to you. And anyway, what about all the gigs we've got in the next few months? Tom said yesterday that Dwayne has finally delivered some quality bookings for next year. Whether you like it or not, we need you and Charlie to at least be on speaking terms because, while I love you both, I need the money. My overdraft is scarier than watching *The Exorcist* in the dark.'

'It'll be fine, I'm sure. It's just awkward at the moment but I don't want it to be difficult for the rest of the band. I'll work it out eventually. But I think I just need to lay low for a couple of days.'

Wren's mobile rang. Turning the screen towards me, her expression was pure seriousness. 'So what do I tell him now?'

Panic froze me to the spot. 'Don't tell him I'm here, please!'

She glared at me and answered the call. 'Hey, dude. Yeah, I'm fine. You? Ah, right . . . Rom? No, hun, I haven't seen her. I spoke to her earlier but . . .' she shot me a look '. . . I think she just needs some time, Charlie. What? I'll tell her – um – when I see her, yeah. Take care, you. Bye.'

I breathed a sigh of relief. 'Thank you.'

'That is absolutely the one and only time I'm doing that for you, Rom. You need to call him. The poor guy's frantic.'

I let out a sigh. 'I'll call him tomorrow.'

Wren picked up my phone from the coffee table and thrust it into my hand. 'No, Rom. Text him tonight, at least. And in the meantime let me work out how you can find the Phantom Kisser of the Christmas Market, OK?'

Of course, I knew she was right. Charlie and I had been friends for too long to let something even as devastatingly embarrassing as this jeopardise our friendship. And *then* there was the band . . .

The Pinstripes have been together for nearly seven years. We formed because of a drunken idea at one of the many house parties hosted by my friends Jack and Sophie. Wren's newly-engaged friend Naomi had been bemoaning the lack of decent wedding bands in the area and joked that we should form a band to fit the bill. To be honest, it was a wonder that none of us had thought of it before; between us we had two singers (one of whom was also a bass player), a drummer, a keyboard player, a lead guitarist and a saxophone player – and all of us were struggling in second-rate bands where we didn't quite fit in. At the time I was singing jazz standards to increasingly bemused diners at a pizza restaurant chain with Jack; Charlie was playing drums in a Jam tribute band (and hating every moment); Sophie was stuck

32

playing saxophone with a group of easy-listening-obsessed over-forties; while Tom and Wren were lying about their age in a teenage thrash metal band called R.T.A. (which truly defined the term 'car crash'). As with many other ideas hatched at three am under the influence of copious amounts of red wine and sambuca, the suggestion was unanimously deemed *brilliant* and The Pinstripes made their magnificent entrance on to the function band scene.

Since then, we have survived nightmare gigs, power-cuts, fistfights (mercifully not involving any of the band) and more than one dodgy middle-aged lothario trying to storm the stage – and have emerged relatively intact and moderately successful. Sophie decided to bow out after two years when she was promoted to Head of Music at the local comprehensive school where she works but we still occasionally coax her back if we're playing a particularly gorgeous venue. While we all hold down day jobs, the band is a bit of fun and a welcome source of extra cash.

Added to this, it's a veritable education in How To and How *Not* To Do a Wedding. It never ceases to amaze me just how awful other people's weddings can be. It's a constant source of amusement to us all, not least to Wren and I, who pore over each successively horrific detail with unrestrained glee. Then there are the weddings that are truly inspirational – when everything seems to come together at once and the adrenalin rush sends your head giddy. These we hold in high regard and recall in hushed tones because they are evidence that what we're doing is more than simply paying the bills. The guys in the band are a bit more cynical about it all, but even they have been known to shed the odd telltale tear at certain moving celebrations.

I've sung with several bands throughout my life, but I can honestly say that nothing beats performing with my best friends. There's a different level of understanding than I've experienced with any other musicians – it's like we all know what the others are thinking. And I love it.

Gig stories form a central part of any conversation when we all get together. It's something that has built a rock-solid bond between the members of the band, but can be a cause of irritation to the non-musician partners among us, who frequently pull faces and moan when tales of songs that went wrong and strange weddings we've played at begin floating across the dinner table on a Saturday night at Jack and Soph's. We all keep saying that we should try harder to curb the stories when non-band members are present, but it's kind of a default setting for us; usually by the time we've realised what we're doing, we've been happily swapping tales for hours. I'm not proud of it, but the gig stories have definitely caused casualties. Although Wren won't admit it, the closeness of the band was one of the major reasons that Matt, her last boyfriend, didn't stick around for long. Sophie told me he asked Wren to choose between The Pinstripes and him. The rest, as they say, is history.

Of course, there are numerous challenges to being in a function band: the sheer logistics of getting five über-busy people together for rehearsals; the internal squabbles that occasionally rear their ugly heads; the stressful load-ins and sound-checks; the late finishes and the often long journeys home in the early hours of the morning, knowing that there's a van packed with equipment to unload before you can get to bed. But despite everything, it's great to be able to hang out with your mates and get paid for it – something that makes all the bad stuff pale into insignificance. Some of my best times have been spent breaking into impromptu jam sessions during sound-checks and discussing obscure music trivia in half-closed motorway service stations at some ungodly hour in the morning. I couldn't bear to lose all that – yet this was what I was risking by continuing to ignore the situation with Charlie.

Staring at my phone alone in my bedroom that night, I knew Wren was right – I had to call him. Mustering every scrap of courage I could, I found Charlie's number and dialled.

I could hear the stress in his voice as soon as he answered.

'Rom – hey.'

'Hi, Charlie.'

'I didn't know what to . . . what to do . . . or say . . .'

'I'm sorry, mate. I was embarrassed.'

'You weren't the only one,' Charlie laughed. My stomach rolled over and I swallowed hard. After a pause, he spoke again. 'You still there?'

'Yes.'

'Look – this is such a mess. Can we meet up tomorrow?'

'I don't know . . .'

'Don't say no, Rom, just listen, OK?'

'OK.'

I heard him breathe out nervously on the other end of the line. 'Cool. What you said yesterday – well, I didn't take it very well.'

No kidding, Charlie.

'I could have handled it better. I definitely shouldn't have stopped following you when you told me to go home.'

'It's fine, honestly.'

'I think we need to talk – to clear the air, Rom. I'd hate this to affect our friendship . . .'

Perish the thought. 'It won't . . .'

'. . . and we've got those gigs coming up. Me and you need to be sorted for those, you know?'

Ever the practical realist, Charlie had managed to turn an awkward moment into an agenda item. 'You're right, we do.'

'Good. So – er – Harry's tomorrow about eight? Breakfast on me, OK?'

I pulled a face at the phone. 'Fine. See you then.'

Ending the call, I threw my phone to the end of my bed, flopped back and placed the pillow over my throbbing eyes.

That night, the stranger from the Christmas Market appeared in my dreams again. There I was, once again, safely cradled in his embrace, inhaling the scent of his skin, gazing at *that look* resplendent across his gorgeous face.

'Hello, beautiful.'

'Hello, you.'

'I'm waiting for you to find me.'

'Really? But you don't know me.'

'Your heart knows me. And my heart has been searching for you.'

'I don't know where to find you.'

He smiled, his face moving closer to mine, his breath tantalisingly warm on my lips. 'Follow your heart, beautiful girl.'

'What is *that* supposed to mean?'

He blinked and shrugged his broad shoulders. 'I have no idea. This is *your* dream. But isn't that what the heroes always say in those rom-coms you insist on watching?'

'That's not helpful.'

His eyes were so full of love as he gently stroked my cheek with velvet fingers that I immediately forgave his unhelpfulness. 'Your heart knows me, beautiful. So follow your heart . . .'

Waking suddenly, I sat up and stared at the pinky-gold dawn breaking through the gap in the curtains. The birds had begun singing outside and the world was starting to wake up. My heart thundered in my ears as the memory of The Kiss magnificently returned.

Wren was right. I had to find him.

But first, I had to face Charlie.

CHAPTER THREE

You've got a friend

The next morning, I bundled myself up in as many layers as I could realistically get away with and set off along the frozen pavements towards the train station. I'd secretly been hoping that the near-arctic conditions would cause considerable delays to the trains, thus keeping me away from the toe-curlingly awful conversation I knew was in store. But the train carried me to Birmingham with perfect punctuality and even though I walked slower than usual to the bus stop, my bus arrived on time. It was clear that nothing was going to keep me from this particular engagement. Accepting my fate, I reluctantly climbed on board.

My mind was distracted as the city suburbs passed by in a hazy blur. All around me, excited children and raucous teens gabbled, the thrill of Christmas tangible in their laughter. Only two days to go before The Big Day, the same topic of conversation buzzed between my fellow passengers: was it going to snow this year?

'*Midlands Today* reckons there's heavy snow heading our way,' the lady behind me was telling her friend, as two chubby tots gurgled on their laps. 'They'd put that poor Shifali out in a park last night to talk about it.'

'Poor love,' the other mother tutted. 'It's a wonder she doesn't catch her death with all those outside broadcasts they make her do. Still, when it comes to the weather she doesn't often get it wrong.'

'Hmm, well, I hope she has this time. Our Dave will go berserk if it snows. He'll be out all hours making snowmen to compete with the neighbours, you watch. It's bad enough with the Christmas lights war in our road without a snowman competition too.'

I smiled into my scarf and took a deep breath as my stop appeared ahead.

There are some places that become landmark locations in your life: for The Pinstripes, Harry's Café is one such place. Ever since Wren, Charlie and I first discovered the greasy, no-frills charms of the small, single-window café as secondary school pupils, Harry's became the setting for countless key (and not-so-key) moments; then we introduced Tom, Jack and Sophie to the café's manifold delights when we met them in our college years. Since The Pinstripes officially formed, Harry's has assumed the status of our unofficial office – most of the major decisions about the band have occurred within its warm, steamy interior.

Given all of this shared history, it was fitting that the inevitable conversation with Charlie should happen here. That and the fact that Harry makes quite possibly the best bacon sandwich around. Not that I was particularly hungry that morning, though, as I stood outside the café willing my stomach to unknot itself. *Take a deep breath, Rom.* Gazing through the steamed-up window I could just make out Charlie's messy mop of chestnut brown hair and the familiar hunch of his shoulders at our usual table by the counter. *Right*, I said to myself, *let's get this over with*.

A humid rush of fried-breakfast-scented air hit me as I pushed open the door and Harry raised a stained tea towel to greet me.

'Romily! Where you been this last week, eh?'

'Oh you know, Harry, Christmas and all that.'

He raised his eyes to heaven. 'Christmas this-and-that – it's all I hear for weeks. You want bacon? I'm a-making one for Charlie now.'

I smiled. 'Go on then.' I looked over to see Charlie raise a self-conscious hand and felt my head spin a little as I approached.

'Morning,' he smiled, half-standing to meet me. He was wearing the dark blue sweater that I like so much because it makes his midnight blue eyes look amazing, with a white t-shirt underneath it and indigo blue jeans. This combination didn't help the butterflies in my stomach one bit.

'Hi.' Not really knowing how to begin the conversation, I bought myself a few precious moments while I removed my coat and slowly unwound my scarf, placing it on the seat beside me.

Charlie resumed his seat and fiddled with an empty sugar packet as he stared at the melamine tabletop. When he lifted his eyes to meet mine, I was surprised to see vulnerability staring back at me.

'It's good to see you.'

I folded my arms protectively. 'I can't stay long.'

'Oh. Right.'

'I've got about forty-five minutes, though, so . . .'

'Good.' He raised a hand to rub the bridge of his nose – something he always does when he's nervous. 'But I'm glad you came. I wasn't sure you would.'

'Neither was I.' Every word felt like extracting teeth without anaesthetic.

He looked away. '*Man*, this is tough.'

'I know.'

'Charlie-boy! You want-a espresso?' Harry called from behind the counter, causing us both to jump.

'Always, Harry,' he replied with a smile, turning back to me and pulling a face. 'Not that I think it'll be any better than usual.'

The in-joke served as a small icebreaker and I felt a modicum of ease in the tension between us. Only for it to instantly disappear when Charlie said: 'Look, Rom, about Saturday . . .'

A sickening rush of nerves swept over me. If the worn olive-green lino beneath our feet had parted to swallow me up at that moment I would have been the happiest woman in the world. Ever since Saturday's debacle I had found myself wishing fervently that I could do that thing Christopher Reeve did in *Superman*, where he flew up into space and reversed the rotation of the earth to turn back time. But the fact remained that this wasn't something that was going to disappear. Gathering what courage I could, I faced him.

'I'm sorry I embarrassed you.'

'You didn't.'

'Yes I did, Charlie. I embarrassed myself, too.'

'Rom . . .'

'No, please let me say this, OK? Because if I don't say it now I never will.'

He nodded and folded his arms.

'You see, the thing is, I got my wires crossed. I obviously thought we were heading a certain way when, clearly, we weren't. It's my mistake. I just don't want to lose your friendship over this.'

41

'You won't.'

'Well, good.'

Charlie was about to say something else when the café door flew open and a large group of builders burst in. Their raucous laughter and loud voices rendered further conversation impossible as they spread themselves liberally around the café. I wondered if this would bring our meeting to a premature end, but Charlie motioned for me to stay where I was and left the table to go to the counter, where a slightly startled Harry was surveying the onslaught on his establishment. A few minutes later, he returned with two takeaway cups and a brown paper bag.

'Come on,' he said, 'I know a better place to have these.'

I followed him out of the noise of the café and out into the High Street. Five minutes later, we were walking down the steep hill towards Cannon Hill Park.

While I wasn't entirely sure that I wanted this conversation to be prolonged, I had to admit that Charlie knew me well. Everywhere I turn memories surround me in this park: summer weekends spent as a kid feeding the ducks; fun bank holiday picnics with Wren, Tom, Jack and Sophie; lunchtime meet-ups on sunny spring days – it's all happened here. Like Harry's, the park is an integral part of our lives.

And what Charlie could never know – but what now stabbed at my heart like sharp winter icicles – was that this park was the place where I first realised I was in love with him.

We had arranged to meet for lunch by the lake on the first Saturday in September, three years ago, just as we had countless times before. The deal – as always – was that he would bring sandwiches if I provided some of my aunt's homemade cake, so I had made a special trip to collect a particularly spectacular white chocolate and elderflower cake from her that morning. Charlie's smile was pure delight when he saw the cake and it made me laugh.

'You're so easy to please,' I mocked him. 'One cake and you're anybody's.'

'Ah, but this isn't just a cake, Rom. It's love at first sight.'

'Blimey. So all those girls who try to get you to go out with them have clearly been missing a trick. All it takes is cake.'

He grinned, broke a piece off the cake and popped it into his mouth. Closing his eyes, he clasped a hand to his heart. 'Find me a woman who makes me cake like this and I'll be hers forever.'

'I'm afraid my aunt's already taken.'

'Shame.' His eyes flicked open and the twinkle in them was unmistakably Charlie. 'Maybe I should settle for a girl who can bring me cake like this, then . . .'

'Yeah, well good luck finding her then,' I grinned back.

He smiled again and his midnight eyes held mine a moment longer than usual. And that was when it happened. I felt my heart skip and the world began to swim a little – and I knew I was in love. The revelation rocked me completely and, when Charlie turned his attention back to the cake moments later, I was left dazed by what had just happened.

In the following days I tried to dismiss it as a freak occurrence and almost managed to convince myself until the next time we met on a Friday night at Jack and Sophie's. As soon as Charlie walked into the room, my pulse began racing and all evening I had to resist the urge to stare at him. Suddenly it was as if I was seeing him for the first time – his easy smile, the twinkle in his eyes as he joked about with Tom and Jack, how he used his hands when he talked. I'd known him all my life but somehow I'd never noticed how wonderful he was.

From that moment on, I fell deeper and deeper in love with him. Every minute we spent together reaffirmed my feelings and then, last year, I began to notice his attitude change towards me. He sought my company more often and when we were together the chemistry was astounding. Or so I'd thought . . .

Today that blissful summer day three years ago felt light years away. The park was covered in a thick layer of frost, the lake an icy winter blue as we walked along the ice-puddled path. I stole a glance at Charlie, trying to work out his feelings from his nondescript expression. The little we had already said to each other this morning clearly wasn't enough for him, otherwise this unscheduled jaunt in the park would not be happening. On the walk down from Harry's our conversation had retreated to safe small talk, Charlie telling me about an art launch his father's gallery had managed to secure and me amusing him with the latest double-glazing advertising jingle I had written for Brum FM.

We walked away from the lake until we reached a Victorian ironwork bandstand. Tiny snowflakes began to swirl about our ears as we climbed the steps and sat down on the wooden bench seats for our alfresco breakfast. Charlie bit into his bacon sandwich and as silence fell between us I felt my stomach begin to knot once more.

'Good sarnie?' I offered, reasoning that any conversation was preferable to none at all.

He nodded and turned the full force of his stare on me. 'Rom . . .'

The excruciation factor shot up a million-fold. 'Charlie, can we just forget Saturday ever happened, please?'

'I still think we need to talk about it. I reacted badly, and I'm sorry.'

'You were just being honest.'

'As you were. And I should have handled it better.'

'You don't have to say that. I know it wasn't what you were expecting.'

He smiled. 'It wasn't. It came totally out of the blue. I mean, one minute we were talking about Quincy Jones and the next . . .'

'I know. I'm sorry, Charlie. I should never have said anything. I don't know what I was thinking.'

Charlie sighed and looked at me. 'I think you're amazing, Rom. I always have. But you're my best friend and that's what matters to me. I'm sorry if I gave you the impression that I . . . that we . . . you know.'

Instantly, I looked away. As I stared at my coffee, a sudden image of the handsome stranger from the Christmas Market flashed into my mind. Despite the intense embarrassment still working its way through my guts, the memory of his lips on mine gave me a welcome boost of hope. I remembered Wren's words to me yesterday, when she gave me the bauble from the scene of the kiss:

'Let this remind you that there is at least one amazing bloke in the city who thinks you're beautiful . . .'

And suddenly, everything came into sharp focus. True, this wasn't particularly helpful right now, seeing as I didn't actually know where he was, or have any idea of where to start looking. But I *was* going to find him. Somehow.

'So where did you go after you left me?' Charlie asked, dragging me back to reality.

I kept my expression steady, despite my heart performing cartwheels. 'Just into the Christmas Market to finish my shopping.'

'Hope you got me something nice,' he quipped, obviously instantly regretting it. 'Sorry.'

'It's fine. Don't worry.' It wasn't fine, of course, but I really didn't want him to be apologising every time any flicker of normality appeared between us.

Charlie studied my face. 'So – what happens now?'

I unwrapped my sandwich to avoid his eyes. 'We enjoy our breakfast before it gets cold.'

'That's not what I meant.'

'I don't know, OK? I haven't ever been in this situation before.'

'Me either.'

I looked at him and attempted a smile. 'I know, I'm sorry.' I didn't want to see the hurt in his eyes, didn't want to face the consequences of my confession, but we needed to move on from this – for the sake of the band, if nothing else.

'We have all these gigs coming up, so maybe we should focus on that.'

'Right.' He paused, carefully selecting his words before he spoke. 'And what about – us?'

'There's nothing to say about us. It's going to be awkward for a while, but I'm willing to carry on as before, if you are?'

The strangest look drifted across his face. 'Sure.'

It was an uneasy truce, but it was a truce nonetheless. As I headed towards the city centre offices of Brum FM later that morning, I consoled myself with the thought that at least I had tackled the subject head on with Charlie before anyone else was involved. Hopefully we could move on from this without the rest of the band noticing too much awkwardness – I really didn't need any more embarrassment.

Ted, the gruff-looking security guard, greeted me at the door as I arrived.

'Morning. Didn't think you'd be in today, what with Christmas and all.'

'I'm only in for a couple of hours, Ted. Looking forward to Christmas?'

He gave an almighty sigh and rolled his eyes heavenwards. 'Well, if by Christmas, you mean being holed up for three days in my mother-in-law's semi in Nuneaton with the wife and all the nutjobs in her family, then no, not particularly.'

'Ah. Well, hope it passes quickly for you.'

'That's all I can hope for, Romily.'

I took the lift down to the depths of Brum FM, known affectionately by our small team of three as the 'Bat Cave', which consists of a production room and a minuscule vocal booth that would make the smallest broom cupboard look capacious.

For the past five years I've worked here writing jingles for the radio adverts that pepper the station's schedule. I'm never likely to win any Brits or Ivor Novello Awards for my daily compositions, but my work never fails to keep my friends entertained.

The Bat Cave was noticeably more pungent than normal today, the stale remnants of late-night curry, sweat and acrylic carpet fug from the soundproofing fabric that covered its doors, floors and walls meeting my nose as I walked in.

Mick, the department's studio engineer, looked up from his already grease-stained copy of the *Mirror*. 'Romily! How the devil are you?'

'Good thanks. What died in here, though?'

He let out a thundering laugh. 'That'll be our esteemed colleague Nev Silver. Apparently he had another row with the wife last night – I found him on the sofa in his sleeping bag this morning.'

I hung my bag up on the rickety coat stand in the corner

and filled a mug with coffee from the filter machine. 'Not again. Does that mean he'll be staying over Christmas?'

Mick sniffed. 'Probably. So, to what do we owe the pleasure of your company this morning?'

'I need to finish the mixes for the New Year campaign so they're ready for next week. Anything else in?'

'Bits and bobs for the new schedule – nothing particularly earth-shattering, I'm afraid. Jane Beckingham wants a new jingle for her morning show, if you don't mind. Oh, and Amanda's on the warpath. *Again.*'

News that my department manager was upset about something didn't surprise me. Amanda Wright-Timpkins is so uptight she makes a coiled spring look relaxed. The twinkle in Mick's eye revealed all I needed to know about his opinion on the matter – there is very little love lost between him and the woman who takes her persistent frustration at being 'sideways-promoted' to our department out on us whenever possible. 'What is it this time?'

'She reckons she's been overlooked for another promotion,' Mick replied, folding his newspaper and rolling his chair over to mine. 'Apparently she was going for the producer job on the *Breakfast Show*.'

'Ah.'

'Exactly. So best to keep your head down, eh?'

The morning passed slowly. As I composed the music for Brum FM's *New Year, New You* campaign, my thoughts strayed back to my conversation with Charlie. What would the year ahead bring for us?

Squeezed into the vocal booth a couple of hours later, I was recording the vocal parts for the jingles when one of the lines struck me:

This could be the year when all your dreams come true.

Instantly Charlie left my mind as I remembered my

handsome stranger. Maybe he was the start of my dreams coming true – after all, hadn't he turned up *exactly* when I needed him? Unlike Charlie. Maybe all the time I had spent waiting for Charlie to notice me was actually preparation for meeting this man. Let's face it, if I hadn't been running away from Charlie, the chances were we would never have met. But was it possible to find him again? I wasn't sure, but I was determined to try. All I had to do was to figure out *how* . . .

'Er, Rom, whenever you're ready?' Mick said in my headphones as I bumped back to reality.

'Sorry. Let's do that line again . . .'

All day, the first sparks of possibility glowed brighter in my mind. It *had* to be possible to find the stranger – even in the sprawl of England's second city. Compared to the situation with Charlie, which I could do no more about, looking for the man who kissed me seemed an enticing alternative. After all, what could be more positive than searching for someone who clearly thought I was beautiful?

'Positivity is key,' Wren said that evening, when she joined me for dinner in my little house in Stourbridge, 'or else you'll never go through with it. Still can't work out where you should start looking, though.'

I handed her a glass of red wine. 'Me either. But I'll think of something.'

'So, things with you and Charlie are a bit better?'

'I'm not sure they're better, but at least we've talked about it. One thing I do know is that I definitely made a mistake. He's only ever seen me as a friend.'

'Yeah right,' Wren muttered into her Merlot.

'Sorry?'

'Who can fathom the minds of men, eh?' she replied

dismissively. 'Charlie will sort it out eventually.' She looked over to my Christmas tree in the corner of the room and smiled. 'I see the bauble has pride of place.'

I followed her gaze and felt a shiver of excitement as I watched the reflections of the tree lights passing smoothly across its surface, remembering the stranger's voice by my ear. 'Yes. It's lovely. Makes me feel Christmassy – I was worried I wouldn't feel like that this year after what happened with Charlie.'

'Everyone should feel Christmassy, no matter what,' Wren said, raising her glass in a flamboyant toast. 'It should be law. Or at least a tradition.'

'Talking of traditions, are you looking forward to the band Christmas meal tomorrow night?'

'Of course, wouldn't miss it. You?'

I shrugged. 'It should be OK. I think Charlie and I will be putting on a united front. Hopefully nobody will notice any difference.'

Wren took a rather large gulp of wine. 'Absolutely. And it will be good to hear about the gigs Dwayne has booked for next year.'

'They'd better be good. He hasn't exactly been successful with bookings this year.'

'Don't pick on him; he's still learning about the business. He hasn't managed us for that long, remember,' she replied, frowning at me. 'Dwayne tries his best. And he needs our support. Anyway, from what he's said, he has some great gigs lined up.'

'You're too nice to him,' I smiled. 'He has to prove himself tomorrow night, that's all I'm saying.'

'Hmm,' Wren replied, her sly expression clear behind her half-empty wine glass. 'And he won't be the only guy there who'll be proving himself, will he?'

CHAPTER FOUR

We are family

Next morning a thick fog shrouded the city centre as I wheeled my bicycle out of the train station. After all the emotion of the past few days I needed to clear my head. A long ride was just what the doctor ordered.

Even in the dim December light, the rolling fields and picturesque villages huddled alongside the road were impossibly gorgeous. I had taken the route to Kingsbury many times since Jack first persuaded me to join the unofficial Pinstripes' pursuit of cycling. He, Charlie and Tom have been bike nuts since university, grabbing any opportunity to tackle increasingly demanding off-road terrain. Following much cajoling and pro-cycling propaganda from the Terrible Three, I had finally surrendered and subsequently spent a very amusing day shopping for bikes with Jack, who spent the whole time skipping like a child in and out of endless cycle shops. While I've still to fully appreciate the delights of mountain bike trails, I've fallen in love with road cycling – especially on days like this when I hadn't a particular schedule to stick to. Plus, this particular route had one distinct advantage: it inevitably involved generous helpings of cake with two of my most favourite people in the world.

As I passed through the lovely village of Shustoke, a single thought played on my mind: the stranger from the Christmas Market. The thrill of his body so close to me, and the glorious memory of his lips on mine, had visited my dreams every night since Saturday and it was beginning to drive me mad. I *needed* to find him . . . but how? After all, we had met in the middle of a bustling Christmas Market on the busiest trading day of the year, surrounded by countless people I would never recognise again. Those kind of odds would make even John McCririck wince. Still, as my old maths teacher Mr Williams used to say, odds of any kind indicated a possibility, however remote.

I've always been the kind of person who believes things are possible before I embark upon them, so searching for my 'Phantom Kisser', as Wren had named him, didn't seem like as big a step of faith as it probably would to other people. In this respect, I am very much like my Uncle Dudley. He's the most positive person I know, always thrilled by the opportunities that life presents and never afraid of a challenge. I sometimes wonder if I should have been his daughter instead of my dad's, whose idea of a risk is something backed up by pages of careful calculations – so not really a risk at all. Uncle Dudley's philosophy of life is that everything turns out well in the end, eventually. His health isn't brilliant, he and Auntie Mags have had to cope with quite a tough series of life problems (including discovering quite early on in their marriage that they were unable to have children – something that I know devastated them both) and they never seem to have quite enough money to be able to fully relax in their retirement, but they are, without a doubt, the happiest couple I know.

Nearing my destination, I crossed over a small humpback bridge spanning a canal. Once on the other side I left the road and turned on to the towpath towards the permanent moorings. The spicy tang of woodburner smoke tickled my nostrils as I dismounted and wheeled past narrowboats with names I knew by heart: *Taliesin*, *The King*, *Barely-A-Wake*, *Adagio*, *Titch*, *Llamedos*. Beside each narrowboat a thin plot of grass revealed a snapshot of the owners' personalities, from a fully stocked vegetable plot to a brick-built barbecue with a greening old picnic table beside it, and what can only be described as a garden gnome shrine. At the end of the row of brightly coloured vessels, stood *Our Pol* – a magnificent 60ft green and red narrowboat crowned with traditionally painted enamel jugs, basins and planters stuffed with winter pansies.

A chirpy whistling from inside made me smile. I knocked three times on the cabin door. 'Anyone aboard?'

The whistling stopped abruptly and the door flew open as Uncle Dudley emerged, blue cap perched at a rakish angle and face in full beam. 'Hello, you!' He ducked his head back inside briefly. 'Mags my love! There's a red-faced cyclist here in need of a cuppa!'

'I'll put the kettle on!' Auntie Mags' disembodied voice replied.

'Hi, Uncle Dud,' I smiled. 'Hope you don't mind me dropping in unannounced?'

'Of course not, bab! We've been looking forward to seeing you. Chuck your bike up above and come on in.'

Uncle Dudley has been in love with narrowboats for as long as anyone can remember. Dad says that his younger brother's favourite toy as a child was a small wooden canal boat (a present from my great-great grandfather), which he insisted accompany him on every outing and family holiday.

Uncle Dudley had his first taste of being aboard the real thing during his time as an engineer on the production lines at Leyland and Rover, when his long-time workmate Eddie bought the rusting hulk of an old coal boat and gradually restored it to full working order. From that moment on, Uncle Dudley's sole ambition was to own a narrowboat, and when, at the age of fifty-two, he elected to take early retirement, he finally realised his dream and bought *The Star* from Eddie's cousin, which he renamed *Our Pol* after Auntie Mags' beloved aunt.

The other great love of his life, Auntie Mags, was considerably less enamoured of the whole idea than her husband, but because it was his dream and because – despite her protestations to the contrary – she dearly loves Uncle Dudley, she went along with it. And continues to go along with it every weekend and holiday or whenever Dudley gets the itch to check on 'the old girl'. Auntie Mags finds spending time on *Our Pol* much more frustrating than she would ever let on to her husband, but it comes out in subtle ways – most notably in her baking. As a simple guide, the level of stress she is experiencing is directly proportional to the amount of baking she produces from the small wood-fuelled oven in the narrowboat's galley.

Judging by the cake tins balanced precariously on every flat surface in *Our Pol*'s interior, Auntie Mags was having a particularly bad day today.

'Spot of baking, Auntie Mags?' I grinned as I entered the warmth of the cabin.

Mags pulled a face. 'Just a tad. Come here and give your poor old landlubber aunt a hug!'

I've always loved hugs from Auntie Mags. She has one of those strong yet soft embraces that makes everything seem better. Not like Mum. My mother's idea of a hug is an air kiss with minimal bodily contact. Causes less creases in one's clothes and removes the need for any embarrassing public displays of affection. Not that I'm a massively 'huggy' person, but hugs from my aunt class as delightful exceptions to the rule – generous treats to be savoured and enjoyed (much like her baking).

There was a whimper and the diminutive, shaking frame of Elvis, my aunt and uncle's rescue poodle, appeared at our feet. Elvis is even less of a fan of being on the water than Auntie Mags and whenever he is spotted aboard *Our Pol* he is not much more than a shivering, terrified bundle of curly grey fur.

Breaking the hug, I reached down to pat his poor terrified body. 'Hey Elvis, how's it going?' Elvis gave my hand a hesitant lick, then fled to the safety of his faded tartan dog bed by the cooker.

Auntie Mags grabbed my shoulders and held me at arm's length. 'Now, let's have a look at you.' Her eyes narrowed. 'Mmmm. Oh dear. You've something serious going on in that mind of yours. There's only one thing I can recommend.'

She wandered over to the pile of old Roses tins haphazardly stacked on the benches and compact table in what Uncle Dudley refers to as 'The Grand Dining Room', and began to search through them, lifting lids and discarding tins until she located the one she was looking for.

'Ah! Here we are.' Brandishing the tin, she thrust it under my nose. 'Coffee and walnut. That's what you need.'

And, like countless times before, she was right.

Maybe it's because she bakes so often – or maybe (as I secretly suspect) she actually has some mystical culinary-based second sight – but Auntie Mags' ability to prescribe exactly the right sweet treat to meet your need is practically legendary. Broken heart? 'Lemon drizzle, pure and simple.' Anxious about something? 'Bakewell tart. It's the only thing that will work.' Tired? 'Triple-layer cappuccino cake – that'll perk you up, chick!'

'You're a genius, Auntie M,' I smiled, as Uncle Dudley poured the tea and Auntie Mags cut an enormous wedge of cake with an ancient, yellow bone-handled butter knife that could only have come from one of my uncle's many car boot sale visits.

'Nonsense. Everybody knows that coffee and walnut cake is vital for making important decisions. Isn't it, Dudley?'

Uncle Dudley nodded sagely. 'Absolutely.'

Dubious as their reasoning may have been, I found myself grinning like a loon. 'And what important decisions do you think I have to make?'

'Cake can't tell you everything,' my aunt replied, wagging the butter knife at me. 'Enlighten us, darling niece.'

I feigned a protest, but inside I was delighted she had asked. The fact was, I needed their advice – and my aunt and uncle were quite possibly the only people I knew who had the ability (and inclination) to fully understand.

They listened intently as I relayed the events of the fateful day, stopping me every now and again to ask questions.

'Why were you running through the Christmas Market?'

'Because I'd just told Charlie I loved him.'

They exchanged raised-eyebrowed glances. 'Oh.'

'But that doesn't matter because it was a mistake. The point *is*, the guy who kissed me changed everything.'

'He kissed you?'

'Yes. It was only for a moment, but . . .' I stopped, suddenly unsure whether this was appropriate territory for a niece to approach with her aunt and uncle. But their mirrored expectant expressions – instantly reminding me of the two china Staffordshire dogs that guard each end of Mum's mock-alabaster mantelpiece – urged me to continue. 'It took my breath away.'

Uncle Dudley patted his wife's hand excitedly. 'Magic! It's just like me and you, love!'

Rolling her eyes, Auntie Mags gave a loud tut. 'Ignore him, Romily, he's deluded. Carry on.'

'That's all, really. I know I should just chalk it up to experience – one of those heart-stopping, fleeting moments that will always give you a thrill. But I keep thinking . . .'

'The attraction of *possibility*,' Uncle Dudley chipped in. 'No matter how unlikely, you can't shake the feeling it *might* happen.'

My heart skipped a beat. 'That's it exactly!'

'And you want to find him again,' Auntie Mags nodded. 'But you don't know where to start.'

'I love you guys. So what do I do?'

Uncle Dudley rose to refill the kettle. 'I reckon you should go for it. What's the worst that could happen, eh?'

'Humiliation, disappointment and an unwanted reputation as a desperate woman?' I ate a forkful of cake and stared at my aunt, who was deep in thought.

'Pah, that's *nothing*,' Uncle Dudley said. 'I've had worse than that in my life and I'm still smiling, aren't I?'

'You were called a desperate woman?'

'Eh? Oh, good one. Our Romily's sharp as a needle, eh, Magsie?'

'Quiet, Dudley, I'm thinking.' She placed her elbows on the table, folded her hands and rested her chin on them.

My uncle clapped his hands in delight. 'Ooh, I know that look, Romily. You're in for a proper treat now if your auntie's got that face on her.'

We waited in silence, the only sounds the lapping of the

canal waters against the side of the boat and the distant chug of a slowly approaching narrowboat, until the shrill ascending whistle of the kettle broke through.

'If you're going to do this, you need to think about how best to let people know you're looking,' Auntie Mags said, finally. 'The more people you can involve in your search, the greater your chances of finding him.'

Uncle Dudley clapped his hands. 'Brilliant, our Mags!'

'That's what I'll do then. But how do I begin?'

Uncle Dudley tapped the side of his nose. 'Now don't you fret about that, bab. You just leave it to your Uncle Dudley.'

Just as I was about to leave home for the band's annual Christmas party, Mum rang.

'I just wanted to check you're still coming for Christmas Day,' she said. I could hear the theme music of *The Great Escape* drifting into the background where Dad was no doubt glued to the television for its umpteenth showing. Rather apt, I thought, given the topic of conversation.

'Yes, I'm looking forward to it,' I lied, putting on my heels as I held the phone against my ear with my shoulder.

'Good. I thought you were going out with your musician friends this evening?'

'I am,' I replied, checking my reflection in the bathroom mirror.

'You're leaving it awfully late, aren't you? It's seven fifteen already.'

I smiled to myself. Mum clearly doesn't know that many musicians.

There are many wonderful skills that my musician friends possess, but accurate timekeeping is not one of them. I can't tell you how many band rehearsals have started with two or three of us waiting for over an hour for the others to roll up. Jack and I are usually there pretty much on time, but Charlie, Wren and Soph can be anything from twenty minutes to well over an hour late. And we almost always start without Tom, who has been known to turn up with only three-quarters of an hour of the rehearsal session remaining.

Every year, the band and their partners meet for a Christmas meal, usually at The Old Gate, a pub and restaurant near Jack and Sophie's house that sells excellent food and locally-brewed ales. This year, however, Jack had left booking the meal to the last minute and, unsurprisingly, discovered that the pub was fully booked. To rescue a few scraps of credibility (although you could lay money on the fact that he wouldn't be allowed to forget this indiscretion *ever*), he and Sophie hastily arranged a meal at their house, begging dining room chairs from family and friends and bringing in the white plastic picnic table from their garden to extend the dinner table in order to accommodate us all. In response to their valiant efforts (and because, despite the constant mocking, we love them both to bits), the rest of the band had divided responsibility for bringing food and drink, each agreeing to bring a component course of the meal. Thankfully, I'd been nominated to provide dessert, which was easy as my mother's beloved Waitrose was only a short drive away from their house.

I picked up two large New York baked cheesecakes and a tub of raspberry compote, remembering to bring a couple of bowls of ready-prepared fruit salad for Sophie, who seems to be permanently on a diet.

True to form, even though I arrived just past nine pm, I was still the first guest at Jack and Sophie's. A grave-looking Sophie met me at the door, apron on and tea towel slung over one shoulder.

'Am I glad to see you,' she said, giving me a huge hug and ushering me inside. 'Jack's being a total nightmare.'

'Oh no. What's up?' I followed her down the hall to their dining room.

'Just my boyfriend doing his best impression of a total muppet. Honestly, you'd think he was entertaining royalty the way he's been carrying on. I swear he's cleaned the kitchen three times, even though it's too minuscule for any of us to spend any time in there tonight.'

'I heard that,' Jack said, emerging from the archway that led to the kitchen. 'I'm just making sure our home is presentable, that's all.'

'I wouldn't mind, but all he's cooking for the meal are some sausage rolls,' Sophie grimaced. 'It's hardly *cordon bleu*, is it?'

'They're pork and herb sausage *filo wraps*, actually.'

His serious expression sent us into a fit of giggles. Sophie threw the tea towel at him. 'Ooh, get *you*, Gordon Ramsay.'

Jack folded his arms and scowled at us. 'Oh, you mock now. But just you wait until you taste them. *Then* we'll see who's laughing.' He leaned in for a kiss. 'Romily, looking gorgeous as ever. Loving the dress, lady.'

I grinned and did a little twirl so that he and Sophie could get a good look at my black sequinned mini-dress and electric blue heels. I had decided to wear something that made me feel fabulous tonight to combat my nerves about seeing Charlie – and so far it was working.

Twenty minutes later, a raucous knocking at the front door heralded the arrival of Charlie, Wren and Tom, who had shared a taxi in order to, as Tom put it, 'be free to quaff muchly'. Charlie and I greeted each other politely, carefully avoiding eye contact, as Wren, resplendent in a bright yellow cocktail dress that looked amazing against her hair, took centre-stage with her witty banter. I knew exactly what she was doing and I loved her for it.

Five minutes later our manager, Dwayne McDougall, appeared bearing a case of red wine, which was welcomed by the assembled Pinstripes with noticeably more warmth and enthusiasm than he was. It isn't that we don't like him – we do immensely – but the band likes to remind him that managing us is very different from running his event management business that helped him make his money. For a start, the events he organises for his eldest brother's hotel tend to stay in one place, unlike we do.

'Hello, Pinstripes!' he boomed as he entered the dining room where drinks had already been handed out. 'How's my favourite wedding band tonight?'

'Don't you mean your *only* wedding band, Dwayne?' Wren asked.

Dwayne's confident countenance faltered slightly. 'It starts with one, Wren,' he mumbled.

It's the cause of much hilarity in the band that Wren (standing at barely five feet two inches tall) can reduce Dwayne (over six feet in stature and a former member of the England judo squad to boot) to a blithering wreck so easily. Fortunately for Dwayne, Wren wasn't looking for a fight this evening. She merely winked at him before wandering into the kitchen to talk to Jack. Quickly recovering his swagger, Dwayne dug in his leather jacket pocket and produced a slim silver business card case. 'Before I forget, I've had some new cards done. You should all have one, in case of emergencies.' He handed cards out to us all.

Tom was the first to laugh. 'Hang on a minute: are you taking a stage name now, "D'Wayne"?'

One by one, each of the band read the name on the

business card in front of them and laughter began to break forth like a wave.

'Changed it by deed poll last week, actually. It's *classy*,' he protested. 'That name will get us openings we've never had before. Top-class stuff. The calibre of engagements that might just take care of all those *pesky bills* of yours . . .'

The room fell silent. All joking aside, the promise of well-paying events was what kept us all going, and Dwayne – sorry, *D'Wayne* – knew this better than anyone.

'Yeah, but it'll still make you sound like a prat,' Jack added, his dry remark reducing the room to unbridled hilarity once more.

Just over a year ago, The Pinstripes decided we needed a manager to take care of our promotion and bookings. I'm still not altogether sure how we managed to find D'Wayne McDougall – but, knowing how most of the band's decisions seem to be made, it was probably through a recommendation from some random musician that one of us met in the pub. Whoever recommended him should, by rights, be given a swift kick up the proverbial, as D'Wayne had so far yet to prove himself in band promotion. And band management. And taking bookings, for that matter. What he had excelled at was giving the impression that big things were just a conversation away and taking the credit for gigs that the band ended up planning ourselves in order to save the booking. (That and having the most impressive array of shave patterns cut into the sides of his shiny black Afro hair which, this evening, appeared to be flames surrounding a large italic D.) Still, The Pinstripes were nothing if not hardened optimists, so we all held out hope that tonight our manager was going to come up trumps.

As we all sat down for our multi-component meal, I watched the interactions between my favourite group of people in the world. Tom, with his dark hair and cyclist physique, always launching into completely improvised impromptu comedy routines at any opportunity; Wren, flame-haired and elfin-framed, confounding the boys with her lightning-fast wit and (it has to be said) utterly *filthy* sense of humour; wise-cracking, tall Jack, with his green-blue eyes, closely-cropped brown hair and a laugh so loud and distinctive that we can tell if he's in a room long before we enter it; Sophie, quiet and contemplative but a great listener, her long blonde hair always piled up on her head in one of those messy-chic hairstyles that look effortless but probably take hours of careful pinning to achieve; and Charlie, chestnut-brown haired with midnight blue eyes that seem to change depending on what colour he wears, sharing increasingly obscure jazz references with Jack. Even though my heart was torn by the sight of him, my embarrassment still raw, I still felt comforted by his presence together with my friends. In their company I have always been able to be myself – fitting in as comfortably as putting on a beloved pair of slippers, sharing the jokes and joining in the light-hearted music trivia debates. The situation with Charlie had definitely brought an edge to it all, but thankfully the others appeared to be completely unaware of it all for the time being.

After the four-course meal of canapés (a.k.a. Jack's posh sausage rolls), baked salmon fillets with lime and fenugreek for the fish course from Charlie, a fantastic rustic pot roast with crispy herb potatoes from Tom (no doubt influenced by Nigel Slater, whose recipe books he worships at the index of), my desserts and coffee with mints provided by Wren (whose idea of culinary skill is knowing where to find things in an M&S food hall, but she gets away with it because we love her so much), we all decamped to the living room.

I love Jack and Sophie's house. An old Edwardian villa,

its rooms are spacious, high-ceilinged affairs with original coving, carved plaster ceiling roses and picture rails. They have rented it for the past four years and it's a place we all end up at some time or other each week. I often visit on Saturday afternoons if we aren't gigging or weekday evenings after work whenever Jack is cooking and the offer of a hearty home-cooked meal is too tempting to resist.

Thankfully, Jack had offered me the use of their spare bed for the night, so I was enjoying the luxury of being able to drink a little more than usual this evening.

Jack chose a Yellowjackets album to play as Sophie and I set out bowls of chocolates, nuts and biscuits on the low wooden coffee table. Charlie and Tom claimed the sofa as usual, with Wren perched up on one arm, and D'Wayne settled himself in the old threadbare armchair that Sophie has made several unsuccessful attempts to retire over the past four years.

'Now we're all together, I want to let you know what I've secured for you next year,' D'Wayne said, pouring himself a large glass of red wine and consulting his iPhone.

Tom brushed biscuit crumbs from his jeans. 'This should be interesting.'

Wren jabbed him in the ribs. 'Shush.'

D'Wayne shot him a look. 'Prepare to be impressed, my friend.'

'Oh, I'm waiting for it, mate.'

'Right. As you know we have the New Year's wedding at the Excelsior in Solihull next week. I think maybe the rock'n'roll medley should be thrown in?' This was met with loud protests from all of us, which D'Wayne lifted his large hands to still. 'I know you hate it but it's what the punters want. Most of the guests at the party are Baby Boomers. You've got to work with your demographic, guys.'

'But it's like *death* on a G-string,' Tom moaned. 'Six songs with identical chord structures. I might as well get Jack to sequence it and just go to the bar for the whole medley.'

I laughed. 'Any excuse, Tom.'

'What can I say? It's a vocation.'

'Maybe we should be looking for gigs that cater for a younger crowd,' Jack muttered, as Wren and Charlie groaned. This was a frequent source of disagreement within the band and was unlikely to be resolved any time soon.

'Older crowds have more disposable income,' Sophie said, topping up her wine glass. 'If you go for younger crowds all the time you'll have to do more gigs to make it financially viable.'

'Which is fortunate, then, that all the gigs in the diary for next year are going to pay well,' D'Wayne interjected, clearly pleased with himself. 'So do you mind if we return to next year's programme?'

Tom shrugged and took a handful of nuts. 'Don't let us stop you, *Duh-Wayne*.'

'Thank you. In January we have a fiftieth birthday gig on the 14th and on the 21st there's a winter wedding at Elstone Farm Estate down in Somerset – smaller crowd but they're all booked into the accommodation onsite so should be in the mood for a party. In February I've managed to get you playing at an exclusive Valentine's Night bash at a venue to be confirmed – two forty-five-minute sets before the DJ comes on and they're happy to pay a premium to secure us, so that should be around £250 each.'

A murmur of surprised approval rippled through the room. February is traditionally a dead month as far as gigs are concerned and, after the usual shock of post-Christmas bills in January, any money coming in during that month is a definite bonus.

'March-wise, bit quiet at the moment but I've almost secured a medieval banquet wedding gig in Northumberland. Bride and groom both work for a big City law firm in London, so it should be more than worthwhile. I'll have more on that next month, hopefully.'

'Ah, the madrigal set then, guys,' Jack quipped.

Tom laughed. 'Must dust off my mandolin.'

'Usual set, *actually*,' D'Wayne countered. 'And the type of younger crowd you're looking for, Tom.' He finished his wine and flicked through the list on his phone. 'Two weddings in April, then May is more or less booked for weddings – three Saturdays and a Sunday, including a very nice one at a Scottish castle near Fort William. There's a Regency wedding in June, a summer ball for a major accountancy firm in London in July and possibly a late July beachside wedding in Devon, so we might blag a free weekend break out of it. Obviously there are more I'm working on but it's all good stuff, I think you'll agree.'

'It's a start,' Charlie said. 'But ideally I think we need to be trying to gig most weeks from May to end of September.'

D'Wayne raised his eyebrows. 'Hey, feel free to do better if you think you can.'

'Actually, I already have,' Charlie replied, his coolness disguising the irritation I knew he was experiencing. We all turned to look at him, including our manager, who looked slightly winded by this. 'My sister's getting married at Combermere Abbey in Shropshire, on the second weekend of September, and she's booked us for the whole day. She's hired a string quartet for the ceremony and wants some smooth jazz for the afternoon reception, so I suggest that Rom, Jack and I do the American Songbook set we put together for Soph's mum's fiftieth last year, and then we'll have the whole band set in the evening. We get £250 each plus travel, two nights' accommodation and expenses. Added to that, the event planner at the venue is an old school friend of hers and is interested in taking us on to her recommended entertainment list, so there's definite potential for repeat gigs. That OK with you, Mr McDougall?'

D'Wayne's voice was small and resigned when it came out. 'Fine. Well done.'

'You kept that quiet, Charlie,' Sophie said. 'Did you know about this, Rom?'

I shook my head, my heart sinking at the fact. Usually, I would be the first to know. After what happened on Saturday, was this how things were going to be between us from now on?

'They're not really talking at the moment,' Wren interjected.

Horrified, I stared at her. '*Wren!*'

'I'm just saying.'

All eyes swung to me, then Charlie, who was looking as uncomfortable as I felt.

'Why? What's up?' Tom demanded.

Charlie's gaze dropped to the carpet. 'Nothing. We're fine.'

Jack pulled a face. 'Awkward!'

I considered throwing out a lame excuse to leave the room, but it would only further fuel my friends' interest. So I remained rooted to the floor, hoping against hope that nobody would pursue it. Luckily for me, Tom had a bigger bombshell to drop.

'Forget Pinstripes' domestics, I can trump your gig, Chas.'

Relief washed over me as all attention switched to our guitarist.

Clearly happy to be let off the hook, Charlie laughed. 'Oh really? Pray tell.'

'I was chatting to my boss Julian last week about the kind of events we do. It was just a bit of small talk on the last day of work and I didn't expect anything to come of it. But yesterday he called me and asked if we would be interested in playing for his daughter's wedding in June. Point is, the guy's loaded – we're talking multi-millionaire – and he's booked an amazing stately home in London not far from Kew Gardens. We had the most mental conversation. He was casually reeling off names of some of the guests who have already accepted, and we're talking *major* celebs.'

It took us all several minutes to process this. It was D'Wayne who finally broke the silence.

'How much?'

Tom's smile was confidence personified. 'Five grand for the full band, and he'll throw in accommodation in Central London.'

'Wow,' Wren breathed. 'That would make a major dent in my credit card debt. And staying in London, too? I'm thinking *shopping* . . .'

'So much for settling the credit cards, Wren,' I laughed.

'How many sets?' Charlie asked.

'Two one-hours with a break for the evening buffet in the middle.'

'Ah, music to my ears,' grinned Jack.

Sophie leant forward. 'When you say "celebs", what calibre are we talking?'

'Put it this way: the happy couple have sold their wedding pictures to *Hello!* magazine for several million pounds. Reckon we could tempt you out of retirement to play some wicked sax for us, Soph?'

Sophie whooped and threw her arms around Tom. 'Yes! Please!'

'How definite a booking is it?' I asked.

'As definite as us saying yes. He listened to the demo tracks on our website and decided we were perfect. Which of course, we are. So I said yes. Was that OK?'

All of us agreed together, even D'Wayne, who was looking decidedly deflated by the news.

Later, I stood in the kitchen with Jack making hot chocolate as the hum of excited conversation drifted through from the other room. Even though he's two months younger than me, Jack's always assumed the role of an older brother, watching out for me at every opportunity. My mother heartily approves of him, I think because he runs his own business (a successful local recording studio) and for several years through my early twenties she wrongly assumed that we were destined for each other – even when I explained that he was already settled with Sophie. As for me, I've always loved the easy friendship we've built, completely free of any kind of romantic undertones. Unlike Charlie and I . . .

'This could be huge for us,' Jack said, as the milk started to steam in the pan. 'If we get recommended to society people it could mean serious money.'

'I know.' I hardly dared to believe it. 'I could certainly use the money.'

'Tell me about it.' He shook several handfuls of Belgian chocolate flakes into the milk while I stirred. 'So what's going on with you and Charlie?'

'Nothing. Just a misunderstanding. But we've sorted it now.'

'Are you sure? Only neither of you seemed yourselves tonight.'

'We're fine, Jack, don't worry. Give it a bit of time and things will be back to normal, you'll see.'

'Right. I don't believe you, but if you say it's fine then so be it.'

In truth, I was no more convinced by my assertion than he was, but I hoped with all my heart that it was true.

CHAPTER FIVE

People get ready

Christmas Day at the Parker house was as strained an affair as usual. Mum and Dad had been biting at each other's heels all morning and by the time Christmas dinner was served (after Her Majesty had summed up the year, of course), the atmosphere between them had descended into recriminatory Punch-and-Judy-style bickering.

Cursing my older brothers Niall and Spence for coming up with plausible excuses for missing the annual Parker family agony, and wishing with all my heart that my parents had relented on their traditional festive snub of Uncle Dudley and Auntie Mags this year, I grimly focused on my Waitrose-provided Christmas dinner in the beige dining room. Mum was describing how close the meal had come to disaster this year due to Dad 'fiddling with the new oven timer' on Christmas Eve.

'Of all the times to experiment with it, your father – of course – chose the very night I was preparing the glazed bacon joint. We had the windows open in the kitchen *all night* to get rid of the smell of burning meat. This after our butchers had closed for the holidays, so no chance of replacing the joint before Christmas. I told him, Romily, I said he's only himself to blame if there's no ham left for supper.'

Dad shrugged. 'I never said I liked the cold meat thing anyway. And besides, we'll have enough cold turkey to last us till March with that organic bird we practically had to remortgage the house to buy.'

'Oh, and *as if* we don't already have precious little time to enjoy the fruits of our labours, you have to complain about *one extravagance* I asked for! Never mind that I work seven days a week to keep the family business going. Never mind that the closest thing I get to a night out these days is my book group on a Thursday night at Moriarty's . . .'

I looked over at Gran, who had obviously switched her hearing aid off and was now giggling at the Christmas film on television, blissfully unaware of World War Three raging around her. If only I'd brought my clear plastic earplugs that I use for rehearsals with the band . . .

As the main course ended and dessert was served, Mum decided to take a quick break from berating my father, turning the maternal spotlight on to me instead.

'I suppose work is still bearable?'

'Not too bad, thanks. The station manager sent my department a bonus for our work this year.'

'Cut-price double-glazing, was it?' Dad sniggered, clearly pleased with his rapier wit.

'Contrary to popular belief, I don't *just* write jingles for double-glazing companies, you know,' I protested. But of course this fell on deaf ears (and I'm not just talking about Gran's).

'I'm sure you don't,' Mum continued, handing round a bowl of over-whipped cream to add to the impossibly stodgy

Christmas pudding slumped resignedly in our cut-glass dishes. 'But writing silly little advertising songs for the "third most popular radio station" in Birmingham is hardly a glittering career choice, is it?'

I had been waiting for this topic to arrive all day and was actually quite impressed that my mother had held back until nearly four o'clock. Being a disappointment to your parents is an occasional hazard for most people. For me – a radio jingle-writer and weekend wedding band vocalist with no sign of anything resembling a five-year career plan – it is practically a vocation. My mother, determined to wear me down over time like water dripping on to solid rock, never varied her tactics: it was always the same, every time I visited.

'The point I'm trying to make is that you are now about to embark on the last year of your twenties, so you should be thinking about a serious career. You know there will always be a place for you at the family firm. Your father has already said he'd happily fund your accountancy training . . .'

'Did I?' Dad's expression changed instantly – no doubt encouraged by the swift meeting of Mum's foot with his shin under the table. 'Er, of course, happy to oblige.'

'You need to think about what you want to do with your life, that's all I'm saying. Thirty is a milestone and you're heading towards it faster than you realise. You should use this time to make a decision about who you want to be.'

Though I hated to admit it, Mum's words had a profound effect on me. Maybe it was because there had been so much soul-searching over the past few days, what with my encounter with the handsome stranger and the intense awkwardness with Charlie, but the thought of making my

73

twenty-ninth year count began to take centre-stage in my mind.

Later that evening, safe in the peaceful surroundings of my home with the soothing tones of Bing, Frank and Nat in the background and the softly twinkling fairy lights from my Christmas tree casting a gently pulsating glow around my living room, I poured a long-overdue glass of red wine and looked at the teardrop-shaped bauble in my hands. Perhaps the events of this week were more significant than I first thought: what if they were part of an as yet unseen pattern leading me to a year that could change the course of my life? The more I considered it, the less convinced I became that it was all a series of unconnected coincidences. Was the universe trying to tell me something?

I grabbed my laptop and logged into Facebook to see if any of the band were online. Nobody was, but one message caught my eye, from an old school friend I had only recently reconnected with:

This time next year, things will be different.
I'm going to make it count.

I took a long sip of wine and stared at the screen. Suddenly, the words seemed to be suspended in the air before my eyes, their sentiment striking a chord. That was it! I was going to make next year – my last year of my twenties – count. I had no idea how this was going to happen or what it would entail, but in a blinding flash of inspiration I realised what I had to do. My journey *had* to begin with the kiss that had changed everything. I was going to find him.

I checked the time – nine thirty pm – and decided to call

my uncle and aunt. I was pretty sure that they would still be up on Christmas Day evening and besides, I needed to share my newfound idea with someone who would understand.

'Hey! Merry Christmas, our bab! Hang on a tick, I'll just pop you on speakerphone . . .' There was a muffled sound as Uncle Dudley fiddled with the controls on his new phone and then I heard the happy greeting of my aunt. 'Right, we're with you, sweetheart! How's your Christmas been so far, eh?'

'Bearable with Mum and Dad. Gran managed to fall asleep in her cheese and biscuits though.'

My uncle's unbridled guffaw reverberated around the room. 'I'll bet she did! Poor Nancy – I hope she did her trick with the hearing aid again.'

'Of course. Good job as well, Mum and Dad were on top form this afternoon. It would've been so much more fun if you two had been there.'

'I don't doubt it! So how are you feeling now you've seen Charlie again?'

I wasn't sure I felt any easier about the situation, but for the time being my new idea was taking the edge off my concerns. 'I've decided to set myself a task for next year,' I told them. 'Starting with finding the man who kissed me.'

I heard my aunt's whoop. 'That's a wonderful idea, Romily! I was just saying to your uncle that I hoped you would.'

'I just think if I could see him again, it could be the start of something.'

'Just like that Hot Chocolate song – "It Started With a Kiss"!' Uncle Dud sang, doing his best impression of Errol Brown. 'I reckon you should set yourself a deadline,

75

chick, and keep a diary of your search for the mystery kisser!'

My aunt giggled. 'Ooh, you're so *twentieth century*, Dudley! Why don't you start a blog, Romily? There must be so many other women out there heading towards thirty and looking to make their twenty-ninth year meaningful. I reckon you could encourage lots of people with it. My friend Oonagh has a blog and she gets comments on it from all over the world. I've been thinking of asking your uncle to set one up for me to share my cake recipes on, even though computers scare me rigid.'

It was a brilliant idea (perhaps made more outstanding by the second large glass of red that I had inadvertently sunk during our conversation). 'That's it! I'll start a blog and give myself until Christmas Eve next year to find the man of my dreams!'

Cheers from the other end of the line warmed my ear as my equally merry aunt and uncle roundly applauded my new idea.

And so it was that, at ten fifteen pm on Christmas Day, my new blog was born.

It Started With a Kiss
Welcome to my new blog!

I've never blogged before, but this is the first new experience for me in what I hope will be a year of discoveries.

As the title suggests, all of this began with a man who stopped to help me when I most needed him. He was gorgeous and he kissed me – but he left and I didn't get a chance to ask his name. I might be mad, but I have to find him again, if for no other reason than to prove that this amazing thing actually happened to me.

So I'm going to spend a year looking for him. I don't know his name, or where he lives: all I know is that I met him on the last Saturday before Christmas in Birmingham's German Christmas Market, when I demolished a toy stall by the Town Hall (long story, I'll explain later). He was amazing: gorgeously handsome, about six feet tall, with hazel-brown eyes and wavy, russet-brown hair. He was wearing a black coat and a green, cream and brown striped scarf, and he helped me to pick up the toys. We spoke for a while and then he gave me the most amazing kiss I've ever received, but he had to leave when his friend called him away.

Were you in the Christmas Market on that Saturday? Do you remember seeing him?

I'm not a desperate woman, or a crazed stalker. I just want to see him again, because I think he felt the same way that I did. So I'm setting myself this challenge in my last year of my twenties: I have between now and the next Christmas Eve to find him.

If you can help – even if it's just an encouraging word to reassure me that I'm not a complete nutter – please let me know.

So, here goes the year of the quest . . . wish me luck!

Love, Romily xx

The next day, I met up with Wren for coffee. We wandered down the canal towpath from her apartment to George, the floating narrowboat café at Brindley Place.

'I really am sorry about the other night,' Wren said, dunking a cinnamon biscuit in the froth of her coffee. She looked so earnest it would have been impossible to be angry with her, even if I was – which I wasn't.

'Don't worry about it,' I smiled, watching two ducks float lazily past the window. 'I think Jack had already guessed something had happened between Charlie and me anyway.'

'And how *is* everything now?'

'We're getting there. To be honest, we haven't spoken much over Christmas, but he texted me yesterday thanking me for his present and it was the normal Charlie-type text.'

'Let me guess: another Yellowjackets album?'

'Ooh, you're good!'

'Nope,' she smiled. 'You two are just predictable.'

'Cheers.'

'Welcome. And what about . . . the *other* thing?'

I knew what she was referring to, but played dumb. 'What other thing?'

Wren's cheeks reddened. 'Oh *please*! The Phantom Kisser?'

The mere mention of my handsome stranger sent a ripple of delight through me. Unable to contain myself any longer, I knew this was time to announce my plan to the world – even if, at that precise moment, that world consisted of Wren, an elderly couple at the table opposite and George's waitress. Baby steps, I told myself.

'I'm going to spend the whole of this year finding him. I've given myself a deadline, too. It's an officially brilliant plan.'

Wren stared at me. 'Tell me more.'

'OK, here it is: I have from now until Christmas Eve next year to find the man who kissed me. I know it's crazy and I know chances are I'll probably fail, but I want to try this because, unless I give it a go, I'll never know if it's possible. No matter how barmy I may sound right now, I honestly believe there's a possibility I *could* find him.' I could feel the adrenalin pumping through me as my heart picked up pace.

Wren shook her head, auburn curls bobbling wildly around her porcelain cheeks. 'Wow. So you're actually going to do this?'

'Yes I am. I've started a blog about it, too.'

'No! When did all this happen?'

'Christmas Day. Something Mum said really made me think.'

'Blimey, I haven't heard you say that before. What did she say?'

'That it's my twenty-ninth year and I should be making it count. And I thought about it and realised that spending the whole of this year looking for the guy from the Christmas Market might be a good place to start. Auntie Mags has been telling me that she was thinking about blogging her cake recipes and I thought a blog would be a great way of documenting the last year of my twenties.'

Wren sat back in her seat, an amused smile wriggling across her lips. 'Wow, Rom, I can't remember the last time I saw you so fired up about something.'

'I feel so positive about it, I really do.'

'That's great . . .' Her smile faded and I knew there was a 'but' coming. 'But what about Charlie? You've been telling me that *he's* the love of your life for the past three years, Rom. How do you know you won't change your mind about this bloke?'

'I don't. But that's all part of the adventure, don't you see? It doesn't matter if I decide halfway through the quest not to pursue it further. What *will* matter is that I tried in the first place.'

Wren giggled. 'You said "quest", Rom.'

'Well, that's what it feels like.'

'I can't believe you just called it a quest, you crazy woman. I think you should go for it. Just promise me you won't do anything silly, OK? And tell me *everything*. Someone needs to be looking out for you.'

'Uncle Dudley's offered to help,' I offered, although it was immediately evident that this did nothing to allay Wren's concerns.

'Even more reason that you should tell me what's happening. Deal?'

I shook her hand. 'Deal.'

Heavy rain had set in by the following morning, washing everything in a dull grey mist, the brave colours of the Christmas lights in the city's streets and houses the only exception to the dimness. After a frustratingly slow journey stuck in endless traffic queues, I finally arrived at the old shoe factory where Tom rents a rehearsal studio. Charlie and Jack were already there, huddled on the curved steps of the peeling Art Deco entrance with identically grumpy expressions.

'Let me guess, we're waiting for Tom?'

Jack grimaced. 'Correct.'

'How long have you been here?'

'Twenty-eight minutes,' Charlie said, pointing at his watch.

'Trust me, he's been counting,' Jack said. 'I've had updates every minute. It's like standing in a doorway with CNN.'

A frigid wind sprang up, blowing sheets of rain into the entrance. I shivered and pushed my hands deeper into my pockets, reprimanding myself for forgetting my gloves this morning. 'I would have been here sooner, but the traffic was horrendous.'

'I wouldn't worry, Rom. It's not like you missed

anything. Wren's running late, too, but no surprise there . . . Oh *finally*,' Charlie announced, looking over my shoulder. I turned to see Tom sprinting through the puddles on the road towards us. 'Leave your watch at home, did you?'

'So-o-o-rry!' Tom chirped. 'Romily, charming as ever.' He kissed my cheek and hugged me, then raised his hand at the lads. 'Jack, Charlie, respect.' Quickly, he unlocked the double doors and propped them open. Clapping his hands together, he grinned at us. 'Care to load in, gentlemen?'

Jack laughed but Charlie strode back out towards his car, muttering unmentionables as he went. Tom pulled a face.

'I see you brought Sarky Git Charlie with you today. I don't like that one. Whatever happened to Nice Friendly Charlie?'

Jack shrugged. 'I've no idea. It's been a while since I've seen him.'

Once all the gear was safely out of the rain, we took turns filling the old service lift, Charlie and I walking up two flights of stairs to unload guitars, drums, amps and cable bags on the first floor, then heading back down to repeat the process.

Thankfully the sheer logistics of getting all the gear to its destination removed the necessity for talking; a blessed relief for me, given that the sight of Charlie had inexplicably brought butterflies to my stomach.

By the time everything was on the first floor, Wren had arrived. We each grabbed a piece of equipment and headed along the high, steel-gabled dusty corridors and towards the heavy riveted steel door into Tom's rehearsal room.

Over the years that The Pinstripes have been performing, we have seen our fair share of rehearsal spaces, ranging from tiny 'sound-proofed garage' affairs to dodgy-looking back rooms in music shops where the mic stands are bolted to the floor. Tom's rehearsal room is a palace by comparison: a sharp contrast to its stark industrial surroundings once you step through the thick steel door. Draped with long white curtains suspended from the ceiling, the room resembles a second-hand furniture shop, with three enormous, incredibly squashed sofas arranged around an old Chinese-patterned rug and a 1940s sideboard that serves as a sound desk stand. A fading rose-painted tray on the gaffer-taped tea crate houses the all-important kettle, mismatched mugs, coffee, tea and dubious-looking scrunched-up sugar bag. Fairy lights are strung up all round the room and a jumble of shaded table lamps illuminate the floor. Tom shares the rent of the room with a heavy metal band called Disaffection and it's a source of great amusement to Wren and I to think of highly tattooed, gruff rockers thrashing out their stuff surrounded by fairy lights and homely soft furnishings.

While the band set up I made tea – something Jack jokily calls 'The Vocalists' Saving Grace', largely because being the singer in a band invariably involves an inordinate amount of standing around while the other band members set up their equipment.

Jack summoned our attention. 'Right, as usual our D'Wayne has been about as useful as a fart in a hurricane and hasn't deigned to enlighten us about what the New Year's Eve wedding organisers want set-wise, apart from the rock'n'roll medley of doom. So I vote we stick to the usual set and add "Auld Lang Syne" for authenticity, followed by the ultimate cheese of Kool and the Gang's "Celebration" for post-midnight.'

'At least it's a bit funky,' Charlie conceded, ignoring Wren who was miming slashing her wrists.

Tom ripped open a packet of chocolate Hobnobs and handed them around. 'Cheese is a necessary evil when it comes to New Year,' he grinned. 'Even more so when it's a wedding on the last day of the year. And anyway, any artistic integrity we once had is a distant memory now. Face it, brothers and sisters, we are *whores* for our art.'

Even considering Tom's legendary lack of tact and decency, this was close to the bone. 'That's terrible, Tom!'

'Yes, but sadly true, Romily. We prostitute our musical selves for the sordid enjoyment of others.' He looked around the room, pleased with the despairing reaction this elicited from the rest of the band. 'OK, Jack, first song in the set?'

'"Love Train". Count us in, Chas.'

Charlie inserted his earphones as Wren and I did the same, watching him for the beat. 'Two, three, four . . .'

My mum can never understand why we need to rehearse before every gig. 'If you play the same songs every time, shouldn't you know them by now?' The fact is that unless we run through the arrangements, medleys and set orders, things can go horribly wrong during the gig. Like the time we played at a particularly raucous wedding where Tom nearly caused a riot by getting stuck in the second verse of 'Love Shack' when he forgot the words for the male vocal part and kept missing the link into the breakdown section. We ended up going round in circles several times until Jack jumped in and brought it to an end. After that, we made it band policy to always rehearse, no matter what.

We took a break between rehearsing sets one and two and Tom produced a tin-foiled parcel from his rucksack while Charlie made coffee.

'Ladies and gentlemen, we have cake!' Tom announced, as we crowded round to witness the unwrapping.

'Please tell me it's your mother's amazing Christmas cake,' Wren said, clapping her hands and whooping when the slab of rich fruitcake nestled within pale marzipan and pure white royal icing was revealed.

'The very same,' Tom grinned. 'Enjoy!'

I wandered over to the jade-green sofa and checked my phone for messages. I was scrolling through my emails when Jack flopped down beside me.

'So.'

'So what?'

He patted my knee. 'So tell me about this guy.'

One look at him confirmed my worst fears. Glancing at Wren, who was engaged in animated debate with Tom, I felt my heart sink. 'When did she tell you?'

'Yesterday, after she'd seen you.'

'Wonderful.'

'She's just concerned about you.'

My hackles were rising. 'Yes, well I wish she'd keep her concerns to herself.'

'Hey, chill. As far as I know, she's only told me. And Sophie, obviously. But that's all.'

'Oh, that's OK then. Only half of my friends know about it.'

'A yearlong search, eh?'

I fixed my eyes on my mobile. 'Yup.'

Jack gave me a gentle nudge. 'I think it's a good thing.'

'You do?'

'Definitely. For one thing it'll take your mind off declaring your undying love to Charlie last week.'

'She told you that, too?'

'Nope. *That* was Charlie.' Jack's smile was warm and

84

comforting, despite the sense of rising panic within me. 'You deserve to be happy, Rom. And if searching for the weirdo in the Christmas Market is going to bring you happiness then I reckon you should go for it. Even if it makes you look like a desperado. Besides, it'll give His Charlieness food for thought.'

This threw me. 'What do you mean by that?'

Jack leaned in and kissed my cheek. 'Never you mind. Just follow your heart, Rom. And be careful, yeah?'

Knowing that Wren had blabbed the details of my plan to Jack and Sophie was annoying, but as I thought about it, I realised that sooner or later all my friends needed to know. If I was going to do this properly, I needed to be loud and proud about it right from the off. As I was mulling this over, Charlie looked up from the far side of the room and caught my eye, causing my heart to perform a somersault. His smile was so quick even a slow-motion camera would have struggled to catch it, but at least it was a smile.

That night, Uncle Dudley sent me a text imbued with so much enthusiasm I could feel it emitting from my handset.

Meet us at Furnace End Car Boot, 6am tomorrow ☺
LOTS to tell! Xx ☺ ☺

The next morning, my uncle was waiting impatiently by the gate in the dark when I arrived at the muddy field, chunky red torch illuminating his bright red cheeks, thick woollen scarf and tweed flat cap. Together we started to walk up the steep path towards the hulking shadows of cars and vans in the darkness of the field beyond.

'No Auntie Mags this morning?' I asked, my breath rising in white clouds as I spoke.

'She's in the car with Elvis and the heater on. Says they're not getting out till the doughnut van opens at seven. You know your auntie. Likes her home comforts too much to fully appreciate the joys of car booting.'

Car booters were laying out their stalls as a surprising number of people milled around.

'I thought we'd be the first ones here.'

'Flippin' 'eck, no! Most of this lot would've turned up at five when the site opened. Got to get here early for the bargains, see. The dealers get here before everyone else to snap up the good stuff. Arrive after eight and all you've got is an outdoor tat sale and a dodgy hot dog van.'

'Wow.'

'Now I just need to see my mate Trev on the military memorabilia stand and then we can grab a cuppa.'

For most people, going to a car boot sale is a leisurely weekend pastime. For Uncle Dudley, it's a highly intricate set of unwritten rules, all designed to lead him to the Holy Grail – the find that will one day make his fortune. And, to give him his due, this approach has paid dividends in the past. A couple of years ago, while rummaging through an old suitcase full of yellowing newspapers and back copies of *Good Housekeeping*, he came across an unassuming notebook, filled with what appeared to be watercolour studies of animals, children and pastoral scenes. The stallholder, keen to shift his stock, agreed to sell Uncle Dudley the suitcase and all its contents for £10. When my uncle took the notebook to an antique dealer, he discovered that the notebook was in fact a pottery artist's personal collection of designs for a major pottery firm in Stoke-on-Trent. At auction, the notebook sold for over £700 – enough to fund a dream trip to Bruges for him and Auntie Mags and a repaint for *Our Pol*.

Watching my uncle at work was an education in strategy. While the casual observer would merely see a fifty-something man engaged in friendly banter with stallholders, to the trained eye it was apparent that Uncle Dudley was a skilful negotiator, cleverly steering the conversation towards a killer deal.

'It's all about *stealth* and *patience*, Romily,' he explained, after I'd seen him barter for a tiny, stylised tank ornament, bringing the price down from £35 to £15. 'I'm like a car boot ninja, ready to strike when they least expect it. This little beauty was made by one of Birmingham's famous armament factories as a salesman's sample during the First World War. Worth about £50, I'd guess. Point is, he wanted £35 for it and I would've happily paid £40. It's the ones who claim to know the most about their stock that know nothing, see. If they don't say anything but the price doesn't move, chances are they know their stuff.'

We walked to 'Dave's Diner' – the grubby-looking refreshment van in the middle of the field – and ordered polystyrene cups of scalding hot tea, the warm steam stinging our faces as we blew on our beverages. Above us, the lightening sky and swelling birdsong heralded the slow arrival of dawn.

'Verdict on Furnace End, then?'

'Nice. In a strangely damp and freezing way.'

Uncle Dudley punched my arm. 'That's why I love you, Romily! You crack me up, you really do.'

'Thanks – I think. So what's the latest on Operation Phantom Kisser?'

His eyes lit up. 'Right. Hold this for us, chick.' He handed me his cup and rifled through his pockets until he found a folded wad of papers. 'Now, I was looking on the web last night and I found *these* . . .' He cleared his throat and started to read from the document in his hands. '"Ellen Adams, 42, has been reunited with a good Samaritan who rescued her car from a snowdrift on Valentine's Day, twenty years ago. A passing remark to a friend led to a blog to find the handsome stranger who had remained in her heart all that time. By chance, the man's sister, Janet Milson, 44, read about the campaign in her local paper and encouraged John Ireland to contact Ellen. When the pair met in August this year, a mutual attraction was obvious. They started to date and, last week, John proposed. 'It just goes to show that true love always wins out,' said a delighted Ellen. 'I never forgot him during all that time and was amazed to discover that he felt the same way.' The couple plan to marry on Valentine's Day next year, exactly twenty-one years since they first met." How about that, our Rom?'

'Wow. That's . . . erm . . .'

'And there's plenty more where that came from! Love, against the odds, couples reunited after thirty, forty, fifty years sometimes, and amazing coincidences bringing old flames back together. Don't you know what this means?'

I had to admit, I didn't. Nice though the story was, what did it mean for my handsome stranger and me? I didn't have twenty years to wait for a reunion: I had a year – no, *less* than a year now – to find him again. 'I'm sorry, Uncle Dud.'

'It *means* it's *possible*, sweetheart! There are so many people who've followed their heart and believed in dreams other folks have written off as plain daft – and those dreams have come up trumps! Now I'm not saying you've got to wait for thirty years to meet this chap again. What I'm saying is that the idea works! And if we can get it in the papers, so much the better!'

'Let's just see how my blog goes first,' I suggested gently, dreading to think what lengths Uncle Dud was considering for publicising my search. 'I don't think I'm ready for large-scale printed public humiliation just yet.'

'Dudley Parker, you promised me doughnuts!' Auntie Mags called as she splodged her way irritably across the field towards us. She had Elvis in tow, resplendent in his baby-blue padded coat, and looking more than a little grateful to have his paws on *terra firma*.

'And doughnuts you shall have, my love. Cup of tea as well?'

Auntie Mags took one look at the refreshment van and shuddered. 'Not likely. I've a flask in the car. There's many things I wouldn't mind picking up here, but listeria isn't one of them.'

As my uncle tripped away to procure doughnuts, Auntie Mags claimed his seat and beamed at me. 'So how's my favourite niece?'

'Good, thanks. Cold, though.' Elvis nudged my knee and when I reached down to pat him he curled up over my feet.

'Yes, well, that's what you get for indulging your uncle in a muddy field before the birds are up. I take it he's told you about his latest findings?'

I nodded and risked a cautious sip at the lava-hot tea in my cup. 'He's very excited.'

'I know.' Auntie Mags pulled a face, but her deep love for her husband was impossible to miss. 'I think this blog of yours could work, though. At any rate, it'll set the ball rolling.'

She was right, of course. I remembered one of the quotes I'd copied down from Dad's desk calendar when I was thirteen: *Every journey begins with a single step*. That's what this was: the first step on the long journey ahead of me. 'Let's do it, then!'

As we high-fived in the middle of a muddy square of Warwickshire countryside, I had no clue of the roller-coaster ride I had unwittingly climbed aboard. If only I'd known . . .

CHAPTER SIX

Get the party started . . .

'I still can't hear anything, Jack.'

'What do you need?'

'Definitely drums, bit of bass and keys, please.'

Jack was hunched over the sound desk at the back of the Excelsior's conference room, tweaking knobs and checking leads. 'I don't understand why you've got no fold-back, Tom.'

'Is it plugged in?' Wren asked.

'Of course it is,' Tom retorted from the stage as I stifled a giggle. 'I connected them all up myself.'

Charlie groaned and left his drum kit to join Jack by the sound desk.

I looked at my watch. Five thirty already and less than an hour left to attempt some kind of a sound-check before the wedding guests descended on the venue. Placing set lists around the stage, I noticed that one of the cables linking Tom's foldback speakers was loose. I pushed the connector back into the socket and a sudden rush of noise blasted out, making him yelp in shock.

'That'll be the cable *you* connected then.' I winked and

Jack, Wren and Charlie launched into a tirade of merciless mocking.

After a single song sound-check, we headed for the Excelsior's luxurious washrooms to get changed. Changing in a toilet cubicle is nothing new for Wren and I: during our time in The Pinstripes we've changed in pub toilets, motorway service station facilities and more than one broom cupboard. I've had to do my make-up bent awkwardly over a compact mirror, sitting on a toilet with one foot wedged against a boltless cubicle door, more often than you would believe.

Already dressed I smiled at my reflection in the large gilt-framed mirror as I applied my make-up. 'Remember those terrible loos we had to change in at the Rock Café in Wigan?' I asked Wren, who was getting dressed in one of the wide toilet stalls.

'With the dodgy flickering lights and that mirror made out of polished steel? How could I forget?' Wren replied, from the other side of the cubicle door. 'It looked like the kind of toilet block where people are murdered on those TV pathology dramas. We were lucky to get out alive.'

'I know. Mind you, the crowd wasn't much better. Remember that embarrassing uncle who was more than a bit pickled, dancing in front of you?' I laughed.

The cubicle door opened and Wren joined me at the mirror, pulling a tube of mascara from her bag. 'Don't remind me.' Adopting a gruff, Lancashire accent, she began to imitate the knock-kneed, middle-aged lothario who had spent most of our second set at the sixtieth birthday party in the dodgy venue wiggling his worryingly snake-like hips just feet away from her, his pink wing-collared shirt open to his exceedingly hairy navel. 'I thought Jack was going to punch him at one point.'

I started to pin up my hair, spraying with hairspray as I went. As Wren and I stood side by side, I couldn't help thinking we both looked good this evening – Wren in her deep green satin cocktail dress, wild red curls piled up on top of her head; and me in my purple strapless dress with dark blue sequinned shrug, my straight dark blonde hair now well and truly held in a slick chignon. Although it can be a pain sometimes, especially when time is short between the sound-check and the start of the first set, I enjoy being able to dress up for gigs. I have more sparkly tops and dresses than I probably need, a still-growing collection of glittery costume jewellery and several pairs of fabulous (but, crucially, comfortable) heels to choose from. It's fun to transform myself before I step on stage, not to mention the terrific boost it gives to my confidence. All part of the magic of performing, I suppose.

'Liking the up-do, Rom.'

'Thanks. I thought I'd try something new.'

'So, how's the search going for mystery man?' She lowered her voice, even though we were the only two people there.

'Good, actually. My aunt and uncle found all these amazing stories about people who have found love against the odds.'

Wren grimaced. 'Watch them, Rom, especially your uncle. If he has his way he'll be trying to get you on *Jeremy Kyle*.'

'Don't worry. I have them under control.'

'In the meantime, like Sophie said to me today, your blog might give Charlie a kick up the proverbial.' She winked and started to gather up her things. Together we headed out into the hotel foyer.

I wasn't sure how I felt about being such a talking point with my friends, I've never been a particularly private person – if anything I'm maybe a little *too* honest sometimes – but knowing that the details of my life were being picked over out of my earshot unnerved me a little. Nothing I could do about it now, I told myself. I was going to have to get used to my life being on show if I stood any chance of finding my stranger again.

In any case, there were much more interesting things to focus on: principally, the wedding reception we were about to perform at. The Excelsior staff had positioned all the tables for the evening event while we had been getting ready, and the whole of the event hall had been transformed.

Contrary to what the guys think, the reason Wren and I love weddings so much is not a pathological urge to get married but an appreciation of the elements that create a magical day. It is impossible not to be swept up in the sheer romanticism of a wedding – even if the bride and groom are dressed as Elvis and Marilyn Monroe, have poodles as bridesmaids or are wearing matching kaftans . . .

Thankfully tonight, for the last wedding of the year, the theme was stunningly elegant: black, white and gold. The dozen round tables set around the polished dance floor were draped in pristine white linen cloths and surrounded by white-covered seats tied with gold bows at the back. Each place setting featured a gold platter, cutlery and fine crystal glassware edged with a single line of gold. Large centrepieces in dark glass vases featured white and yellow lilies, roses and sprays of deep green ivy trailing out along the table. Tea lights flickered from clear crystal holders, reflected in the gold sequins and crystal beads scattered across the tablecloths. In the dimmed light of the event hall, this gave the stunning effect of lavish tables at a prestigious award ceremony.

The conference hall was steadily filling up with well-heeled guests – women in expensive black, white and gold evening gowns that appeared to make them float on air as they moved around the room, and men in black evening suits so perfectly tailored that I half-expected George Clooney to stroll in at any moment.

We took in as much of the scene as we could, knowing that Sophie was going to demand a detailed account of it all when we next saw her, and then Wren and I reluctantly left the glamorous scene and made our way across the dance floor towards the stage. A black curtain hanging from one side created a small backstage area where Charlie, Jack and Tom were gathered, sitting on flight cases and a couple of chairs stolen from front of house. They were smartly dressed in freshly-pressed black shirts, black trousers and white ties.

'Wow, Rom, great dress.' Tom nodded approvingly as I joined them. 'Nice to see those legs of yours out for a change.'

I gave a little spin and smiled at him. 'You don't look so bad yourself.'

'See? She knows class when she sees it. Are you ladies ready?'

Wren nodded. 'What time are we on?'

Charlie consulted his watch. 'I reckon we start about eight fifteen. There's a buffet break at nine fifteen and the DJ goes on until eleven. Then we're back on again until just after the big Happy New Year bit and the DJ will take over until about two.'

Tom scowled. 'It's going to be a long night, guys. Don't suppose we can start to pack down while "Disco Paul" is doing his thing?'

Jack shook his head. 'Sorry. I had a word with Eric, the wedding planner, but no joy, I'm afraid. He said it would "spoil the aesthetics of the atmosphere", whatever that means.'

'Heaven *forbid* we spoil anyone's aesthetics,' I said.

'Especially if we're "going with the demographic",' Wren added.

Charlie groaned. 'Anyone have any idea where our great and noble manager is this evening?'

Nobody did.

'He'd better show,' Tom said, picking up his guitar and beginning to tune it.

'He will,' Wren quickly replied. 'He said he would be here.'

The curtain pulled back and Eric looked in. 'All ready, guys?'

There was a tangible change in the atmosphere as the band moved into action. I could feel my pulse rate increase and the familiar flutter of anticipation in my stomach. I hummed through a couple of scales and shook the tension from my hands – two pre-gig rituals that help to calm my nerves.

No matter where the gig is, how large the audience or which songs I'm about to perform, this moment is always the same: it's like standing on a precipice, daring yourself to jump. Even though I have waited in the wings on count- less stages, and even though I know the set backwards, there remains a small element of the unknown, which I will only discover when I stand before the audience. It's an intoxicating mix of risk and possibility – and it's impossible not to feel its fire.

On stage, the Master of Ceremonies was welcoming the guests and calling them forward on to the dance floor. The rising sense of expectation fuelled the adrenalin rush I knew that all of us were experiencing at that precise moment. Charlie pulled his drumsticks from his back pocket and hopped up the steps on to the stage. Jack picked up his music folder, waiting for Tom to take the steps before him. Wren and I fitted our in-ear monitors and switched on our power-packs as we headed on stage.

'Ladies and gentlemen, let's have a warm welcome for your band for this evening – The Pinstripes!'

As New Year's Eve gigs go, the Excelsior event was relatively uneventful. There was the usual good-natured heckling, lairy behaviour and embarrassing 'Dad-dancing' that come with the territory when there are two hundred and fifty sozzled wedding guests in the mood for a party. The bride and groom surprised everyone with a well-choreographed American Smooth-inspired first dance to 'It Had to Be You', the bride's flowing 1930s-style dress making her look every inch like Ginger Rogers. Later on, the Hollywood sheen slipped somewhat when she and her new husband joined their friends in frenzied moshing to Reef's 'Place Your Hands' – one of the stranger song requests of the night. Wren and I enjoyed a good banter with the crowd, encouraging them to dance and sing along with us, and the band were summoned back on stage for an encore at the end of our performance.

The only downside of the night was the extremely late pack-down time, after 'Disco Paul' the DJ decided he was such a hit with the merry crowd that it warranted another hour's worth of 'yesteryear hits'. Trust me, keeping your cool backstage when you're tired, longing for bed and forced to listen to 'Build Me Up Buttercup', 'Oops Upside Your Head' and 'Agadoo' is an *art* . . .

At 4.15 am, we loaded the last of the gear into Jack's van and shut the doors. Charlie flopped against the van's side and I looked around at my near-comatose bandmates.

'Happy New Year, everyone.'

A weary set of murmurs were sent back in my direction.

'This time next year,' Wren began, only to be met with protestations. 'No, *listen*. This time next year, we will have done the millionaire gig and we might just be looking at a full diary for the year ahead.'

'Amen to that,' Jack said, raising his half-empty plastic water bottle.

Tom buttoned his jacket against the bitter night air. 'I can't believe *Duh-Wayne* didn't even show his face tonight. The organiser was expecting him to be here.'

Charlie grunted. 'He wasn't the only one.

'He texted me at midnight to say he'd been majorly delayed and wouldn't make it,' Wren offered. 'He was really upset about it – no, Charlie, don't look like that – he did.'

I could feel the rumblings of an argument beginning – an occupational hazard when there are five knackered musicians all with short tempers, a journey back and a van to unpack before anyone can go home – so I stepped in. 'This is a conversation for another time. Let's just get the gear back to Jack and Soph's so we can all get to bed, OK?'

Jack slung his battered rucksack over his shoulder. '*Thank you*, Rom. I'm heading off. See you at the house, guys? I'll put the kettle on.'

'Smashing,' Tom replied. 'Fancy a lift, Rom?'

Charlie stepped forward. 'Actually, why don't you take Wren with you to help Jack get the garage ready for the gear? Rom can come back with me.'

A sinking feeling claimed my insides. 'I'm fine to go with Tom.'

Tom exchanged glances with Charlie and held up his hands. 'Hey, I'm cool whatever. The sooner we get this lot sorted the sooner I can get to bed.'

Charlie was clearly set on his suggestion. 'It'll just be better if Wren goes with you. I mean, her bass is already in the boot of your car.'

A clearly relieved Wren ignored my silent pleas to not let this happen. 'Cheers, mate.'

I watched helplessly as my friends swiftly deserted me and an excruciatingly awful silence fell between Charlie and I. He just stood there, frozen to the spot, staring at me. What was I supposed to do now? I avoided his stare, looking over to the yellow wheelie bins at the back of the hotel, suddenly vulnerable. This, I realised, was the first time we had been alone since our talk in the park and I had no idea what to say to him. I stamped my feet to coax the circulation back into my toes, which tonight had endured the triple-whammy of hours of standing about, dancing on stage and now freezing in the wee small hours of New Year's Day. One thing was certain, if I wanted to get home before daylight I had to chivvy things along a bit.

He opened his mouth to speak but I got there first.

'Let's move then, shall we?' It was my best attempt at chirpiness, given that I was exhausted and cold.

He looked at me for a moment, frowned and climbed into the driver's seat without a word.

'Great,' I muttered to myself, as I got into the passenger side, balking at the ripe aroma wafting from the bins, 'of all the men in the city tonight I had to choose the strong silent type to hitch a ride with.'

Eyes fixed on the road ahead, Charlie started the engine and we pulled into the thickly frosted darkness. I thanked heaven that this was only a short journey, even if it was likely to be the longest twenty-five minutes of my entire life. Was he angry with me? And if so, why wasn't he using this opportunity to say so? With no audible communication forthcoming, I huddled up against the passenger door and stared out at the passing streets. I could feel the lack of sleep and the retreat of post-performance adrenalin sapping my strength, but Charlie's behaviour irked me. Why go to all the trouble of requesting that I travel with him, only to sit in stony silence? Within five minutes, it was too much. One thing all my bandmates know about me is that I never back away if there's an argument brewing.

'Right. I've had enough of the silent treatment. What is your problem?'

The sharpness of my tone and suddenness of its entrance into the van made Charlie jump. His head jerked round to stare at me and the van swerved a little. 'What did you do that for?'

'What, *talk* to you? Oh, I don't know, Charlie. I just thought that's what two friends tend to do when they share a journey home.'

His frame tensed as my sarcasm hit its target square on. 'You nearly made me go off the road. Are you mad?'

'Yes, I am, actually. I'm mad at you.'

'Me? What for?'

Prepare yourself for a tirade, Mr Wakeley. 'Because I've been hanging around for hours, while you and the others faffed about with the gear, then even longer when you all decided to start arguing about our manager. I'm cold and I'm tired and I was all set to go with Tom until you stepped in. And now we're here and you can't even speak to me.'

'We're all tired, Rom. I'm sorry that I'm not "chat-central" right now. I just want to get this van back to Jack's and go home.'

'So why ask me to come with you? What was wrong with Wren and Tom?'

'Nothing, it was . . . You know, I wish I *had* asked them

100

now. I doubt either of them would be having a hissy fit at me for being quiet.'

'You haven't answered my question.'

'You haven't asked me a credible one yet.'

The classic red-rag-to-bull moment had arrived. 'Excuse me? You *specifically* ask me to come with you, proceed to ignore me completely and when I finally say something, you accuse me of overreacting? I think you're the one having the hissy fit, Wakeley, not me. I thought we'd sorted what happened at Christmas. So what the hell do you want from me?'

Charlie braked sharply at a red light and faced me. 'I thought we might have some time alone, OK?'

I opened my mouth to speak, but words had deserted me. I didn't know what this meant and I wasn't sure I wanted to find out.

'There are things I wanted to say, but I've been racking my brains since we set off trying to work out where to begin.'

'I'm sorry.' My voice was weak and pathetic when it returned. 'I thought . . .'

'I know what you thought.'

I took a breath. 'What did you want to say?'

Charlie shook his head. 'It doesn't matter.'

'It does.' Tentatively, I reached forward and let my fingers brush against his warm hand on the steering wheel. The sensation of it was momentarily comforting before he flinched and I quickly withdrew my hand.

'I just wanted to say that this year's going to be better. For both of us. Things will get back to normal and there won't be *this* . . .' He swallowed hard. 'I hate that there's this invisible – *thing* – between us. I wanted to let you know I won't let it stay there forever. That's all.'

This threw me completely. I don't know what I was expecting, but this wasn't it. I watched his face in the darkness, the passing streetlights washing alternate waves of orange light and inky shadow across his features. There were a million things I wanted to say to him, but I didn't know where to begin. Did he feel the same? I couldn't be sure: his face was frustratingly expressionless, but there was something in his eyes that I couldn't quite make out. For a moment I almost said something, but instantly thought better of it. 'Thank you . . . um, for saying that,' I managed, finally. And then, because I couldn't come up with anything better to say: 'Happy New Year, Charlie.'

His sigh was heavier than an anvil. 'Happy New Year, Rom.'

January blew through the city with a freezer-like blast – first with an amazing hoar frost, which coated each branch and blade of grass in long, spidery ice crystals, and then the snow descended. Roads became impassable, kids were granted a few more days before their schools opened after the Christmas break and even grown-ups who weren't badly affected called into their workplaces and claimed a day off anyway.

Having spent two hours on an impossibly slow-moving bus that eventually came to a halt half a mile away from my destination, I was trudging along the main road to work when Amanda called.

'The water's frozen at the studio,' she told me. 'Maintenance have got all the heating on trying to defrost the pipes. Needless to say, don't bother coming in today.'

I should have been annoyed at her calling me so late with this news, but actually it felt like a reprieve. The workload at Brum FM had been slightly crazy for the past

102

week, so a surprise day off was more than welcome. With nothing else to do, I decided to walk into the city centre. I crunched through the pristine powder as whisper-light flakes fell thick and fast, gently patting against my nose and cheeks.

The rate at which the snow was falling, together with the considerable depth of snow on the main roads already, had brought the city to a standstill. Row upon row of frustrated motorists waited in immobile, steaming jams under thick white shrouds. It was almost as if every family was trying to leave the city at once, like a scene from a disaster movie where everybody is frantically trying to escape some apocalyptic calamity.

As I pressed on I noticed a distinct difference between the people who were walking and the people stuck in their cars. The motorists were stony-faced, glaring at each flake of snow – now nearing blizzard proportions – as it lashed against their windscreens. By contrast, the people who walked alongside me were smiling, relaxed and visibly proud of themselves, chatting and laughing with passers-by as they walked past. It was almost as if we had recaptured a little of the famed wartime 'bulldog spirit' our grandparents had spoken so fondly of: utter strangers uniting together in the face of a common threat.

By the time I reached Wren's apartment block, I was grinning like a kid, although my eyes stung from the whiteness of everything.

'Come up, come up!' Wren's ecstatic tones crackled through the intercom at the entrance to the building when I buzzed her apartment.

She was positively bubbling with excitement when I walked in. 'A whole day off school and it's almost the weekend too!' she whooped, flitting past me into the kitchen.

'I'm making mocha with squirty cream and marshmallows! Want one?'

I stepped into the black granite and walnut kitchen. 'Are you sure that extra sugar is a good idea when you're this hyper already?'

She giggled, curls the colour of a new penny bouncing around her face. 'I don't care. There's no school, it's snowing and all is well with the world!'

Leaving her to prepare the kamikaze sugar rush, I pulled off my boots and sank into the sofa, gazing out towards the window at the sheets of snow covering the chic buildings outside.

Wren brought in two enormous mugs of bobbling cream-topped mocha and sat down beside me. 'I meant to ask you, were you OK after the New Year gig?'

'Just tired. I didn't get home till gone six am.'

My nonchalance didn't wash with Wren. She knows me too well. 'It was more than that. You were really quiet when you got out of the van. Did Charlie say something to upset you?'

'No, not really.' I scooped a spoonful of cream and ate it. 'Things are odd between us at the moment.' I decided to ask the question that had been tapping on my shoulder since the aftermath of the gig. 'You don't think he knows about my plan to find the Phantom Kisser, do you?'

'Of course he doesn't.'

'Well, the rest of the band seems to know.'

Wren's eyes narrowed. 'Would it matter if he did?'

I was about to answer when Stevie Wonder started singing 'Sir Duke' from my mobile. 'Hello?'

'Alright, our bab!'

I had to smile. Uncle Dudley's enthusiasm is infectious

even on the other end of a phone line. 'Aye aye, Cap'n! How's everything going?'

'It's up! Operation Phantom Kisser is officially in action. Are you near a computer?'

I looked around the room to see if I could spot Wren's laptop. I couldn't. 'Um . . .'

'What do you need?' she asked.

'Laptop?' I mouthed.

Jumping to her feet, Wren started a comedic search around the living room, lifting cushions off the sofa and tipping her large handbag upside down on the oak floor, sending coins and keys and paper skidding in all directions. Never let it be said that Wren Malloy is invisible when she's trying to help . . .

'What on earth was that?' asked Uncle Dudley when he heard the crash.

'It's just Wren. *Quietly helping*, as usual. Oh, looks like she's found it.'

'Oh, bless her! Right, I'll ping you the link.'

Did my uncle just say 'ping'? Surely not . . . Mind you, nothing Uncle Dudley does surprises me now. Since he bought *Our Pol* and discovered the joys of mobile broadband he's become a genuine silver surfer, a champion of social media and a fiend on Facebook. Hearing him casually mentioning 'DM-ing' someone, or 'RT-ing' something interesting he's read from a 'fellow Tweeter' never fails to amuse me.

I signed into my email and waited. 'It's here,' I told my uncle, exchanging an anxious look with Wren as she rejoined me.

'Click the link, sweetheart, and see what your old uncle's been busy with!'

Opening the email, I felt my heart stop.

There, in the middle of the screen was what looked like

an explosion in a flash animation studio. Somehow my uncle had uploaded a whole host of flashing, scrolling and rotating images into a single page that bore the legend: 'FIND THE PHANTOM KISSER!' It was, to put it bluntly, a migraine in visual form.

Wren and I stared at the screen. After some time, Wren said, 'Wow.'

'Good, eh?' Uncle Dudley's voice was full of pride. 'Your Auntie Mags came up with the strap-line. And the dancing bears, you see? Proper clever she is. We thought you could load it up as a gadget on your blog. I've been reading online about how to do all that and it looks like a doddle. Do you like it?'

'It's – um – it's . . .'

'Different,' Wren said slowly.

A moment like this required diplomacy. I desperately didn't want to offend him, even if his handiwork was, at that precise moment, filling every last filament of my being with a sense of slowly undulating nausea. 'You've put so much effort into it. Thank you.'

'No probs, our bab. Least me and your auntie could do for you, especially after the Charlie thing.'

'Sorry?'

'Listen, Romily, just because one fool didn't want you, it doesn't mean there isn't someone out there who will. This chappy you met at Christmas might just be the love of your life. You're on the brink of an adventure that could maybe change everything. Take it from someone who knows, chick, it's worth putting your neck on the line to find that kind of happiness.'

His faith in me – and his complete understanding of why I wanted to pursue the possibility of finding my handsome stranger – was truly inspirational. And about as far removed from the reaction my parents were likely to have when they found out.

Wren saw the change in my expression and, concerned, gripped my hand. I could feel tears welling as I fought to steady myself. 'Thank you,' I whispered. 'That means a lot to me.'

'Aw, don't you start blubbing, our bab, you'll have me going off if you're not careful! So you like it?'

This was it, I knew it: the official start of my yearlong quest. (Sorry, Wren, but there was really no other way of describing what I was about to undertake.) I had taken the first step of telling people close to me. No more hiding, no turning back. I was on my way to destiny.

'It's perfect, Uncle Dud.'

'Right, kidda. Let's go find him!'

CHAPTER SEVEN

Keep on moving . . .

I'm a singer with a wedding band, did I mention that?

At New Year my band was booked to perform for a New Year's Eve wedding. It made quite a nice change from the usual New Year bashes we play at, although some things remained the same – people drinking too much, embarrassing dancing and blatant lechery breaking out on the stroke of midnight.

I was watching the scrum for the first kiss of the New Year (which was quite monumental with two hundred and fifty guests merrily launching themselves at each other) and while it was amusing to see of course, I couldn't help thinking about the man who kissed me nearly two weeks ago.

I can't believe almost a fortnight has passed since I met him. He's on my mind all the time. I know this will probably make me sound like a total desperado, but that's the way it is.

My best friend Wren said something at the wedding that really made me think. We were standing at the front of the stage, dancing away as always, when she leaned over to me during an instrumental break and yelled, 'Just think, your mystery guy could be at this wedding!' I immediately scanned the guests across the room to see if she was right and, needless to say, he wasn't there. But the point is, he could have been. That's what makes this situation so irresistibly compelling: he could be anywhere. I mean, he was there almost two weeks ago, wandering around just like I was. Perhaps he lives on the next street to me, visits the same coffee shop for his morning cappuccino, or catches the same train. He could be literally anywhere I go from now on – and that just makes me more determined to find him . . .

'So, how's the search for the Phantom Kisser going?' Jack grinned, as we were carrying speakers into the elegant venue for our next wedding gig, a large Georgian mansion set in acres of beautiful parkland on the outskirts of Stratford-upon-Avon.

'I wish people would stop calling him that,' I replied. 'Honestly, you, Wren, my aunt and uncle . . . It makes him sound creepy. And he wasn't.'

Jack's smile was warm and instantly forgivable. 'Well, we need to call him *something*. "Mystery bloke" doesn't have an alluring ring to it.'

'How about PK?' Wren interjected as she arrived with an armful of microphone stands and bent down to stack them on the ballroom floor.

I liked that. It somehow made my handsome stranger seem, well, *less* of a stranger. I smiled at my friends. 'Excellent, PK it is!'

Charlie stuck his head between Jack and Wren. 'Who's PK?'

'Oh, just a new make of amp we were talking about,' Jack said, as quick as a flash.

Charlie's midnight blue eyes narrowed. 'Why is Rom buying an amp?'

'I'm not,' I said, noticing Wren pull a face and leave. 'I just read about it and, you know, thought I'd ask . . .' It was an awful reply and quite obviously a lie, but thankfully Charlie had other things on his mind and didn't notice.

'Whatever. Anyone know what's got into Tom today? He's scarily quiet.'

We all looked to the other side of the room where Tom was slumped over his guitar retuning the strings.

Wren shook her head. 'No idea. He's definitely not himself, though.'

D'Wayne strolled into the ballroom, iPhone glued to his ear. Wren waved and he approached us. 'Great news, guys. That gig at the Scottish castle has just been confirmed for May.'

'Blimey, nice one.' Charlie couldn't hide his surprise at the news.

'Good money, is it?' Jack asked.

D'Wayne grinned. 'Oh yes, my friends. Four hundred each, plus expenses, so I'll book us into a local hotel for the night and whoever drives will have their petrol costs covered.'

'Well, I think that's brilliant. Well done, D'Wayne,' Wren said. Her eyes shone with mischief when she saw the effect her praise had on our manager, who had all of a sudden become a bashful fifteen-year-old.

I left them chatting and walked over to Tom.

'Hey.'

He didn't look up. 'Hey.'

'You OK?'

110

'Peachy, Rom.'

I folded my arms. 'Don't ever go into acting, will you? That was dreadful.'

He gave a hollow laugh as he raised his head, and immediately I could see sadness paling his face. 'Thanks, loser.'

'What's going on? You haven't been yourself all day.'

It was some time before he answered. Tom and I have always had an understanding. While we were at university together, we both worked on Saturdays at his granddad's pub and during that time we developed a close friendship, talking about everything from music to relationships and whatever other random topics we happened to fall upon. He likes to think that he's enigmatic and able to shield his feelings from other people, but he's about as mysterious as a glass box. So when he tells the rest of the band that being an IT specialist in a job with few promotion prospects doesn't bother him, I know he's lying. Or when he insists he doesn't mind that one of his best friends chucked him out of a band just before they landed a huge recording contract and became global stars, I don't believe a word of it. This latest attempt to avoid the truth was doomed and he knew it.

'It's Anya and me. We're over.'

This was a shock. Tom and Anya had been together since they met at college and though things hadn't been great between them for a while, we'd all assumed they would work through it. 'Oh hun, no! What happened?'

He shrugged. 'She's met someone else. At work. I mean, a solicitor, for heaven's sake. I met him once – the guy's a jerk. His idea of cutting-edge music is James Blunt.'

I placed my hand on his arm and gave it a squeeze. 'That's dreadful. When did you . . .?'

'Last night. She said we'd run our course and wanted

something new. I wasn't likely to argue with her, not with her mind made up like that. I mean, it sucks, but I guess I'll get over it eventually.'

'Yes, you will. Absolutely. In fact,' I looked out at the venue for tonight's wedding gig, as people milled around setting tables and arranging flowers underneath an enormous glittering crystal chandelier, 'I reckon there could be plenty of options for you here tonight.'

That elicited a wry smile. 'At least some eye candy will keep my mind off stuff.' He put his hand on my shoulder. 'Cheers, Rom. Um . . . would you tell the others and ask them to give me a bit of space? The way Charlie and Jack were looking at me just now I might end up with my head kicked in otherwise.'

'Sure. The wedding organiser's just brought us some leftovers from the wedding breakfast. Can I get you anything?'

'In a totally film-clichéd way, I'm not hungry. Thanks, though.'

I left him and rejoined the others who were enjoying the surprise gift of food at the back of the room.

'He's fine,' I said, when they all looked up at me. 'But we should just be a bit sensitive around him today, OK?'

'Fine by me,' Jack replied through a huge mouthful of food. 'If he's not eating it means more for us.'

You never know how a wedding gig will go, and tonight was no exception. Despite the beautiful surroundings, impeccably attired bridal party and equally elegant guests, the atmosphere was noticeably muted and – worse for us – the dance floor remained frustratingly empty after the first dance. D'Wayne offered an unhelpful shrug from the side of the stage whenever I looked over at him. Tom was defiantly quiet and Jack and Charlie wore identical thunderous expressions. Still, Wren and I pressed on regardless, smiling and dancing for all we were worth.

'Why was nobody dancing?' Jack asked D'Wayne, as we congregated by the side of the stage while the buffet was served.

'I don't understand it,' he replied. 'When I booked the gig the bride and groom were adamant their guests would be dancing all night.'

'Well they weren't,' Wren said, stepping out of her impossibly high gold sequinned heels and reaching down to rub her aching feet. 'I felt like a right prat up there smiling like a loon.'

'Aye aye,' Jack nodded in the direction of the groom who was walking towards us. 'This should be interesting.'

'Guys, I'm so sorry. I don't know what's got into them. Karen's really upset.'

Charlie smiled at him. 'Hey, don't worry, Josh. It happens sometimes.'

'Is there anything we can do to help?' D'Wayne suggested.

Josh shrugged. 'You're all great. I can't think of what more you could do for us.'

Tom threw his hat into the ring. 'Maybe the set list isn't exciting your guests? Are there any songs that you and your friends like?'

Josh considered this for a moment. 'I'm a bit of a fan of Bon Jovi,' he admitted. 'My mates always rib me about it.'

Tom, Jack and Charlie shared a look. 'You reckon you can handle a bit of classic rock, Wren?'

Wren sniggered. 'Their back catalogue was the first thing I learned to play. My bass teacher was obsessed with them.'

Charlie turned to me with a cheeky smile that momentarily threw me. 'Think you can manage it, Rom?'

I had never previously found a good time to confess my thorough knowledge of all things BJ (thanks to my brothers playing little else as we were growing up), but now seemed like an opportune moment. 'I'll be fine. You call it and I'll sing it.'

So that's what we did. And it was as if a switch had been flicked to bring the room to life. Delighted, the guests abandoned the chairs they had been so resolutely glued to and crowded on to the dance floor in an enthusiastic jumble of grooving bodies. Halfway through 'Living On a Prayer', Tom sidled up to me, clearly loving the unexpected opportunity of full-on eighties axe-wielding, and yelled: 'This is the best gig in ages!'

It was great to see Tom's demeanour so transformed, and fantastic to witness the change in The Pinstripes as a whole. The feeling when you connect with an audience is completely wonderful and unlike any other. There's an invisible energy that links you to them, an understanding that moves the performance and drives their response. That's what happened that night and we all felt it. By the end of the night, everybody in the room was smiling – and none broader than Karen and Josh, the radiant bride and groom.

'That was hilarious,' Jack said later, as he and I were coiling up microphone leads. 'Who knew that Bon Jovi had the ability to save a wedding gig?'

I laughed. 'I can't get over us doing three encores. *Three!* When was the last time that happened?'

'Er, *never*,' Wren said. 'You know, I reckon we're in the wrong line of business. Maybe we should start a Bon Jovi tribute act.'

'Or maybe not,' D'Wayne interrupted. 'I've given out five cards tonight. You're stuck doing wedding gigs for the time being, I'm afraid.'

'Perhaps we should make it policy to always ask the bride and groom to nominate their favourite songs,' I suggested. 'I don't want another first set like tonight. It was excruciating.'

'Amen, sister!' Charlie brought his drum cases to the front of the stage and hopped off to carry them across the ball-room to the fire exit at the back of the room.

'Forget that for a second. I want to know how the blog is going,' Jack said, with a cheeky smile.

I groaned. 'You saw it then?'

'Saw it? I'm following it!'

'Me too,' Tom added. 'And I've tweeted the link to my Twitter followers.'

'You mean all the desperate bridesmaids you've met at our wedding gigs who are still lusting after you?' Wren chuckled.

Tom winked back. 'Hey, what can I tell you? Girls love a guitarist.'

'Great. So is it safe to assume that the entire band knows about it, then?' I asked.

'Knows about what?' We hadn't seen Charlie come back in and there was an incredibly awkward pause as he stared at us. I had made a point of not thinking about what would happen when Charlie found out and now, with a sinking heart, I realised why.

'Rom's searching for a bloke who kissed her,' Wren informed him.

I couldn't tell whether his expression was that of shock or surprise. 'Oh? When?'

Jack glanced at me. 'The last Saturday before Christmas. In the Christmas Market.'

Charlie stared at me, a million questions in his eyes. 'Right.' My heart went out to him, but I couldn't find the words to do the same.

115

'It's so sweet,' Wren continued mercilessly, clearly on a mission. 'Her mad Uncle Dudley's concocting all these crazy schemes to try to find him.'

'So this guy didn't leave a number?' Charlie asked.

'Didn't hang about, did he, Rom?' D'Wayne grinned.

'Blimey, have you seen the time? We need to be out of here by twelve,' I said quickly, grabbing an armful of microphone stands and making my way off the stage as fast as I could. Dropping them with the stack of equipment by the fire exit doors, I ran out into the frosty car park to my car, leaning against it as I tried to calm my thudding heart. I was angry with myself for not considering how Charlie might react to the news. He had made his feelings towards me abundantly clear; but even so, discovering that the girl who had so openly declared her affections for him had then been kissed by someone else barely twenty minutes later might, understandably, be an unwelcome revelation.

'Rom.'

I jumped and looked up to see Charlie walking towards me. *Great.* 'Hey.'

'You're serious about finding this bloke, are you?'

I nodded. 'I should have told you.'

'You should have.'

Please, car park tarmac, swallow me now. 'I'm sorry.'

He shrugged. 'Don't be. You've every right to do whatever you want. Just be careful, OK? The guy might be an idiot.'

'Right. Absolutely. Thanks.' Was that the best I could do? The tension between us was excruciating and alien, and might as well have been a ten-foot-high brick wall for the separation it made me feel from him.

'Good.' He regarded me for a moment and then, unexpectedly, leaned in for what was, quite possibly, the world's most awkward hug. 'Let's get back in, shall we?'

Taking a deep breath to combat the shaking in my legs, I followed him into the warmth of the mansion.

CHAPTER EIGHT

Love is all around . . .

It's been four weeks since The Kiss and I am now
more determined than ever to find him.

Now that all my friends know about it, I'm actually
feeling more positive about the quest. It's like it's out
in the open now and I can be honest and proud about
it. It was a little tricky to begin with – I mean, I know
how I'd probably react if one of my friends said they
were spending the next year searching for someone
they barely knew – but I think now they're rooting for
me. Well, most of them anyway.

And it's not before time. Tomorrow is the first day
of my twenty-ninth year – the year I'm hoping will
mark the start of big things for me. It feels weird to
be having the last birthday of my twenties, but I'm
going to make it count. Whether or not I find PK is
immaterial: what matters is that I try to follow my
heart. That's what I'm telling myself anyway. And if it
all goes horribly wrong, at least I will have kept you
entertained, dear four faithful followers. Or should I
say Tom, Wren, Jack and someone else I suspect is a

friend of Tom's. I'm glad you're all coming on this
daft adventure with me. Please say hello in the
comments beneath this post if you get a moment – it
would be nice to hear from you.
Rom x

'A toast!' Jack said, pushing back his chair and raising his glass, much to the bemusement of the other diners in the cosy French bistro. 'To our wonderful Romily Parker. May all her dreams come true this year and may she not be arrested for stalking the poor fella who kissed her at Christmas.'

Laughing, my friends rose to their feet and joined the toast. 'To Romily!'

'Speech!' Tom called and Wren whistled.

There was no point refusing, so I stood up. 'Thank you, you nutters. Well, seeing as I now have less than a year of my twenties left, I would just like to thank you all for being my fabulous friends through almost three decades of my life. And I know the quest might seem certifiable to some of you . . .' I couldn't help noticing that Charlie skilfully avoided my eye at this point, 'but I'd like to say I value your support. Um, that's it really. I think we should eat now before it gets cold.'

'Hear hear!' Jack shouted as I sat down amid the applause of my friends. 'But before you do, we've bought you this to help with your search.' Beaming, he produced a large gift box from under the table and presented it to me.

Casting a cursory glance at the collected grins around the table, I untied the ribbon bow and lifted the lid. I laughed as I drew out a large deerstalker hat, magnifying glass and pair of plastic kid's binoculars. 'Hilarious,' I said, popping the hat on my head. 'I'm sure these will come in very handy.'

D'Wayne coughed self-consciously to summon my attention. 'While we're on the subject of presents, I've got you this.' He handed me a small, flat package wrapped in jelly-bean-printed paper. When I opened it, I was surprised to find a reporter's notebook, Bic biro and pencil.

'I thought it might be useful, you know, for writing your jingles. Or keeping notes about this bloke you're looking for.'

'Where did you pick that up, D'Wayne?' Tom laughed. 'A twenty-four-hour garage?'

D'Wayne picked at the edge of his napkin. 'It was the only place to stop on the way here.'

The rest of my friends fell about laughing, whooping at the opportunity to joke at D'Wayne's expense, but I reached across the table and patted his hand.

'Well, I think it's wonderful. And very useful. Thanks, D'Wayne.'

As we ate, laughed and drank, I couldn't resist sneaking a glance at Charlie from time to time. He didn't look at me, and although his smile had returned and the jokes were once again bouncing back and forth between him, Jack and Tom, I knew what he was thinking. Or suspected, anyhow. It felt odd to see him acting normally with everyone else when I knew he was still being careful around me. This time last year, he would have been sharing those jokes with me . . .

But it didn't matter. I couldn't worry about what Charlie did or didn't think about me. I needed to focus on happy things – like finding PK again. Instinctively, I took a quick look around the packed Friday night restaurant, just in case he might be one of the diners tonight. Now *that* would be a great birthday present, I mused to myself, closing my eyes for a moment and summoning the memory of his lips on mine.

'You look happy.' Jack nudged me.

'I am happy.'

'Good for you. And things with you and Charlie are . . .?'

I shrugged. 'No different. Anyway, what he thinks doesn't worry me.'

I couldn't exactly make out what Jack's reaction to this was. Maybe he couldn't either, because he changed the subject as quickly as he'd brought it up. 'Listen, I've a confession to make. You remember the tracks we wrote last year for that ad client of yours at Brum FM who wanted pop songs for a campaign?'

'Vaguely. I remember that the client didn't use them in the end and went for some awful disco covers instead.'

'Well, I came across them at the studio last week when I was sorting through old files and kind of re-jigged them a little. They're good, Rom. All they needed was a new arrangement, so I did that and sent it off.'

My heart did a little skip. 'Sent it off where?'

'One of my clients works with a music lawyer in London, who places songs with record companies looking for material for their artists. I don't know if it will be what he's looking for, but I thought it was worth a shot. I haven't heard back yet, but I thought you should know.'

Wow. This was a lot to take in. But as Jack proceeded to describe in detail the changes he had made to the arrangements, it all seemed to fall into place. I had committed to making this year count, and what better than to push the songs I had written with Jack? Regardless of whether this led anywhere or not, I felt the move had a greater significance than Jack realised: it was a sign that I was doing the right thing. Maybe this *was* going to be my best year so far . . .

* * *

121

The following Saturday morning, we packed the van and headed down the M5 to the West Country. Several of us had raised concerns about travelling to the Somerset countryside for a late January wedding, especially given the ominous weather forecasts threatening more snow. Much to everyone's relief, however, the morning of the wedding was clear and cold, pale winter-blue skies and bright sunshine greeted us as we drove in convoy towards the venue.

D'Wayne had surprised everyone by turning up at Jack and Soph's that morning in time to help load the van, instead of turning up at the venue to meet us as usual. To give him his due, he certainly seemed to be embracing the responsibilities of being our manager. It must have been a bit of a baptism of fire after years organising events in one venue.

'I just thought I should be more involved in the whole operation,' he explained when he saw our genuine shock at his arrival.

As we climbed into the van, Jack winked at me. 'You know, I seem to remember Wren making a sideways comment to D'Wayne at your birthday meal about him never helping with the heavy lifting bits. Don't suppose *that* could have had any bearing on his decision this morning, do you?'

As venues go, Elstone Farm Estate was surprisingly different. Set in the middle of the one-hundred-and-fifty-acre estate, surrounded by rolling Somerset countryside, the venue for the wedding was an impressive sixteenth-century tithe barn made of honey-hued stone with huge oak doors and beams. When we stepped inside, we were delighted to discover how warm the building was, due to the underfloor heating installed beneath the large flagstone floor.

'It's sort of like sixteenth-century history with twenty-first-century comforts,' Liesl, the attractive wedding co-ordinator commented, as she took us on a tour around the barn. Large round tables covered with crisp white linen cloths and surrounded by gold chairs were already laid out for the reception, and a team of florists was putting the finishing touches to table arrangements that rose from the centre of each table in high glass vases, filled with pure white roses and lilies, deep blue agapanthus and palest pink hydrangea, the beautiful scent of which filled the vaulted space.

'In the summer, there's a meadow at the back that the guests use,' Liesl continued. 'But obviously they won't be out there today. If you can set up at the far end of the bar, we'll clear the tables back this evening so that this whole central run becomes the dance floor. Acoustic-wise, it's a bit echoey, I'm afraid.'

'That's fine. We'll work from in-ear monitors and keep front of house sound at a good volume,' Charlie suggested. 'And I'll watch the level on my drums.'

'That'll be a first,' Tom sniggered. He was decidedly happier today than the last time we played. Since his breakup with Anya, Tom's sparkle had started to make a welcome return and it was good to see my friend heading back to his old self.

Liesl smiled politely, but I'm sure I detected the merest blush in her cheeks. Tom caught it immediately and extended his hand. 'I'm Tom, by the way. I play guitar.'

'I'm trying to learn at the moment,' she confessed.

'Really? Well, perhaps I could help with that,' he smoothed. 'Tell me more . . .'

Jack and Wren rolled their eyes as we watched Tom leading the pretty blonde away towards the bar. 'Since he and Anya split he's been dreadful,' Jack said. 'He was helping me on a wiring job yesterday and he spent his lunch break chatting up one of the office girls. I think he may be starting to enjoy his new-found freedom.'

'Watch out world,' I laughed. 'This place is amazing, isn't it?'

'It's gorgeous,' Wren breathed, as we carried equipment in from the van, fifteen minutes later. 'If I ever – you know – I reckon somewhere like this would be perfect.'

'Isn't it just? If only I had a *man*, this could all be *mine*!' Jack slapped a hand to his heart and pretended to swoon at the surroundings.

Wren punched his arm and he yelped. 'That'll teach you to mock, Jack Williams. Ignore him, Rom. We have every right to lust after the venue.'

'Absolutely.' I linked my arm through Wren's and poked my tongue out at Jack. 'This is the main reason we come, you know.'

Rating wedding venues is an essential part of enjoying the wedding band experience for Wren and me. Neither of us are desperate to trip down the aisle – far from it – but there's an irresistibly girly pleasure in enjoying the details of someone else's big day. Especially when we find a lovely one like this. Needless to say, the boys in the band are more than happy to mock us for this, but we press on regardless, even occasionally eliciting agreement from some of them if they think the others aren't looking. At the end of the day, all of us are romantics at heart, however hard we try to hide the fact.

The only exception to this is our esteemed manager.

'How much has this cost them?' he scoffed, as we set up the band around him. 'Over twenty grand, for sure. And for what? A day of someone else's ideas to launch a marriage that probably won't last more than two years.'

Wren looked aghast. Even by D'Wayne's standards, this was a harsh assessment. 'You can't say that! How can you possibly know?'

D'Wayne nodded sagely. 'I know.'

'He's only saying that because he can't get a woman to stay with him for long enough to consider marriage,' I said, tightening the adjuster on a microphone stand.

'Hey, I date,' D'Wayne protested. 'I just choose to leave when the fun's over.'

I winked at Wren. 'What a catch. No wonder the ladies are queuing up for the McDougall love-in.'

D'Wayne glared at me. 'See, this is why I don't come early to your gigs. If anyone wants me I'll be in the car.' Grabbing his keys and phone from the top of a speaker cab, he stormed off.

'Nice one, ladies. That's the *D'Wayne Diva* taken care of,' said Jack, rubbing his hands together. 'Now let's find the caterers and blag food! Wren – you're the drama specialist – I want to see poor, starving musician and big, baby doll eyes, please.'

Wren smirked. 'No problem. So what's my motivation, Mr Scorsese?'

'Grub, my dear. And lots of it!'

An hour before the start of the set, Jack gathered us together behind the tithe barn by the catering van, which had very kindly provided us with some spare portions of the wedding breakfast being served inside.

'Right. We're doing "What a Difference a Day Made" for the first dance – Rom can lead that. OK with you, Wren?'

Wren grinned. 'Fine by me. I can never remember the words.'

'OK, you and I'll do some harmony pads behind, then.'

'Standard oohs and aahs, people,' Tom joked, referring to the in-joke we have about Jack only being trusted to provide random sounds as harmonies, owing to the fact that he often muddles up lyrics which throws everyone else off completely.

Jack pulled a face. '*Thank you*. Happy couple's names are Andrew and Sarah, so make a note of that. Then it's standard first set, ending with "Lovely Day" into "Valerie". They reckon everyone will be up for dancing, so let's try to get the dance floor occupied as soon as we can. Wren, are you happy to tag-team with Rom on hosting?'

'Sure.'

'Chas, if you count us in on the first dance and then I'll lead it from there.'

Charlie saluted his agreement.

Jack consulted the set list. 'O-K. So, I'll start off "Ain't Nobody", but can you nod me in so I don't get the speed wrong, Chas?'

'What, you mean like you did last week at The Quiet Gig?' Charlie grinned. A ripple of laughter passed round the band.

'Man, that's the only time I've heard a Chaka Khan song played as a funeral march,' agreed Tom.

'Is this International Pick on Jack Day?' Jack protested.

I patted his back. 'Nope. It's just a regular Saturday, honey.'

'I get no thanks . . .' Our dejected keyboard player didn't have the opportunity to wallow for long, as we all piled on to him in an overly sympathetic group hug.

Every now and again at a wedding, we witness something truly lovely – and this gig turned out to be just that. It's like the very edge of a curtain is lifted up to allow you a

126

rare glimpse of real-life magic. Andrew and Sarah were obviously in love – but the scene we witnessed was far more than just a happy couple taking to the floor for their first dance. It was as if the whole space was filled with a rush of love, not only from the couple waltzing slowly to the Dinah Washington song, but also from every wedding guest standing silently around the room watching them. I'll never know if the guests were party to information about this couple that made this moment so poignant, but the atmosphere in the high, vaulted interior of the sixteenth-century building was so full of heartfelt emotion, it almost stole my voice.

Singing someone's first dance song is one of the most nerve-racking, adrenalin-pumped experiences I think you can have as a vocalist. There are no second chances: if you make a mistake you can never go back and do it again. Not to mention the fact that, with so many camera phones recording the moment, any slip-ups you make will be recorded for posterity and probably immortalised in perennial playback hell on YouTube and Facebook. But perform it right and you know you'll pass into history as the soundtrack to one of the most precious moments a couple can share. The song choice is immaterial – and, trust me, some of the requests we get are inexplicably odd, from the theme tune to *Shrek*, to 'The Chapel of Love', to 'Sex on Fire'. At the end of the day, it's all about what it means to the two people dancing together as you sing.

As I reached the end of the first refrain, I could feel a mass of unexpected emotion building in my throat, and I struggled to contain it as Jack played an instrumental run of the song. Casting my gaze around the band, I could see the others sensed it, too; all eyes were reverently trained on the handsome, dark-haired groom and his beautiful auburn-haired bride in her exquisite silk taffeta and lace gown, as they traversed the floor as if on air.

Watching the way Andrew held Sarah – as if cradling a priceless diamond in his arms – my thoughts inevitably drifted back to the sensation of being surrounded by PK's strong arms in the Christmas Market. Suddenly, my memories brilliantly returned, clear as light through a prism: prickling my senses into life. I could smell his cologne, see the colours from the twinkling lights over our heads reflected in his wavy hair, hear the beating of my own heart as the crowd noise fell away to a pin-drop. I could hear his voice, see the way he looked at me: as if he had found what he'd been searching for his whole life. It was the same expression the groom dancing in front of me now wore as he gazed upon his bride.

I closed my eyes as I reached the end of the refrain for the second time, and my handsome stranger was there, holding me again, my whole world becoming the size of his embrace as his lips fell on mine . . .

When I find him again, I made a silent promise in the ancient building warmly lit by candles and fairy lights, *I'll run back into those arms and never leave.*

After the icy numbness of December and January, an unexpectedly warm February came as a welcome surprise. For two weeks almost spring-like weather bathed everything, soothing away the stress of winter. Mornings were lighter, birds seemed to sing louder and people smiled more when you passed them in the street.

On the second Saturday of the month, Uncle Dudley, Auntie Mags and Elvis made the twenty-eight-mile journey from *Our Pol*'s Kingsbury mooring to visit me at home in Stourbridge. When they arrived, Elvis was a far more confident version of himself than his waterborne alter-ego.

I love it when people visit my home. Somehow it feels more alive when it's filled with people. I've always loved my little house. From the moment I first walked through the archway from the small car park by the canal and entered Number 83b, Harvest Court, I knew I was home. The small estate where I live consists mostly of largely unremarkable early nineties buildings, but the corner of the courtyard where my maisonette stands has a distinct charm about it. From the deep green ivy draping itself around the entrance, to the small circular stained glass window to the right of the bright purple front door, every detail is perfect in my eyes. I've often laughed at those property search programmes on TV when misty-eyed house hunters declare a house to be a perfect home – but when I laid eyes on this place four years ago, I finally understood the feeling they were describing.

'Now, we've something rather fantastic to report,' Uncle Dudley said, perched so far on the edge of the sofa seat that he looked as if he could fly off it at any moment. 'A bit of a breakthrough, you could say.'

This set butterflies cavorting around my stomach. Since my flash of memory at the beautiful tithe barn wedding, I had thought of little else but finding the handsome stranger. 'What's happened?'

Uncle Dudley and Auntie Mags exchanged Cheshire Cat grins and faced me like overexcited bookends on my sofa. 'I had a call from a mate of mine I used to work with at Rover. His wife heard about your blog and told him to get in touch. Been ten years since I last saw him, can you believe it?'

Auntie Mags tutted. 'For heaven's sake, get to the good stuff, Dudley!'

'I'm sorry, my beloved. You know me – getting carried away and everything. Anyway,' his pale blue eyes twinkled, 'Barry is now working as a security guard and you'll never guess where . . .'

'He mans the CCTV cameras in the city centre!' Auntie Mags cut in. 'Including one by the Town Hall, near where you met your handsome chap. Can you believe it?'

Now I was the one on the edge of my seat – or as much as anyone can be in a beanbag. 'Now that *is* interesting.' My heart had begun beating like a troupe of Irish dancers doing Riverdance on fast-forward.

'So, he's had a word with his boss, who, it turns out, is a bit of an old romantic himself.' Uncle Dudley took a deep breath, beaming like a 500kw spotlight. 'And they're going to go through the security camera logs for the day you met Mystery Man!'

My heart jumped into my mouth. 'Seriously? Can they do that?'

Auntie Mags chuckled. 'Legally, it's probably dubious, but when there's a former Rover man involved, things can happen that wouldn't otherwise. You just trust your Uncle Dudley, sweetheart.'

'Wow,' I breathed, my head a whirligig of thoughts as I soaked in the news. Of course, I knew that the likelihood of the CCTV camera actually capturing us on the busiest shopping day of the year was nigh on negligible. But the barely perceptible glimmer of possibility caught my eye like a scrap of tin foil in a magpie's nest. *If* we just happened to be in the right place at the right time, *if* the camera could get a shot, however hazy, it would mean that I would have irrefutable proof that PK existed and I would finally be able to hold an image in my hand as well as the frustratingly sparse one in my head.

'So when will we know?'

'They're going to start looking next weekend. Baz reckons that where you met Mr Mystery was right under the Town Hall security camera. It just depends if it was pointing in the right direction at the time.'

Heart going ten to the dozen, I mentally crossed everything I could find to cross.

I think I might be on the verge of a breakthrough!

I can't say much at the moment because it's early days and I don't want to jinx anything, but it looks like the strongest lead I've had so far and I'm really excited about it.

My Uncle Dudley and Auntie Mags have been helping me from day one and they've been a tremendous help to me. Uncle Dudley has been designing bits for the blog, finding encouraging stories and generally being brilliant, while Auntie Mags has been using her almost magical skill for baking exactly the right cakes at exactly the right time. For instance, this week she had made raspberry meringue cake, which she said was perfect for anticipation. And she was right! Honestly, it's a gift. If you don't believe me, why not leave a comment on this post, tell me how you're feeling at the moment and I'll ask Auntie Mags to recommend a cake. Believe me, she'll prescribe the perfect remedy!

Thank you for your lovely comments, by the way. I'm amazed that thirty of you have found my blog now and I really value your support. Hopefully I'll have some exciting news to report soon!

Rom x

'Let me get this straight: D'Wayne *still* hasn't said where the venue is?' Jack's incredulous expression spoke volumes.

I shook my head as I handed him a mug of coffee. 'Nope. Wren assures me that he's on to it, and I hope for his sake she's right.'

We walked out of the minuscule kitchen above Jack's studio and teetered down the rickety iron fire escape steps to the warmth of the control room, where we sank into the battered yet immensely comfortable black leather office chairs by the sound desk.

'After all the effort he's put in lately, it doesn't make sense.' Jack flicked a switch on the desk and a demo arrangement of drums, bass and keys began to play. 'Surely he's got to know whereabouts the gig is?'

'You'd think so, but he's being very cagey about the whole thing. Anyway, forget D'Wayne. Tell me about this track.'

Jack pulled a face. 'It's something I did for this guy who came in last week. He brings his ideas in on a dictaphone and I have to try to make sense of it all. It's like piecing shattered crockery together: I'm not entirely convinced it's worth the effort.'

I laughed. 'Wow, you're *so* lucky to have your own recording studio, aren't you?' It's a long-running joke among the band that people think Jack has the most glamorous job in the world when, in reality, most of his working life is spent battling with would-be musicians who possess more money than talent.

He grimaced. 'Livin' the dream, baby. Livin' the dream . . .'

I listened to the chord sequence playing through the large studio speakers and a thought occurred to me. Jack caught it immediately.

'What?'

He knows me too well. We've been songwriting since we were at college – and even though strangely both of us ended up writing music for a living, in a manner of speaking, our own songs have always just been for fun. Now, eight years later, we have an understanding that Jack's girlfriend Sophie likes to refer to as our 'married couple's intuition'. When we're working together, or talking about music, we often finish each other's sentences and know instinctively what the other one is thinking, even before we say it. I'm more at home in his studio than almost anywhere else on earth: because here I can be me, unhindered, free, completely able to immerse myself in creativity. There's no need for explanations or justifications – I just turn up, be who I am and watch magic happen.

Everything in me was buzzing, as if electricity was pumping through every atom of my being. It's hard to explain, but when something creative starts to happen it feels like my senses shift into another gear entirely. All of a sudden, I'm working almost subconsciously, caught in the slipstream of an idea, letting it take me where it will.

'These chords – they fit a song idea I've had for a while.'

A warm smile made its slow progress across my friend's lips. 'Yeah?'

I nodded quickly, my thoughts racing at two hundred miles an hour. 'Slow it down a little, maybe a relaxed Jack-Johnson-style beat, add close harmonies on the chorus . . .'

'Go on.' He clicked the mouse to loop the sequence as he observed me.

I started to hum, closing my eyes to let the sparse arrangement of the demo track merge with the fully produced song playing in my head. The song had been growing steadily since my encounter with PK and wouldn't leave me alone. I'd wake up with it playing in my mind and catch myself

133

singing it as I worked on jingles for builders' merchants and ear-wax drops, absent-mindedly scribbling snippets of lyric ideas down on scraps of paper to hand. Consequently, the song was currently scattered across an eccentric collection of old envelopes, coffee shop serviettes and crumpled till receipts stuffed into my bag.

Without even looking, I knew Jack was feeling it, too – that first spark of an idea beckoning invitingly to us.

After a few runs through the sequence, I opened my eyes and stared at the sound waves running across the screen, allowing my thoughts space to run about in.

'Fancy singing it through? Got any words yet?'

'Just a bit of the chorus so far.'

'Cool, let's hear that, then.'

Pulse crashing loud in my ears, I launched into the unknown.

'Be my last first kiss, let's start forever, you and me, perfectly . . .'

'Love it!' Jack proclaimed, the suddenness of his response making me jump. Grabbing an acoustic guitar from its stand by the desk, he started to play a half-picked, half-strummed rhythm, nodding appreciatively as he played.

We jammed through the chorus a few times, adding bits here and there as we went, Jack's smile widening with each run. Finally, after five minutes, he hit the stop button on the loop and turned to me. 'I think we could do something with that one. Put it into our unplugged set, maybe.' He grinned. 'Pretty obvious who that little ditty's about.'

'It might not be,' I smiled, failing to look even the slightest bit innocent.

'Doesn't matter anyway. I like the new Rom I'm seeing.'

His swift subject change took me aback for a few seconds.

'I mean it, Rom. Since you've started this search of yours you've been different. Confident, positive – we've all noticed it. Don't look at me like I'm a nut job, I'm trying to pay you a compliment.'

'Thanks. But I don't think I'm any different.'

'Well, you are. And you must be if Tom's noticed it too. Normally if it doesn't have two wheels and an expensive carbon fibre body he doesn't notice anything.'

Bracing myself, I asked the question now rotating magnificently like a glitter ball in my mind. 'And Charlie?'

Jack grabbed his mug. 'Another coffee?'

I opened my mouth to speak, but Jack was already halfway up the stairs to the kitchen. Stunned, I stared in the direction he had left. What did Charlie think?

Jack didn't answer my question then or later, although judging by Charlie's brooding silences at the band rehearsal and meal out at our local balti restaurant in the week that followed, I could hazard a pretty good guess. Part of me was pleased that the internal optimism I felt about my quest was evident externally too, but a stubborn part of me still wished that I could talk to Charlie about it. In any other situation, his opinion would have been the first I sought.

The Valentine's gig arrived and, true to form, our manager was still keeping the pertinent details close to his chest. Mumbling something unconvincing about 'last-minute planning issues', he arranged to meet us in the car park of an immense twenty-four-hour supermarket on the outskirts of Birmingham. This in itself was nothing new – D'Wayne often met us in random car parks and motorway service stations on our way to an event. But this particular evening the lack of detail was beginning to fray my bandmates' patience.

'Where is he?' Tom demanded, pacing furiously at the back of the van. 'We're meant to be loaded in and sound-checked in two hours.'

'He'll be here,' Wren said gently, although her anxious observation of the car park entrance undermined her professed confidence.

Ten minutes later, D'Wayne's silver BMW roared into view, driving across the rows of empty parking spaces and screeching to a halt alongside Jack's van. Holding his hands up in apology, he joined us.

'Traffic was crazy,' he offered.

'Funny, we didn't have any problems *twenty-five minutes ago*,' Tom sneered.

D'Wayne pressed on regardless. 'Anyway, we're all here now, yeah? So no harm done.'

'Except the one, very small detail of where the venue is for the gig,' Charlie reminded him. 'We've less than two hours now, and if there's a long drive involved we're going to be in deep crap.'

'It's very near.' D'Wayne's reply was so cool it was practically Alaskan.

'How near?' We all observed him carefully.

Triumphant, D'Wayne opened his hands. 'Right here, guys!'

Stunned, The Pinstripes stared at him.

'In the *car park*?' I asked.

'No, not the car park. That would just be stupid. It's in *there*.' He pointed in the direction of the supermarket, where two workers were parking impressively lengthy stacks of metal trolleys as shoppers milled in and out of the automatic doors.

'Where, exactly? The frozen food aisle? The deli counter?' Tom was so incensed he was almost incandescent.

136

'They've rigged up a stage in the entrance,' D'Wayne proudly informed his incredulous charges. 'It's a "Lonely Hearts Valentine's Shopping Event" and you're the headline band.'

D'Wayne McDougall had pulled some stunts in his just-over twelve months managing the band, but this had to be up there with the craziest of them. As we set up on the low, bolt-together riser stage in the wide entrance to the store, it transpired that he had taken the 'executive decision' to withhold crucial information concerning the venue because he felt it would 'impair our approach' to the gig. Fortunately for D'Wayne, time was not on our side so setting up for the gig had to take precedence over the reckoning he should have faced.

Crazy as the idea seemed, it certainly had attracted some attention from shoppers. By the time we began our first set, at least two hundred single people were walking round the store, embarrassingly pink heart name badges pinned to their chests. That said, their response to find a live band bopping around a makeshift stage by the automatic doors was less than rapturous. For the first four songs, we had to contend with bemused looks from the shoppers, not to mention the odd Tannoy announcement cutting in through the supermarket speakers. As I sang, trying to ignore the small child observing me suspiciously at the front of the stage with his middle finger jammed up one nostril, I looked around at the band. Their identical resigned expressions told me all I needed to know.

After a while more lonely heart shoppers stopped to watch and by the end of the first set we were rewarded with polite applause. Relieved, we left the stage to enjoy the refreshments laid on for us by Frank, the cheerful and immensely rotund store manager.

'Excellent set, *dudes*,' he enthused, handing round a tray of drinks. 'The crowd's loving it.'

'Not like you'd know,' Jack mumbled between mouthfuls of food, his previously dark mood placated by the considerable spread at his disposal.

D'Wayne walked up to us, chatting to the beautiful blonde with him. Tom instantly forgot his anger and deployed his most devastating smile. 'D'Wayne, mate, aren't you going to introduce us to this lovely lady?'

Charlie groaned and shot me a weary look as he retreated to the relative safety of the buffet table. The woman in question smiled serenely.

'Hi, I'm Cayte Brogan, reporter with Midlands Radio – we're covering tonight's event. I love your music, by the way.'

'Thanks,' Tom accepted, although the compliment was clearly meant for all of us. 'So, are you Kate with a "K" or a "C"?' His charm was more dairy-laden than the entire contents of the cheese counter just behind the stage.

'Actually, I have a "C" *and* a "Y",' Cayte purred, indicating the shocking pink heart-shaped name badge on the lapel of her exquisitely fitted suit.

Tom was only too happy to accept this invitation to observe her ample chest. 'Ah, two of my favourite members of the alphabet.'

The palpable chemistry between them transformed this Sesame-Street-style discussion of pertinent letters into something more akin to an 18-certificate movie.

Jack rolled his eyes and turned to Frank, who was failing to disguise his disappointment at being deserted in favour of Tom. 'What time do you want us back on?'

'As soon as possible,' he replied a little too forcefully as he glared at Tom.

We launched into set two, the groove of 'Love Train' attracting more lonely heart shoppers to the area in front of the stage. Although this gig probably rated as one of the most unusual venues we had ever played, I had to admit that the idea appeared to be working. Certainly the assembled singles dancing and milling around the store with their ridiculous name badges seemed to be enjoying the opportunity to window-shop their fellow attendees as they bought their groceries. Nevertheless, as we worked through our repertoire, I knew that all of us were dearly hoping that D'Wayne would never book another gig like it. Weddings were undeniably safer territory . . .

'At least one person's definitely pulled tonight,' Wren whispered to me as the intro to 'Sunny' began. She nodded towards the right of the stage, where a rapt Cayte was gazing up at Tom as he played.

I picked up a tambourine and kept the beat as I danced, Wren stepping up to the microphone to take the lead. While she was singing, I let my gaze drift casually across the crowd, pausing to add stabs of harmony here and there. Towards the end of the second verse, I was about to sing when something caught my eye.

A striped scarf – green, brown and cream – identical to the one I had seen on the day I met PK.

I noticed it at the far end of the dance floor area, by the start of the fresh produce aisle. It was unmistakably familiar and draped around the neck of a shopper with his back to me. Squinting against the spotlight glare, I tried to make out more of the figure. His russet-brown hair was wavy, but could it be the same man I'd met? All around me, the music continued, the band reaching the instrumental and Tom delighting in the opportunity to show off his considerable guitar skills for the benefit of the gorgeous blonde reporter. Turning back to the crowd, my heart plummeted when I saw that the man in the striped scarf was no longer standing there.

It couldn't be him, I scolded myself, willing my head to stop spinning. *Concentrate on what you're here to do.*

The final verse arrived and Wren began to improvise while Jack and I picked up the melody. As we reached the three repeats of the last line, I suddenly saw the man again, this time walking from the checkouts towards the door. This time, there was no mistake: his hair, his scarf, the black wool coat . . . all exactly as I remembered. The song came to an end and, without thinking, I dropped the tambourine and ran down the steps at the side of the stage, weaving through the dancing shoppers and out into the car park. I gasped as the intense chill of the night air hit me. *Where was he?*

Scanning left to right, my heart sank. How could he have disappeared so quickly? Dismayed, I was starting to walk back inside when the loud blast of a car horn spun me back around. A white taxi was pulling up about thirty feet away. I watched, heart in mouth, as the man with the scarf strolled from the canopied entrance and opened the car door. I started to walk quickly, praying that the taxi would remain parked by the kerb. The thud of my pulse competed in my ears with the beat of Charlie's drums coming from inside the store. I had no idea what I would say, and no clue about how I would handle the situation. But I wasn't going to let him get away this time without at least trying to say something.

He was placing his shopping bags on the back seat as I neared the boot of the car.

'Cheers, mate,' I heard him say and I recognised his voice immediately. I wasn't mistaken – it was him! *Please don't leave yet*, I begged him silently, breaking into a run. *Please stay where you are* . . . Just a few more steps . . .

'Wait!' I called, but my voice was no more than a whisper when it came out and I watched with helpless despair as he ducked inside and the taxi door slammed shut. My fingers brushed the paintwork of the boot, then thin air, and the car roared away, leaving me devastated on the pavement, my breath short and painful as the taxi's red rear lights shrunk from view.

I was *so close* . . . How could I have missed him? Shivering as a shudder of chill passed down my spine, I hugged my arms to myself and swallowed back my tears that threatened to flood forth. Then, heart heavy, I slowly retreated into the warmth of the store.

CHAPTER NINE

Help!

If there is one thing you can rely on my friends to do, no matter what, it's to leap gleefully on any opportunity to mock each other. Tom's preposterous strutting around stage for the beautiful Cayte's benefit at the Valentine's gig should have elicited hilarity: it was akin to a cross between Mick Jagger (in his latter years) and AC/DC's Angus Young in full plank-spanking mode, and certainly not attractive in any sense. However, thanks to my impromptu exit from the stage, Tom's misdemeanours had paled into insignificance.

By the time the first signs of spring began to appear at the beginning of March, the jokes at my expense were firmly entrenched in The Pinstripes' psyche.

'Hey, Rom, are you staying with us for lunch?' Jack asked innocently as I arrived on the small green where my friends had gathered to make the most of the mild weather.

'Of course. Hence the fact that it's lunchtime and I've come over to meet you,' I smiled.

'Right. I just wanted to check, you know, in case you have to *dash off* . . .'

I raised my eyebrows grudgingly as my assembled

142

bandmates collapsed in fits of giggles. 'Hilarious. Don't you think three weeks of this is a little much, now?'

'We haven't even started,' Tom grinned, stretching his long legs out in front of the bench and fiddling with his tie. It's always a little strange to see my friends in their work clothes – especially Charlie and Tom, who spend so much of their spare time in t-shirts, hoodies and jeans. Of course they dress smartly for our gigs, but all our outfits are co-ordinated to create an overall effect so there isn't much scope for personal expression. Work clothes, however, highlight the differences. Tom is referred to by all of us as 'Man at Next' – owing to the fact that almost all his work wardrobe for the IT firm hails from that store. Charlie is perhaps the most arty of the guys – which is just as well considering that he manages his father's art gallery. His blue suit, blue checked shirt, silver tie and Converse sneakers were typical of his eclectic work wardrobe. Jack is the only one of us who can legitimately not dress up for his job, but even he likes to ring the changes sometimes, pairing jeans with a shirt and tie. Wren, of course, would have outshone us all, had she not been teaching today and therefore unable to join us; I have it on good authority that her work wardrobe is every bit as eclectic as the outfits we see her in at evenings and weekends.

'Aw, Rom, sit down,' Jack said, pulling me on to his lap. 'If you want to run away from our gigs on a whim, then who are we to mock you for it?'

'Thanks.'

'You're welcome. So was it him?'

I noticed that Charlie, seated on the far end of the bench, had flicked open his newspaper and was studying it intently. 'I think so. No, I'm sure of it.'

Reclining magnificently on the grass, Tom flicked crumbs off his shirt from the enormous baguette he was demolishing.

'Shame we didn't get a good look. You know I like to vet all your dates.'

'Like who? I haven't dated in over a year.'

He smirked. 'Yes, well, when you do finally find a bloke who's brave enough to stick around, Rom, I'll be ready to do my vetting *thang*.'

I shot him a withering look. 'You know, I'm so glad I sacrificed my lunch hour to be here this afternoon.'

Jack hugged me. 'It's only because we love you. I think you're right to search for this fella.'

'Well, thank you, Jack.'

There was a dangerous glint in Jack's eye, which could mean only one thing: and, sure enough it happened. 'It's about time someone noticed how wonderful you are. Don't you think, Chas?'

Subtle as a lump hammer, Jack's overt challenge brought Charlie's head snapping upright, and I noticed a deep flush across his cheeks. 'Sorry?'

Oh dear. Cue round two: 'I said Rom should find someone who appreciates her.'

Charlie's midnight blue eyes flicked from Jack to me, holding my gaze for a second before he blinked the moment away. 'Sorry, mate, didn't hear you. So when are we meeting for rehearsal this week?'

His snub hit a nerve and I bit into my sandwich to hide it. Tom caught my reaction and winked at me, patting the grass beside him in invitation. Gratefully, I accepted, moving away from Charlie and Jack's discussion.

'Ignore him, babes. He's just being a prat about everything.'

'I know.'

'Good. I think it's cool, honestly. Borderline crackers, but still cool. How's the blog going?'

144

'Great, actually. I've had about ten messages from supporters, which is nice.'

Tom's smile was like warm honey. No wonder he was always a hit with the ladies at gigs. 'Well, seeing your chap at the gig was a great thing, I reckon.'

'You do?'

'Definitely. Because now you know it's possible to find him again. He's in this city and that means he could be closer than you think. He could live above Ricky WahWah's.' He pointed at the popular music shop, where he and Charlie teach occasional music lessons. 'He could drink in The Garter over there. Something suitably rubbish, probably, like Sol or Leffe – not real ale like us proper men.' I laughed as his attention switched to an old lady approaching us with a scratty dog in tow. 'And *that* could be his nan . . .'

I love the way that Tom can make me forget I'm angry or stressed, just with a well-placed phrase. He has an amazing eye for the comical in any situation. I know it was once a career contender for him, too. Just before we started university, he took a stand-up show to Edinburgh Fringe and, by all accounts, was a bit of a hit. But the lure of music soon usurped his love of comedy and now only we are treated to his comic skills.

'Thanks, hun.'

He stroked my hand. 'Listen, if this chap has any sense, he'll be hunting for you, too. So let's keep everything crossed that something turns up soon, OK?'

Pleased by his vote of confidence, I agreed. But little did I know how effective his wish would turn out to be . . .

Just wanted to say, I think your quest is brilliant.
Keep going! **Maisie x**

145

*A friend told me about your blog and I'm so glad
I came to see it. What you're doing is great, like
a real-life fairytale!* **C. Smith**
*Don't worry that you haven't found him yet.
Something will turn up. Everyone at work is
rooting for you – can't wait to see what happens
in your quest!* **Kathy96**
*You are crazy but if you don't try you'll never
know. Good luck to you.* **GR007**

The messages of support had started to appear from my
fourth blog post and were increasing in number. It amazed
me how all these complete strangers came across my blog
– especially now that my followers had grown from just
my kind bandmates to people I'd never met. That very fact
filled me with hope about my quest: after all, if these
strangers could find me, then it was completely conceivable
that PK could find me, too.

As I worked on the week's quota of jingles, my growing
excitement at the burgeoning popularity of my blog took
the edge off the lyrical challenge of purporting the virtues
of vertical blind suppliers, coach tour operators and even
a well-known haemorrhoid preparation.

Wren's face was a picture when I met up with her one
evening at Petito's, a bright, modern canalside restaurant
in Brindley Place, not far from her home.

'I can't believe you had to sing about *piles*,' she exclaimed,
eliciting a disapproving stare from the older couple seated
at the table next to us.

'Say it a bit louder, hun – the ducks on the other side of
the canal didn't quite catch that,' I grimaced, ducking my
head behind the menu.

Wren giggled and raised her glass of wine. 'Romily Parker, I salute you. You're the only person I know who can write a song about embarrassing medical conditions. Whatever next, diarrhoea?'

'Did one for that last month.'

'Awesome.' She topped up our glasses with red wine. 'Anyway, enough about the day job. What's happening with the quest?'

'I'm getting more supporters every week. Someone has to know who he is.'

'I certainly hope so. I mean, it's March and you haven't exactly made much headway yet, have you? Apart from the fleeting glimpse that may or may not have been the man in question last month.'

'It's still early in the year. There's time.'

'Yes, there is. But there's also time to conclude that it was a lovely, romantic notion that just won't stand up to the test of time. We *all* have our "what-if" memories, Rom. I still think about that guy I met on holiday in New York when I was eighteen. He took me on a horse-drawn carriage tour of Central Park and gave me a single yellow rose. But it was *one day* – and I knew I wouldn't see him again. It's just a nice memory. And we need nice memories for the days when we think nobody will ever be interested in us. Not to chase after indefinitely.' She squeezed my hand. 'And I really don't want to be the one to say it because, you know, I desperately want this all to come good for you. I would hate you to be hurt by this, you know.'

'I know, hun, but it's just a year of my life. If I can do this, regardless of whether I'm successful or not, then it proves I can set my mind to something and see it through.'

Wren observed me intently. 'You've really thought about this, haven't you?'

'Yes, I have.'

'Then we need to up the ante. I'll think of something.'

The Garter pub was packed when I walked in the following evening. As usual, there was the odd combination of patrons: well-to-do diners enjoying the expensive gastro-pub food, raucous locals indulging in a few pints after work and pockets of students downing pints as they crowded around tiny tables or playing darts in the pub's newly renovated interior.

'Remind me what we're doing here?' I asked Wren, as she ducked through a gap in the crowd to claim a small table by a slot machine in one corner.

'We're *here* because it's just possible that your handsome stranger might be.'

'How do you figure that?'

Wren hung her coat over the back of the chair. 'If he's local, he's likely to *have* a local – a pub, I mean – and this could be it.'

I laughed at her seriousness. 'It could be, or it could be any other pub anywhere across the city. Are you suggesting we visit all of them? Because I think we might need more than a year to do that. Not to mention the fact that we might end up alcoholics in the process.'

Wren was undeterred by my amusement. 'Well then in *that case* you could meet him at an AA meeting, so it could all be worth it after all.'

I looked around the packed pub. 'I don't think he's in here, Wren.'

'You didn't think he'd be in that supermarket on Valentine's Night, but he was, wasn't he? Think of the *possibility*, Rom! Now, I'm going to get us some drinks, so you keep looking, OK?'

I smiled as she headed to the bar. I knew the chances of us just happening to bump into PK here were slim at best, but her belief in what I was doing was touching nevertheless. I flicked to my emails on my phone and saw that I had received another three messages on my most recent blog post. I was just about to look at them when the pub door opened and in walked Charlie and Jack.

Of course, they spotted me straight away, Charlie's expression more of surprise than delight to see me, unlike Jack, who beamed brightly and bounded over.

'I didn't know you were going to be in here tonight,' he said as he and Charlie approached.

'Ditto,' I replied. 'Wren thought it was a good idea.'

'Ah right,' Jack replied, clearly confused. 'Why?'

'We're here on official quest business.'

Charlie shifted uncomfortably and stared in the direction of the bar. Jack raised an eyebrow and sat down on Wren's empty chair.

'You've had another sighting?'

I couldn't ignore Charlie's discomfort as I answered. 'No, nothing like that. Wren just thought . . .'

'Aha! Spying on us, are you?' Wren interjected as she arrived back with two shots of JD and Coke.

Jack vacated the seat and rejoined Charlie. 'Perish the thought. We just fancied a blokes' night out, didn't we, Chas?'

Charlie muttered something unintelligible, and avoided eye contact with me.

Wren and Jack exchanged looks and I stared resolutely at my drink.

Jack slapped Charlie's back. 'Well,' he said, a little too brightly, 'we have an appointment with a rather lovely local ale, so we'll love you and leave you, OK?'

'Have a good night,' I offered.

Charlie lifted his eyes to mine momentarily. 'You too.' And then they were gone, Jack pushing Charlie into the crowd by the bar.

Wren giggled and leaned towards me. 'Blimey, how awkward was *that*?'

Glumly, I twisted my glass in the puddle of water on the dark, shiny table surface. 'I know.'

'Stuff him, Rom. He needs to grow a pair. You'll show him when you find the mystery man and live happy ever after.'

I smiled back. But as the night wore on, ultimately proving fruitless for me (although Wren managed to elicit the phone number of the rather cute barman, so perhaps not a total loss), my thoughts kept returning to Charlie's expression. Lately, I had begun to hope that things were becoming more settled between us, but his reaction tonight harked back to that awful argument in Jack's van after the New Year's Eve wedding. Was this how it would be with us from now on, I wondered?

After a bus ride back to Wren's, I said goodnight and hailed a taxi home. As the bright lights of the city passed by in a bright blur, I sank into the back seat and my thoughts returned to PK. Forget what Charlie Wakeley thought, I was going to carry on searching. Wren was right: I had to believe that I could bump into him again anywhere, at any time. After all, if it had happened once, why not again?

Reaching into my bag, I retrieved my mobile and was surprised to find a text from Charlie.

Hope the search went well. Sorry for being a moron. See you tomorrow Cx

As messages of support continued to appear on the comments section of my blog posts, I found myself increasingly touched by the enthusiasm and unshakeable belief of complete strangers in what I was doing.

Jack's girlfriend Sophie certainly seemed to think so. After The Pinstripes' gig rehearsal next day, she arrived bearing three large pizza boxes, much to the delight of everyone present.

'Seriously, Rom, *everyone* at work is following your blog now. I mentioned it in the staffroom last week and it turned out most of the teachers had heard about it already. Two of my colleagues mentioned your quest today without any prompting from me, and then proceeded to tell me about their "what-if" stories.'

This was the second time I had heard that phrase this week. 'Wren said that. She thinks my handsome stranger is my "what-if".'

Sophie smiled. 'Could be. But it turns out this kind of thing has happened to lots of girls. It's just that none of them were brave enough to try to pursue it, unlike you.'

'Wow. I had no idea.'

'I reckon if you do this and find him, you'll be a hero for a lot of women who want to believe that once-in-a-lifetime romances like that can happen.'

I poured boiling water from the kettle into Tom's battered yellow teapot and gave it a stir. 'Well, if Wren has her way we'll be spending an awful lot of time visiting local pubs in order to find him.'

Sophie's black-brown eyes twinkled. 'Ah, I heard about that. Jack and Charlie were full of it when they went out for their ride this morning.'

'Oh? What did they say?'

'Well, when Charlie first saw you sitting there by yourself he thought you'd located the mystery man and were on your first date. I think he was a bit miffed about it, although of course he didn't admit it after he realised his mistake. Jack ribbed him all night apparently, and it was still going on this morning.'

Charlie was laughing with Tom and Jack at the other side of the shoe factory rehearsal room. I lowered my voice in case he could hear me. 'I don't know why he would think that. He only needs to read my blog to see that the Valentine's Night sighting is the closest I've got to PK so far.'

'Don't worry what Charlie thinks, Rom. You go for it with this quest.'

'Thanks, Sophie. So have you had a "what-if", then?'

Sophie visibly sparkled. 'About a year before I met Jack I was in London on a drama trip. We were visiting Covent Garden when this beautiful man with the most amazing azure blue eyes bowed to me by the entrance to Neal's Yard. That's all he did: just bowed – a flamboyant, full Shakespearean bow. And then he left. But it took my breath away. I still wonder what would have happened if he had said something, or if I'd met him again.'

I had no idea if Charlie had heard what I said, but his mood was markedly different that evening as we ploughed our way through the boxes of pizza and copious mugs of tea. He made an effort to smile at me whenever I caught his eye and he even offered me a lift to the wedding gig that Saturday. Although I was still irritated by his earlier attitude, the apparent white flag he was waving came as a blessed relief, so I agreed. Despite all that had gone between us since Christmas, I couldn't deny that Charlie in charming mode was impossible not to like.

Just after eight on Saturday morning, The Pinstripes piled into a motorway service station on the M6 after a criminally early pre-dawn van loading. The wedding venue we were travelling to was a medieval manor house in Northumberland

and we had been asked to arrive and set up as early as possible. It would be a five-hour drive from door to door, but at least D'Wayne had arranged accommodation for us nearby after the gig – even if we would have another early start book tomorrow.

After all the recent weirdness between Charlie and I, the journey so far had been surprisingly jovial. Steering well clear of any possibly contentious issues, we resorted to gig stories and memories from school, college and university – far safer territory for both of us. As the miles passed by, I began to relax in the heated seats of his dark green Volvo estate, carefully enjoying our conversation.

Most of the food concessions in the service station were only just coming to life, so the band descended on WHSmith's for crisps, chocolate bars, fruit juice and cans of drink. Charlie and Jack, coffee snobs to the last, opted to wait for the Italian coffee concession to open, refusing to consume anything produced by the automatic machine in the shop. Meanwhile Wren incurred the wit of Tom for insisting on buying *The Times* to do the crossword.

'Call yourself an honest, working-class woman?' he lambasted her. 'Anyone else would buy *Puzzler* or *Take a Break*, but – oh no – not you! Well, you know what you can do with your bourgeois, middle-class word games. Give me good, honest Hangman and I-Spy any day of the week!'

Half an hour later, we had all given in to the inevitable and purchased coffee and cake from the counter after our junk food choices paled beside Charlie and Jack's far superior offerings.

'Why have they booked a band if it's a medieval wedding?' Wren asked, taking a bite of an enormous double chocolate chip muffin that was almost as big as her head.

Tom smiled. 'Apparently it's a compromise the bride made

153

for the groom. She gets the medieval theme, he gets music he and his friends can dance to.'

'Sounds like a marriage built on good, solid foundations then,' I replied.

'Shame D'Wayne couldn't be here this morning,' said Jack, 'otherwise he'd be able to suggest how long the marriage is likely to last.' He hunched his shoulders up to give the appearance of a too-muscular neck, adopted a broad Handsworth accent and shook his head sagely: '"I give them twelve months *maximum*."'

'Do you think they'll all be dressed up, though?' Wren asked. 'I'm not quite sure how a hundred and fifty guests are going to manage moshing to "I Kissed a Girl" in full medieval garb.'

'That's another thing: who requests "I Kissed a Girl" for a wedding? It's hardly a song you want your granny dancing to, is it?' Jack offered. The mental picture this created sent us all into helpless giggles.

'It's the groom's friends' favourite song,' Tom informed us, his seemingly encyclopedic knowledge of the gig's final details taking us all aback. 'It was the anthem of the stag weekend.'

'Has D'Wayne got you on the payroll now?' Charlie asked with surprise. 'Do we need to start calling you T'Om?'

This was met with the kind of hilarity that can only be created by a group of people with sleep deficiency coupled with a caffeine and sugar overload. When the laughter finally subsided once more, Tom enlightened us. 'I only know because Cayte's covering the back story of the wedding for a freelance thing she's doing for *Brides Magazine*.'

Since the Valentine's Night gig, Tom and Cayte's attraction had blossomed into a full-blown relationship and she

154

was now a regular face whenever we got together for food or a night out. Tom liked to refer to her as 'a little something I picked up with my groceries' – a joke that never seemed to lose its allure for the two of them, despite it wearing thin for Jack and Charlie.

'Honestly, Rom, if he uses that flippin' line one more time when we're out riding, I'm going to push him off his singlespeed,' Charlie grumbled once we were back in the car and heading north.

'Give him a break. He's happy again – that's a good thing, isn't it?'

Charlie pulled a face. 'I guess so.'

I leaned back and listened to the metallic clunking of the equipment stacked up to the roof as the car bumped over the changing tarmacs of the motorway. 'I reckon this gig is destined to be another D'Wayne McDougall extravaganza – medieval wedding, bride and groom fighting over the entertainment choices, everyone in tights . . . It already carries the hallmarks of a classic.'

Charlie laughed. 'You may well be right. Still, let's just think about the millionaire gig.'

The thought of the Gig That Could Change Everything was enough to send lightning bolts of thrill careering up my spine. 'Has Tom found out any more details yet?'

'He was telling me the latest last night. The venue is a country palace just over the Thames from Kew Gardens. It's called Syon Park and by all accounts it's stunning. Countless celebrities have been married there and it's been used as a location for feature films and TV shows. I think some duke and his family still own it. Tom was gushing – I think he's more excited about getting to play there than he is about how much we're getting paid.' He paused and I sensed a subtle change in the atmosphere. 'Look, Rom,

I was a total idiot on Wednesday night. I just didn't expect to see you there. To be honest, I thought you were on a date. So you can see why I was a bit quiet?'

I couldn't really. Any right Charlie had to comment on what I did had surely been surrendered when he passed up the opportunity for us to be together. As far as I was concerned, he could think whatever he liked, just as long as he didn't tell me what to do with my life. But his sincerity made me swallow my objections and simply smile in return.

'Thanks for saying that. I appreciate it.'

This polite answer seemed sufficient reward and I watched him relax as he drove.

'I don't reckon you'd find anyone in The Garter, though,' he added.

'You don't? Wren did – she got the barman's number. Anyway, it's the thought that counts. She's determined to help me find my man.'

His not-so-silent groan was impossible to miss. 'You still believe that's possible?'

'Yes, I do. I definitely saw him at that gig.'

'Fair enough.'

Unwilling to discuss what was already a highly uncomfortable topic further, I changed the subject as the motorway stretched out before us.

By the time we arrived at Beauforden Manor, Charlie and I had established unspoken boundaries for our conversation and I felt considerably calmer as a result. When we were discussing non-contentious issues, the old magic between us was back: the jokes that sparked off each other's comments, creating layer upon layer of wit. When it was like this, it was almost as if our conversation at Christmas had never happened. Almost . . .

The medieval manor house was darkly beautiful, its walls rising from wildly romantic gardens edged with cedars, willows and oaks that led to the silver expanse of a river, which wound its way around the hill on which the building stood. We set up in the grand central hall of the manor, which had been significantly embellished with overtly Gothic splendour by its owners during the Victorian era. Candles burned at every window and along the length of three sixty-foot dining tables that stretched from the top table. Gold-painted platters were set at every place and earthenware jugs of peonies, ivy and roses adorned each table. It was certainly impressive, although Wren, Jack and Tom struggled to take it seriously once they had spotted the venue's staff walking around sulkily in full medieval dress.

'You've got to hope they're being paid sufficiently for the ignominy of having to be seen in public like *that*,' Jack gasped, wiping tears from his eyes. 'No wonder they all look so miserable.'

'There are times when I realise how lucky I am not to have to wear a uniform for work,' Tom agreed, lowering his voice as a particularly surly older gentleman in bulging smock and pea-green tights walked past carrying a stack of chairs. 'This is one of those times!'

'Alright, lads and lasses.' A gruff-looking man in a baron's outfit was approaching us. Grasping a very un-twelfth-century clipboard, he surveyed the half-assembled equipment. 'I'm Gary, event organiser at Beauforden. This is looking good. You've got everything you need?'

Jack shook his hand. 'I think so. Jack Williams – I think we spoke on the phone earlier?'

A broad smile spread across Gary's face. 'Oh yes, the keyboard player with the dodgy sat-nav. Don't worry, lad, you're not the first to get taken the wrong way on the moors by one of them contraptions.'

Jack dropped his head as the rest of us launched into raucous laughter at his expense. 'I ended up in a *field*. The only thing I could do was call here and ask them to guide me in. Thanks, mate.'

'No worries. Now you've got a dressing room just through that door and I've laid out your costumes in there. Any probs, give us a shout.' He began to stride away.

Shock ricocheted round the band. 'Costumes?' Charlie repeated weakly.

Gary turned back. 'Aye, lad. The ones your manager sent.'

Wren paled. 'Did anyone know about this?'

'No,' Jack said, 'and I only spoke to D'Wayne this morning. He never mentioned it.'

Tom's face was the colour of the crimson roses that framed the stage. 'I'll kill him!'

'Maybe they aren't that bad,' I offered, even though I suspected I was wrong. 'Perhaps we should just go and see them before we all start to panic?'

Five minutes later, we were staring at the most garish collection of quasi-medieval garments ever assembled. These monstrosities made the staff costumes we had been mocking not ten minutes beforehand look almost fashionable.

'D'Wayne is *history*, man,' Tom growled. 'Nobody gives me canary-yellow tights and lives to laugh about it.'

'You think you have problems.' Jack held a purple velvet tunic aloft. 'I'm going to look like an aubergine in this.'

'The green tights and matching hat will help with that,' Wren giggled.

'Yous lot all getting on OK?' Gary's smiling face appeared at the door.

Tom smiled hopefully. 'We don't have to wear these if we don't want to, right?'

''Fraid so, lad,' Gary answered, his mirth barely hidden. 'S'all in the contract. Your manager agreed it when we booked you. Those tights are surprisingly comfy when you get used to them, you know.' Chortling, he departed, leaving us helplessly staring after him.

Wren picked up her mustard-yellow velvet dress, burgundy twisted rope headband and veil. 'The way I see it, we don't have a choice. I vote we get changed, do the gig and then plan all the truly nasty ways we're going to wreak our revenge on D'Wayne.'

Only one good thing could be said about the outlandish outfits: at least we didn't look out of place. Whichever sadistic fancy dress emporium supplied The Pinstripes' garb for the evening had obviously also been responsible for clothing every guest and member of the bridal party.

Halfway through the second set, we launched into 'Love Shack' and the assembled guests (particularly enthusiastic about dancing owing to the prohibitive amounts of mead they had consumed) started bopping about in their ridiculous outfits. Half of them began an energetic conga line around the great hall, the stragglers at the end running as best they could in brightly hued hose and preposterous curling-toed shoes, while the rest of our audience were frantically moshing in a manner more akin to a rock concert crowd. As we looked out at the completely bizarre scene before us, we all suddenly realised how hilarious the situation was. Charlie was the first to snigger, struggling to sing the male lead in the song from behind the drum kit. Wren and I followed suit and Tom had to stop playing his guitar as the wave of mirth hit him next. By the time we reached the end of the song, tears were rolling down our faces and we couldn't look at each other for fear of losing the plot entirely.

At the end of the gig, we were all on a high.

'I'm thinking burnt orange might be my colour,' Tom said, twirling around the stage in his tunic and yellow tights as we packed away.

'Yeah, mate, it matches your eyes,' Charlie replied from behind the stacks of his drum cases.

I walked back into the dressing room to change out of the pale blue velvet gown and tall lilac hennin hat. As far as our costumes for the evening went, I think I'd received the best – Wren's mustard yellow and burgundy braid number resembled a product from an occupational therapy class for depressed colour-blind seamstresses, while the less said about Charlie's harlequin brown, cream and puce velvet tunic with slate-grey tights the better.

As I folded up my costume, Stevie Wonder started warbling from the front pocket of my bag. I retrieved my mobile and saw that I had three calls and a voicemail message from Uncle Dudley.

'Bab, it's happening! Baz called me tonight to say he has some stills of you and your fella! He's bringing them round to the boat tomorrow afternoon, so get yourself over here as soon as you can. It might just be the breakthrough we've been waiting for and . . .' His voice trailed off and I could hear Auntie Mags' muffled voice in the background. 'Yes . . . I know, I said that, Magsie . . . say what? Righty-ho. Sorry about that, our Rom. Your auntie says she tried out a new recipe today that is exactly what you'll need when you see the pictures. Tarar-a-bit!'

'Everything OK?' Charlie asked, taking me by surprise.

I smiled, feeling a strange fluttering in the pit of my stomach. 'Yes, I think it is now.'

160

He stared at me and for a moment I thought he was going to say something more, but he simply nodded and left. I wasn't altogether sure whether I was relieved or disappointed by this – to have such a breakthrough happen and not to share it with him was yet another reminder of how things had changed between us. But I couldn't think about that now: the news from Uncle Dudley was far too exciting to ignore.

Alone once more in the dark wood-panelled room, I sank down on to the oak bench that ran round three of the four walls. I could hardly believe it. I was finally going to see him again – not a fleeting glimpse like before, but an irrefutable image that time couldn't fade.

There had been so many happenings lately that were now linking together – the Valentine's Night gig sighting, the growing support for my quest, the collective 'what-if' stories from Sophie and her colleagues at school – surely these were confirmations that spending my year searching for him was right?

There was only one way to test this theory: I needed to see those photos.

I can't remember much of the ride over to Kingsbury next day. My head was consumed by a multitude of thoughts, elbowing and jostling for position like cramped commuters jammed into a morning train. In fact, it nearly wasn't a ride at all: I was tempted to drive straight from home to *Our Pol*, but a sense of duty to my parents and two weeks without giving my bike a decent outing led me instead to choose Sunday lunch in the beige kingdom first.

Thankfully, my parents were still blissfully unaware of my blog and Uncle Dudley's one-man mission to locate PK. And it was likely to remain the case for the foreseeable future, especially given that Mum and Dad (who only used their aged home PC for work spreadsheets and wouldn't know how to Google anything if their beige lives depended on it) were resolutely against social media in any form.

The delicious naughtiness of concealing something from them was impossible to resist. Of course, my principle is always to tell my parents about the latest developments in my life, just not necessarily *right away* . . .

Crossing over the canal bridge and turning on to the towpath, I shivered as my stomach somersaulted for the umpteenth time that day, knowing the inevitable moment of truth was accelerating towards me. Knocking on *Our Pol*'s bow doors, I hoisted my bike on to the narrowboat's roof, removed my gloves and cycle helmet and stepped inside.

If there was ever an Oscar awarded for 'Most Ineffective Attempt at Nonchalance', my aunt and uncle would be guests of honour at Elton John's winners' afterparty. They stood rigidly by the kitchen sink, identikit fixed grins across their faces.

'Cup of tea?' Auntie Mags asked, her voice almost squeaking as she battled the excitement evident in every syllable of her body language.

I tried to answer as calmly as I could. 'Yes, please. Just what I need after my ride. Everything good with you, Uncle Dud?'

My uncle was even worse, fidgeting like a coiled spring about to unravel. 'Fine, bab, just peachy.'

'You are rubbish at waiting, aren't you?' I laughed, as my aunt and uncle rushed to the table and pushed a brown, A4 envelope towards me.

Clasping her hands to her chin, Auntie Mags fixed me with her gaze. 'Are you ready?'

'I think so.' Holding the envelope in front of me, I realised my hands were shaking. I made a conscious effort to slow my breathing, ignoring the insistent flutter of my pulse, and turned the envelope over to break its seal.

Please let this be him.

Uncle Dudley wrapped a nervous arm around my aunt. So much hope and love were mixed in their encouraging smiles that I had to close my eyes for a second to push the mass of emotion away.

My fingers clumsy with impatience, I pulled back the envelope flap, the salt and vinegar scent of brown paper rising to my nostrils as I did so. I felt the cool glossiness of photo paper and I slowly pulled the picture out, its white reverse appearing first.

Here goes . . .

I flipped over the image, scanning its hazy black and white detail. Before my eyes were the familiar shapes of the Christmas Market stalls where we had met, the blurry faces of Christmas shoppers crowded around us. And there, in the midst of it all, were two figures, one of whom I instantly recognised . . .

'*Well?*'

'It's – a wonderful photo . . .' I looked up at my rapt audience and held it out to them, tears welling in my eyes '. . . of *me.*'

The silence in *Our Pol* was deafening.

CHAPTER TEN

Gimme! Gimme! Gimme! (a man after midnight)

'It's the back of his head.'

'Yes, I know it is, Wren.'

'The *back* of his head, Rom! That's all you have?'

'Oh, look, Fat Face has a sale on. Shall we go in?'

Wren wasn't listening, staring at the photo in her hands as we travelled down a vivid pink-lit escalator in The Mailbox. 'I suppose one consolation is that you can compare the back of this guy's head with the bloke you saw the back of at the Valentine's gig.' She cracked up, oblivious to the disapproving looks she was getting from two well-heeled ladies walking out of Harvey Nic's. 'You have to admit it's funny.'

'Hilarious. Where did you want to go for coffee?'

She gathered herself together long enough to give me a sensible answer. 'Let's head for New Street, then we can take our pick.' As her eyes met mine, her mirth vanished. 'Oh Rom, are you upset? I shouldn't have laughed, I'm sorry.' Linking her arm through mine, she gave me a squeeze. 'Right. We're going to think about lovely, girly things now and for the rest of the afternoon, OK?'

A week after I first laid eyes on the photo, I was feeling decidedly calmer about the whole thing – in fact, I even found myself laughing with Jack and Soph when I shared the photo with them yesterday evening. Yes, I was disappointed, but what mattered was that he *was* in the photo, which meant that he *was* real and it *had* happened. However I looked at it, I couldn't escape the positives in this situation.

'It's one more piece of the puzzle,' I explained to Wren when we sat down in a coffee shop ten minutes later, watching shoppers milling about outside as a street performer played his tenor sax, accompanied by a sound-activated dancing reggae cat.

Wren stirred the whipped cream into her *venti* hot chocolate. 'You're amazing, Rom. I'd have given up months ago. So what happens now?'

'I don't know. We keep looking, I suppose. Uncle Dudley reckons the blog will bear fruit soon, especially as the number of followers keeps growing.'

'How many do you have now?'

'Nearly forty. I don't know how they find it, but they're certainly very enthusiastic when they arrive. If my chances of success were directly proportionate to the level of belief in my followers, I'd be on to a dead cert.'

'Hmm . . .' She was flicking through an old local paper, left on our table. 'I guess your problem now is that the supporters you have aren't much good for anything other than cheering you on. What you need is . . .' She broke off as something caught her eye.

Wren possesses the type of creative brain that operates at a zillion miles an hour, all day, every day. Consequently people assume she's a ditzy redhead, owing to her apparent inability to finish sentences or follow the thread of a discussion. In reality, she is probably more intelligent than the rest of us put together, capable of multitasking several different trains of thought and physical actions at once. One school report famously suggested that Wren had the potential to become 'either a prodigiously gifted young woman or a despot in the making' – a description she frequently reminds us of with unbridled pride.

'Anyway, at least I know that the man I met was real. Wren?' I waved my hand in front of her face, but her eyes would not be moved from the crumpled newspaper spread out between our coffee mugs. 'Hello? Earth to Wren . . .'

'That's it!' she exclaimed, stabbing page 12 with her finger. Lifting her head, she beamed, triumph igniting her expression. 'I know how we can find him! Why didn't I think about this before?' She slapped the heel of her hand to her forehead. 'Dumbnut! I apologise, Rom, for being so bloomin' slow on the uptake here. *This* is perfect!' Any moment, I expected Wren to lift off and bump up against the ceiling, like a newly filled helium balloon.

'Wren, calm down. What are you talking about?'

'This!' She rotated the newspaper and indicated a page.

'The Encounters section?'

'Yes! We put an ad in there, saying where you were, what you were both wearing and what happened, and then when he reads it he'll get in touch and that will be it!'

'As long as he reads this paper.'

'Rom, *everyone* reads this paper. Anyway, that's just details. I want you to find him again. I think you deserve to have a gorgeous man rescuing you, especially after all that time you waited for Charlie.'

Out of all of my closest friends, Wren's opinion of me was one of those I cherished the most. It was unspeakably touching to see her so passionate about my happiness.

'In fact, I think we should write the advert now and I'll email it in.'

Now it was my turn to be cautious. 'Don't you think we should maybe take some time to consider this properly?'

'Oh come on, sweets, where's your famous sense of adventure? Grab a pen and let's get writing!'

Even though I had my reservations about Wren's latest plan, I had to admit that I couldn't think of anything else that might work. Since Baz's not-so-great photographic evidence of the meeting with my stranger, developments had been scarcer than promotion opportunities for my boss at work. Wren's Encounters advert was due to go in the following weekend's paper (after she had insisted on rewriting it at least five times since our first draft a few days ago), and Uncle Dudley had nothing to report, apart from a new batch of lovely messages from my ever-growing crowd of supporters:

> *Go for it Romily – you carry our dreams of fairytale endings with you! xx* **rosieNYC**
> *Hope you find your chap. Best of luck* ☺ **dave_carter**
> *I go 2 the city every wknd and all the blokes r proper mingers LOL. Gd luck finding the only fit one! :D x* **chelC**
> *This is a great campaign! All my friends at school are watching you xoxoxo* **Jenna96**

Such enthusiastic encouragement was going to take some getting used to, unaccustomed as I was to sharing the intricate details of my love life with half of cyberspace. But then, as Uncle Dudley reminded me, 'The wider the net, the more chance you've got of catching your fella.'

I had to believe that was possible, even though the trail had gone cold – temporarily, I hoped. At least Wren was a gold-card-bearing member of the quest, and my other friends, though happy to make kind-hearted jokes at my expense, were supportive too. The only person yet to be convinced was Charlie.

Following our discussion on the way to the medieval wedding, the tension between him and I had noticeably eased, but we were far from the level of honesty we had shared before the quest began. My instinct was to tell him everything – fifteen years of doing so wasn't easy to forget – but the subject remained firmly out of bounds. Not wishing to be the unwitting instigator of an argument, I resolved to avoid it entirely when Charlie and I were together.

Meanwhile, the wedding gigs began to increase in frequency. As March passed into April, one wedding emerged that was to pass into Pinstripes' history: 'The Bunny Wedding'.

Set in a hotel on the outskirts of Leeds, the Easter Saturday gig had appeared promising enough when D'Wayne provided us with the details. But when we gathered together mid-rehearsal in the old shoe factory to listen to the couple's requirements, we had no inkling of the delights that lurked in store for us.

'OK, we're looking at a standard set but the couple have vetoed the Motown medley in favour of the Bee Gees one – they think their guests will be up for a bit of "Saturday Night Fever" and "Grease" rather than "Heard it Through the Grapevine". First dance will be "Better Together".'

'*Ugh.* Jack Johnson. Bo-o-o-o-oring,' Tom groaned.

I stared at him. 'It's a lovely song.'

'To sing, maybe. To play it's the musical equivalent of watching paint dry.' Tom and Wren launched into an impression of playing the song, *bm-bm*ing the bass line whilst miming yawning, looking at their watches and slipping a noose around their necks. Charlie and Jack found this utterly hilarious and joined in, motioning drums and keyboard with the same reactions.

'You're all cynics,' I reprimanded them, although it was impossible not to be amused by their act.

'And you're sure there aren't any tights this time?' Jack asked D'Wayne, whose shoulders instantly drooped. He had been relentlessly ribbed about the medieval outfits since our costumed spectacular.

'Look, I've said I'm sorry about the medieval gig,' he replied. 'The wedding planner assures me that this is a straightforward event today.'

As it turned out, the wedding planner lied.

What better way to celebrate your commitment to the love of your life on Easter Saturday than an Easter Bunny theme? To our collective horror, we discovered that not only were the entire bridal party resplendent in baby-pink furry bunny-ear headbands, but every guest was expected to wear them, too. According to the wedding planner, each invitation had stated firmly that nobody, be they bridal party member or guest, would be admitted to the nuptials if they failed to come attired in the correct headgear. Needless to say, the wedding entertainment wasn't exempt from this edict and the best man insisted we comply before we were allowed to set foot in the country club venue.

Tom's expression conveyed what we were all feeling. 'I used to think I was a serious musician,' he thundered, the impact of his fury dampened somewhat by the ridiculous fluffy appendages strapped to his head that bobbed as he spoke. 'What kind of strange, demented psycho demands bunny ears for their wedding? It just makes a mockery of the whole event.'

I would love to say that the Easter theme ended with the fluffy ears, but I'm afraid I would be lying. Yellow, fluffy toy chicks marked each place setting and were scattered across the top table; pastel pink, blue, yellow and green ribbons were tied around the white chair covers and looped round the marble pillars at the entrance to the reception hall; cuddly toy rabbits were *everywhere* – nestling round the Easter-egg-topped wedding cake, sitting in the middle of tables holding baskets stuffed with daffodils and white tulips; and real white rabbits sat dejectedly in a caged area on a strip of sickening green Astroturf in the middle of the room. For bridal favours, each guest received a box of Cadbury Mini Eggs and an Easter egg hunt had been organised for the children between the afternoon and evening receptions. Worst of all, garishly pink fluffy rabbit tails were fixed to the back of each chair. It was *hideous* – a case of a funny idea being taken way too far, eventually taking precedence over everything that should have been lovely about a spring wedding.

And as for the gig – well, *you* try giving a polished performance with two hundred blatted guests John Travolta-ing to 'Night Fever' in matching leporine accessories . . .

Our task was not helped by the thoroughly unpleasant selection of guests who moaned, bitched and shouted their way through the majority of our set. The bride – highly spray-tanned and sporting at least four sets of false eyelashes – pouted constantly because she was being ignored by her three chunky bridesmaids who were desperately attempting to grab anything remotely male. Meanwhile, her new husband – who had the legend 'Wolfman' blue-tattooed across the back of his neck – almost caused a full-on fistfight when he very publicly fell out with his best man, two of the ushers and the mother of the bride.

It doesn't happen very often, but all of us were thoroughly relieved to reach the end of the gig and leave as soon as possible. However, the night was saved by Tom's timely summation of the event, as we sat in Jack and Soph's living room nursing huge mugs of hot chocolate:

'Look at this way: at least we got out of there alive. Pity the bunnies, people!'

BRIEF ENCOUNTER?

I was the girl in the red coat and cream scarf who crashed into a toy stall in the Christmas Market, Victoria Square, Birmingham, on Saturday 17th December.
I have shoulder-length dark blonde hair, sea green eyes and I'm 5ft 5ins tall. You were the man in the black coat wearing a green, brown and cream striped scarf who came to my rescue. You had wavy, russet-brown hair, hazel eyes and were around 6ft tall. If you don't want this to remain a brief encounter, please contact me.
Email encounters@brumnews.co.uk quoting
Box No: **BE1712**

'I think it's good,' Tom said slowly, his eyebrows raised far too high for this to be what he truly thought.

I don't often wish for alcohol at ten thirty on a Saturday morning, but today the presence of a nice glass of red in the middle of the band rehearsal might just have helped to take the edge off the sinking feeling I was now experiencing.

'I think it's cheesy beyond belief,' I admitted, 'but it might help to jog someone's memory.'

Tom handed me a strong cup of tea as Jack joined us. 'I can't believe we're the first ones to show it to you.'

'To be honest, I hadn't made that much of an effort to get hold of a copy,' I confessed.

While I was touched that Wren was supporting me, I remained unconvinced about placing the advert in the paper. Still, at least someone was doing *something* – and, like Auntie Mags had put it recently (over the most amazingly sticky St Clements cake that, unsurprisingly, turned out to be exactly what I needed): 'It's any port in a storm now, kid.'

'But do you think he'll still remember meeting you, bearing in mind it's three and a half months since it happened?' Jack asked, yelping as Wren clipped his ear.

'Don't listen to him. He's being pedantic.'

'That *hurt*. You're vicious, Wren.'

'Well, consider it your just reward for overt pessimism, Jack. Seriously, Rom, I think this could work. And if he was as bowled over with you as you said he was, he'll be searching for you, too.'

With every last ounce of optimism within me, I hoped he was.

Two hours later we broke for lunch, Wren, Tom and Jack heading into town to grab food for us. With the rehearsal room empty, I grabbed the kettle and walked to the tiny kitchen down the hall to refill it.

When I returned, I was shocked to see Charlie standing on the far side of the rehearsal room, head bent over the open newspaper where Jack had left it on the amp beside his keyboard. I had wrongly assumed he had joined the others on the food run. I stopped in the doorway, kettle in hand, debating whether or not to leave. As I stepped back, the floorboard creaked and Charlie looked up.

'Brief Encounter, huh?'

I walked into the rehearsal room and replaced the kettle on its base, flicking the switch to boil it. 'It was Wren's idea.'

'Hm. Any replies yet?'

I shrugged. 'It's only just come out. This morning was the first time I'd seen it.' That frustrating barrier had appeared again between us, blocking the usual flow of conversation, forcing every word to be considered before it could pass. 'Cup of tea?' I offered, desperate to find anything to recapture some of the easiness I so longed for between us.

'Probably should wait until the others get back.'

'Oh.' Unsure whether to leave him reading the offending column and occupy myself with tea-making duties anyway, or wait for his next comment, I remained where I was, goosebumps prickling along my arms as I searched for something else to say.

Why was this so hard? Even though I absolutely believed in my quest and nothing would persuade me otherwise, the atmosphere between Charlie and I sat uncomfortably with my soul. Unfinished business, I suppose. After being convinced that I loved him for the best part of the last three years, perhaps this was understandable: feelings harboured and nurtured for all that time didn't disappear overnight, did they? As no more was said, I busied myself with making tea, hoping fervently that Wren's crazy advert would encourage some kind of response soon. I needed to focus on the quest: rogue thoughts about Charlie were most definitely *not* welcome.

* * *

In the event, the first response arrived far sooner than anyone could have predicted:

Hey
I saw your ad in the Encounters section and had to reply. I remember meeting you in the Christmas Market and I'd like to pick up where we left off. If you're interested, let me know.
Sebastian.

'I don't think that's him,' I said, peering at the reply. My heart was beating like the Duracell Bunny at a rave and my palms were damp.

'How do you know? He answered the ad, didn't he?'

'But *Sebastian*?' I pleaded.

'What's wrong with Sebastian? It's a lovely name.'

'There's nothing wrong with Sebastian on the whole. My stranger didn't strike me as a *Sebastian*, that's all.'

Wren scowled at me. 'Romily Parker, I can't believe what I'm hearing.'

'What do you mean?'

'You're a *name racist*!'

A group of businessmen at the next table were now staring at us. Embarrassed, I lowered my voice. 'No I'm *not*. I'm just trying to get my head around the fact that my handsome stranger might be called Sebastian.'

'Well, what name were you expecting?'

This was an interesting question, one I had mulled over many times since the day I met him. Is it possible to guess someone's name merely on the strength of two words, a gorgeous face and a striped scarf? He could be a Matt, or a Ben, or maybe a Joe at a push – but he couldn't be a Sebastian, could he?

Wren's eyes were sparkling dangerously. 'There's only one way to find out.'

'I know. But I need a little more time to prepare myself before I decide whether or not to reply.'

'Too late. I replied this morning.'

'*What?*'

Wren sipped her tea with self-satisfaction. 'Well, if I'd left it up to you it would never happen. So you're meeting Sebastian tomorrow evening in the café overlooking St Martin's church. All you have to do is to decide what you're going to wear to meet the man of your dreams.'

Robbed of my usual arsenal of witticisms, I nodded blankly. One thing I know about Wren: when she sets her mind to do something, nothing short of a freak meteor strike will dissuade her from seeing it through. The die was cast. I was meeting Sebastian tomorrow.

CHAPTER ELEVEN

Rescue me

It's funny the things that hurtle through your brain when you're heading towards a possibly life-changing situation. All day, alongside the usual 'Will he turn up?', 'Will he like me?' and 'What will we talk about?' questions, other issues – such as whether the blue printed White Stuff dress and orange scarf I had chosen after several hours of trying on seemingly every item of clothing I possessed was, in fact, the correct choice – joined in the onslaught on my consciousness.

Mick had noticed my distractedness as soon as I arrived at work, but left it until almost the end of the day to question me.

'Alright, Parker, what's up?' he asked, striding back into the Bat Cave with a mug of tea and an air that said he wasn't going to let me go until he received a satisfactory answer.

As it was less than an hour before I was due to meet Sebastian, nerves were threatening to remove any remaining shreds of sanity I still possessed and support was badly needed. So I told him everything: Wren's advert, the speedy reply, the unexpected name of my possible stranger and the worries I had been battling since yesterday.

'Wow. No wonder you haven't been with it today. Are you excited?'

'Yes, of course I am. I've thought about this guy so much since Christmas and gone through about every scenario possible in my mind. I want it so much to be him that I'm meeting today . . .'

'But?'

I searched his face for reassurance. 'But what if the picture and the person I've built up in my mind don't match the reality?'

Mick rubbed the stubble along his square jawline. 'You can't worry about things like that, Rom. I guess what's important is that you're willing to find out either way. Just focus on the excitement and you'll be fine.'

His pep talk certainly helped to bolster my self-confidence. An hour later, walking towards the venue for our meeting, I felt like a changed woman. It was *just a coffee*, I reminded myself, not a marriage proposal. I could do this!

I was almost at the entrance to the glass-fronted café when my mobile rang. 'Are you there yet, bab?' Uncle Dudley asked, his exuberance instantly making me smile.

'About three steps away,' I whispered.

'Ooh, we're so chuffed for you, we are. Your aunt has been cooking all day she's been that nervous. The galley looks like the swanky cake counter in Selfridges Food Hall now.'

'I'll have to pop over and sample some of those, then.'

'Make sure you do. We're proper rooting for you, sweetheart. You have a fantastic time and let us know how you get on, OK?'

Ending the call, I paused at the entrance to the coffee shop, straightened my dress and, heart in mouth, walked in.

With ten minutes to spare, I ordered a caramel macchiato and found a seat by the window. The lights around the beautiful red sandstone church in the centre of the modern shopping centre were starting to come on as dusk began to fall, making everything feel magical, while a cloudless sky arced over the considerable crowds of people as they made their way home from the city shops, banks and offices. As I watched them I thought about the stranger, about *Sebastian* – that name was going to take some getting used to – and wondered how close he was to me right now. Was he as nervous as me?

A polite cough summoned me from my reverie. Standing next to my table was a well-dressed man with wavy blond hair and blue eyes. By my estimate, he must have been in his mid- to late thirties and appeared to be rather nervous.

'Can I help you?'

'I very much hope so. I'm Sebastian. Sebastian Myers. May I sit down?'

The weight of crushing disappointment was breath-stealing as I forced a smile at the random stranger who wasn't *my* random stranger, mentally kicking myself for investing so much thought and emotion into this meeting. I felt like the whole coffee shop could see just how much of an idiot I was feeling.

'I'm sorry, I don't know your name. Your reply only had your Encounters box number on it,' Sebastian smiled, 'and I can't spend all night referring to you as "BE1712", can I?'

Wait a minute – *all night*? Who said anything about all night? As far as I was aware, this was just a coffee. Either Sebastian was getting ahead of himself or else Wren was guilty of gross misrepresentation on my behalf.

'I'm Romily. Nice to meet you, er, Sebastian.' There was one bright spark in the quagmire of discouragement I was experiencing at that moment – at least now there was little danger of me ending up as one half of a couple that would have sounded more at home in the register of a home for retired theatre luvvies. *Have you met Sebastian and Romily, two of our most senior residents?*

'Can I say, before we do anything else, how attractive you're looking this evening?'

'Thank you.' More than a little concerned by the lascivious twinkle in his eye, I decided to cut to the chase. 'Look, there's clearly been some mistake here. You're not the stranger I met at Christmas.'

From his nonchalant expression it was blatantly apparent that Sebastian had no intention of even trying to pretend he was. 'I know I'm not. But I could be just what you're looking for.'

Argh! Standing quickly I clutched my bag to myself. 'Well, thank you very much for meeting me. Um, have a nice life.'

'Romily! Wait!' he called after me as I bolted out of the coffee shop. 'We could have a brief encounter all of our own!'

No, *thank you*!

I didn't stop running until I was several hundred feet away. My head was spinning, the disappointment of finding a dead-end in my quest tempered by the utter hilarity of meeting Sleazy Sebastian. I was just about to call Wren when I heard running footsteps and heavy panting behind me. Turning, I was amazed to see my aunt and uncle dashing towards me, faces flushed and bodies protesting at the effort.

'What on earth are you doing?'

'Well,' Uncle Dudley panted, leaning his hands on his knees to catch his breath, 'you left the coffee shop so fast we had to run to keep up with you.'

'Hang on, you were just in there?'

Auntie Mags flashed a contrite smile at me. 'It was my idea. I was worried about you meeting a stranger all alone. We were just round the corner from your table. I'm sorry, chick.'

'We even had disguises,' Uncle Dudley admitted, holding up a threadbare trilby and a pair of dark glasses.

The thought of my aunt and uncle engaged in a covert surveillance operation was too funny for words, its effect magnified by their guilty expressions. I burst out laughing, startling a Hare Krishna follower who was handing out leaflets outside Primark. And such was the release after all the recent tension, anticipation and disappointment that, for a full five minutes, I shook with laughter, tears streaming down my face and my sides aching, while Uncle Dudley and Auntie Mags stood helplessly by. When it finally subsided I was exhausted, but feeling a million times better.

'I take it you're not too upset it wasn't him?' Auntie Mags asked as she hugged me.

'I'm *relieved* it wasn't him. He was so sleazy and suggestive he made Leslie Phillips look reserved.'

'And it means your chap is still out there,' Uncle Dudley added.

'Absolutely. Onwards and upwards.'

Initial disappointment (and cringe-worthy conversations) aside, today had turned out to be an important step for me. As I mulled everything over later that night, I realised that the experience had only served to strengthen my determination to find the man who kissed me. I had seen him for the briefest of moments in February, I now possessed photographic proof that I hadn't dreamed the whole thing and I carried with me the well-wishes of the people who loved me and the countless strangers who believed in what I was doing. With all this in my favour, how could the quest fail?

Well, I said I might have a breakthrough to report, and in a way I have. I now know that my mystery stranger is not *called Sebastian!*

Considering how nervous I was before meeting the man who'd replied to the Encounters ad, you would think I'd be devastated to find that it wasn't the man I met. But honestly, it was the best ever result. My handsome stranger was kind, honest and completely gorgeous – but the guy I met today had none of these qualities. He was an opportunist who didn't even match the description in the advert.

So my handsome stranger is back to being PK for the time being, which feels a much better name than Sebastian! It did make me wonder what his name is (and kick myself for the millionth time that I didn't ask him what it was at Christmas). I suppose the point is that his name doesn't really matter. When I find this lovely guy, I won't care a bean if he's a Rupert, Bill, Dave or even Juan. (It would be quite fun to introduce a Juan to my parents, though . . .) The important thing will be that I'll have found the man who made my whole world stop when I met him.

Like Uncle Dudley says, this whole episode just goes to prove that my handsome stranger is still out there – so keep your fingers crossed for me!

Rom x

'How many more times do you want me to apologise? The wedding planner lied, not me. I'm sorry about the bunny ears, but what could I do?' D'Wayne faced us, his brow furrowed as he protested his innocence once more. To be fair to our manager, we knew it wasn't his fault, but Jack and Tom found D'Wayne's propensity to rise to the bait just too tempting to ignore.

We were sitting in the melamine splendour of Harry's, primarily to hear the latest juicy details of the millionaire gig after Tom had called an impromptu band meeting.

'I think we should let up on him now,' Wren said, shaking off the 'oooohs' from Charlie and Jack. 'No, I'm just saying. D'Wayne's arranged some really good bookings for us this year – apart from the tights gig and the bunny gig – and let's face it, it's a lot better for us than when Jack and Tom were organising things.'

'Hey!' Tom protested.

'She has a point,' Charlie conceded, receiving an accusatory glance from Jack. 'Although Tom might just have come up trumps with this gig, eh, mate?'

Tom made no attempt to disguise his disdain. 'Cheers.'

With perfect timing, Harry chose that very moment to bring over his mama's secret recipe doughnuts.

'I take it you all kissy-kissy made up, now huh?' he grinned as we descended like locusts on the hugely calorific but thoroughly amazing golden twists of sugary gorgeousness. 'Good. I need my customers to be 'appy, you know? All this English down-in-the-mouth I am seeing from you is not so good for my business.'

Jack brushed sugar from his chin and grinned at Tom. 'So what's the news about the millionaire gig?'

'It looks like everything is set,' Tom said, in between mouthfuls of doughnut. 'Justin – my boss – told me he's arranged it all for us, including a dressing room, a P.A. so we don't have to bring ours, accommodation nearby the day before and the night after the gig. He's even covering our travel expenses. So what we're basically looking at, people, is an all-expenses-paid trip to London!'

This was fantastic news, and exactly the thing to take my mind off the temporary hiatus in my quest. I could see the excitement washing over my friends; even D'Wayne's eyes were sparkling at the prospect.

Wren squealed. 'It's like a *dream*! I can't believe they want us. This is serious stuff.'

'Yes, it is,' D'Wayne conceded. 'It's a great coup, Tom. You did good.'

'Good? I did more than good, I think you'll find. Julian said that he'd recommended us to two friends already, purely on the strength of our demo CD and our "can-do" attitude. And trust me, Jules is the kind of guy that doesn't get impressed very often.'

Wren clasped her hands together and closed her eyes. 'Please *heaven* let us get more of these! I want to kiss my credit card bills goodbye!'

'I hear you, sister!' Tom adopted a Southern Baptist drawl. 'And all the people said . . .'

We raised our hands and chorused: 'A-men!'

CHAPTER TWELVE

Move on up . . .

The following Saturday was Sophie's birthday. In addition to the meal planned for the evening, Wren and I had arranged a 'girly day' of shopping, chatting and eating – or, as Sophie calls it, 'the holy trinity of girlieness'. After Tom revealed that Cayte felt she didn't know us well enough yet, Sophie decided to ask her to join us. So at nine am, the four of us met for breakfast in the chic restaurant in Selfridges.

One of the most endearing things about Sophie (and, believe me, there are many to choose from) is how excited she gets about her birthday. I don't think I've ever met anyone who adores their special day quite as much. No matter what she does or where she spends it, she has an astounding ability to transform herself into a giggling child, finding wonder and awe in everything.

This birthday was no exception. When Sophie laid eyes on the pale pink and green balloons we had tied to her chair, she whooped so loudly that she nearly gave an elderly gentleman sitting by the window heart failure. The barista, who Wren had sweet-talked earlier into helping us (helping herself to his phone number in the process), brought over a heart-shaped cookie and a cappuccino topped with an 'S' dusted in cocoa, which earned him a kiss from Sophie.

By the time she'd been treated to a manicure, a slice of elegant Swiss gateau for elevenses in Drucker's patisserie and a good two hours' worth of shopping, Sophie was practically effervescent. Over lunch in the Chinese quarter, she finally paused for breath.

'I am having the *best* day. Thank you so much!'

Wren hugged her. 'Just as long as you're having fun, that's all that matters.'

'Is she *always* like this?' Cayte whispered to me, when Sophie and Wren were animatedly extolling the attractions of the hunky barista from breakfast.

I smiled. 'Always. Birthdays do this to her – it's so sweet.'

'It's *exhausting*,' Cayte laughed, adding quickly, 'but sweet, too.'

Perhaps it was because I didn't know Cayte well enough yet, but her forthrightness and ability to pass wry judgement on any and every subject was taking some getting used to. Wren and I would make wry observations on things we saw around us, but Cayte would take it to the next level, mercilessly dissecting everything within her sight. Even Sophie, in the midst of all her girly birthday glee, commented on it later that afternoon.

We were wandering around the Ikon Gallery, people-watching as much as appreciating the art, when a group of three ladies in their forties came in, talking and laughing loudly. Instantly, our attention was drawn to them and Wren nudged me.

'That'll be me, you and Sophie in twenty years' time.'

I laughed. 'Bring it on. I think I'd be the one in the green with the perma-tan and the Fendi suit.'

'Not to mention the embarrassingly loud voice echoing around the gallery. What a nightmare,' Cayte added, her smile vanishing in an instant when Sophie, Wren and I turned in shock to face her.

Sophie's perennial brightness dimmed noticeably. 'You don't take any prisoners, do you?'

Cayte gave a nervous giggle. 'I was only saying . . . I didn't mean anything by it, I just . . .'

'No, I get it, Cayte. But we're here to have fun, not engage in character assassinations.'

'OK, look I'm sorry. I don't want to ruin your birthday.'

As suddenly as it had disappeared, Sophie's smile returned. 'You haven't at all. Let's just have fun, yeah?'

Uncomfortable moment thus averted, our afternoon continued, although I was aware of Cayte approaching each topic of conversation with pronounced caution from then on.

An hour later, we collapsed in the opulent sofas of a Brindley Place wine bar for an end-of-shopping drink before going home to get ready for the evening.

Sophie piled her shopping bags beside her and smiled at us. 'What a lovely day. Thanks, girls, it was just what I needed.'

'Glad you had fun – and it's not over yet,' I smiled.

Sophie's eyes sparkled. 'I know. So, how goes the quest?'

All eyes turned to me. 'It's still going. There have been a couple of dead-ends that threw me a little, but I'm staying positive.'

'I looked at your blog the other day and I couldn't believe how many fans you have now,' Sophie said, taking a sip of her sunset-coloured Bellini.

'They're not *fans* . . .' I protested.

'What quest is this?' Cayte asked, her eyes suddenly alive.

'Romily's searching for a gorgeous stranger who rescued her at the Christmas Market last year,' Sophie squeaked. 'It's *so* romantic!'

'Oh? Tell me more.'

Sophie and Wren then launched into an enthusiastic briefing of the pertinent details of the quest, sparing no twist, turn or disappointment. Cayte, meanwhile, listened on the edge of her seat, drinking it all in.

'And you're spending the whole year searching for him?'

I nodded. 'It's more than just looking for a random stranger. It's about following my heart. And it wasn't until I started my blog that I understood how many people have had a similar thing happen to them, except they didn't pursue it. I know people will think I'm crazy, but if I don't try to find him I think I'll always wonder what might have happened if I'd taken the chance.'

Explaining my quest to Cayte reminded me of the excitement I had felt about it before the disappointing CCTV photo and the Sebastian dead-end. With a kick of joy I realised that my desire to find him was as strong as ever, the setbacks of recent weeks serving only to further increase my determination.

That evening, we gathered around a large circular table at Bella, the Italian restaurant not far from my parents' house, for the culmination of Sophie's birthday celebrations. After the recent tensions regarding D'Wayne, it was wonderful to see my friends relaxed and happy again. Once we had finished eating and Sophie had squealed her way through the box of presents we had pooled our money to buy, Jack – who had been busy tapping various glasses, wine bottles and the blue-glass bud vases on the table, pouring water in and out to establish the correct pitches – proudly performed 'Happy Birthday' for his delighted girlfriend, accompanied by the rest of us singing in four-part harmony, much to the amusement of the other diners. This one moment perfectly summed up everything I love about my friends. And it must have been the only time in that restaurant when a rendition of 'Happy Birthday' has elicited calls for an encore . . .

While Wren and Charlie were working out the bill, Cayte swapped seats with Tom to sit next to me.

'I had fun today, Rom, thanks for having me.'

'You're welcome.'

'And, hey, I'm sorry if I upset anyone. I know I can be a bit opinionated – it's an occupational hazard, I'm afraid.' She pushed her long blonde hair behind her ears, suddenly looking so contrite that my heart went out to her. I often forget how daunting it must be for new partners to enter into our close-knit group, especially if they are unsure of the boundaries.

'You didn't upset anyone. It was nice to get to know you.'

She smiled. 'Thanks. Look, I was thinking about what you told me this afternoon – your quest? I reckon there's more you can do to get it out there. You need to achieve the most exposure you can to increase your chances of reaching the man in question.'

I twisted in my seat to face her. 'What were you thinking?'

Cayte's baby blue eyes lit up and she clapped her hands. 'OK, this is what I was thinking: I write freelance articles for Newsfast – the group that owns most of the local papers in the region. The features that I write are syndicated across the Midlands, both in print and online. I think, if you agree, I should write an article about you and your quest. Like you say, it's obviously something that lots of women experience but few act upon, and I think your story is inspiring.'

It was a bit of an unexpected suggestion, but the thought

of spreading the word further had definite appeal. 'So what do you need from me?'

Cayte's smile lit up her already perfect face as she pulled a notebook and pen from her handbag. 'Tell me *everything*.'

The next day the warm late spring sunshine was dancing in glistening globes on the ripples of the deep blue-green canal as I wheeled my bike along the hard-pack ground of the towpath. After a night spent at my parents' a ride out was exactly what I needed – as was the joy of having some real quest-related news to share with my uncle and aunt. Cayte and I had talked for almost an hour in total, beginning in Bella and continuing at Jack and Sophie's into the early hours.

Auntie Mags was in the throes of a mammoth baking session when I arrived. Clouds of flour dust rose and swirled in the air and the irresistible smell of baking filled the whole interior of *Our Pol*. Elvis, trembling as much as ever, was curled dejectedly in his bed by the cooker, his grey furry chin slumped on one of my uncle's slippers, a weariness in his terrified canine eyes.

'Everything good here?' I asked cautiously, taking tentative steps around the stacks of cake tins on the floor.

My aunt wiped her floury hands on her blue polka-dot apron and hugged me. 'Your uncle is driving me loopy.'

I hid my smile. 'Why? What's he up to now?'

'He's only gone and found a website for "love against the odds" stories. Well, several, to be precise. He's been holed up in the bedroom for three days and nearly killed our printer with all the things he's been printing out. I can't get any sense out of him, daft old beggar. I tell you, Romily, he's obsessed.'

'Oh dear. Shall I put the kettle on?'

Auntie Mags sighed. 'Might as well. I'm at a loss to know what else to do.'

'Is that you, bab?' Uncle Dudley's voice drifted in from the bedroom at the far end of the narrowboat.

'Morning, Uncle Dud,' I called back.

'With you in a tick. I'm just getting things together.'

Auntie Mags rolled her eyes. 'Honestly, you'd think he was researching for flippin' *Panorama* the way he's carrying on. Anyway, let me look at you.'

Obediently, I did a little twirl, grinning as I did so. 'What do you see?'

A warm smile greeted me. 'Well, that's one determined niece of mine.' She bent down and began to sort through the cake tins until she stood with an oblong Tupperware box. 'Perfect! This is the only thing you need when you're as focused as you are today.'

I would never have thought of millionaire's shortbread as synonymous with determination before, but when I tasted the rich chocolate, creamy caramel and salty-sweet short-bread, my aunt's uncanny skill proved correct again.

'I had a bit of a revelation yesterday,' I told her, proceeding to explain about the conversation with Cayte and the resulting plan for her article. 'I think this could really work.'

Auntie Mags chewed her square of chocolate caramel shortbread thoughtfully. 'It has potential, I grant you. But are you sure this Cayte is the right person to write it?'

'I don't see why not. By all accounts she's a talented journalist – Tom reckons she'll end up on a national news programme within five years. She certainly seems to know her stuff, so an article from her is likely to gain the attention we need.'

'When is it going to be published?'

'I'm not sure. She seems to be so busy at the moment that I guess it'll be whenever she can fit it in. But we still have seven months of the quest left, so there's no need to rush.'

There was a loud crash, followed by a muffled curse, and Uncle Dudley emerged from the bedroom, an enormous stack of printed sheets clutched haphazardly in his arms. 'Flaming ship's wheel of yours, Magsie,' he grumbled, dumping the jumbled wad of paper in the middle of the table. 'Just stubbed my toe on it again.'

Auntie Mags folded her arms and surveyed him sternly. 'First off, it's not *my* ship's wheel, Dudley, it's the frankly silly ship's wheel you decided I needed from one of your blessed car boots. And secondly, if you wore your glasses like the optician told you to, you wouldn't trip over things in the first place.'

Chastened, Uncle Dudley sank down next to me on to the bench seat. 'You're lovely when you're angry, Magsie.'

'Oh *stop* it!' Auntie Mags reddened and poured him a cup of tea to distract him from her blushes.

I sipped my builder's-strength tea and listened to the dull *thwummph* of canal waves hitting the side of the barge as Uncle Dudley and Auntie Mags shared smiles that bore a whole story behind them.

'Now, I've been a bit busy on the tinterweb,' Uncle Dudley said, spreading out the sheets of paper on the table. 'After that terrible date with the fake stranger, I thought you could do with a spot of *uppage*.'

Even with my uncle's famous creativity when it comes to words, I hadn't heard this one before. 'Uppage?'

Uncle Dudley looked aghast. 'Don't tell me you don't know what uppage is? It's the only thing that works when life's been dumping its rubbish on you.'

191

'You and your made-up words,' my aunt tutted.

'It is *not* made up! My mother said it for years.'

'Oh well, if your *mother* said it then it must be right, seeing as she was so well-known for *not* being a fruitcake.'

Shaking his head, my uncle pressed on regardless. 'Uppage is when you find things that lift your spirits from the doldrums. Like when I've had a tough week with my arthritis and then I find something special at a car boot. Or when I found out my department needed to lose half its workforce, but then discovered I could take early retirement and not lose any of my money. It's like finding a shiny penny on a rainy day, or when Magsie cooks a new cake, just when I need it. You've had some big downs lately. It's high time for some *ups*.'

There are times I love my uncle so much I could squish him. 'So what do you recommend, uppage-wise for me?'

He beamed as brightly as the May sunshine pouring in through *Our Pol*'s windows. 'Ah, good question. Now I was thinking you might be wondering what the chances of you finding your fella are, now that you've hit a few snags. So I did a bit of virtual digging. And you are going to be amazed at what I found!' He pulled a sheet from the stack spread before me. 'Listen to this: "A Solihull man has been reunited with his childhood sweetheart after the discovery of a letter she wrote to him thirty years ago. Al Cunningham lost contact with first love, Ruth Lucas, when her family moved to Leicestershire. After six months with no contact, Mr Cunningham assumed she had forgotten him, going on to marry and have a family. Following the death of his mother, Alan – now divorced – was amazed to find a letter behind a sideboard, written thirty years ago by his child-hood sweetheart. 'I know my mother didn't approve of

Ruth so I think she kept the letter from me, hoping that I would forget her,' said Mr Cunningham, 46. Visiting the address Ms Lucas gave in her letter, Mr Cunningham met a neighbour who was still in contact with the family. The couple were reunited five months ago and are now planning a fairytale wedding in St Lucia, later this year. 'I couldn't believe it when Alan called me,' Ms Lucas said yesterday, speaking from the home the couple now shares in Solihull. 'When we met again it was as if the years melted away. I never stopped thinking about him, even though he didn't respond to my letter. He's my soul mate and now we're looking forward to the rest of our lives together.'" See? True love overcomes every barrier!'

I must admit that for my first taste of uppage, this was hard to beat. But there were more – at least fifty more instances of love triumphing over the odds that Uncle Dudley had collected to lift our spirits. For the next hour and a half, the three of us pored over the details of real-life love stories, some of which were so beautiful that all of us were reduced to tears.

'Ooh, look at us,' Auntie Mags laughed, wiping her eyes with the edge of her apron. 'We're like a season finale from *Dynasty*! A bunch of soppy gets, the lot of us.'

'If we carry on like this, *Our Pol* will sink to the bottom of the Cut,' Uncle Dudley agreed. 'But what's important, bab, is that you realise this stuff happens. You just keep believing and who knows what might happen.' He patted the stack of evidence on the table. 'By Christmas Eve, one of these stories could be *you*.'

In the same way that Auntie Mags' baking matched every mood perfectly, Uncle Dudley's true love research was exactly what I needed to see. With so many people willing me to find the man I was looking for, the promise of Cayte's article and just under seven months remaining of the quest, I felt more positive than ever that success was within my grasp.

I could be on the verge of a breakthrough. Yes, I know I've said it before, but this time it's a real possibility. One of my bandmates has started dating a journalist and she wants to do a piece on my quest! I think she's going to include this blog, too, so you're all going to be stars (in a way).

I've noticed something over the past couple of weeks that I never would have expected to be an outcome of my search for PK. People keep telling me how different I am, how the quest is changing me. And they like the change. I've always felt like I was a confident person, but recently my friends have said how much they've noticed it in me. I have to say that following my heart for almost five months seems to suit me. I'm less willing to accept disappointments, and despite the dead-ends and false alarms I've encountered so far, my hope is stronger than ever.

So when the opportunity came to widen the net with this article, I jumped at it. I'm not sure exactly when it's going to be published, but when it happens you'll be the first to know.

Exciting, eh?

Rom x

'I think you just pulled the best man!' Wren's eyes were wider than saucers.

'No, I didn't.'

'You did! He just totally hit on you!'

'All he said was that he was looking forward to hearing

me sing,' I protested as we crunched across the gravel of the staff car park towards Jack's van.

'But it was the *way* he said it, like "hearing you sing" was a euphemism for what he'd *really* like to see you do . . .'

'Wren!'

Tom passed by with an armful of mic stands. 'What's happened?'

'The best man just tried to chat Rom up.' Wren's amusement was unbridled.

'Well, you know what *that* is,' Jack grinned, arriving at my side as I stared helplessly at Wren, who was carrying the sound desk bag towards the stone archway of the impossibly gorgeous Scottish castle, the venue for our gig today. The speed of the Wren Malloy Grapevine would make Jensen Button pale.

'No. But I've a feeling you're about to enlighten me.'

'That's the Jim Bowen Theory of Attraction.'

Halfway to the door, I stopped and turned back. 'What on earth are you talking about? Isn't he the comedian who used to present that darts quiz show?'

Jack nodded, carrying three drum cases. 'The very same. It's the "Let's Have a Look At What You Could've Won" effect.'

I still had no idea what he meant. 'Which means?'

'It means that the minute you're looking elsewhere, that's the moment that you become completely irresistible to the opposite sex.'

'Why is that?'

He smirked. 'Who knows? I guess it's because you aren't checking out every bloke as a potential date – you relax, become more yourself, and the fact you aren't bothered is the ultimate challenge. We like the "Quest Rom". She rocks.'

It touched me that my friends had noticed the positive effects of my quest.

'Cayte says her article should be live at the start of June,' Tom told me, as we set up in the limited space available between two giant pink Cadillac cut-outs that were taking pride of place on the small stage. 'Her editor loves the idea. It could turn out to be a much bigger feature than she first thought.'

This was fantastic news. More column inches meant more of a chance that the man in question would read it.

I have to say that when D'Wayne first mentioned the wedding gig in a beautiful Scottish castle nestled between heather-crowned mountains with a silver loch lapping at its feet, the last thing I expected was to find a rockabilly theme inside. Yet here it was, resplendent in fifties kitsch, from the diner-style stools at the bar to the Rat Pack and Teddy Boy outfits worn by the groom's party – including the best man whose polite comment about my singing was responsible for Wren's current amusement.

'Hope you've brought your bobby socks, Rom,' Charlie quipped, dropping a coil of leads by my mic stand.

'Absolutely. Wren and I found our outfits at a fancy dress shop last week. I think you'll be impressed.'

'No doubt I will.' There was a definite twinkle in his eye when he looked at me over his shoulder. I shook away the thought bouncing around my mind like a kid on a space-hopper and jumped down from the stage to go and find Wren.

After much fruitless searching around the giant fifties-themed props in the grand ballroom, I eventually found her in the car park. She was talking and giggling on her phone, oblivious to the world around her, and from her demeanour and lowered, flirtatious tone, I knew there was a man involved.

As she ended the call, she seemed surprised to see me. 'I thought you were inside.'

'I was. But then I thought I'd find you. So, who's the lucky guy this time?'

She shoved her hands into her pockets and glared despairingly at me. 'I don't know why, whenever I'm on the phone, you lot assume there's a man on the other end. Do you think so little of me?'

I waited until she had finished her impassioned speech. 'Right. So what's his name then?'

Her pale cheeks became rosebud pink. 'Seth. The barista from Selfridges who we met on Sophie's birthday.'

'Wren Malloy, what are you like?'

'Oh I know, but he's so cute and I couldn't resist! Talk about "wake up and smell the coffee"!'

'Too much information, thanks!'

'Noted.'

'Has D'Wayne arrived yet?' I asked. 'I didn't see him when we were having breakfast at the hotel this morning.'

'I think he may be a little delicate after Tom persuaded him to take part in a whisky tasting in the bar last night.' Wren rolled her eyes. 'I think it's part of his attempt to fit in.'

'Oh, bless him. Nobody should take Tom on in a drinking competition.'

'I would imagine he's well aware of that now.' Her eyes followed a delivery driver who was carrying a huge fibre-glass Fender guitar into the venue. 'Question is, how will Jack and Tom cope with our fifties and sixties set tonight? The first hour is non-stop rock'n'roll.'

'I would imagine they'll be thinking of the money, the same way we do every time we perform "9 to 5" and "Copacabana".'

197

Wren wrinkled her nose disapprovingly. 'Tell me about it! Talking of money, though, I was thinking – when we've been paid for the millionaire gig, how do you fancy going on a girly weekend to Paris?'

Saving money is about as alien to Wren as quantum physics is to me. 'You're meant to be clearing your overdraft and credit card bills with that, remember.' We walked in through the fire exit into the main hall.

'I know. But the way I see it, those bills aren't going anywhere anytime soon, whereas the opportunity for a bit of European culture doesn't come around very often, and . . . what the heck is *that*?'

I followed her pointed finger towards the stage. 'Ah. That's the wedding cake.'

Wren giggled. 'But it's an Elvis figure. A three-tiered Elvis head and shoulders cake!'

It certainly was. At this rock'n'roll-themed wedding, every vaguely relevant music and culture theme had been referenced, from the *High Society*-style champagne glasses and early Audrey Hepburn posters around the room, to the table names laid out like the diner menus from *Happy Days*, and the giant multi-coloured Wurlitzer juke box by the top table. Appearing in our set list for the evening were retro delights such as Little Richard's 'Good Golly Miss Molly', Jerry Lee Lewis' 'Great Balls of Fire' and medleys of songs by Elvis, Buddy Holly and Eddie Cochran.

An hour before the event was due to begin, with guests beginning to mill around, The Pinstripes gathered by the bar with Ailsa, the venue's wedding co-ordinator, for final checks on the evening's running order.

'Lucy and Rick have asked for some extra photos to be taken as guests are arriving, so if you can do three or four songs before the first dance, that would be good.'

'Not a problem,' Jack nodded. 'We've more than enough be-bop to do that tonight.'

'It's a good crowd,' Ailsa said, as a group of guests looking like extras from *Grease* passed by. 'You know, I don't think I've enjoyed planning a wedding so much as I have this one.'

'Do you get a lot of unusual weddings here?' I asked.

Ailsa smiled. 'Not very many. Mostly people want the full "kilts and haggis" experience, although we also had a spate of *Lord of the Rings*-themed ceremonies a couple of years ago. This makes a nice change for me.'

A man in his mid-fifties walked over and flung a clearly unwelcome arm around the wedding co-ordinator. 'Ahhh, lovely *Ailsa*,' he breathed, sending a waft of stale-cigar-and-whisky odour in our direction. 'Handling all the fine details of this h-h-happy, h-h-happy day, eh? She's a wonder, this one. Can handle *my* requirements any day of the week.'

Ailsa's smile was pure professional grit as the man coughed a guttural laugh.

'All part of the service,' she replied, perhaps ill-advisedly, given the guest's wicked smile that seeped across his face like an oil slick.

'H-h-h-ha, *h-h-haaa*! I'll bet!'

As he wandered off towards the bride and groom who were greeting their guests by the entrance to the ballroom, Ailsa visibly shuddered.

'Occupational hazard?' Charlie asked.

'Exactly. He's the stepfather of the bride and was three sheets to the wind when he arrived for the ceremony this morning. I dread to think how much he's consumed by now.' She winked at Wren and me. 'I'd watch out for that one, if I were you.'

Wren laughed. 'Don't worry. Rom and I have fended off

more than our fair share of lecherous relatives in our time. We can handle him.'

While the boys in the band had made no secret of their feelings towards rock'n'roll songs in rehearsal, the enthusiastic reaction from the entirely fifties-attired guests made it a thoroughly enjoyable experience for all of us when we performed that night. As a vocalist, I actually relish the opportunity to sing well-known songs that I wouldn't have the opportunity to perform otherwise. Especially if the guests are as appreciative as our audience were that night. The wedding had a truly retro vibe, with every guest entering into the spirit of things with their brightly coloured costumes – ladies in full circle skirts and bobby socks, or Grace Kelly evening gowns, and gentlemen in fitted suits and trilbies. Lucy, the bride, wore a vintage Dior 'New Look' strapless wedding gown, its bodice covered in guipure lace roses and studded with pearls, over a full tulle skirt, with long white silk gloves; while her new husband Rick was every inch a Gregory Peck in his grey flannel suit. Watching them dancing with their guests to an era-specific set list was inspiring.

Not wanting to stand out from the crowd, Wren and I had hired two circle-skirt dresses from a fancy dress shop and looked as if we had stepped off the set of *Happy Days*. Getting into character really helped the show that night, particularly when it came to performing the songs. Fronting a band is very similar to acting: it's about playing a role – one which, in any other circumstance, you perhaps wouldn't dream of portraying. On stage, I can be confident, flirty and in control – much more than in real life. I'm happy to chivvy the audience to step on to the dance floor, answering back the obligatory hecklers and keeping the show running smoothly. The key is to ensure that once people are on the dance floor, the band and I make it harder for them to leave. The whole task becomes much easier when Wren is helping me and it's one of the many things I love about singing with her. If one of us needs a break, the other can take the melody; if one forgets the words, the other can jump in. We call it 'tag-teaming' and it's wonderful to know that my friend has my back during a performance.

In the break between the two sets, Wren and I wandered out into the grounds of the castle to cool down. The air was so fresh it almost hurt my lungs as I gazed out at the beautiful scenery. The last glow of sunset was beginning to dip beneath the shining waters of the loch, bright stars already appearing overhead.

'This is quite an amazing place. Not a bad setting for your wedding.'

Wren nudged me. 'Thinking about your mystery man, are you?'

I couldn't deny it. In such unbelievably romantic surroundings, it was impossible not to think of the man who had burst into my life in such a romantic way. But what was strange was that in all the time I had been in love with Charlie, I had never even considered marrying him. Yet as soon as PK appeared, the thought had become a regular occurrence at our wedding gigs. Which was completely barmy in itself, but there it is. The memory of how he had looked at me had somehow made plausible the possibility of one day spending the rest of my life with him.

'A-h-h-h-ha!' boomed a throaty voice behind us. Wren and I turned to see the repulsive stepfather-of-the-bride wheeling his way across the lawn towards us. 'So *this* is where you lovely ladies are h-h-hiding yourselves. Naughty, naughty!'

Wren groaned but granted him her brightest smile. 'Actually, we were just going back inside for the next set.'

Unfortunately, the inebriated man wasn't likely to be deterred so easily. 'No h-h-hurry,' he slurred, grabbing hold of Wren's arm. 'After all, you're being *paid* to entertain us. So I was thinking of a little *private* show, if you get my meaning.'

'I'm sorry. We really have to go . . .' Wren balked at his breath as he leaned towards her, lips pursed, making the most gut-wrenching kissy-kissy noises.

'I think you should let my friend go,' I said with as much confidence as I could muster, but the tremor at the edge of my voice betrayed my mounting unease.

He didn't take the hint, instead catching hold of my wrist with his other arm. 'Two for the price of one, eh?'

'With respect, I think you should let my artists go,' said a voice to our right. Wren and I looked over and, to our surprise, saw D'Wayne standing with his arms folded across his chest, looking every inch the scary bouncer.

'And what is it to you?' sneered the stepfather.

'I'm their manager,' he replied, moving closer. 'And dealing with dirty old men is not in their contract.'

'Cost extra, does it?' His grip on my wrist tightened as I tried to wrench it away.

'Right, that does it.'

What happened next was so fast it was almost a blur. D'Wayne stepped forward in a single movement, thrusting his arm between the stepfather and me. Our unwelcome guest let go of us in surprise and D'Wayne flipped him over on his back. Wren and I stared down at the stunned man sprawled on the grass.

'*Wow*. How on earth did you do that?'

D'Wayne shrugged. 'I studied judo for a long time. You

never forget.' He looked down at the man at his feet. 'Now, we're going back to the reception, sir, and I suggest you do the same. Are we clear?'

Eyes wide with terror, the man nodded dumbly. D'Wayne led us quickly towards the castle doors.

'Where have you guys been?' Charlie asked when we rejoined them, his smile vanishing when he saw our expressions. 'What happened?'

'D'Wayne has just been a complete hero, that's what happened,' Wren replied. 'Believe me, you don't want to mess with this man!'

D'Wayne gave a nervous laugh. 'I didn't do anything.'

'Yes, you did,' she replied, a little too forcefully, making our manager stare at her. 'He totally karate-chopped that sleazy stepfather of the bride! It was like something from a Kung Fu movie!'

'It was *judo*,' D'Wayne corrected, but Wren wasn't listening, enthusiastically re-enacting her version of what had just happened as D'Wayne's embarrassment increased.

The second set passed without further drama, the response from the guests soon removing any thoughts of the sleazy stepfather. When the last bars of the final song ended, our audience applauded and whistled until we gave in and performed 'Can't Take My Eyes Off You', much to their delight as they sang along with all the vigour of a football crowd.

'Thank you so much,' the flushed bride smiled as we began to pack away. 'Everybody's had the best time tonight.'

When the van was packed, Jack gave us the thumbs-up. 'Job done. I vote we look for a chippy in that town we pass through on the way back to the hotel.'

D'Wayne pulled a face. 'Greasy chips? Not my choice of late night food.'

'Well, don't feel you have to join us,' Tom replied, a little too vehemently.

'I think he *should* join us,' Wren cut in, linking her arm around our manager's considerable bicep – a move that terrified him as much as it amused the rest of us.

'Um, yeah, I'm cool with that.'

As D'Wayne obediently followed Wren to his car, she looked over her shoulder at us and mouthed, 'Putty in my hands!'

Tom slung an arm around my shoulder. 'Now that's one lady who never needs the Jim Bowen Effect. Just decides what she wants and goes for it. No man is safe, trust me.' He ruffled my hair. 'Watch and learn, Rom.'

I pondered this conundrum for most of the week following our return from Scotland, in the spare moments I stole between juggling work and rehearsals for our next wedding booking. Tom had obviously been alluding to something when he made that comment, but I could not for the life of me work out what it was. One thing I did conclude, however, was that when I found my man, I would hold on to him with a stubbornness that Wren – and Tom – would be proud of.

CHAPTER THIRTEEN

Could it be magic?

Hi. My brother told me about your Encounters advert and I had to contact you. I think we should meet. Please email me (address below).
Thanks, Mark.

The late reply to Wren's Encounters advert took both of us completely by surprise. Wren was so beside herself with excitement that she rushed over to the radio station after work, clutching a printout of the email, and blagged her way to the Bat Cave in order to personally deliver the news. Meanwhile, Uncle Dudley was thrilled when he heard about it – proof, as he put it, of 'uppage being at work'.

The weekend after Mark's email arrived, I found myself sitting on a bench on the canal towpath just outside my house, trying my hardest to stay calm as I listened to the ringing tone on the other end of the mobile line. It was Saturday afternoon and already Mark and I had exchanged several emails since his Encounters reply yesterday lunchtime. Unlike Sleazy Sebastian, I had high hopes for Mark: his emails, while brief, indicated that he remembered me and was keen for us to meet. All that remained now was to hear his voice.

The ringing ended and I held my breath.

'Hello?'

It *sounded* deep enough, but was it *his* voice? 'Hi, is that Mark?'

'Yes it is. Romily, right?'

'Yes. Hi.'

'Hi.'

As conversations go, this one wasn't likely to win any awards, but what we talked about was immaterial. I needed to hear his voice to be sure.

'I think we should meet,' I said finally, after a few more awkward minutes of stilted conversation. 'Do you know George – the narrowboat café at Brindley Place?'

'Yes, I know it well. Let's say ten am tomorrow?' The more I heard his voice, the more convinced I became.

'Perfect. I'll see you then.'

'Great. Till tomorrow, beautiful.'

Everything within me froze in time, as Mark's last word reverberated around my mind. *Beautiful* – that was the word I'd been longing to hear! There was no way he could have known the significance of the word unless he was my PK.

Shaking a little, I dialled Wren's number.

'Hey, this is Wren. I'm hopefully out doing *unspeakable* things to a gorgeous man right now, or maybe I'm wrangling a class of fourteen-year-old drama students – you decide. Anyway, I can't answer my phone, so if you're still listening, leave a message. Or, if you're my boss, this answerphone message was recorded as part of a Stanislavskian improvisation exercise designed to investigate how close drama can be to reality before it actually becomes reality itself. Bye!'

I smiled. Only Wren could turn something as mundane as an answerphone message into a piece worthy of an Olivier Award.

'Wren, it's me. The voice fits, I repeat, the voice fits. I'm meeting him tomorrow morning in Brindley Place, so I'll come straight to yours afterwards. I think this could be it!'

Next morning I caught the train into the city, reasoning that I would arrive calmer if I didn't make the journey by car. Nerves had been steadily building within me since the early hours and now, as I walked through the city streets, the butterflies in my stomach were reaching a fluttery crescendo. Unfortunately for me, I had inadvertently chosen one of the wettest days of the year so far for this meeting, so my gorgeous red Monsoon dress was now spattered with raindrops and starting to crease.

My umbrella barely shielded me from the rain as I walked across Victoria Square, past the cascading water feature with the female statue known locally as 'The Floosie in the Jacuzzi'. I paused for a moment at the place where PK had kissed me, feeling a cold rush of nerves as I gazed up at the ornate little fountain that as a child I thought was a princess's castle. I'd believed in fairytale endings then: could this be the beginning of my own?

By the time I reached Brindley Place, my hair had transformed itself from sleek, dark-blonde straightness to mousey frizz. *Great.* I was quite possibly about to meet the future love of my life and he would probably take one look at me and jump straight into the BCN Mainline Canal . . .

I stopped for a moment outside George to try to catch my breath and straighten myself into some kind of presentable state. This was somewhat of a losing battle in the now torrential rain lashing the canal towpath, but it was the thought that counted, right?

When I could delay the inevitable no longer, I stepped into the narrowboat. Scanning the tables, my eyes fell on the figure seated at the far end. His back was to me, but his wavy hair and striped scarf were unmistakable.

Oh. My. *Life*. This was it: the moment I had been waiting for. Taking off my coat, I walked slowly towards my destiny . . .

'Hi, Mark?' I asked, placing my hand gently on his shoulder.

'Yes,' he said, turning to face me.

If, at that moment, a seven-tentacled alien had suddenly beamed itself into the cosy narrowboat café and started singing a Tom Jones medley, I couldn't have been more surprised. Because while the voice, the scarf, the build and the hair matched the memory of the man who had stolen my heart, the face did not.

Maybe I'd remembered him wrong. After all, I'd only spent a few minutes in his company and five months had passed since then. Perhaps, in my rose-tinted recollections, I had subconsciously embellished his appearance, seeing the man I *wanted* to see, not the man he actually was. I had been in a bit of a state when I'd met him, so what if the shock of Charlie's rebuttal and my collision with the toy stall had altered my perception of reality?

I realised I was staring at him like a crazy person, so I smiled my friendliest smile and sat down. I needed to accept reality and leave the dream image of him behind.

'I've ordered coffee, I hope that was OK?' he asked, and I tried my best not to notice how crooked his teeth were – yet another detail I'd failed to remember, probably.

'That's fine.' Weren't his eyes more of a hazel colour in

the Christmas Market? But, now I came to think of it, I wasn't altogether sure I remembered his exact eye colour at all. 'Thanks for getting in touch.'

'Well, my brother saw the advert and told me about it.'

'Is that who you were with on the day we met?'

'Yes.' Was his eyebrow twitching?

'Coffee for two?' the young waitress asked, interrupting our conversation. As she placed cups, cafetière, milk jug and spoons on the table between us, I took the opportunity to regroup. Perhaps this was the Almighty's way of repri-manding me for being so superficial about looks – to look deeper and find the beauty within.

We chatted vaguely for about ten minutes, my discomfort growing steadily all the time. Everything I thought I knew had been shaken; the allure of my quest was dimming a little as I sat opposite this man who didn't quite fit the picture in my head. Finally, I decided to cut to the chase.

'What I really want to know is why you had to leave so quickly?' It was the question I had been toying with ever since it happened and, if Mark was my handsome(ish) stranger, he was the only one who could provide the answer.

His expression clouded a little. 'I didn't.'

Eh? 'Yes, you did. That's why I wanted to find you again.'

'Ah . . .'

'Not that I blame you – I mean, it was busy and I expect you had a lot of shopping to do, what with it being so close to Christmas and everything . . .' Was I babbling? This was not how I'd envisaged this meeting and I felt like I was fast losing the plot.

'Er, yeah.' He busied himself with pouring a second cup of coffee.

Excellent. Now I was boring him.

All the same, I needed to know. 'So – um – what made you leave?'

He stared at me. 'I'm sorry, I really don't know what you're talking about.'

'But I . . .'

'No!' I was silenced by Mark's hand slapping the table. Running a hand through his hair, he took a minute to compose himself as I stared at him like a complete dummy. 'I'm sorry. I can't do this.'

'Can't do what?'

His eyes were wild as he spoke. 'I never met you.'

'Sorry? B-but you said . . .'

'I know what I said. I lied. My brother saw the advert and the resemblance to me was startling. I've not had that much success with relationships lately and Phil – my brother – said this was too much of a coincidence to ignore.'

Hurt, confused and increasingly angry, I eyeballed him. 'Well, you could have just *said* that in the first place. I've been sitting here like . . . like a *lunatic,* beating myself up over not being able to remember you properly and now you tell me you're not *you* – I mean, *him*?'

'I'm sorry. The last thing I wanted to do was to hurt you.'

Fury raging within me, I picked up my coat and bag and rose to my feet. 'Well, how did you expect to carry this off, hmm? Surely you knew that I'd work it out eventually?'

'Look, you can't blame me for trying. I mean, a beautiful woman like you searching for a bloke who looks just like me? I thought that maybe you might see something in me that you liked.'

'And suppose I had, would you ever have told me the truth?'

He looked away – and that was enough of an answer for me. Without saying another word, I left.

I couldn't face Wren, I decided, not yet. Still reeling from the experience, I wrapped my coat around myself, ran up the steps from the canalside and headed across the bridge back into the city centre. Buying a bottle of water in a department store atrium café, I found a seat away from other customers, under the slope of an escalator. Smooth jazz was oozing from the café sound system and the blankness of the space in the building gave my surroundings an anonymity that slowly calmed my now throbbing head.

I was relieved that Mark wasn't my stranger, but meeting him had called into question my memories of PK. Before today I had been so completely sure of what he'd looked like, but after almost believing I had been mistaken, how sure could I be now? There could be any number of guys with striped scarves and wavy hair that looked like him – and, with a thudding blow, I realised that the man I had seen at the Valentine's gig could well have been Mark, not the man I was looking for.

'Rom? Hi, I thought it was you!' I looked up to see Charlie's smile. He had a copy of *The Times* tucked under one arm and a takeaway coffee cup in his hand. 'Can I sit down?'

Great. The absolute last person I needed to see at that moment was Charlie Wakeley. But I couldn't very well refuse him, especially given that he seemed so pleased to see me. Gathering myself together, I smiled at him as he sat down.

'I didn't mean to make you jump, sorry.'

'You didn't. What brings you here today?'

'Oh you know, it was a quiet Sunday and I fancied getting out of the house for a bit. My neighbour's bought a lawn-mower that sounds like an aircraft engine so a lie-in was out of the question. How about you?'

'I – er . . .' The pain in my head was getting worse and a warm flush began to spread up the back of my neck. All of a sudden, I felt sick.

Concern washed over his face. 'Hey, are you OK?'

I dismissed this with a wave of my hand. 'I'm fine. Sorry. Bit of a late night last night.'

'Liar.'

That was *so* annoying. Why couldn't he – just for today – *forget* he was my best friend who knows me so well? Instead of sitting there, looking effortlessly relaxed with his tousled hair, jawline edged with weekend stubble and cool, sky blue sweater over jeans, when I knew I was doing my best impression of a half-drenched madwoman. The way I saw it, I had two options: make up an excuse and stick to it (unlikely to work, considering he had already rumbled one of my fibs), or tell him the truth. All things considered, the latter was the only one that made sense.

Screwing my eyes up – less because of the pain and more because of the impending embarrassment I was about to heap upon myself – I confessed all.

To be fair to Charlie, he listened impassively and didn't once succumb to the temptation to mock me. 'Wow. You've had an eventful morning, haven't you?'

'I certainly have.' I took a long drink of water, my mouth inexplicably dry. 'What's worse is that I think it might have been Mark that I saw at the gig.'

He frowned. 'And that's a problem because?'

'Because I thought it was the man I was looking for.'

He sipped his coffee. 'Right.'

Discussing this with Charlie felt odd, especially given our recent history. I decided the best thing to do was to make my excuses.

'Anyway, Wren's expecting me, so . . .'

He sat forward. 'Yes, absolutely. Good to bump into you, though.'

I stood. 'You too.'

I was just about to leave when he touched my arm. 'Look, Rom, if this mystery man is as into you as you believe he was when you met him, he'll be trying to find you too. And if he isn't, well, he's an idiot.'

His words touched me more than I wanted him to see.

'How could it *not* be him?' Wren demanded, hands on hips, as she stood like a particularly miffed three-year-old in the middle of her ultra-modern living room.

'It just wasn't. But I thought it was and that was why it was so dreadful.'

'You're a gut-truster like me, Rom. You should have listened to your intuition.'

I slumped back into Wren's sofa. 'But what if my intuition is wrong? My memories of PK are so vague . . .'

She stomped over and sat down next to me. 'Now listen, missy. I don't want to hear any of this from you, OK? What you're doing – what you're believing is possible – is nothing short of inspirational. I looked at your blog today. Have you seen it lately? There are over fifty messages of support on there from men and women you've never even met! They believe in you. And they believe in your memories of the guy, too – however vague they might be. This is just a temporary wobble; you have to expect this. But the Romily Parker I know and adore isn't the kind of person who gives up just because she's found a couple of dead-ends. Time for some bridge building, I think.'

'What is that supposed to mean?'

Wren looked despairingly at me. 'Have you learned nothing from your many hours wasted watching *The Hills*

213

and *The O.C.*?' She puffed out her chest, flicked her hair and mimicked a slow, Californian drawl. 'Honey, you gotta build a bridge and Get. Over. It.'

I knew she was right. So much of what had happened recently presented more questions than had been answered, but underneath it all my belief remained. I had lost sight of it momentarily but I was not going to let that happen again.

When you get to see as many weddings as we do, a sense of déjà vu becomes an occupational hazard. There are only so many ways someone can offer a toast, arrange a room, perform a first dance or bid an emotional farewell at the end of the night: eventually, some overlap becomes inevitable.

Granted, as more locations gain licences to hold nuptials, the scope of themed weddings becomes wider – and we have certainly performed in some strange venues, from a social club in a naturist holiday park (mercifully most of the guests opted for some form of clothing), to a former mental hospital, a fire station and even a restored GWR railway station (the bride and groom tied the knot in the signal box before joining their guests on the marquee-covered platform for a 1940s-themed reception). But at every wedding reception there are universal constants: food, drink, music, flowers, relatives, friends and at least one embarrassing uncle/father/friend of the family/bridesmaid/mother-in-law/former partner of the bride or groom.

Our second wedding in May was a cookie-cutter stately home affair at a rambling Oxfordshire pile we have played at several times before. It's awful to say it – and I know for the guests it was a perfect day that they'll remember forever – but from our point of view there was nothing about it to set the event apart. The bride wore an unremarkable strapless gown and her flowers were regulation pink and white. The mother of the bride wore a big hat; the mother of the groom sported a feather and ribbon fascinator. The groom, best man, father of the bride and ushers were squeezed into light grey full morning dress with matching pink cravats they were uncomfortable in and grey top hats they didn't know what to do with. The speeches overran, the evening buffet was delayed and the guests were pacified with champagne and canapés on the croquet lawn outside.

The worst thing about the event was that the bride and groom appeared to spend less and less time together as the evening went on. To the casual observer, all the elements of a typical wedding were there and they had obviously invested a great deal of money in the day. But something was missing from the perfect, predictable picture: I felt it as soon as we arrived, but it was confirmed when the couple stepped on to the dance floor for their first dance. The groom fixed his gaze above his new wife's head and she stared resolutely at his shoulder as they made a half-hearted waltz around the floor. Their families and friends looked on approvingly from the sidelines, apparently fooled by the act. But I saw it, and so did the band. It felt hollow, as if the heart of the occasion had been omitted from the list of material requirements.

'That whole gig felt false,' Jack said later, as we were driving home. 'It was like turning up at a station to meet someone and them not being there.'

'I know. It's been a while since we had one that bad,' I agreed.

'Remember the one where the couple had fallen out on the way to the reception?' he chuckled. 'I don't think I've ever seen a his'n'hers receiving line before.'

In contrast, the wedding booking for the last Saturday in May was anything but predictable. Held at Maudlem Hall, a Regency house in the heart of Jane Austen's Hampshire, the event that was to pass into Pinstripes' posterity as the 'P&P Wedding' was the costume drama to end them all.

Much to the band's relief, we learned that we were exempt from the dressing-up requirement of the other guests – although I think Wren and I had secretly quite fancied the idea of flitting around the stage in empire-line frocks and bonnets. Two hundred guests had gathered for the event, which was taking place over two days; the happy couple had booked the Hall's 'Regency Weekend Package', according to Gianni, the flamboyant wedding planner charged with orchestrating the whole event.

'The package is simply *to – die – for*,' he gushed as he tripped joyfully around the grand ballroom where the evening reception was due to take place. 'Costumes, carriages, *heeeeaving* bosoms as far as the eye can see, handsome gents and blushing bonnets at every turn – for a whole weekend! Can you believe it? And as for the fabulous price – don't get me *staarted*!'

'He isn't real, surely?' Charlie whispered to me as we followed behind our guide.

Wren leaned in. 'Oh, he's real – I'm taking character notes on him for my drama class.'

I'm not sure if Jane Austen, even considering her delight in the ridiculous, would have been entirely comfortable with the twenty-first-century, middle-class version of the world she created in her novels that we were presented with. I would lay odds on the fact that none of her heroines ever arrived at a ball in a clear Perspex horse-drawn carriage, cavorted for the benefit of a liveried footman with an HD camcorder, quaffed a 'Pemberley Pimms' or knocked back a 'Bennet Bourbon' at the bar, before bopping in her corset to 'Mustang Sally' . . .

However, the most remarkable element of this wedding was beyond the dubious delights of the Maudlem Hall wedding package – and something I think Miss Austen would have heartily approved of.

Wren was the first one to notice it, three songs into the first set. Just as Tom was beginning the guitar solo for '(Everything I Do) I Do It For You', Wren nudged me.

'The groom's grumpier than Mr Darcy – I don't think I've seen him crack a smile since we started.'

I looked over to the questionably happy couple by the bar (garishly pink Pemberley Pimms in hand) and, sure enough, the groom had a facial expression more suited to a divorce than a wedding. The bride – wearing an exact replica of Jennifer Ehle's *Pride and Prejudice* wedding gown from the classic BBC adaptation – didn't appear much perkier herself, scowling at her new husband as he haughtily surveyed the strutting guests on the dance floor. Considering the song we were currently performing, the whole scene possessed a delicious irony that would have had Miss Austen reaching for her quill to preserve it.

But this was only the start of the startling similarities between the gathered party and the famous novel's cast. There was a cousin of the bride who spent the entire night trying to entice all the single female guests to dance with him, with about as much finesse as Mr Collins could have mustered; two teenage girls who set their sights on the handsome best man and wouldn't leave him alone, giggling louder than Kitty and Lydia; and the poor father of the bride who sat almost unnoticed for most of the night, no doubt wishing he had Mr Bennet's study to disappear into.

Added to this, the mother of the bride was a huge and decidedly overbearing woman who had been shoe-horned into a corset and spray-tanned to within an inch of her life. She was blessed with quite possibly the loudest voice we had ever heard, and had an uncanny knack of making booming bitchy remarks just as the music ended. In fact, had Mrs Bennet herself been in attendance, I suspect even she would have felt obliged to take the lady in question aside and suggest she tone it down a little . . .

Driving home in the early hours of the morning with Wren and Tom, our thoughts turned to what lay ahead for us in the coming month. The millionaire gig was getting closer, rising majestically on the horizon, luminous with the promise of bigger and better things.

Wren snuggled down in the passenger seat and closed her eyes. 'I can't wait till we're there, on that stage.'

'I can't wait till the money's in my account,' Tom added sleepily from the back seat. 'Maybe then my bank will like me again.'

I smiled as I kept my eyes on the road. The prospect of the gig was undeniably exciting, but for me it took second place to the thought of what Cayte's article would achieve. Thinking of that brought my thoughts back to PK. What was he doing now? Probably sleeping, given that it was two in the morning. But was he dreaming of me? Or had I slipped from his thoughts months ago, like the motorway miles disappearing behind us? Whatever the truth was, I reasoned, June promised to be a crucial month, both for me and for the band.

Staring at the red rear lights of Jack's van ahead of me in the blue-black predawn darkness, I could never have envisaged how true this prediction would be.

CHAPTER FOURTEEN

Please don't stop the music . . .

> Hi everyone. Sorry for mass text. Millionaire
> gig is OFF. Not our fault but nothing we can
> do about it. Will explain at rehearsal on
> Thursday. Tom x

I was staring at the text in disbelief when my phone rang.

'Rom, it's Charlie. Have you seen Tom's message?'

Despite my shock, it was good to know that Charlie's first response was to call me. 'Just. What's going on?'

Charlie sounded as shaken as I was. 'I've no idea. I just tried calling him but it was engaged.'

'If you find out anything, will you let me know?'

'Sure. Talk to you soon.'

Mick was looking at me as I ended the call. 'Everything OK?'

'No, it's not actually. My band just lost the biggest gig and I've no idea why.'

'Not the one for the millionaire bloke?' Mick's capacity for remembering random bits of conversation never ceased to amaze me.

'Yes.'

'That sucks, kid. Bet you're gutted.'

I nodded, twisting my chair back to face my monitor and feeling my heart bobbling about somewhere around my toes. Suddenly writing a jingle about underarm deodorant seemed like a booby prize. 'We all will be.'

Thursday was one of the most depressing days I had endured for a very long time. It didn't help that I had spent all day battling with the advertising manager of an agency drafted in by a client to 'pep-up' their radio campaigns – which, in non-idiot speak, meant interfering with every decision when he had very little creative input to offer. I wouldn't have minded so much if the product in question hadn't been a well-known brand of earwax softener . . .

My day went from bad to worse, especially when my boss Amanda waded into the debate.

'What Romily is *trying* to say, in her own way – not very well, admittedly – is that the concept you've suggested is impossible to realise in a thirty-second commercial. And if you want that commercial to be entirely sung in the style of Sigur Rós, your message will be completely lost on our audience. Most of whom, I would dare to suggest, will have little grasp of the Icelandic language.'

Great. As if the tension in the Bat Cave wasn't sliceable enough already.

'Maybe there's another way around this?' I suggested. 'We can write something that sounds like an art-house piece to use as a bed underneath your script – in English, of course. Would that keep the feel you're looking for?'

For the smallest of moments, I honestly thought the advertising manager was impressed. But my optimism was short-lived.

'It stays as the agency has designed it,' he sneered, 'or we pull the campaign.'

Amanda's face said it all as she flounced out of the studio. I groaned and let my head drop to the desk as Mick uttered a few choice words.

The thought of seeing my friends after such a tough day should have been comforting, but given the stony silence that had settled over us all since Tom's text, our impending rehearsal hung over me like a hail-heavy thundercloud.

We gathered in Tom's rehearsal studio in the old shoe factory at six pm, after the quietest load-in of equipment in the band's history. We set everything up, but the futility of the act was not lost on anyone in the room. This was supposed to be our final rehearsal before the gig that could lead to bright things for the band; yet now, in light of this week's developments, it was little more than going through the motions before the inevitable post-mortem of what had happened.

Charlie and Jack slumped against guitar and bass amps in one corner of the room, while Wren and Tom sat motionless on the sofa. I stood by the kettle and mugs, not really knowing what else to do. After ten minutes of this, the door opened and D'Wayne arrived, his expression as stone-hewn as everyone else's. He managed the briefest of smiles when his eyes met mine, but it was over as quickly as it had appeared.

'What happened, Tom?' he asked, finally giving voice to the question we all had.

Tom shook his head. 'Jules phoned me to say that the wedding's been postponed, perhaps indefinitely.'

'How come?'

'His daughter has been recovering from injuries she sustained in a car crash recently, but on Monday night she took a turn for the worse. Apparently the nerves in her legs sustained more damage than they first thought and she now needs a major operation to repair her injuries. The doctors have advised against her going through with the wedding until her condition has stabilised. They reckon it could take up to a year for her to be able to walk unaided again.'

Charlie groaned. 'Man, I feel bad now. I thought he'd just changed his mind and booked someone else.'

'I think that's what we all thought, Chas,' Jack reassured him. 'Tom, mate, next time you see Jules would you pass on our best wishes to his daughter?'

Tom nodded. 'I'm so sorry, guys. I feel like this is my fault. I mean, if I'd never mentioned us to Jules then he wouldn't have offered us the gig and we wouldn't have all built up our expectations.'

'We probably wouldn't have been good enough anyway,' Wren said, picking at a thread in her distressed jeans.

'Wren, don't say that.'

'You know what I mean, Rom! We've never handled a gig that prestigious before. Maybe the responsibility would've been too much.'

Suddenly everyone began to protest at once, the rehearsal space ringing to the sound of impassioned disagreement. D'Wayne held up his hands to silence us once more.

'It's nobody's fault and you're more than good enough. So let's just do what we came here to do and run the rehearsal, OK? Romily, can I have a word?' He opened the door and stepped out into the corridor beyond. Leaving the others reluctantly beginning the rehearsal, I followed him outside.

He smiled the same half-smile that he'd flashed at me earlier. 'I didn't know if you'd seen this, but I thought it was important you did.'

He reached into his back pocket and pulled out a folded piece of paper. Intrigued, I reached out for it, but he held it back for a moment, fixing his deep brown eyes on me. 'I just want to say, I think this is unwarranted and you should ignore it.'

What an odd thing to say. If he thought I should ignore it, why had he brought me out of the rehearsal to show me? I took it from him and unfolded it to reveal a printout of a news article. Looking closer, I recognised, with utter horror, my photo from The Pinstripes' website at the centre of it:

DESPERATELY SEEKING . . . ANYONE!

*How far **should** you go to find love?*
They say that The One is out there somewhere for everyone. But how far is too far to look? CAYTE BROGAN thinks she's found the answer.
Like many women, I believe in true love. I cry as much as the next girl when Elizabeth marries Darcy, or Bridget snogs Mark in a snowy London street; I listen to songs about the pursuit of love and use them to soothe my broken heart when love goes wrong for me; and I will admit, in the past, I've accepted the odd blind date on the off-chance that the stranger I'm about to meet is the man of my dreams.

But would you spend an *entire year of your life* searching for a stranger you'd only met once?

Romily Parker is doing just that. Following a chance meeting with a handsome stranger in Birmingham's Christmas Market last December, she is convinced he is The One and has embarked on a desperate quest to locate him again. And 'quest' is exactly the word she chooses to explain it.

'I know people will think my quest is mad, but I'm determined to find him,' she told me. 'When something like this happens in your life, I believe you shouldn't let it go.'

Ms Parker, 29, is not undertaking this mission alone. Her blog about the search has, to date, attracted over a hundred followers, keen to see if her real-life fairytale gets its happy ending. So far the mystery man remains at large, but Ms Parker – who hasn't been in a relationship for over a year – is undeterred. 'Love doesn't come along every day. This may be my only chance of happiness,' she said.

However, not all of her friends and family share her enthusiasm. 'Romily seems to have latched on to this "quest" on a bit of a whim,' a close friend confided. 'One minute she was declaring undying love for a mate of ours, the next she was starting this search for a random stranger. If you ask me, she's desperate.'

Alice Parker, 49, Ms Parker's mother, expressed horror at her daughter's yearlong search. 'She's done some preposterous things in her time, but this takes the biscuit. It's a real embarrassment to the family.'

Die-hard romantics might argue that Ms Parker is simply following her heart and that all's fair in love. But I believe her 'quest' carries a darker, more sinister undertone for women today.

While womankind has progressed far in terms of career choice, civil liberties and recognition, what of our personal lives and relationships? Have we been reduced to this? Wasting our lives searching for some outdated, utopian ideal forced down our throats by society and the media?

Whether Romily Parker succeeds in her 'quest' or not, the picture this kind of desperate act paints of today's young women is not a pretty one. Happily-ever-after? I don't think so.

I couldn't breathe. My eyes scanned the scathing article over and over, as if this would eventually wear it away completely. Insult piled upon offending words as Cayte's damning verdict of my life screamed out at me from every line. A sickening cold rush gripped my stomach and my head was giddy as I held the paper with shaking hands that didn't look like mine any more.

'This is – a *disaster* . . .' I spluttered. 'It wasn't supposed to be like this!'

D'Wayne watched me impotently, his face full of concern. 'I'm just so sorry.'

'She told my *mother*.' I shuddered as the full force of the implications hit me like a landslide. 'And one of my friends called me *desperate* . . .' Who was it? Tom most probably. But what if it was Jack or Wren, or *worse* – what if it was Charlie? I closed my eyes as tears flooded in. Whoever it was knew me well enough to know how long it had been since my last relationship. Why on earth would any of them share something like that with a viciously ambitious journalist baying for fresh blood?

Unwilling to consider this further, my mind switched into damage limitation mode. I needed to stop panicking and try to think clearly: this was a local article in a local paper that only relatively few people would see. Granted, I might encounter some problems with people who knew me and

225

the inevitable conversation with my parents was going to be *hell* – but once the initial interest had died down, surely it would pass?

'Where did you get this?' I asked him, wiping my eyes.

'My sister Shenice saw it on the *Edgevale Gazette*'s website this morning and when I checked the local paper it was on their website, too.'

'Right. Well, that's not too bad. Cayte said to me that the articles she wrote were often syndicated locally. Edgevale – that's Stone Yardley way, isn't it?'

'I think so. But . . .'

I took a breath to steady myself. 'OK, good, that's local at least . . .'

'Romily.' I stopped speaking and stared at D'Wayne, suddenly chilled by the tone of his voice. 'It gets worse, I'm afraid.'

'Define "worse".'

'I think – no, I know – it's gone viral.'

I blinked. 'What does that mean?'

'I Googled the article to see which papers it was in. It's *everywhere*. Websites, newspapers, blogs . . . It turns out some columnist at the *Daily Mail* picked up on it and wrote her own opinion this morning. I didn't bother to print out that one, but you can imagine how bad it was.'

When Cayte said her article would achieve the most exposure possible for my quest, she wasn't kidding. 'I can't believe it. I didn't say any of what she quoted me as saying.'

'Why did you agree to speak to her in the first place?'

'She said she could help me. She said I was an inspiration to other women,' I replied, even though in the light of what she had written in the article, my reasons now carried about as much weight as a feather in the wind.

D'Wayne laughed in disbelief. 'She's a *journalist*. She'll say anything to get the story she wants. I can't believe you trusted her.'

'She's dating one of my closest friends and she offered to help. What was I supposed to do?' I stared back at her article, feeling like the biggest fool in the world. 'Do you think I'm desperate?'

'No.' His smile was kind. 'Not at all.'

When I walked back into the rehearsal room, I couldn't bring myself to look at Tom. If he was going to find out exactly what sort of woman he was dating, I decided, I wasn't going to be the one to tell him. Besides, I was too angry to be able to make any kind of coherent sense. So, although it hurt me to conceal it, I endured the rest of the rehearsal keeping the truth of Cayte's betrayal secret.

I don't know if you've seen it, but I'm a laughing stock . . .

No, that wasn't right.

Ever felt like you've been stabbed in the back?

That didn't work, either.

Frustrated, I stared at my laptop's screen on the kitchen table, as if I could summon the right words on to my blog with just the power of my eyes. After the tensest rehearsal in Pinstripes history, I had made my excuses as soon as I could and fled to the safety of my little house. How I'd managed not to tell Wren or Jack was a minor miracle in itself. I think in the end the only thing that stopped me was the fear of saying something that I would later regret. The band was in enough of a state without me kicking off and making things worse.

Now, with my third glass of wine well underway and Cayte's words resounding in my head, all I wanted to do was to express the turmoil I now felt. But the words wouldn't come. Admitting defeat, I pushed back my chair and, wine glass in hand, opened the front door to step out into the warm night.

This was a disaster, in more ways than one. Ignore the utter embarrassment this was bound to cause me when people read the article; the worst thing was that, if PK did happen to read it, he was more likely to run away than into my arms. I felt helpless to know what to do next and as I leaned against the wall watching bats flitting about over the darkened waters of the Stourbridge canal, it occurred to me that in any other situation Charlie would have been the first person to ask for advice. Knowing that this road was no longer available to me filled me with the deepest sadness. There was only one thing to do. Pulling my phone from my pocket, I made a call.

'Hi, it's me. Cayte's article has just come out and it's . . .' I swallowed hard, '. . . *awful*. I don't know what to do.'

'You come over and see us straight after work tomorrow, our bab. We'll sort you out.'

Next day I headed to work, my head in a bruised fug from the dodgy combination of far too much red wine and far too little sleep. Although it was still early, my mobile was annoyingly message-free from my friends. Was this just because they hadn't seen Cayte's article yet, or were they lying low after seeing their words about me committed to print? Determined to get through the day with as few reminders of the annoying piece as possible, I shook my concerns away as I walked into the bright June sunshine.

I knew something was up the moment I arrived at Brum FM. Ted was as gloomily cheery as ever, but I swear he was smirking as the lift doors shut the lobby from my view.

People in the corridors averted their eyes and muffled laughter broke out behind me as they passed by. But it was only when I walked into the Bat Cave that Mick gave the game away.

'You should probably go and have a look at the notice-board in the staffroom,' he said, an annoying half-grin on his face.

Heart plummeting, I walked into the small room and, as I suspected, found Cayte's article slapped right in the middle of it.

'Makes quite interesting reading, doesn't it?' asked a self-satisfied voice behind me.

Amanda Wright-Timpkins, every inch the personification of smugness and a severe seniority complex. *Fantastic*.

I shrugged. 'If you like that sort of thing.'

She snorted. 'I imagine *you* don't.'

Oh, how witty of you . . . 'Yes, well, now you've had your fun . . .' I reached out, pulled the article down and screwed it up. 'There. That's much better.' I smiled sweetly at her and started to leave the room.

'That's fine, Romily, I quite understand. Of course, the *others* are still up.'

I stopped in the doorway and turned slowly to face her. 'The others?'

'You mean you didn't know? They're up on *every* notice-board in the building, sweetie!'

Deflated, I walked back to the Bat Cave with Amanda prancing along in my wake.

'Well, you know, we like to celebrate our colleagues' *success* at Brum FM. It's only fair that everyone gets to share your fifteen minutes of fame.'

Mick looked up as we entered the studio. 'You look pleased with yourself, Amanda.'

'Do I? Well, I must admit it gave me the smallest little boost this morning when I read the article. I mean, *how embarrassing* for you, Romily. Having your sad little love life broadcast to all and sundry. But you really only have yourself to blame. I mean, spending a whole year searching for a man who's clearly not interested? I know pickings are getting slim now you're almost *thirty*, but even you've got to admit it's a bit desperate.'

'Don't you have a broom to ride or something?' Mick growled, handing me a takeaway cup of coffee and a grease-proof-paper-wrapped bacon roll. 'We're actually quite busy in here.'

'Fine, I can take a hint,' she said, holding up her square-tipped acrylic nails in surrender, leaning towards me before she left. 'Maybe *some other people* in here should learn to do the same.'

'That woman has a stick *so far* up her jac . . .'

'It's cool. Let her have her fun,' I replied, looking through the work roster to see which delights were lined up for us today. 'Cereal bars, driving lessons and constipation relief – hmm. Nobody can say our job isn't varied.'

'We are nothing if not versatile,' Mick grinned. 'Are you sure you're OK?'

'I'm just hoping this all blows over. In the meantime, I'm just going to rise above it.'

Mick grinned. 'You do that. Actually, I have the very thing to help you . . .' He opened the music library on his screen and selected a track, ducking to avoid my empty coffee cup that flew towards his head when 'Desperado' began to play.

By the time I reached *Our Pol* later that afternoon, I was thoroughly sick of the jokes and thinly veiled amusement of my colleagues. It was all good-natured, of course, but it still rankled.

Auntie Mags was waiting anxiously by the cabin doors and when she saw me she hopped off the boat and hurried towards me in her slippers, a tea towel flapping from her hand as she ran. When she reached me, she scooped me up into the biggest, best hug.

'Ooooh, poppet! Give me a hug! That horrible woman! Poor, poor you!' Breaking the embrace she took a long, hard look at me. 'You need carrot cake. Nothing else will do.' She grabbed my hand and led me into the comforting interior of *Our Pol*. Uncle Dudley was already making a pot of tea in the old yellow teapot as we entered the galley.

'There she is! Our little media star!'

'*Quiet*, Dudley, you're not helping.' Auntie Mags made a tea towel swipe at my uncle, which he expertly ducked, the result of years of training. 'Romily is here for cheering up, not mickey-taking.'

'Don't worry, I've had lots of that today,' I said, flopping down on the bench by the table as Elvis hopped up on to my lap.

'You see? Even the dog has more sensitivity than you,' my aunt tutted.

Uncle Dudley looked so crestfallen that I had to hug him when he sat down. 'It's fine, Uncle Dud. I'm just in desperate need of some of your famous *uppage*.'

He brightened instantly. 'Well, in that case, bab, you've come to the right narrowboat!'

It is a thing of real beauty to me that even five minutes in the company of my aunt and uncle can completely change my perspective. They should bottle it, or maybe open a 'positivity spa' – somewhere where people could book

231

themselves in for an exclusive 'uppage boost' while luxuriating in delicious, emotion-specific baked goods . . .

'The point is, our kid, this does nothing to harm your quest,' Uncle Dudley said, pouring me a third mug of tea.

'But what if he's seen it and takes out a restraining order or something?'

'Romily Louise Parker, stop that! It's in a few local papers and the odd internet site,' Auntie Mags said. 'If he did happen to see it – which I highly doubt – he wouldn't recognise you from the lies *that woman* wrote about you. You've come through six months of your quest – are you really going to let one silly woman take the rest of it away from you?'

'And besides, this isn't just about you any more,' Uncle Dudley added. 'Have you seen the comments on your blog lately? No? Right!' He made a flourishing gesture with his hand as if summoning a vast army. 'Magsie, fetch the laptop!'

Auntie Mags didn't move. 'I don't know where it is.'

His face fell. 'Didn't I leave it in the bedroom?'

'I've no idea, Dudley, on account of not yet being able to see through walls, even if they are chipboard. Did you want me to go and look for you?'

Blushing slightly, Uncle Dudley nodded. 'If you wouldn't mind, *lovely* wife of mine.'

Patting his balding head, Auntie Mags winked at me as she headed off to locate the lost laptop. When she returned with it, my uncle logged into my blog.

'There,' he said, spinning the laptop to face me. 'Read those.'

To my utter surprise, the last blog post I'd written (before the article appeared) now had about twenty new messages. It transpired that several of my blog followers had seen the article and taken to the social networks to drum up support. Their number had now risen to almost one hundred and fifty and the comments were nothing short of lovely.

Keep going and ignore what that stupid journalist said about you. We believe! X **rosienyc**
All you are doing is following your heart. I think that's fab x **MissEmsie**
I haven't seen your blog before but when I saw that article I had to come and say that I thought it was very rude. I'm going to follow your progress from now on. Hope you find him xx **pasha353**
Romily, I'd just like to say that you're not on your own in your quest. There are LOTS of people willing you to find this guy, so keep going! xx **Ysobabe8**

And there were more of the same. I could hardly believe it.

'You've struck a chord with people, dear,' Auntie Mags smiled.

'And she's not the only one,' Uncle Dudley grinned, scrolling to the bottom of the comments and sliding the laptop towards my aunt.

Can I have the recipe for some of your auntie's cakes? They sound proper lush! x **cupcakefairy**

'Well, gracious me! Whatever does she want that for?' Auntie Mags feigned shock, but the deep flush of her cheeks told a different story.

'You should write them down, Magsie, I've been saying this for years.'

'Maybe I should . . . If I type out some recipes, would you email them to that young lady, Romily?'

'Of course I will. This is amazing, Uncle Dud. Thanks for showing me. I've been feeling so rotten about it all day, but knowing that people are supporting me still has really helped.'

We moved to the squashy seats of the living area and Auntie Mags brought more tea and cake. Before long, the conversation moved into not-so-positive territory.

'So have you spoken to your parents yet?'

Oh yes. Mercifully, only by phone so far. I had been putting off the evil moment, but finally bit the bullet in my lunchbreak earlier that day.

There are few certainties in this world, but when it comes to my mother, one immovable truth exists: when she is angry, *everyone* knows about it. Mum had made sure that she called as many people as possible to tell them how mortified she was about me. Consequently, the first ten minutes of our conversation had been filled with details of just how horrified everyone else had been.

'A *blog*, Romily? Do you have any idea how cheap and tacky that appears to the world? We didn't bring you up to air your dirty laundry in public. This is a complete embarrassment – everyone I have spoken to today says the same thing.'

I had apologised, of course, especially for the way she found out. But Mum was unwilling to let the matter drop and an argument thus ensued that began with her blaming the band, my aunt and uncle and more or less everyone else who had offended her over the years, and ended with her demanding that I cancel the quest.

'I'm sorry, I can't do that, Mum.'

'But what good is it doing you if you're nothing but a joke with your friends?'

That had hurt – after all, if Cayte's article was to be believed, one of my closest friends had been less than supportive of me. 'There are people who still believe in what I'm doing. And I happen to be one of them.'

'Well, more fool you. Fine. Go ahead. Show yourself up in front of everyone. But don't expect your father and I to pick up the pieces for you when it all goes wrong.'

'She said that?' Auntie Mags stared at me. 'I know she's not the most supportive mother on the planet but even for her that's harsh.'

'I just told her that this is my life and she has to let me take charge of it.'

Uncle Dudley grasped my hand between both of his. 'Now you listen to me, bab, this is just a little setback. I can't shake the feeling that you're going to find him. As for your parents, just leave them be. The only person you have to answer to for who you are is *you*. Don't you forget that.'

On my way home that evening, I felt distinctly brighter about the situation. Sometimes, it's only when your beliefs and values are challenged that you understand how important they are in your life. The exchange with my parents, while heartbreaking, confirmed what I had suspected all along: I was never going to be the person they assumed I should be. Instead, I felt free: I had found out that I could believe in who I actually was. And that was a girl who was going to carry on following her heart . . .

I heard nothing from any of the band the next day, save for a couple of concerned texts from D'Wayne. Bless him, he seemed to feel personally responsible for the hurt the article had inflicted on me. I really wasn't looking forward to the next band rehearsal, not least because I still couldn't be certain whom the 'close friend' quoted in Cayte's article was.

Of course this was assuming that Cayte had broken with tradition and actually bothered to source a genuine quote from anyone, instead of making it up like the rest of her article. I was still shocked at how blatant her betrayal had been. Did she imagine that I was going to thank her for what she wrote? Did she even care what I thought?

Later that afternoon, Charlie smiled as I walked into Tom's rehearsal room, but it was short-lived and did nothing to reassure me of his innocence. Jack looked up from his keyboard and was more forthcoming, leaving his instrument and walking quickly across the room to wrap his arms around me.

'Oh mate, I saw it yesterday. What a total bitch! Sophie was so angry I had to stop her going round to Tom's to confront Cayte. I think she probably fired off some choicely worded texts, though.'

'But you didn't text me.' I glanced over at Charlie, who was staring at me. 'Nobody did.'

Jack stepped back, guilt staining his features. 'I know. We just didn't . . . I wasn't sure what to say. I should have called. I'm sorry.'

'Doesn't matter. I don't think I would have known what to say if it had happened to one of you instead. But I'd like to think I would have tried to say *something*.' I looked him straight in the eye. 'You didn't tell Cayte anything, did you?'

Utter shock filled his face. 'No! Never! Hell, did you think that quote was from me?'

Instantly I felt terrible for even entertaining the possibility. 'No – well, I don't know who it was, so . . .'

'It wasn't me, either,' Charlie said, joining us. 'I hope you believe that.' His eyes were earnest as he spoke and I sensed he was telling the truth.

'I know she probably invented the whole thing. I just hate that it's made me question my friends.'

The door creaked and Charlie nodded in its direction. 'I would imagine this is the person who can tell you more.'

Tom didn't smile as he carried in his battered guitar case and placed it beside the drum kit. Jack, Charlie and I watched him as he busied himself with unpacking his guitar and connecting its lead to the amp. Our eyes must have been burning into him, however, because after a few moments he let out a massive sigh and returned our collective stare.

'So say it.'

Jack seemed taken aback by his defensiveness. 'Hey, steady on . . .'

'There's no point messing about. Just say what you're all dying to say.'

'Tom,' Charlie began, but Tom had clearly decided to dig in.

'Look, I had no idea what she was writing. It's not my fault it went viral. I don't control her and I'm not responsible for her actions. OK?'

Incensed, Jack stared at him. 'What, that's it? It doesn't matter to you that your stupid airhead girlfriend has attacked one of your best friends?'

I didn't want this. Animosity between us wouldn't achieve anything. 'Jack, let's not fight. In fact, can we just not mention it, please? I'd like to forget the whole thing and move on.'

'No, I'm sorry, Rom. You've been attacked and humiliated and *he* doesn't even seem to care. I think that needs dealing with.'

'That's *it*.' Tom slammed his guitar down on top of the

amp and leapt across the room, stopping inches away from Jack's face. 'If you've something to say to me, you can say it to my face.'

'Fine by me,' Jack growled back, squaring up to him.

'You start on Jack and you start on me,' Charlie threatened.

That was the last straw. Cayte was *not* going to rob me of my closest friends. 'Enough!' I shouted, surprising them sufficiently to cease the standoff. 'Look, she's your girlfriend, Tom. If you want to defend her, that's fine. Jack, I don't need you to fight my battles for me. And, Charlie, you should know better than to rise to the bait. So stop this now, because I will *not* have a bust-up laid at my feet on top of everything else. Just flippin' well grow up!'

They were still gawping at me dumbly as I walked out.

I didn't go far – just the small coffee shop in a former jewellery workshop around the corner from the old shoe factory – but it was far enough to make my point. I ordered a caramel latte and let the scents of fresh coffee, old worn wood and vintage dust soothe my racing pulse. I knew that the tension wasn't wholly due to the fallout from Cayte's article: we were all still reeling from the loss of the millionaire gig, suffering the sudden disappearance of its promise for our fortunes and the gaping hole in our diaries it had left behind. And since we couldn't blame anyone for its postponement, especially given the awful circumstances that had necessitated it, the resulting pent-up emotions were finding another outlet.

Ten minutes after my departure, I received a text.

Rom, where are you? We're sacking off the rehearsal. Do you want to talk? Jack x

Unwilling to reopen the conversation for today, I quickly sent a text back.

Sounds like a plan. Don't worry about me, just didn't want to stay in the middle of a row. Talk soon. Rom x

Your comments are amazing, thank you so much.

I feel like a total idiot for believing Cayte Brogan when she offered to help me. Looking back it was so obvious what she was planning to do. But then I'm not a suspicious person and I don't have time for people who are constantly looking for conspiracy theories. I trust people – is that a bad thing?

My aunt and uncle helped a lot, though, especially when the story first appeared. They always have a positive answer for everything. Of course, some people I know haven't taken it well, but I've realised I can't worry about what they think because, ultimately, it's up to me to decide what to do with my life.

Am I angry? Yes, actually, I would be lying if I said otherwise. But I think I'm angry that I got sucked in more than anything. And I'm upset that what she said about me made me question myself – and, worse, people that I care about. But feeling like this has made me understand how much this search means to me and I'm not going to let this stop me. I've come too far for it to be taken away by someone who doesn't see me as anything more than a meal ticket. If I let her words stall me then she's won. So I'm going to prove her wrong.

Thank you for believing in me. This is not the end!
Rom x

*Don't give up! I know you're going to find him
x* **pasha353**
*You have to carry on Romily and don't let that
woman win. Go for it! xx* **Ysobabe8**
*Keep going hun, you'll get there x p.s. I made
your auntie's ginger cake last night and it's
amazing* ☺ **cupcakefairy**
*In all the great chick-flicks there's a bit where
the main character gets her faith rocked by
something and she has to bounce back. This is
just yours. I know you're going to have a
happy ending! x* **MissEmsie**

The next day, I met up with Wren and we walked into the
city centre. She was horrified and upset that she had been
one of the last of my friends to hear about Cayte's article
– not to mention the ensuing row between Charlie, Jack
and Tom.

'I can't believe you didn't call me straight away,' she said,
setting two mugs of cappuccino and two white sparkly
cake-pops on the table. 'The first I heard of it was when
Jack called me to say the rehearsal was off. I've tried calling
Tom but his phone's going straight to answerphone. It's
such a mess.'

'I know. I just left them to it. I know it's not Tom's fault
for what Cayte's done but Jack seemed to think it was.'

Wren raised her eyebrows. 'And you're surprised? Tom
should have defended you, not her. You and he go way
back – that woman has only been in his life five minutes.
And what's to say that she wasn't just using him for her
next scoop, hmm? The way I see it, it's about time he got
his priorities straight.'

This wasn't my idea of a relaxing Sunday morning. 'Wren,

240

stop it. I don't want us all breaking up over this. It's done and it's out there: can we not just all move on?'

'But she's a total *bitch* . . .' Wren protested.

'That's as maybe, but she's not worth losing all my friends over.'

That evening, I noticed the email inbox flashing on my mobile. Flicking it open, I caught my breath . . .

To: jack@funkster-studio.com, mistertom@gmail.com, charliew@galleryQ.co.uk
CC: romilyp@bubblemail.co.uk
From: ladywren@hotmail.com
Subject: Pinstripes unite!

Guys,

We are all idiots. I just thought you should know. Our lovely Rom is hurting enough without us all joining in the kicking. So Jack, reel your head in. Tom, regardless of what your girlfriend says, let Rom know what she means to you. And Charlie, be the old head that we need right now. Otherwise, we'll tear ourselves apart and for what?

This stops now. Do something about it.

Wren xx

To: romilyp@bubblemail.co.uk, mistertom@gmail.com, charliew@galleryQ.co.uk
CC: ladywren@hotmail.com
From: jack@funkster-studio.com
Subject: RE: Pinstripes unite!

Rom – I'm so sorry. You didn't need me weighing in like that. You're wonderful and we're all here for you.

Tom – sorry for being a knob. I was just angry but that's not your fault.

Charlie – you're a mate and I value you, but you shouldn't have to make a prat of yourself to support me.

Wren – thanks for making me see sense. You're right. (But don't make a habit of it. It's not good for my pride.)

Jack x

To: romilyp@bubblemail.co.uk, charliew@galleryQ.co.uk, jack@funkster-studio.com, ladywren@hotmail.com
From: mistertom@gmail.com
Subject: RE: Pinstripes unite!

Guys
Wren's right. I don't want to fight with you. But you have to see it from my point of view. Cayte's my girlfriend and it's only right that I defend her. All the same, what she wrote about Rom in that article was shocking and we've done nothing but argue about it since it came out. Rom, I do care about you, more than you realise, and I hate that you're in this position because of someone I invited in. I had no idea what she was planning and I don't think I could have stopped her even if I did. But I hate that she hurt you and I hate that you thought I said those

things about you. I didn't say anything
at all.

   This is such a mess. I need to sort out what
happens next with Cayte and me and right now
I have no idea what that's going to be. But
that's not your problem. I love you guys and I
don't want this fight any more than you do.
   Big love
   Tom x

To: romilyp@bubblemail.co.uk, mistertom@gmail.
com, jack@funkster-studio.com,
ladywren@hotmail.com
From: charliew@galleryQ.co.uk
Subject: RE: Pinstripes unite!

So much love in the room today!
Seriously, this is good stuff, people. We
shouldn't be arguing.
   Rom, I'm sorry for being an idiot the other
day. You're right, I rise to the bait too easily
and I should know better. Jack, sorry for
egging you on when you were doing the big
square-up. And Tom, I'm sorry for taking
sides. We're all here for you, too. Wren, well
said about everything. Glad we've got you to
sort us all out. Can we get back to having a
laugh now? Good.
   Biggest love
   Chas ☺

To see my friends reunited gave me the biggest boost.
At least I didn't have the breakup of The Pinstripes on

my head on top of everything else. Now all I had to do was weather the storm of my unwelcome sudden celebrity . . .

'I'm *sure* I know you,' the lady in the supermarket queue for the self-service checkouts said again, screwing up her eyes and leaning her head to one side, as if this was going to aid her memory.

I smiled politely, wishing I'd gone to an out-of-town store instead. 'I don't think so,' I answered, hoping this would be sufficient.

'Have you been on the telly? Ooh, I know – were you on *Casualty* last week?'

Please get bored and leave it, I pleaded, but the woman in the cerise velour tracksuit obviously wasn't on the same ESP frequency. Time to try another angle: 'Um, I think that till's free now . . .'

'*Million Pound Drop*? *EastEnders*?'

What next, *Crimewatch*? *Wife Swap*? At this rate I would be here until Christmas until she had named all the television programmes she'd watched lately. Looking into my basket I was dismayed to see nothing that could legitimately aid my escape from this conversation, unless you counted poking her in the eye with a baguette or throwing tampons at her as possible options.

This was the fifth such conversation I had endured today and it was beginning to wear thin. The problem with celebrity status, I was discovering, was that although people recognised you, they didn't necessarily know where from. Consequently, they had to embark on the same thought process every time: did we go to school together, are you from work, do you know my husband, do you know my mother, are you my sister's best friend, have you been on an advert, are you off the telly, have you been on *Big Brother*, were you in *Heat* magazine last week . . .?

A week after 'Cayte-gate' (as Wren christened it), the instances of people thinking they recognised me showed no signs of slowing. It had happened everywhere – from the trains I caught, to the shops I had visited during the week, including one very embarrassing incident in M&S while being measured for a new bra. I was at the point of seriously considering having a t-shirt made up with Cayte's article emblazoned across it to save me from this random game of *Guess Who*.

Jack told me that the day after the *Daily Mail* columnist covered the article, '#desperatewoman' was briefly a UK trending topic on Twitter and the subject of several phone-in debates on local and national radio shows.

My uncle and aunt, as ever, managed to find a positive spin on the situation, with Auntie Mags assuring me that all publicity was good for spreading the word. I wanted to share her enthusiasm but, as far as I was concerned, the reality of being recognised was proving decidedly less positive than the promise of what it might lead to. But I was about to discover how wrong I was . . .

Almost two weeks after the article, I received a breathless answerphone message from Uncle Dudley:

'Bab! It's me. I think your journalist friend might have done you a favour. We've just had an email that could possibly be the break we've been hoping for! Call me back as *soon* as you get this . . .'

CHAPTER FIFTEEN

I will survive

I couldn't believe it.

'Well?' Auntie Mags asked, as Uncle Dudley hovered by her side in *Our Pol* with a be-cosied teapot in hand. 'Is it . . .?'

I focused on the laptop screen again, my heart thudding so hard it was threatening to crash clean out of my chest. I'd been wrong before; could I trust my eyes now? The image was a little out of focus, and taken from side-on, but it was *him*, I was sure of it.

'I think so,' I said finally, as Uncle Dudley cheered and did a little jig, almost showering Auntie Mags with scalding hot tea.

'Dudley Parker, calm down! It's just a photo, for heaven's sake.'

But this was so much more than just a photo: it was almost clear, conclusive proof that the man I wanted to find was real. This time, it wasn't the back of his head in a grainy monochrome CCTV still – it was my handsome stranger in glorious Technicolor. His russet hair, the faint line of stubble along his chin, his beautiful hazel eyes gazing out at me, and the lips of his broad mouth parted slightly, as if startled by the camera shot.

'Where did she get this?' I asked, my voice trembling as the thrill of seeing him again reverberated through me.

'The lady said she was changing her mobile phone, so was sorting through her stored photos and videos and found this. She'd forgotten she had taken it, apparently. That woman your chap's looking over the shoulder of is her best friend and she'd taken the photo while they were Christmas shopping. It's a fluke that he happened to turn around just as she took the photo.'

'It's a bit blurry,' Auntie Mags said, squinting at the image on Uncle Dudley's laptop. 'Are you certain that's him?'

I nodded, my palms suddenly sweaty. After the frustration of an apparently cooling trail and the still-sore bruises of Cayte's article, this was an unexpected breakthrough.

'Did she give a phone number at all?' I wanted to know more about how the photo came to exist, just to be sure.

'Way ahead of you, chick.' Uncle Dudley handed me a scrap of paper. 'Give her a ring now, go on!'

'Wait, before you do, have some of this . . .' Auntie Mags placed a plate in front of me with a thick slab of sticky ginger cake '. . . for courage.'

'Here goes nothing.' Smiling at both of them, I dialled the number.

'Hello?'

'Hi, can I speak to Natalie, please?'

'Speaking.'

I gave my aunt and uncle a thumbs-up. 'Hello, this is Romily Parker. You very kindly sent me a . . .'

I didn't get the chance to finish.

'Ooh hello!' Natalie screamed down the phone, half-deafening me. 'I am, like, your biggest fan!'

247

'Are you?'

'Absolutely! I've been following your blog since the end of January – I'm so excited about your quest!'

'Erm, thanks . . .'

'All my friends love you too, and we all wanted to scratch that Cayte Brogan's eyes out for what she wrote about you. You're not desperate at all. You're just looking for your handsome stranger. It's *so* romantic! Is it him in my photo? I'm going to be *so* chuffed if I'm the one who found him for you!'

Winded by this barrage of support, it took me a moment to process everything Natalie had said. 'I think it is, yes, tha—'

'*Wheeeee-e-e-e-e-e-eeee!*'

I held my mobile away from my ear as Natalie's celebratory scream split the calmness of *Our Pol*'s interior. Elvis, shaking mournfully in his dog bed by the cooker, looked alarmed and buried himself under Uncle Dudley's old lumberjack shirt that he had stolen from the washing pile.

'I'm going to tell *all* my friends! This is so exciting!'

'Can you remember anything about the day you took the photo?'

Natalie paused for breath long enough to regain some of her faculties. 'I was in town shopping with Cass – she's the girl in the photo – and we ended up in the Christmas Market about half past two. We were mucking around and I took a photo of her – that's all I remember. Like I said in my email, I didn't realise that the bloke was in it until yesterday when I found it again. I remembered the description on your blog. He fitted so perfectly that I knew I had to send the pic to you.'

Seeing him again meant more to me than I could

248

adequately express. 'Well, thank you so much, you've been a fantastic help.'

'It's the least I could do,' Natalie replied. 'Me and my friends have had so much fun following you so far. You are going to keep going, aren't you?'

I smiled at my aunt and uncle who were nodding frantically at me like a pair of Churchill dogs. 'Of course I am.'

'*Wow*.'

'I know.'

'No wonder you're looking for him. Even given the blurriness the guy is *sex on legs . . .*'

I wasn't sure I would class him exactly in those terms, but Wren's summation was justified. 'He is gorgeous, isn't he?'

'Gorgeous doesn't begin to cover it, hun. Put it this way, I wouldn't kick him out of bed for eating crackers.'

I smiled into my toasted teacake as the lady at the next table in George shot her a filthy look. 'Delicately put.'

Wren grinned. 'I say it like it is, me. Seriously though, *he-e-llo*! Well, that's one in the eye for bitch-face anyway.'

'Wren!'

My best friend was unapologetic. 'She deserves it. Trashing your dreams like that to move her poxy career on. Tell you what though, you're a better woman than I am: if she'd pulled that stunt on me she'd be making a close inspection of the bottom of this canal by now. You know Tom's dumped her, don't you?'

'I had heard.'

'Mind you, he's miserable. I'm thinking of friends of mine I could set him up with. So,' she squeezed my hand, 'how are you?'

Apart from still being regularly recognised in the street,

249

I was feeling more positive than I had in a long time. I had survived the aftermath of Cayte's article and been rewarded with an almost-clear image of my stranger. I had spent almost seven months of the year working from memory – and had fallen foul of it twice with Sebastian and Mark – so it was wonderful to be able to see PK and remember just how gorgeous he looked.

It was no coincidence that I had received his photo just after the shock and humiliation of 'Cayte-gate'. This, I decided, was destiny's way of getting me back on track. I *must* be fated to find him again.

D'Wayne brought some better news for The Pinstripes the following week, having secured two late bookings – one in September, one in October. As for July and August, things were looking decidedly sparse, but D'Wayne's brother offered some promotional weekend work for any of us wanting to earn a little extra money. In the event, only Charlie and I accepted, turning up at his cramped office at eight am on an overcast Saturday morning.

'Have you any idea what this is going to entail?' Charlie asked me as we walked from the small car park at the back of the office complex towards the entrance.

'None at all. D'Wayne said it was a "brand awareness" job, whatever that means.'

Charlie rubbed his chin. 'Perhaps it's manning one of those stands where you give out free samples of a product. That's fine by me – I don't mind doing that for seventy quid on a Saturday.'

Colson McDougall was a shorter, squatter version of his younger brother, with the same wide grin and air of self-assurance, but slightly less hair.

'Guys! So pleased you could help me with this. It's a new client and I'm keen to impress them, you know how it is.'

Charlie and I nodded.

'Excellent.' Colson handed me a sheet of paper. 'Now, everything you need is in the box by the door and here's your route. Good luck!'

'I'm a *pizza box*.'

Charlie's face was a picture as we trudged slowly out on to the street, car horns honking at us and amused passers-by stopping to point and laugh.

'It could be worse,' I smiled, adjusting the cardboard costume so it chafed a little less on my shoulders.

He stared at me like I was a lunatic. 'How, exactly, could it be worse?'

'We could be *pizzas*.'

Charlie shook his head and kicked a stone on the pavement in front of him. 'I don't know how you can be so cheerful considering what we look like.' A car full of teenagers honked loudly as they leaned out of open windows to shout abuse. Charlie sent them a clear message back with some questionable sign language.

'Oh come on, Charlie, you have to admit this is funny.'

'No, I don't. I look like a pillock and we have *eight hours* of this torture to endure. I officially have no dignity left.'

'No, mate, I think you'll find the tights gig and the bunny gig removed any scrap of remaining dignity you had this year.'

He had to smile at that. 'Well at least I'm not making a bizarre spectacle of myself all alone,' he said, knocking on the back of my pizza box.

Comedy promotional costumes aside, I relished the opportunity to spend some time with Charlie. As we chatted and joked, it was as if all the awkwardness and embarrassment of the last seven months had drifted away and we had rediscovered the easy friendship we'd enjoyed before. There was definitely something to be said for wearing large cardboard boxes to walk the city streets: it removed the usual boundaries of what we felt comfortable talking about. After all, when you're both stripped of your dignity, circumspection seems pretty pointless.

We stopped for lunch at a canalside gastro-pub in the centre of town. Owing to our large and cumbersome cardboard appendages, we were obliged to sit outside, but thankfully the sun had decided to appear and the day was now drenched in glorious sunshine.

'This,' Charlie said, holding his glass of golden ale aloft like Excalibur, 'is officially the World's Most Deserved Pint.'

'Indeed. Accompanied by the World's Most Expensive Ploughman's,' I agreed, pointing at our £15 gastro-pub lunch.

'Yes, well, seeing as CM Promotions is kindly footing the bill, it's only fair. How long do we have left of this prestige promotional job?'

I looked at my watch. 'Three and a half hours. Think you can stand the pace?'

His dark blue eyes flashed mischievously over the top of his pint glass. 'What, having to work with you? Hmm, not sure.'

'Loser. I can always let you finish the round alone if you'd prefer . . .'

'You're not going anywhere, thank you very much. If I have to degrade myself in public I'm not doing it alone.'

I watched Charlie as we enjoyed our lunch, loving the easy atmosphere and good-natured mockery as it ebbed and flowed naturally between us. I think he felt it, too; a satisfied smile settling on his face as we ate.

When we set off for our final stint, the conversation fell away into a comfortable silence for a while and I became aware of him casting glances in my direction as we walked.

A lady coming the other way chuckled when she passed us. 'Are you deep pan or stuffed cheese?' she laughed.

'Thin and crispy, I'll have you know,' Charlie called back. His hand bumped against mine. 'I like this.'

'What? Being a pizza box?'

'No, this – *us*. It's good.'

I nodded. 'It is.'

He sniffed and raised his hand as another car horn sounded. 'You seem really different, Rom.'

This took me by surprise. 'Oh?'

'Good different. Happy. Confident. That kind of stuff . . .' He laughed at himself. 'Ever the eloquent drummer, eh?'

'No – thanks, that means a lot. I feel different. It's been a bit of a crazy year, but I know I've made some really important decisions and learned a lot about myself. Blimey, I sound like an *X Factor* contestant. Vote for me!'

'I would – um, . . . but you're too good for that show anyway.'

What was he going on about? 'Thanks – I think.'

He halted and faced me. 'The thing is, I've been an idiot about – you know – Christmas and that. I just wanted you to know that I'm sorry. I should have noticed you before . . . I mean, who you're becoming, not who you are in my head. I think what you're doing with this whole quest thing is brilliant. Whether you find him or not, it's just *you* through and through. And you deserve to be happy, Rom, I really mean that.' He looked down at his feet. 'That's all I wanted to say.'

Wow. Out of all the possible conversation topics I could

have envisaged for today, that one was never even on my radar. Unsure of how to handle what he had just said, I gave him a long hug – which is no mean feat when you're both two-thirds cardboard.

After this, normal conversation service was resumed, but Charlie's words buzzed about in my mind for the rest of the day.

CHAPTER SIXTEEN

Spinning around . . .

August blew into the city with a freshness welcomed by everyone. Blue cloudless skies presided over comfortably warm days, kissed by bright sunlight and soothed with cool breezes. For once, I didn't mind not being able to afford a holiday, instead taking the opportunity to spend as much time out in the glorious weather as I could. I cycled into work twice a week, went for long walks, rides and runs along the towpath by my house and lazed in various back gardens, beer gardens and restaurant terraces with my friends.

I also took the impromptu break from our gigging calendar to consider my next move for the quest. Following the shock and fallout of 'Cayte-gate' last month, I had been so thrilled to receive the photo of PK that enjoying its existence had been the extent of my interaction with the search to find him. But now, with only four months of my quest remaining, it was time to step up the search.

I booked a week off work and spent a couple of days aboard *Our Pol* in my aunt and uncle's ultra-compact single-berth spare bedroom. It had been years since I had stayed on the narrowboat and it was a treat to be able to hang out with them. We went for long walks in the beautiful water park next to the canal, Uncle Dudley pointing out all the varieties of waterfowl from cosy pine-scented hides amid the reeds and lakes, while Auntie Mags read her book with Elvis curled happily around her feet. We spent lazy afternoons in their makeshift canalside garden chatting with the other narrowboat owners over homemade lemonade in the bright sunshine. We lay on *Old Pol*'s roof stargazing up at the breathtakingly bright constellations in the indigo blackness. And we talked – *lots* – about everything and anything under the sun. All the time we spent together, I soaked up the constant positivity that seemed to shine out of them.

Auntie Mags was thrilled with the enthusiasm my blog followers were showing for her recipes and I persuaded her to start a blog of her own, posting the recipes for the world to see. Each one was rapturously received, much to her surprise.

'This was such a good idea of yours,' she said to me one afternoon, as we were enjoying generous slices of sticky fruit bread spread with real butter. 'It's almost like my own little baking circle.'

'Your recipes are too good not to share.' I smiled and pointed at a comment from someone in Michigan. 'This lady thinks you should open a chain of English tea shops!'

Uncle Dudley placed a new pot of tea on the table and paused to kiss the top of her head. 'Now there's an idea, Magsie! You could be one of those *entrepreneurials*, like that Richard Branson. My Magsie, taking on the world!'

'Don't be daft, Dudley. I can't be starting empires at my age.'

I smiled at her as a thought occurred to me. 'You could

always start with one tea shop. If the reception on here is anything to go by, I reckon people would flock to it.'

Auntie Mags wrinkled her nose but her eyes were twinkling. 'You're very kind, but I can't see myself baking for a living. It's a lot of hard work.'

'And since when have you ever been put off by hard work?' I asked her. 'Your cakes are like therapy – that's a skill that should be shared with the world.'

Uncle Dudley hugged her. 'Magsie, if you put your mind to something you always do it. That's why I love you!'

The thing that I loved hearing my aunt and uncle talk about most was the story of how they met and fell in love. In many ways, what they went through in order to be together made sense of why they believed so wholeheartedly in my quest. It was impossible not to draw parallels between their experience and what I hoped would be mine.

Uncle Dudley had been working as an apprentice at the Longbridge car plant when he first laid eyes on the shy but beautiful girl in the admin office. He was twenty years old and Auntie Mags had just turned sixteen – barely out of school and making her first tentative steps into the world of work. For my uncle, it was love at first sight: he lost his appetite and took every opportunity to visit the teak-clad office where Mags worked, trying unsuccessfully to talk to her.

'I wanted to be all Clark Gable or Cary Grant, but every time I opened my mouth, I turned into a gibbering wreck,' he laughed, tickling Elvis behind the ear as we relaxed in their old striped plastic folding chairs on the edge of the towpath throwing bread for the ducks. 'Your auntie was so gorgeous she took my breath away. It was like I was staring at the rest of my life, daft as it sounds.'

However, when Dudley finally summoned enough courage

to ask Mags to a works' social, she politely refused. Devastated, he vowed to cease his pursuit of her.

'She broke my heart, that Magsie of mine. I went off to lick my wounds and didn't speak to her again.' He gave my aunt a hangdog expression, to which she responded with a sharp tut.

'I was sixteen years old, Dudley, and scared of my own shadow, let alone a handsome boy. First day I started work at the plant my mother told me nice girls didn't date factory workers. You know what she was like – I was terrified of letting her down. That's the only reason I said no, and you know it.'

Two years passed, during which time Uncle Dudley had a string of girlfriends, creating a bit of a reputation for himself as a ladies' man within the car plant. He heard from a friend at his local pub that Mags had married the heir to one of the city's large baking firms (a match more or less arranged by her social-climbing mother) and had quit her job in order to keep his home. Uncle Dudley met and married Eilish Quinn, a strong-willed girl from a large Irish family who worked in the staff canteen and stole his heart with her black hair and emerald eyes. Unfortunately for my uncle, she also attracted the attention of several other men after they were married, and within a year she had left him for someone with a bigger car and more money.

Then, a chance encounter with a friend of Mags, seven years after Dudley had last seen her, led to them meeting again on Christmas Eve in The Old Contemptibles, one of Birmingham's historic pubs. The transformation of Mags from the shy schoolgirl he had fallen in love with into the twenty-three-year-old woman she was now shocked my uncle. Mags was almost unrecognisable, painfully thin with eyes hollowed out by years of pain. His heart breaking over what she had become, Uncle Dudley gently coaxed her into a conversation, slowly gaining her trust. They began to meet on Saturday afternoons at the pub, talking for hours at a time, before she had to catch the train home to her husband. The details of her life that transpired during these conversations revealed the extent of my aunt's unhappy marriage – and made my uncle determined to help her escape.

The man Auntie Mags married had turned out to be a vicious abuser, taking out his frustration at the world on my aunt's fragile body. Terrified to confess the abuse she was enduring to her family – who all thought her husband was a wonderful man – Mags closed her mouth and accepted the blows in silence. When she discovered she was pregnant, her 'loving' husband took her to a backstreet abortion clinic, the complications from which left her in agony and would eventually lead to her remaining childless for the rest of her life.

It was hard for me to hear what my lovely, inspirational aunt had gone through, but the very fact that she is still here, strong and beautiful, is testament to what an amazing woman she is.

'I was too scared to leave, but still I woke every morning planning my escape,' she said, when I asked her about it. 'It was only when your uncle came back into my life that I started to believe it was possible.'

Almost a year to the day since they had met again, Uncle Dudley pulled his aged Austin Seven up outside Auntie Mags' marital home while her husband was out playing darts, bundled her scant belongings into the car and drove my aunt to her freedom.

Their decision was roundly condemned by both their families – my dad's parents refusing to acknowledge Auntie Mags for the first ten years they were together. Her former husband divorced her with no financial settlement and for quite a few years they struggled to make ends meet. But despite all of this, one thing remained, as Uncle Dudley put it: 'We had each other – and we were richer than Midas for that.'

'Which is why you have to try harder to find your man.' Auntie Mags winked at me, serving up a slice of what she called her 'spontaneity-encouraging' fruitcake. 'If he's the man for you, don't let anything stand in the way of being with him.'

After much discussion, it was agreed that we would post PK's photo on to the blog page, encouraging my ardent band of followers – now almost two-hundred strong – to help me track him down. Looking at his face half-smiling up at me from my blog, a renewed sense of determination welled up within me.

'PK, your days of elusiveness are numbered. I'm going to find you!'

Towards the end of August, my new tactic initially appeared to be bearing some fruit, with several of my blog supporters claiming to have seen him in and around the city. Two people independently reported sighting a man who closely fit PK's description in Harborne – ten minutes away from where I worked – and, while I couldn't be sure whether this was Mark, the Encounters impostor or not, I was greatly encouraged by the shimmering possibility that he might be almost on my doorstep.

Jack and Sophie had insisted on walking around Harborne on the last Saturday of August 'just in case we bump into him'. This led to Jack thoroughly embarrassing himself by chasing one man down the High Street, believing him to be PK, only to discover his mistake and have to frantically concoct a cover story. It meant a lot to me that they wanted to get involved though, especially at this late stage.

However, the early signs of progress began to quickly wane and, by the beginning of September, the trail had all but gone cold once more. Undeterred, I decided to leave the blog crowd to their searches, reasoning that these things obviously took time to filter into people's consciousnesses. After all, PK's photo had been found long after I had abandoned hope of having a clear image of him, so there was still time for someone to discover his identity . . . wasn't there?

Charlie's sister's wedding took place on the second weekend in September and was something I had been looking forward to for months.

From the moment we pulled on to the grand drive that led to Combermere Abbey, I knew this was a special place. I'm a big believer in first impressions, and this venue seemed to be infused with romance from first sight. Driving in the van with Charlie and Wren, I noticed that we all fell silent as we drove along the winding drive towards the Victorian gothic house with its fairytale-turreted cottages in the converted stable block.

The wedding planner, Ellie, was waiting for us when Charlie pulled Jack's van into the cobbled courtyard. Slightly stiff after our journey, I was relieved to be able to stretch my legs. The first thing I noticed was how fresh the air was – so startlingly crisp that it almost hurt my lungs as I inhaled. The stillness of the place was remarkable, surrounded by romantic rolling fields with a stretch of silver lake that snaked away into the distance. Birdsong was the only sound around us, a blessed relief after two hours of droning road noise and Radio 2 playlists.

Charlie discussed the arrangements for setting up with Ellie as Wren and I made a brief exploration of our immediate surroundings, unashamedly girly in our enthusiastic reactions to everything we saw.

'It's just so peaceful here,' Wren breathed, 'and those turrets at the entrance – they're like something straight out of a Disney film!'

'If you think this is impressive, wait until you see the Glasshouse,' Ellie grinned, approaching us to introduce herself. 'In fact, it's probably best we head there first, so you can see where you'll be playing.'

We followed her out along a wide gravel path the colour of clotted cream towards an ornate set of gates that led into the Victorian walled garden. It was as if we had stepped into another world. Roses of all sizes and colours were everywhere – adorning the high red brick walls, rising in beautifully tended bushes from the lawns and nestling amid lavender-edged borders. Honeysuckle dripped from the arches and arbours that arced gracefully over the path, while lilac bushes imbued the garden with their scent. Beyond the walls, tall ancient cedars spread their dark green branches wide in the pale blue sky and, through another set of white gates, apple, pear, plum and apricot fruit trees had been trained into a maze in front of the focal point of the garden – a restored, half-moon-shaped, iron-frame Glasshouse.

'At night we have thousands of white fairy lights in and among the fruit tree maze, along the pathways and around the walls,' Ellie explained, as we slowly navigated the gardens. 'It's quite a magical place, I think.'

Considering all the different venues we had played in over the past three years, I had never experienced anything like this before. The high walls enclosing the space bestowed a sense of seclusion and safety – making me feel as if I had stumbled upon a secret garden all of my own. As we walked, I noticed Charlie's eyes straying to me whenever he thought I wasn't looking. Wren noticed it too, and raised her eyebrows at me.

Ellie then led us into the large white pavilion marquee where we would be playing for both the afternoon and evening receptions next day. Wren and I gasped like eight-year-olds when we saw the draped ceiling dotted with hundreds of tiny white LED lights, sparkling like magical stars. Everything inside the pavilion was white: tablecloths, chair covers, huge sparkling chandeliers and even the ceramic dance floor on the other side of a curtained parti-tion. The overall effect was breathtaking – simple yet elegant, with a touch of magical glamour sprinkled into the mix.

'There's no event this evening, so feel free to set up as you want to,' Ellie told us. 'If you need any help loading in, just give me a shout. There should be people around until six. I'll take you to see the accommodation and then you're free to do whatever you want.'

It isn't very often we have our accommodation provided for us, but because Charlie's family were our clients this week, we were being spoiled. Setting up the day before and loading out the day after the wedding was a fantastic luxury and made the whole weekend seem incredibly relaxed: knowing that we wouldn't have to pack the van and drive home at stupid o'clock was simply bliss.

We were all staying in one of the courtyard cottages, converted from the abbey's former stable block. By the time we were settled in and the kettle was on, Jack, Tom and Sophie had arrived, whooping with delight when they saw our luxurious digs for the next two nights. It was so nice to have Sophie with us – a last-minute surprise from

Charlie's parents who were very fond of Jack's girlfriend and had insisted the day before that she join us to enjoy the wedding.

'I can't believe we get to stay here *and* get paid,' Jack beamed, flopping into one of the cottage's generous armchairs and kicking off his shoes. 'This is what we should be aiming for with every gig, I reckon.'

'In your dreams,' Sophie retorted, flinging a cushion at him. 'You just need gigs, full stop.'

Tom sat cross-legged on the plush rug by the open fireplace. 'Just think what our accommodation would have been like for the millionaire gig.'

This prompted a volley of cushions, coats, jumpers and one of Jack's shoes to rain down on him as he yelped.

'Serves you right for reminding us of the one that got away,' Wren retorted. 'At least we have *this* gig and I fully intend to enjoy it.'

Tom harrumphed and nodded in Charlie's direction. 'Fine. I bow to your supreme gig-booking abilities, Chas.'

Charlie gave a reverential bow. 'I am honoured, oh Mighty Axe-Wielder.' As he lifted back up he caught my eye and winked. The gesture made my stomach flip and the temperature in the room suddenly became stifling. I needed some fresh air – and fast.

Thankfully, Sophie and Wren had already launched into girlish eulogies about the cottage and the grounds, much to the collective amusement of the guys, so I was able to vacate my seat unnoticed. Swinging the heavy oak front door open, I stepped out into the warm early evening sunshine, taking a deep lungful of honeysuckle-scented air as I made my way across the courtyard cobbles to lean against the fence and admire the view across wood-fringed fields with the abbey in the distance, proud as an elder statesman.

An unexpected wave of doubt had blown into my mind for the first time today and I couldn't pinpoint its cause. Charlie's odd demeanour was only adding to the swirling mass of conflicting thoughts and I needed space to think.

What was it with Charlie today? His behaviour had been noticeably different since our pizza-box-attired discussion a few weeks ago. Normally you could rely on Charlie to be the straight man of the outfit when the band was together, acting as a foil to the slapstick humour of Jack and Tom. But recently it was as if somebody had granted him permission to become one of the lads and he had moved himself into the centre of their tomfoolery.

More unusual, however, was his apparent desire to include me in his newfound jokes – whether covertly with a secret wink or overtly by dragging me into them. Driving here this afternoon, he had been trying to wind me up about my stage persona, comparing me to a schmoozy lounge-singer and laughing like a drain when I rose to the bait. Of course, I knew what the problem was: the hiatus in the quest's progress had given me too much time for obsessing about other things. Charlie, I told myself firmly, was just one of those distractions. It was only a matter of time until the quest picked up momentum again, and then all of these thoughts waltzing around inside my head would be forgotten.

I closed my eyes and pictured PK, as birdsong swelled around me.

Where are you? I silently pleaded his frozen image in my mind. When I had embarked on this quest, eight and a half months ago, all rosy hope and great expectations, it never occurred to me that I might still be searching for him when autumn arrived. Sure, I had pledged a whole year, but deep down I think I expected to have located him within two or three months, four at the outside.

Given the time that had passed, was it still worth the effort? I hated myself for even asking the question.

'Penny for 'em?' Jack's familiar voice brushed my ear as he leaned on the fence beside me.

'Oh, nothing. I'm just thinking.'

He drew a sharp intake of breath. 'You want to watch that, matey. Very dangerous stuff to attempt without the benefit of cakeybuns.' His eyes twinkled. 'Sophie's mum sent us one of her fabled Sachertortes. Seriously, it's one mean chocolate cake. You fancy some?'

That was the best news I had heard all day. 'How could I refuse?'

We turned to walk back to the cottage, but Jack paused in the courtyard a few feet away from the front door. 'Rom, I've been meaning to say something.'

'Go ahead.'

He glanced at the cottage. 'Don't give up on Charlie.'

My nerves snapped to attention. 'What is that supposed to mean?'

'Don't take offence. All I mean is that he's . . . working things out at the moment. It's going to take a while, but he'll get there in the end.'

I crossed my arms, a chill passing across my shoulders. 'I have no idea what you're talking about.'

I could see he was battling with something he couldn't – or wouldn't – convey at that point. After a few more moments of wrestling, he gave up. 'Forget it. I'm just being over-protective.' He drew me into a long hug and I could feel the tension across his back as I returned it. 'You both mean the world to me. I just don't want to see either of you unhappy, that's all.' Breaking free, it was business as usual for his broad smile. 'Enough with the slushy stuff. Let's do cake!'

*   *   *

The following morning was clear-skied and sun-kissed, the perfect early autumn day for Francesca and Owen's wedding. Most of us were awake early, enjoying a full English breakfast courtesy of Jack, whose early morning vittle-rustling skills are legendary. His years as a scout leader have stood him in excellent stead for this role, and his ability to organise us into a military-style production line is a truly a sight to behold. This morning I had been on egg duty, while Wren and Sophie and Tom were charged with beans, buttering and toast responsibilities. Meanwhile, Jack kept expert watch over sausages and bacon under the grill. The only exception was Charlie, who had awarded himself a lie-in, although this might have had something to do with the bottles of real ale supplied by Tom and enthusiastically consumed by the pair of them last night . . .

At nine, joined by a very ruffle-haired Charlie munching a sausage sandwich, we all walked into the beautiful gardens towards the pavilion for our sound check. Florists, caterers and the abbey staff were dressing tables with extravagant centre-pieces of white roses, delphiniums, gardenias, freesias and crisp green apples, laying out elegant gold platters at each place setting and winding yet more fairy lights through white rose and lavender garlands swathed along the front of the top table and draped over white trellis arches over the pavilion entrance. In the middle of all the activity stood Francesca, Charlie's sister, dressed in a large checked shirt, yoga pants and Ugg boots. Her exquisite wedding hairstyle was already in place, a pearl tiara and miniature white roses dotted through her piled-up dark curls to stunning effect.

'Morning, lovelies,' she glowed. 'How lush is this?'

Sophie, Wren and I took turns to hug her. 'It's gorgeous,' I said. 'And you look amazing, Frankie.'

She laughed. 'If I had it my way, this is what I'd be

wearing today. But I suppose Owen's shirt and my workout pants don't really go with the colour scheme. Plus, my mother would have heart failure. It's taken almost a year to get me in a dress – if I renege now I can kiss goodbye to her good books forever.'

'You scrub up well, don't you?' Charlie said, scooping his sister up in his arms.

'I suppose I'll do.' She cast a critical eye over her brother. 'Unlike you. Who dragged you through a hedge backwards?'

Charlie grimaced. 'Don't worry, I'll be presentable for the ceremony.'

'Hmm, you'd better be. Otherwise the Wrath of Mum will be upon you.'

I watched as Charlie and Francesca mocked each other, thinking how alike they looked. I have known Frankie almost as long as her brother, and like her immensely. Seeing her in the middle of her wedding day preparations was odd though, not least because she's two years younger than Charlie and me, but was today embarking on the next great stage of her life. A thought strolled casually across my subconscious: would I ever be in her position? Quickly, I dismissed it. Considering I was currently doing my best not to obsess about the focus of my quest, thinking that far ahead was not a good idea.

'Charles William Wakeley, what on *earth* do you look like?' came a voice from the far end of the pavilion, and I turned to see Charlie and Frankie's mum striding across the floor to join us.

It always amuses me how Charlie reverts to a naughty little five-year-old whenever his mother is around. It's all incredibly affectionate, of course, but funny nevertheless to see tall, self-assured Charlie blushing and embarrassed.

Especially as Glynis stands barely four feet seven inches tall in her stockinged feet.

'I've still got to get ready, don't worry.' His shoulders slumped and he thrust his hands in his pockets as Glynis hugged him.

'I should think so, Charlie-boy. Honestly, Romily, have you ever in all your days met somebody so utterly averse to dressing up?' She winked at me. 'Remember his graduation?'

Charlie rubbed the back of his neck. 'Mu-u-um . . .!'

Jack, Sophie and Tom observed our squirming bandmate with unmitigated delight. I've known Charlie's parents for many years and the collected tales we have about him are innumerable.

'He looked alright in the end,' I offered, but Glynis was having none of it.

'It's only because I managed to find a decent hairbrush. Like a messy woodland creature, wasn't he? Now I know you can get away with being all nonconformist and *avant garde* at that gallery of your father's, Charlie, but I need you to be groomed today. Romily, promise me you won't let him out until he's halfway decent?'

I nodded as Charlie heaved a sigh of frustration. I don't know if Glynis and Henry ever harboured hopes that Charlie and I would end up together, but as we stood in the elegant pavilion it was clear that they considered me part of the family – something that both thrilled me and scared me simultaneously.

At two o'clock the ceremony began in the beautiful Glasshouse. White orchids, roses and gardenias were every-where: spilling over planters, framing the doors and fastened to the end of each row with white and pale gold ribbons. As our services were not required for the ceremony, Wren,

Sophie, Jack, Tom and I sat on the bride's side of the seating, craning our necks to watch the string quartet who were playing a beautiful set of classical wedding favourites: Bach's *Air on a G string*, Vivaldi's *Largo* from the Winter Concerto, Debussy's *Clair de Lune* and the *Minuet* from Boccherini's String Quintet and another piece that caused a heated debate amongst us.

'That's Grieg,' Tom whispered.

Wren shook her head. 'No, I'm sure it's someone like Handel.'

Tom pulled a face. 'Three years of a music degree and you think I can't recognise Grieg when I hear him? Soph, you're the music teacher, what do you think?'

'Don't look at me. I thought it was Mendelssohn. I know, I'm officially rubbish. But I'm not on duty today, so my Head will never know.'

Wren wasn't budging. 'I tell you, it's Handel.'

Tom frowned. 'Fiver says it isn't.'

'Done.' Wren and Tom sealed the bet with a competitive handshake.

Jack coughed and held up his iPhone. 'Hate to say it, Wren, but the guitarist has it. I just whistled the tune into my music recognition app and it's confirmed it, look: "*Grieg: Wedding Day At Troldhaugen*".' He saw our expressions at this revelation. 'What? It solved the debate, didn't it?'

I laughed. 'You are such a techie loser, Jack.'

'I am a slave to the creative whims of Mr Jobs, it's true.' Jack's eyes drifted towards the front, where Owen and Charlie were standing joking with guests and miming checking their watches. 'Man, Charlie looks good today. And I'm saying this as a confirmed heterosexual.'

I had to admit that Jack was right. Charlie had successfully tamed his wild chestnut morning hair and was dressed almost entirely in black, from the collarless shirt and Nehru jacket to his high patent Church's shoes (of which I knew he would be very proud) – the only exception being the large white rose and orchid flower buttonhole pinned to his chest. Owen, by contrast, was completely in white, a golden yellow rose and a sprig of purple lavender providing a vivid splash of colour across his heart. I shouldn't have been looking at Charlie, I knew it, but at that moment his eyes met mine and I felt the familiar quiver in the pit of my stomach. Did he see it in my expression? I couldn't tell.

I was about to avert my gaze when the registrar stood, summoning Charlie's attention away from me – and suddenly the mood in the Glasshouse changed, relaxed conversation ebbing to anticipatory whispers.

'Ladies and gentlemen, please stand for the arrival of the bride.'

On cue, the string quartet began a reverential rendition of Pachelbel's *Canon in D*, summoning an unexpected well of tears that I blinked away. I put it down to the romance of the ceremony – or maybe it was the hope of my quest succeeding that still tugged insistently at my heart like a child pulling its mother's hand.

The doors to the garden opened and two tiny bridesmaids in white tulle dresses with green and pale gold sashes appeared from the fruit tree maze before us. They were followed by Francesca, who weaved in and out of the green foliage heavy with ripening apples, pears and plums. She was serene in fitted white silk, an apple-green ribbon tied at her waist, its long lengths trailing down on to her train underneath her three-quarter-length veil. Her arm was linked through the proud arm of her father, who winked at his son, suddenly so serious by Owen's side.

The service was simple but beautiful: Owen and Francesca

in a pool of golden sunlight reflecting through the glass roof, the guests rapt by the scene. An immense sense of peace flooded the entire room, the surety of real, life-changing love. I saw Jack and Sophie's hands squeeze tighter together and the wistfulness in Tom's eyes as his thoughts no doubt drifted to the uncertain situation with Cayte. Wren smiled at me, but her eyes were sad – and for the first time in months I realised how alone I felt. It was a nanosecond of reality, but enough to jolt me alert. I shook it away. I have never been much of an emotional wallower in the past and I didn't intend to start now.

Rings were exchanged and the couple were declared husband and wife. Owen didn't wait for the registrar's invitation to kiss his bride, sweeping a giggling Frankie into a full Hollywood-style Errol Flynn kiss as the whoops, whistles and applause swelled around them. The formalities thus completed, Owen and Frankie's own personalities were free to emerge, evident when Charlie produced a pair of bongos from under his chair, crouching on the floor in the middle of the string quartet to perform a completely unique rendition of Feeder's 'Buck Rogers' as the couple danced their way out into the garden followed by their highly amused guests.

Following an afternoon reception filled with a great deal of laughter, some tears and a hundred happy people, accompanied by Jack, Charlie and my American Songbook set, the band walked back through Combermere's beautiful secret gardens to our cottage.

'How fab is it that we can have tea in between performances?' Sophie asked, bringing a tray of fine bone china mugs and a rather splendid Royal Doulton teapot into the living room. 'I could definitely get used to this.'

I took off my high pink satin platform heels and enjoyed

the rush of relief as my toes luxuriated in the lush pile of the cream wool carpet. The shoes had seemed like a brilliant idea this morning but I had forgotten how much standing around was involved in a daylong event and now the balls of my feet were burning ferociously. Taking my mug of tea, I padded out through the French doors in the dining room into the small private garden of the cottage, walking into the middle of the token square of lawn.

I was trying to pick a daisy with my toes when a pair of shiny black shoes came into view. Lifting my head, I came face to face with Charlie – his laid-back smile and rolled up shirtsleeves befitting our restful surroundings.

'Great stuff this afternoon. Frankie loves your voice.'

'Thanks. It was fun. Respect for the bongo playing, by the way. When did you arrange that?'

He flopped down on the grass and took a gulp of tea. 'Last week. Over the phone, anyway. We didn't practise until today while you lot were getting ready. Imogen, the cellist, is Frankie's friend from uni and it was her idea to do the Feeder song because my sister and Owen love it.' He picked a blade of grass and started to weave it in and out of his fingers. 'I don't find this kind of thing easy, you know.'

His sudden subject switch was so fast that it took my brain a few moments to catch up. Assuming he was still referring to the previous conversation, I smiled. 'Well, I did think it was brave of you to wing it, knowing how much you love your rehearsals.'

'Eh? Oh, not the bongo playing. I mean –' he gestured to his surroundings, '– *this*. The wedding. Seeing my kid sister making a huge leap in her life, while I'm . . .' His voice faltered and he coughed sharply. 'Change and me don't get on.'

Such candidness was practically unheard of and it had certainly been a long time since Charlie had been as remotely open as this with me. 'We all have to go through it sooner or later, I suppose.'

Excellent. Now I sounded like a daytime TV agony aunt . . .

'Mmm.'

The bees in the surrounding hedges seemed to have pushed their amplifier settings up to eleven as we struggled to make conversation.

'Oi! You two! How long have we got till we need to be back over at the pavilion?' Tom called from the French doors.

Slightly shaken, Charlie jumped to his feet, the motion of which gave the impression that he had been caught doing something he shouldn't have. Tom's smirk confirmed that he had caught it and that the incident was likely to be mentioned relentlessly from this day forth.

'Hope I didn't interrupt anything there?'

'No, Rom and I were just chatting.' Charlie brushed a clump of mown grass from his trouser leg. 'I think if we head over at about seven that should give us plenty of time to check everything before the evening reception begins.'

'Cool.' Tom winked at me. 'As you were.'

Charlie sank his hands into his pockets and looked down at me. 'He's a sarky git.' He fell silent again and I was reminded of the kind of weighted silences we shared before Christmas, where there had seemed to be a tide of unspoken things being held at bay. Those silences had been responsible for my confession of love, believing them to be confirmation of his feelings for me. But those assumptions had been proven to be spectacularly wrong then – so why take notice of them now?

I felt goosebumps beginning to rise on my forearms and took this as my cue to stand. 'I think I might grab a nap for an hour or so before we're back on duty.'

'Cool. I might join you –' his eyes widened in shock, '– um, I mean, the sleep, not the . . . erm . . .'

Great digging, Charlie. Next stop Australia. 'You're going red.'

His eyes moved away. 'I am not.'

'Don't worry, I didn't take that as an invitation.' The rush of amusement felt good, even if it was a mask hastily pinned over my own embarrassment. 'Anyway, it's a single, so there's only room for me . . .'

His blush intensified. 'Rom! I can't believe you said that!'

'Lighten up, will you? We have to laugh about Christmas sometime – and, let's face it, I'm the one who has the most right to be upset by it.'

'But you were only saying how you felt. That's nothing to reproach yourself for.'

I couldn't work out whether he was being condescending or not, but either way his tone irritated me. Did he think I was still in love with him, despite all I had done to pursue my quest? If he did, how bigheaded was that? 'I'm not reproaching myself for anything. I'm just trying to get back to where we were before I declared my undying love for you.'

'Oh.'

'Yes. So cut me some slack and at least let me joke about my mistake.' I made to walk back inside, but Charlie caught my arm.

'What if it wasn't a mistake?'

I glared at him. 'It was.'

His voice softened. 'But you were so sure about it at Christmas . . .'

275

I shrugged my arm free. 'Charlie, enough! Can't you take a joke any more? This . . . it's not fair.' I bent down to collect my empty mug, straightening back up until my face was inches away from his. 'I thought you wanted us to be like we were before? Well, this is me trying to do that.'

He said nothing in return. All of a sudden he seemed vulnerable, in a way I had never seen – as if one more word from me might shatter him into a hundred million pieces.

This was getting us nowhere. Relaxing a little, I pulled back and patted his chest lightly. 'Sorry. I really need a lie-down. I'll catch you later.'

I walked away, but could feel him watching my every step.

'Toast?' Tom asked, next morning. It was seven thirty and I had decided to venture into the kitchen after a night of broken sleep. I was surprised to find Tom already there.

I declined, my stomach decidedly queasy. 'Just a cup of tea, if there's one going.'

He feigned offence. 'If I'm in the kitchen, there's *always* tea going.' He picked up the rose-covered teapot and poured out a mug for me. As I sat down at the large oak kitchen table, he looked concerned. 'You OK, Rom?'

'I'm really tired. I didn't sleep much last night.'

'Strange bed, I imagine. I'm the same – hence the early morning breakfast. You look rough, though.'

'Cheers.' I wrapped my hands around the mug, the warmth from the bone china soothing on my hands. 'What time did everyone get to bed last night?'

'No idea. I went about two and I don't think Wren and Soph were too far behind me. But Jack and Charlie were up a lot longer – I got up to go to the bathroom at four and could still hear their voices in the lounge.'

There was nothing remarkable about this. After a gig it can be really difficult to relax for a few hours, the adrenalin rush from the performance still coursing through our veins. Added to this, we usually have a long journey home and a van to unload, so our bodies have learned to maintain the adrenalin flow longer than it would normally. Last night, after a wonderful evening reception, it was such a gift to simply walk back to our cosy cottage, crack open a bottle of wine, demolish the platter of leftover buffet food and relax, chatting in the warm afterglow of a good performance.

Of course, it *would* have been the perfect end to the day had it not been for my conversation with Charlie being on constant repeat in my head. During the evening's performance there was nothing in the way he interacted with me that would suggest anything was different, but I couldn't get away from the questions his sudden outburst had left hanging in my head. As the jovial conversation from the others surrounded us, we had walked back through the fairy-light-illuminated garden together without speaking. But when we met in the kitchen later, he was seemingly back to his old self – no awkward silences, no carefully avoided eye contact – so much so that I wasn't sure whether I had imagined it all.

'What time do we have to be out of here?' I asked Tom, needing to wrench my weary mind away from the Charlie conundrum.

'Midday, I think. Loads of time.' He pointed at me with the edge of his toast. 'You should eat something. Can't have you passing out on us when we're loading the van.'

Charlie didn't surface until nine, looking remarkably fresh considering his late-night conversation with Jack, who emerged looking dishevelled and grumpy half an hour later.

'I don't know how you two do it,' he muttered, shuffling into the kitchen and banging cupboard doors until I handed him a cup of tea and gently steered him towards a seat.

Charlie finished buttering three rounds of toast and joined us at the kitchen table. 'How "we two" do what?' He winked at me and I instantly lost my appetite again.

Jack scratched his messy hair. 'You know what. Look so annoyingly sober the night after you've been drinking. You knocked back more than me, Chas.'

'Must be good genes,' Charlie answered. 'You saw how much my folks put away last night? I guarantee they'll be as fresh as daisies this morning, probably making breakfast for everybody.'

I left them chatting and went back to my room to finish packing. As I folded my trusty black John Rocha dress, I noticed a thread hanging from the hem and sat down on the bed to bite it off.

'Toast would probably have been a better choice, but each to their own.' Charlie was leaning against the door-frame, that annoying smirk on his face again.

'Very funny. Haven't you got a keyboard player to cheer up?'

'Jack will be fine when he's had a shower and rediscovered his mojo.' He took a step into the room. 'I'm more concerned about you.'

I closed my eyes and wished with all my might that he would take the hint and disappear. 'I didn't sleep well last night, that's all.'

His face fell. 'Oh? How come?'

'Haven't the foggiest.'

'Adrenalin overload from last night perhaps? Or was it something you ate?'

'Charlie, I don't know!' I snapped, then quickly checked

278

myself. 'Sorry. I'm not the friendliest person when I'm lacking sleep.'

'Right.' His brow furrowed. 'I'll – um – let you get back to . . .'

I watched him leave, my heart heavy. Yesterday I believed we were returning to the friendship I'd missed so much – but now it was as if new complications were queuing up to pile on top of each other.

CHAPTER SEVENTEEN

Here come the girls . . .

Monday in the Bat Cave was a quiet one, which was just as well, seeing as my head was still trying to piece together the jigsaw puzzle of the weekend. Mick seemed unusually preoccupied, his trusty one-liners absent as we tried to find things to do to look busy in case Amanda stuck her nose in.

'Good weekend?' I asked, attempting to start a conversation.

'Not bad. You?'

'Great, actually. We were playing at my friend's sister's wedding in Shropshire.'

'Nice. Well, *I* got chatted up on Saturday night.'

'You did? Fantastic! Tell me details.'

Mick smiled a shy smile. 'She's someone I've known for a while, actually. She comes into my local with her friends and there's always a bit of banter. It's fun.'

'So have you asked her out yet?'

'No.'

'Why not?'

He stared at his screen. 'It just hasn't been the right time yet.'

'But you think she'd say yes if you did?'

'I'd like to think so.'

'Then what are you waiting for? If you don't say something now, how will she ever know?'

He grunted. 'Maybe I'm waiting for her to take the hint.'

'Mick!' I laughed. 'If you like her you should ask her out. Or someone else might get there before you.'

He swivelled in his chair to face me. 'When did you get so clever, eh?'

Leaning forward, I stretched out a knot in my lower back. 'Call it almost a year of searching for someone I should have held on to when I had the chance.'

Lately, the thought had crossed my mind more than once that maybe I should have done something more on the day I met PK. I should have run after him through the snowy streets, or scribbled my number on the back of his hand in eyeliner – the kind of things that characters in chick-flicks do when they are about to be separated from the one they are meant to be with. But it had all happened so quickly that by the time I had processed the details he was gone, swallowed up into the Christmas crowds.

Since Frankie and Owen's wedding, the uncertainty I felt about Charlie had definitely unnerved me – not least because I thought I had put my feelings for him to bed months ago. Truth was, I didn't want to be thinking about him; I wanted to be absolutely focused on finding PK, putting all my hopes and dreams and energies into the quest. From Charlie's hot and cold reactions at the weekend, it was impossible to gauge where he stood on the matter, and I was well aware that the only person likely to be losing sleep over it all was me.

Curled up in front of the television later that night, my attention drifted from Lorelai and Luke's 'will-they-won't-they' scenes in *Gilmore Girls* to a delightful intrusion of

281

PK's face in my thoughts. The memory of being in his arms had to become my sole focus. Get this right, I reasoned, and Charlie-centred musings would cease to be relevant.

In the meantime, Charlie was going to return to the only role I wanted him to assume in my life: that of my best friend.

To: romilyp@bubblemail.com
From: caytebrogan@gmail.com
Hi Romily

I know you probably don't want to talk to me, but I wanted to say how truly sorry I am for betraying your trust.

I can't defend my actions, so I won't even try. I got caught up in the whirlwind of everything and my stupid ambition got the better of me. But I had no idea what damage it would cause, both to your own reputation and to my personal life. I deserve it, I know, and believe me I'm under no illusions that this is anyone's fault but mine.

The thing is, I lost Tom, and it's killing me to know that I threw away something so special in the name of a scoop. He won't even speak to me, or hear me out. I love him and I'm lost without him. I want to put things right. I'm not thinking that this will bring him back to me at all, but it's the right thing to do. He won't listen to me. But he might listen to you.

I know he loves you to bits, Romily, and he respects you. If you could forgive me, then maybe he would at least listen to what I want to say to him. That's all I'm asking – and I know it's a big ask. It's not your problem and I don't deserve you to even be reading this email (maybe you aren't).

Please forgive me. I have no idea what to do to make amends for the pain and embarrassment I caused you, but I'll find some way of making it up to you, I promise.

That's all. Thanks for reading.

Cayte

I stared at the email at work, thinking that maybe if I looked at it for long and hard enough it would disappear. Because it couldn't be real, could it? I must have had my mouth open because the next thing I knew a screwed-up ball of paper bounced off my lips, followed by the raucous laughter of my colleague.

'Denied! No, don't close it, Rom. One more shot.'

'Loser.'

'You have to admit, that was funny? No?' Mick shook his head. 'My comic genius is *wasted* in here. So what's up? You won the lottery or something?'

I smiled and threw the paper ball back at him. 'Do you really think I'd be still sitting here if I was?'

'Fair point. What is it, then?' He wheeled his chair over to mine and swore loudly when he saw the email. 'She's having a laugh, isn't she? I hope you're going to tell her to take a running jump.'

I stared back at the screen. 'Hmm.'

Mick's eyes narrowed. 'You *are* going to tell her to get lost, aren't you?'

I faked a smile. 'Yes, absolutely. Blimmin' cheek.'

He was far from convinced. 'Well make sure you do. That woman doesn't deserve a minute more of your time.'

Through the rest of the day, Cayte's email played on my mind. While Mick and I worked on jingles for a loan company, a bingo site and yet another double-glazing firm, my thoughts were somewhere else entirely. By the time I arrived home that evening, my mind was made up.

Yes, Cayte didn't deserve it, but this was the right thing to do – for me and for Tom. He'd been utterly miserable without her and, whatever else I thought about her, I could see that she'd made him happy. I suspected that the main reason he wasn't talking to her now was out of loyalty to me. I didn't want revenge – even though most of my friends seemed to want it for me – so it was up to me to be the bigger person. Besides, Cayte had mocked me for my belief in true love. Perhaps the best comeback I could make was to demonstrate how wrong she was . . .

'You have *got* to be kidding me!' Wren's indignation lit up her apartment brighter than the floodlights at Villa Park.

'I thought it was a good idea,' I protested, but Wren wasn't listening.

'You're unbelievable! This woman *wrecked your life* more or less and now you're playing Cilla Black so she can have a happy-ever-after? So Cayte flamin' Brogan is unhappy after qualifying for Bitch of the Year and stuffing up her own life? Diddums – my heart bleeds. Perhaps she should have thought of what might happen *before* she humiliated you.'

I didn't have an answer for that, agreeing with pretty much everything Wren was articulating. 'To be fair, I think she's actually moved on quite a lot since Cayte-gate.'

Wren snorted. 'Don't make me laugh. As if a woman

like that is capable of moving on with anything except her own motives. Of course, you realise she's talking through her cheeks, don't you? She's playing you as easily as she played you last time and you're just rolling over and taking it.'

I flopped down on the sofa, watching any remaining chances I had of winning this argument slinking out of the room in shame. 'I don't expect you to understand, Wren. I just wanted to tell you about it.'

Hands on hips in the middle of the living room, she frowned at me, but I sensed her fury was dying down. 'I'm just so mad at the woman for how little she thought of you when it was all about getting an exclusive story. She should have seen you for the courageous, beautiful go-getter you truly are, but instead all she saw was her ticket to the big-time. That angers me, and I won't forgive her for it.' She pulled a hairband from her wrist and wound her red curls into a loose bun at the back of her head. 'What on earth is Tom going to say about all this? He is so gutted about what she did.'

I averted my eyes. 'Yes – he *was*.'

Slowly, the realisation dawned. 'You've already done this, haven't you?'

My apologetic smile condemned me and I knew it. 'Yes.'

'When?'

'This afternoon, just before I came here. I'm sorry I didn't tell you before, but Tom needed to be the first to hear it.'

'I can't believe you! How was he?'

How many words did she want? Angry, hurt, incensed, disbelieving, quiet, cold, emotional, lost . . . all of these and more in the space of a thirty-minute conversation. I hated inflicting this on him, loathed that I was the one witnessing his struggle between bitterness and longing when Cayte should have had to endure this. After his initial reaction, Tom had become very still, staring at a sight a hundred thousand miles away from the compact front room of his terraced house. I wanted to hug him, but suddenly wasn't sure whether he now felt I had betrayed our friendship by bringing this literally to his door. I was debating what to say when he spoke, his voice strained and low.

'Tell me why I should.'

'I don't think I can . . .'

He raised his head. 'Then tell me why you agreed to talk to me.'

I desperately hoped that this would make sense when it came out – because I was having trouble deciphering my motives as well.

'All I can say is that I recognised something in her that I've seen in myself since I started my quest. I don't like what she did to me – and I *hate* what she did to you. I don't know if I can ever forgive her for that. But what I do know is that she's realised how amazing you are. And I know it may be too little, too late, but this is her last chance to put everything right. And I don't know, but I think if I was in her position and I'd hurt someone I knew I was in love with I'd move heaven and earth to make amends. I would do whatever it took to make him hear me. I can't tell you to take her back; I wouldn't dream of it even if I could. But I promised I would talk to you, and that's what I've done. What happens now is none of my business.'

He had looked at me for a long time. 'You're one of my best friends and you mean the world to me. You've always been fair and I know you wouldn't be here if you hadn't thought it through first.' He rubbed his chin and nodded.

'Tell her to call me tonight. But I'm making no promises about anything.'

'I still think she's a proper cowbag for making you do her dirty work,' Wren shook her head. 'But I've got to hand it to you, Rom, you've more balls than me. I bet she was over the moon when you called her.'

'There were a lot of tears and thanks.'

'Hmm. Well I hope she realises how gracious you've been. If there's such a thing as karma then I reckon PK is already on his way to find you.'

'Let's hope there's a stealth jet nearby so he can get here tonight!'

Joking aside, the thought that my actions might influence events regarding PK gave me an immense shot of hope. Regardless of the result of Tom and Cayte's tentative cease-fire, I knew I'd done the right thing. Once again, I'd followed my heart – even though it led me towards the most difficult path – and I had stayed true to myself.

As I considered everything that had happened, something Auntie Mags had said to me suddenly came back into sharp focus:

'You must always be yourself, Romily, no matter what. Because, at the end of the day, that's all you have.'

The beginning of October brought gale force winds that lashed the city and brought several centenarian trees crashing to the ground. Uncle Dudley called to tell me that the main road had been blocked for the best part of a day while council workers struggled to dissect and remove a four-hundred-year-old oak tree felled by the wind overnight. In the end, he and a group of narrowboat skippers had offered their assistance, finally clearing the road at six pm. Always one to spot an opportunity, Uncle Dudley managed to secure a large section of the fallen tree from the grateful council staff, who were only too happy to transport it half a mile to the narrowboat moorings, thus providing a significant amount of free firewood that would keep the stoves of everyone's galleys toasty for several weeks.

While my uncle was battling the elements outside, my aunt was engaged in a battle of her own of an altogether different kind – although just as potentially tempestuous. The first I heard of it was when she unexpectedly called me at work and asked if we could meet for lunch.

It was a pleasant surprise and a well-timed interruption from the wonders of writing something suitably annoying for a corn plaster commercial. I arranged to meet her at Chez Henri, a small family-run French bistro just off New Street that I know she particularly likes.

During the first course, we chatted about everything and nothing: work, the weather, Uncle Dudley's valiant struggle with the fallen tree, Elvis' ear infection which had led to him crashing about *Our Pol* in a wide plastic moon collar to stop him scratching . . . All the time, I could see something unspoken causing the corners of her smile to tighten.

When our desserts arrived (the *real* reason my aunt loves Chez Henri) I watched as she carefully rotated the plate, studying its construction as closely as the Jewellery Quarter jeweller inspecting an antique diamond necklace.

'Faultless, *effortless* . . .' she breathed, shaking her head in awe. 'This is the highest order of confectionery skill.' Then, quite out of the blue, she burst into tears.

'Auntie Mags, what's wrong?' I pleaded, shocked to see such an intense flood of emotion coming from my usually level-headed aunt. Her loud, full-body sobs were startling the other diners in the restaurant.

'I'll never be able to compete with this! What was I *thinking*?'

'What do you mean? Why do you have to compete?' For a moment I half-wondered if Auntie Mags had entered *MasterChef* – something Uncle Dudley drives her mad suggesting whenever they're watching it.

'Ooh, ignore your old batty auntie,' she sniffed, wiping her eyes with her napkin. 'It's just that I've . . . well, I've gone and done something a bit silly.'

'Madame Parker, are you well?' asked Jean-Jacques, the assistant manager and son of the restaurant owner, arriving at our table after being alerted by one of the waitresses, who now half-hid behind him. The family is great friends with Auntie Mags and Uncle Dudley, who have been coming to this restaurant since they first got together.

Blushing, she smiled up at him. 'I am now, JJ. I'm so sorry for scaring your customers.'

'You mustn't worry about that. We are concerned about you,' Jean-Jacques replied, with the waitress and now the wine waiter and the maître d' all nodding their agreement either side of him. 'Please, tell us what has happened to make you so sad?'

Auntie Mags sniffed again and addressed her growing audience at the table. 'I was just explaining to my niece that I've been a little . . . impulsive.' Her smile was apologetic as she looked at me. 'It was something you said in the summer when you came to stay with us, Romily, about my cakes being like therapy? Well, I haven't been able to get that thought out of my mind ever since. And then when your blog followers started asking me for my recipes, it all seemed to point to one obvious thing. I mean, life's too short to put things off, isn't it?'

Jean-Jacques, the waitress, the wine waiter, the maître d',

the couple at the next table (who had now turned their chairs to face us) and I all nodded.

'Well, that's what I thought until . . . But I'm getting ahead of myself.' She smoothed the napkin into a neat triangle beside her plate and took a deep breath. 'Yesterday morning, I signed the lease on a small tea shop in Kingsbury village, with some of the inheritance money from my mother that I've been squirrelling away for a rainy day. And I know what you're going to say, Jean-Jacques, and I agree *totally* – it was impetuous . . .'

'*No*, Madame!' The assembled staff shook their heads in unison with their boss.

'But it *was*! What do I know about food service?'

'That's nonsense, Auntie M. You bake all the time and your meals are always wonderful,' I protested.

'For my family and friends, yes, but I don't know the first thing about health and safety regulations, or food hygiene thingies! And how will I know what to make every day, or how much to make? I'm starting a business in the premises of a former tea shop that went bust in six months – that's not a great omen to begin with, is it?' Tears welled in her lovely grey eyes once more and she gave a helpless shrug. 'You see? It's hopeless.'

The waitress and the wine waiter placed sympathetic hands on her shoulders as Jean-Jacques, the other diners and the maître d' offered their best sympathetic smiles.

'I think it's a brilliant idea,' I said, reaching across to take hold of her hand. 'Your cakes *are* like magic. You should be sharing them with the world. I'll help you to sort everything out – and so will Uncle Dudley.'

'And you must come to the kitchens after service one day for my father to tell you about the regulations,' Jean-Jacques agreed. 'You can ask us anything.'

Hope glistened in Auntie Mags' eyes as she looked around at the impromptu team of cheerleaders gathered round her chair. 'Do you really think it could work?'

It was impossible not to grin as I reassured her with the very words she had said to me when I was launching into the unknown at the beginning of my quest: 'Absolutely. You just have to believe that it's *possible*.'

I love your blog posts so much, Romily! The way you believe in possibility is really inspirational. I've been trying to do the same and I really think it's helping. I've already found my happy-ever-after, although everything else in my life has been challenged. What I know is that when you find the one for you, nothing can shake it. I wish for you what I've found. Keep going! xx **Ysobabe8**

Thanks for your encouragement! That means a lot. It's great to know that you're feeling positive about things, too. I'm glad I've helped, even if it's just in a little way. As for me, even though right now I can't see what's ahead for the quest and things have definitely gone quiet, I'm not giving up hope. xx **RomilyP**

The following Tuesday, an excited phone message from Jack summoned me to his studio after work. He was waiting by the fire exit when I arrived in the car park.

'Is everything OK?' I asked, a little unnerved by this enthusiastic welcoming committee. Jack is usually so laid-back he makes snails look like they're in a hurry.

'Fine, fine – *excellent*,' he gabbled, ushering me inside and slamming the door behind us. When I sat down in the black leather office chair, Jack was practically hovering off the edge of his seat.

Amused, I giggled. 'What on earth is up with you?'

His smile was wider than I've ever seen it before (excepting, perhaps, the time we surprised him with front row tickets to see Prince in concert for his birthday). 'We might just have had a breakthrough.'

'Who might have?'

'*Us* – me and you, Rom! Keep up, will you?'

'What kind of breakthrough?'

'A *music* kind of breakthrough . . .'

Now my interest was fully switched on. 'Tell me.'

He rubbed his hands together. 'Right. You know those two songs we sent to the music lawyer ages back? Well, I had a very enlightening phone conversation this afternoon with one of the music buyers for Integral – they handle some of the biggest names in the industry. Turns out someone there listened to our tracks and passed them on to Mitchell, the senior music buyer.'

My heart was racing. I knew Integral well – they had been one of the labels we had always joked about being signed to when we were in our teens and writing truly awful songs together. Could it really be possible that they were interested in us? 'So what did they say?'

He took a breath. 'They liked what they heard. And they want more. Six more, to be precise. They have an artist in development at the moment and they're looking for something fresh that will set them apart. I can hardly believe I'm saying this – but they think our stuff is what they've been looking for!'

I let out a yelp as Jack jumped up and wrapped his arms around me, the pair of us jumping around like children, until we fell back breathless into our chairs, mirroring dopey grins at each other. This was crazy – our songs had become something we did for fun and we had long since put our unrealistic teenage dreams of chart-storming stardom behind us. I knew we were good, but I never in my wildest dreams thought that anyone else would be interested in them but us.

'Who'd have thought it, eh? Our tunes being *commercial*,' Jack grinned. 'I've been in a daze since I spoke to them. But I know we can do it. We totally rock!'

'We so do!' Trying to get a grip on my emotions, I made a concerted effort to calm my racing pulse. 'Wait – OK, what does this *actually* mean for us? In terms of time frames . . .?'

Jack calmed himself sufficiently to talk shop. 'Realistically, Integral are looking to receive the extra tracks in the New Year. The guy I spoke to reckons they'll be searching in earnest for the album tracks from around mid-January. We're just lucky to have come to his attention while they're in the planning stages. I don't think this is "give up your day job" stuff just yet – but if they like them, and this artist turns out to be suitable, who knows where it might lead? So, what you think?'

It was a lot to take in, but the easiest decision I've ever made. 'I'm in if you are.'

Jack reached out and shook my hand. 'Deal.'

'So what happens now?'

'We work out when we're actually going to write these songs,' Jack replied. 'I reckon we give ourselves six weeks – aiming to deliver them by the end of the second week of January.' He flashed a wry smile at me. 'I suppose it'll be good for you to focus *past* the end of this year for a change.'

Wow. That was a new thought to add to the mix. I hadn't really considered what I would be doing after my Christmas

Eve deadline. I had lived with the quest and my thoughts of PK day in, day out for the past ten months and had come to rely on them always being with me. But the truth was, time was running out and, come Christmas Day, the quest would be over. What would I do then? I hadn't considered how I would walk away into the rest of my life if he didn't show up. I had so many people rooting for me, believing in what I'd pledged my year to achieve: what would they do after midnight on Christmas Eve if I failed to find my mystery man? Would it be like the scene in *Forrest Gump* where he just stops running and everyone following him is left standing when he turns to begin the long walk home?

The prospect of at least a foot in the door at Integral was exciting. It wasn't the career in music that I dreamed of – not yet. But it was a start: and that, surely, was something we could build on. As we excitedly discussed how we would go about this, I marvelled at how far I had come in almost a year. Searching for PK, no matter how fruitless it had proved to be so far, had undeniably stood me in good stead for learning to wholeheartedly pursue my heart's desires. And if I could get to the end of this year knowing I'd remained true to myself, then all boded well for next year . . . whatever it might bring.

With a free weekend that week, The Pinstripes arranged a weekend gathering at Jack and Soph's, beginning with a meal on Friday night, followed by a bike ride at Cannock Chase the next day. One good thing that had come out of our gig drought of late was that we had been able to spend a lot more time together doing non-music-related things. I arrived before everyone else and helped Jack prepare the component parts of the meal. By the time Sophie arrived home, an impressive selection of delicious tapas was laid out on the table in the dining room.

Sophie was grave-faced when I handed her a freshly brewed mug of tea. 'You know Tom's bringing *her* tonight, don't you?'

I didn't have to ask to whom she was referring. Since Tom and Cayte announced their tentative intentions to give their relationship a second chance, my friends had been sharply divided over the decision. Sophie was unrepentant in her opinion: 'I don't think she deserves to come back. Frankly, I'm surprised at Tom for believing her.'

'It was his choice, hun. We have to support him.'

She wrinkled her nose in disgust. 'That's as maybe. But I don't have to *like* it – or her.'

Right on cue, Tom and Cayte entered, he looking a lot more relaxed than she was. His eyes lit up when he saw me. 'Hey you,' he said, giving me what Uncle Dudley would call a 'hug that could crush walnuts', 'thanks – you know, for this.'

I hugged him back. 'You're welcome.'

Cayte hesitantly offered a hug, which I accepted briefly. 'Romily, I . . .'

'I know. Hi.' I might have been instrumental in bringing them back together, but I wasn't quite ready to be bosom buddies just yet.

Wren and Charlie arrived an hour later, after a meeting at Charlie's dad Henry's art gallery.

'I'm doing a jazz gig there next month,' she told me. 'Henry reckons it could be a regular thing.' Her eyes were sad tonight – noticeably so.

'That's great – isn't it?' I asked.

Wren's smile said otherwise. 'Yeah, of course it is. It'll make my bank manager a little happier at least.'

Sophie clapped her hands. 'OK, everyone, food's ready.'

We dutifully filed through into the dining room, everyone making approving noises about the spread of tapas before us. As we moved around filling our plates, I could see the dynamics change around Cayte. Sophie avoided her entirely, watched carefully by Jack; Tom stayed close behind her, his right hand protectively at the small of her back and his eyes flicking to each of us, trying to gauge our reactions; Wren was in a world of her own and seemed oblivious to everything going on around her; while Charlie made an effort to include Cayte in the conversation drifting between us all.

'Bet you've never seen so much tapas in one room before, eh, Cayte?'

'I haven't. You've done a great job, Sophie.'

Sophie muttered something and walked into the kitchen. Cayte's smile remained in place, but the tension in her expression was unmissable.

'Guys, don't feel you have to stand up in here,' Jack said quickly, smiling broadly. 'Let's go into the living room where we can all relax, yeah?'

Tom and Cayte were the first to leave, with Charlie following close behind. Jack gave me a despairing smile and headed into the kitchen to pacify his girlfriend, leaving Wren and I alone by the mountain of buffet food.

'I don't think Cayte's in for an easy ride tonight,' I said.

'Hmm.' Wren was absent-mindedly picking at a pile of salad on her plate.

'Right, what's up?'

'What? Nothing, I'm fine.' She popped an olive into her mouth and chewed vigorously. 'See? I'm eating and everything. So no need to worry.'

'Wren . . .'

Her face fell instantly. 'Oh, OK. Seth broke it off last night.'

'The barista? How come?'

Her curls bounced as she shook her head. 'I don't know. One minute he was über-keen, the next he announces we're not working and he's found someone else. Guys just don't seem to want to hang around for me after the initial chase. What am I doing wrong, Rom? I mean, am I hideous or something?' Tears sparkled at the corners of her impossibly large, cocoa brown eyes.

I hugged her, feeling the shudder of her shoulders as her tears began to fall. 'The right one is out there for you, I know he is. He might be closer than you think. You just have to focus on what makes you happy until he arrives, that's all, instead of putting your life on hold indefinitely.'

She sniffed. 'I know. I'd just like a man I could keep hold of, you know?'

Right at that moment, I knew exactly what she meant.

CHAPTER EIGHTEEN

Respect

'Welcome one and all to the beautiful surroundings of Cannock Chase,' Jack announced next day, leaping on to a rock by the car park as we gathered together. 'As you are no doubt aware, we are gathered here today to help our very good friend Wren Malloy in her quest for the perfect school outing.'

We broke into hammy applause as Wren took a bow.

'Thanks, Jack. Now as you know, I do not do bikes in any shape or form and I really, really need to impress my Head so that he might consider giving me a pay rise some-time before I retire. So I need you bikey people to tell me how you find the trails, if you think a bunch of fourteen-year-olds would enjoy it here and how good the facilities are. Also let me know if there's anything you think could be a problem. Honest opinions, please.'

Jack jumped down from the boulder. 'Right, so the idea today is that we complete at least three circuits, following the white and yellow arrow bike trails. If you fancy a breather at any time, come back from the road crossing on the orange trail, which will conveniently deposit you at the refreshment cabin. I'd suggest people wait there anyway once they're done and then we'll head back to ours tonight to compare notes.'

Clutching the handlebars of our mountain bikes, we all sounded our agreement and disbanded – D'Wayne and Tom racing off first due to a bet they had made that morning to try to get four circuits in before lunch. Wren and Sophie, both confirmed non-bikers, headed in the opposite direction to start the foot trail, while Cayte, the latest convert to The Pinstripes' bike club, rode steadily towards the easier bike trail with Jack, who last night had promised to accompany her – no doubt as part of his attempt to build bridges. With everyone else thus occupied, Charlie and I were left together. He fastened his cycle helmet and put on his gloves. 'Well, looks like just thee and me, kid. Thanks for keeping me company.'

I adjusted the knee support on my left leg. 'You're welcome.' Noticing he was fiddling with the water bottle clipped to the frame of his bike, I decided to take advantage. 'Shame you're going to come last, though!' I called over my shoulder as I rode quickly away over the ginger-brown pine-needled floor of the forest, feeling the rush of pine-scented air against my face.

'Oi!' I heard him shout after me. 'Alright, Parker, you want a race? I'll give you a race!'

We sped through the undulating terrain of the trail, dodging the low-hanging tree branches and roots that jutted out into the path, attempting to negotiate the obstacles with some finesse, but more often than not resorting to what amounted to 'falling with style'. As I neared the start of a hairpin right-hand bend, I misjudged the angle and skidded, feet flailing, over to one edge of the steep drop that fell away from the path, just about recovering in time to see Charlie overtaking me, laughing triumphantly as he did so.

'You've asked for it now!' I yelled, the rush of adrenalin intoxicating as I pedalled quickly in his wake.

I was inches away from his back wheel, but he managed to stay just a fraction ahead of me. At this point, some of Dick Dastardly's sabotage contraptions would have come in rather handy, I mused to myself, pushing my legs as fast as I could to move alongside Charlie, just as the trail levelled out.

'Your ass is mine, Wakeley!' I grinned.

Charlie's smile lit up the forest clearer than a spotlight on a night ride. 'Tempting, Parker, but I think I'd rather woop yours.' He found a reserve of energy from nowhere and pushed a length ahead of me, laughing like a loon as he looked back over his shoulder.

Schoolboy error, right there. Because unfortunately he didn't see the rather large and pointed granite boulder directly in front of him until it was too late. With a yelp, his front wheel hit the rock head on, flipping him clean over the handlebars to land and skid a few metres down the sandy path on his bottom. It was so hilarious a sight that I guffawed with laughter, sensing my victory was near.

Unfortunately for me, nearer still was the exact same rock he had collided with moments before, and my front wheel crashed into it, flinging me to the ground inches away from Charlie's winded but guffawing body. Rocked with gasping breaths of laughter, I lay on the ground for a time, my backside complaining vehemently.

When our mirth subsided, Charlie hauled himself upright, offering me his hand. 'Are you OK?'

I checked myself and, apart from an incredibly dirty

behind and a shallow scrape along the length of my thigh, I appeared to have survived the fall. 'Yes, thanks. You?'

'I'll live.' He gave a rueful smile and rested his tall frame on a verdant, fern-fringed grassy bank at the edge of the trail.

Still amused, I flopped down next to him and picked a dried beech leaf from the lace of my shoe. With its tall, majestic trees stretching up from the lush green foliage, the forest around us was breathtaking in both appearance and size – stretching in all directions as far as the eye could see.

'I've come here all my life, but I'm always amazed by this place,' Charlie said, watching the kerfuffle of two crows scrapping for supremacy in the branches of a pine tree opposite. He turned to look at me. 'I know that sounds lame.'

'No, not at all. I think you should be proud of how you feel.'

'Like you are with your quest, you mean?'

It came completely out of the blue. I blinked away my surprise. 'Yes, I suppose so. I'm a big believer that you should be able to express your feelings, whatever situation you find yourself in.' Suddenly self-conscious, I added, 'It works for me, anyway.'

His blue eyes were very still. 'It's a good plan. That bloke is lucky to have someone like you searching for him.'

The intensity of his gaze unsettled me a little. I looked away. 'Yes, well. At the moment I don't know if he would even remember me.'

'Well, in that case he's a fool. All the same, it's good that you have the support of those people on your blog.' There was a pause. 'I support you, too. I hope you know that.'

I turned back to meet his gaze. 'Thank you. I appreciate that.'

301

A gentle smile broke across his lips. 'Even if you do have half the forest floor plastered to your face.' Reaching up, he brushed the dirt from my cheek with the deftest of strokes, his midnight blue eyes never leaving mine. My breath quickened a little as his fingers came to a gentle rest on the con tour of my cheekbone, and I could see the pronounced rise and fall of his chest in reply to mine. Suddenly, it was as if the whole forest was filled with sparks of electricity, as an invisible force began to pull us gradually, instinctively closer . . .

'SLACKERS!!!'

Tom's shout as he approached us shattered the moment and we jumped back from each other, startled by the intrusion. He skidded to a stop by us. 'Come on, Charlie-boy – just because you're not riding with D'Wayne and me doesn't mean you're not expected to maintain your excellent trail record.'

There was a loud yell and D'Wayne jumped the rock that had floored us both, pulling up by Tom. 'What are you doing, guys? This is our second circuit and you two haven't even done one yet!'

'Getting old, that's what it is,' Tom agreed, jumping on his bike and speeding away when Charlie rose to the bait and grabbed his bike.

'I'll give you "getting old", you sarky git!' He grinned at me as he started to ride away. 'Catch you later, yeah?'

Still shell-shocked by what may or may not have just happened, I nodded blankly. 'Cool.'

Tom shot me a quizzical look, but the call of competition was too strong for him to resist, so he straightened his cycle helmet and set off in hot pursuit, leaving me more than a little dazed at the side of the track.

When I finally remounted and rode after them, my

302

thoughts were in dire need of direction. I decided to take my time on a single circuit of the trail. Negotiating the twists and turns, I replayed the moment over and over, drawing a blank every time. I must have imagined it. He'd said he supported my quest, so why then would a moment like that happen? Perhaps I was more winded from my fall than I realised, or maybe . . . I pushed the thought firmly to the back of my mind. By the time I reached the others at the picnic tables outside the refreshment cabin, I had convinced myself that nothing had happened. And so, it seemed, had Charlie.

For the rest of the day, and on into the evening back at Jack and Sophie's, Charlie and I resumed normal service, mocking each other, joking around with the others and enjoying being with our friends. There were no longing looks or stolen glances, awkward pauses or touchy subjects.

When I eventually climbed into my bed in the early hours of the morning, my mind was set: I had obviously misread the moment and everything remained as it had been before.

Over the next few weeks, I tried not to think about Charlie, finding as many things as I could do to distract my mind. Work was incredibly busy as we began to compose the station's festive jingles for furniture sales, catalogue stores and indulgent food ranges at major supermarkets. Mick jokingly covered the whole of the Bat Cave in tinsel and coloured fairy lights, '. . . to get us in the Festive Zone', which Amanda hated, of course, grumbling about a lack of respect for health and safety regulations, but Mick refused to take them down, knowing full well that Amanda wouldn't challenge it, needing to keep us on side and productive in order to impress her bosses. I found the decorations amusing,

303

but their presence inevitably reminded me that time for my quest was running out.

Meanwhile, Auntie Mags and Uncle Dudley were on the verge of a new adventure in their lives, with my aunt's tea shop – Tea and Sympathy – opening imminently. I spent most evenings after work helping them to paint, furnish and prepare the small shop unit, another welcome distraction from conflicting thoughts about Charlie and PK. On the night before the big opening, we gathered in the tea shop with celebratory glasses of wine and a freshly baked strawberry and white chocolate cake 'for new beginnings'.

'Well, Magsie, we did it,' Uncle Dudley beamed, hugging her to him.

'Yes, I think we did. This is going to work, isn't it?'

'Of course!' I reassured her. 'Look at this place – it's so homely and welcoming. I reckon you'll be fending people off.'

Painted in soft green, pale pink and duck egg blue, the café was a haven of all things sweet. Vintage teacups filled with silk flowers and primrose yellow tablecloths were placed on every table, glass cloches covered rose-painted chintz china cake stands on the whitewashed wood counter top, old books from Uncle Dudley's car boot forages were stacked on shelves along the walls and large wicker floor-baskets were stuffed with extra cushions – everything a customer could need to feel extra welcome and at home. It was every inch my aunt, even down to the framed pictures of Uncle Dudley, Elvis, *Our Pol* and me behind the counter.

I raised my glass. 'I'd like to propose a toast. To Auntie Mags and her amazing cakes!'

Uncle Dudley joined the toast, but Auntie Mags stopped us.

'No, I've got a better one.' She lifted her glass. 'To dreams. And believing they're possible.'

Whatever reservations I may have harboured about Cayte being back in Tom's life, I had to admit that she was definitely making an effort to repair the damage she had done with her article. Now working freelance, she had written a positive article on love-against-the-odds stories and had linked to my blog at the end. The fresh swell of interest and support this generated really helped to boost my resolve for the quest. Every time I looked at the site, there were a few new messages of support and, as October passed into November, the site's regular visitors began to have conversations with each other via the comment boxes, forming a virtual community all of their own.

Bridges were even being built between Sophie and Cayte, much to Jack and Tom's relief. A Saturday night out at The Garter unexpectedly revealed their shared love of karaoke when Jack persuaded them to sing a duet of 'Don't Go Breaking My Heart'. I half-expected a full-on catfight to break out mid-song, but to my surprise they ended up hugging when they received a standing ovation from the regulars. The following weekend, Cayte brought her copy of *SingStar* to a meal at Jack and Soph's, leading to the two of them taking centre-stage in the living room, singing away into the early hours of the morning – and that was it. Having found a language both could understand, they looked to be well on the way to becoming firm friends.

Uncle Dudley and Auntie Mags meanwhile were busy drumming up support from their ever-growing number of customers at Tea and Sympathy. Conversations with my aunt and uncle soon began to include familiar names of the people who were now travelling from all over

Warwickshire to visit Auntie Mags' little shop of culinary magic in Kingsbury.

'You know, it's just like Suzi was saying last week . . .'

'That reminds me, Rich Robbins recommended a great new artisan jam for my Victoria sponge that a farm shop near him sells . . .'

'If Davey suggests we let him and his strange Goth friends make a movie of the quest one more time, I think I'll scream . . .'

Discussions would begin in the tea shop and pass over to my blog, and vice-versa. It was lovely to see my aunt and uncle acting as self-appointed surrogate parents to their tea shop kids by answering questions, offering timely advice and – in my aunt's case – prescribing cakes for various emotional ailments.

Focusing on the quest – in particular, my virtual supporters' enthusiasm for it – was good for my mind, too. It meant that my goal of finding PK was uppermost in my thinking, reminding me of why I was searching for him in the first place and reinforcing the still-glowing possibility that I would find him again. With every new follower, I knew I could be one step closer to finding PK.

Since our conversation on the bike trail at Cannock Chase, Charlie had said no more about what I was doing. Neither did he reference or acknowledge what happened in the forest, leading me to assume that it was just another red herring on the long road to finding the man I was meant to be with. We had spent most of the past year learning to be friends again – the last thing we needed was for one of us to decide we wanted more. Even if the memory of what I *thought* had happened in the forest still burned more brightly than it should in its far corner of my mind . . .

As November set in, D'Wayne was proud to announce

that he had secured a golden wedding anniversary booking for The Pinstripes. As the happy couple were fans of fifties and sixties crooners, we had great fun putting together a laid-back set of swing and classic American Songbook songs. Wren and I took turns to lead, Charlie played a simplified drum kit with brushes and Jack indulged in some smooth jazz improvisation. Classics like 'My Baby Just Cares for Me', 'Fly Me to the Moon', 'Stormy Weather', 'Autumn Leaves', 'Let There Be Love', 'The Lady is a Tramp' and 'Summertime' flowed as easily as the guests traversing the polished hotel ballroom floor in their long evening gowns and full dinner suits. To do justice to the style of songs we would be singing this evening, all of us had gone to town on our stage outfits: the boys wore tuxedos, Wren looked stunning in a figure-skimming gold floor-length gown and I chose a gorgeous crimson satin 1930s-style dress that draped beautifully and made me feel unspeakably glamorous. In fact, the whole event felt like a scene from a classic Hollywood movie. I could almost imagine a full MGM orchestra supporting me as I sang.

For the final song of the first set, we received a request for Nat King Cole's 'When I Fall in Love', which I was duly elected to sing. I adore this song, not least because it's one of Uncle Dudley's favourites and one of the few he knows all of the lyrics to. It's a long-standing joke between my uncle, aunt and myself that Uncle Dudley can never remember more than one line of lyrics to any song. Auntie Mags and I once caught him falling into the famous pitfall of forgetting the words to 'Unforgettable': 'Unforgettable . . . la la la laaa . . .' – which, as you can imagine, he has never been allowed to forget.

Singing 'When I Fall in Love', I was instantly reminded of Uncle Dudley serenading Auntie Mags with it in the tiny living quarters of *Our Pol*, waltzing her around in his Simpsons slippers. I closed my eyes and imagined waltzing through the Christmas crowds in the arms of my russet-haired partner, every line from the song a promise to him . . . I reached the instrumental and looked back at Jack and Charlie as they played. Jack, his eyes closed, was lost in the moment, playing almost unconsciously. But Charlie was looking straight back at me, his midnight blue eyes dark in the coloured stage lights that threw shadows along the con tours of his face.

We took a break while the buffet was served and Jack, Tom and Wren made a beeline for the bar. D'Wayne strolled over to Charlie and me, chatting with the couple celebrating their anniversary.

'Charlie, Romily, can I introduce you to Trisha and Les?'

Les shook our hands and Trisha hugged us, much to Charlie's surprise. 'It's just so *wonderful*,' she gushed. 'It's the kind of wedding we dreamed of fifty years ago.'

Her husband squeezed her arm. 'Not that we would've had it any other way though, eh?'

She patted his hand. 'Absolutely not. We didn't have anything as fancy as this,' she told us. 'A fish supper with our families and a couple of friends in Stone Yardley Village Hall and his mother made the cake. I made my wedding dress at evening class and we walked from the church to the reception because my mum and dad didn't have a car. But it was a lovely day.'

'Made me the happiest man alive, my Patricia did, when she said she'd be my wife. And we've never looked back, have we, sweetness?'

'No. Happy-ever-after, us, aren't we, Leslie?'

When they left, Charlie bought me a drink and we sat at a table by the side of the stage, chatting and laughing.

I couldn't help thinking how different this was to when Charlie insisted I accompany him back from the New Year's Eve gig, ten months ago. It was wonderful to be able to laugh and joke together, even if unfinished business still lurked forebodingly around the peripheries.

After a lull in the conversation, Charlie cleared his throat. 'I have to say, you sound awesome tonight.'

Taken aback by the sudden compliment, heat began to spread up the back of my neck and I focused hard on my glass. 'Thanks. You're playing well, too.'

'That's not what I mean. We've performed these songs before, but I've never seen you so lost in a song as you were with the last one.'

'I was just thinking about my uncle and aunt,' I replied truthfully. 'It's one of their favourites.'

He was quiet for a while. 'I thought . . . No, forget it.'

'Go on.'

He smiled. 'I was wondering if you were thinking of *him.*'

I considered my response for a moment, this being new territory for both of us. How odd that he'd read my thoughts like that . . . 'I was, actually.'

'Oh. Spooky, huh?'

I smiled at him. 'Very.'

Nothing more was said on the subject, but I sensed a taboo had been broken. And it felt good. As we joined the others on stage for the second set, I couldn't stop smiling.

But as we embarked on the second set, things began to change. I noticed it about four songs in, when I looked over to Charlie during an instrumental break and noticed that he wasn't smiling. Initially dismissing it, I turned back to the audience and focused on my performance. But, three songs later, it became obvious that a dark mood had settled

309

across him. Everyone else in the band was laughing and enjoying the moment – so why couldn't he?

As we reached the end of the gig and began to pack away, I tried to think back over what we talked about during the break and couldn't find anything that I might have said to offend him. Annoyed, I timed my journeys back and forth to the van in order to incur minimal meeting points with him. This tactic appeared to be working until Les and Trisha's family accosted the others, leaving the task of the equipment pack-down to Charlie and me. With no spare bodies to watch the van, I was forced to remain by its open back doors, as Charlie brought the remainder of the equipment out.

I fitted the speakers, flight cases and bags into the van as best I could, but Charlie insisted on taking out what I had packed and huffily replacing them. Incensed by his silent hostility, feeling utterly useless and disregarded, I resorted to handing him items as he crouched inside. When he shook his head in exasperation at me for the fifth time, it was the last straw.

'Maybe I should leave this to you, seeing as I'm obviously causing more problems by helping,' I snapped.

His head jerked round. 'What?'

'I don't see the point of me standing here like a total lemon while you tut and sigh at everything I do.'

'I wasn't aware that I was.'

'Like hell you weren't. Honestly, Charlie, I don't know what's worse: you blowing hot and cold or you ignoring me entirely.'

The blue touch-paper well and truly lit, he jumped down from the van and faced me, anger firing through him. 'That's rich coming from you.'

'Pardon me?'

'You heard.'

He pushed past me and stormed back into the hotel, leaving me raging by the van. How on earth could he accuse me of being the one at fault? It was *his* attitude from out of nowhere that had caused this tension, not mine. And if he thought I was going to take the blame, then he was seriously mistaken.

Reasoning that the best thing I could do now was to make my excuses and leave, I slammed the van doors and turned to head back – just as Charlie strode out again.

'See, the thing is, Romily, I don't get it. I'm sorry, but I don't.'

If he was after a fight, he was most certainly going to get one now. *Seconds out, round two* . . . 'Oh, *please* enlighten me.'

His midnight eyes were aflame as they seared into mine. 'I don't get how you can spend a year of your life looking for someone you barely know, when the someone you *should* be looking for is right in front of you.'

The world around me skidded to a halt. My anger vaporised, leaving me numb and defenceless. 'Sorry?'

'This guy you think you're in love with doesn't exist. Only up here,' he pointed to his temple. 'You're asking him to be someone he isn't. He can't be what you want him to be because he doesn't know who you are. This isn't what you need, Rom, and you know it.' His voice softened. 'Deep down, you *know* who you need. I think you've known it all along.'

What on earth was he talking about? He knew how much my quest meant to me – and if he didn't, then why did he seem to be supporting me at the Chase last week?

'Don't you dare say that now, after everything we talked about,' I countered, hurt and confusion mixing with anger

311

to form a dangerously flammable cocktail. 'You have no right to . . .'

'I have every right!' he shouted back. 'Why are you still searching, Rom? Why won't you admit how you feel?'

'I *am* saying how I feel! The difference is, Charlie, the man I'm looking for sees me for who I am – and yes, it was only for a second, but in that time I saw all I needed to know. *That's* why I'm still searching.'

'But he doesn't deserve you like . . .' he broke off.

'Like *who*, Charlie?'

'Like *me*!'

Winded by this blindside blow, I reeled for a moment then regrouped. 'This is ridiculous. I gave you the opportunity to be with me at Christmas and you didn't want me!'

'Well, I do now!'

And there it was, his final shot reverberating around the buildings that surrounded us as we faced each other.

Gone was the fire from his eyes; instead they met mine with the startling vulnerability I had seen for the first time in the cottage garden at Combermere Abbey, two months ago. But what was I supposed to say? Did he expect me to fall into his arms now, after he so roundly rejected me almost a year ago?

'I don't know what to say to that,' I said.

His shoulders dropped. 'Don't say anything now. Just think about it, OK? I know everything's a mess and I don't blame you for being cautious. But what happened at the Chase – I *know* you felt something too.'

He was right, of course, but I needed time to think, to weigh up the evidence before me and work out where all the pieces belonged: Charlie, PK, my quest, the possibility of a burgeoning new career . . . 'I don't know how I feel.'

He took a breath. 'But you'll think about it?'

I nodded.

Even though it had been one of Mum's pet sayings as I was growing up, the phrase 'be careful what you wish for' had never really made sense to me before. I had always assumed it was just my mother's way of discouraging any illogical, heart-led notions I might be harbouring.

But now I understood. I had invested at least three years of my life fostering what I thought was true love for Charlie, only to have it thrown in my face last year and then newly resurrected now. On the other hand, I had devoted almost a year of my life – along with everything that had entailed – searching for someone who appeared to want my love, only for him to disappear instantly and remain stubbornly at large. It was nearly the end of November, a month before the quest deadline. If I was honest with myself, what chance did I realistically have of finding him now?

Of course I loved Charlie: you don't spend three years of your life pining after someone without it leaving any lasting mark. But after a year of looking in the opposite direction, did enough of it remain to support a relationship? And what of my feelings for PK? The intoxicating, gleaming prize awaiting me at the close of my quest, the promise of which had dictated my every move this year; waiting, longing, sure in the knowledge that it could be mine?

When I confided in Uncle Dudley and Auntie Mags, they told me to follow my heart. But the only problem was that my heart was twice as confused as my head. Wren suggested that I imagine which of them I'd like to wake up next to in the morning, but that didn't exactly narrow the choice down either.

In the end, the best advice I received came from a most unexpected source.

The aged laptop I had been using at home finally decided it had tired of slaving over my photographs, freezing one evening and stubbornly refusing to turn itself off or reboot. When it comes to anything computer-related, there is only ever one person my friends and I turn to.

'Hello, Tom Rushton.'

'Hi, it's Rom.'

'*Romulus!* How goes it in the land of jingling? Still immortalising dodgy products in song?'

'I'm afraid so. Sorry to do this to you, but my laptop's playing hardball. Is there any chance you could take a look at it for me?'

'Sure, bring it over any time. In fact, what are you up to tonight?'

'Nothing, I think.'

'Excellent! Come to mine for tea! Cayte bought me the new Gordon Ramsay cookbook and I'm experimenting tonight. You up for it?'

I smiled. 'Absolutely. Thanks, mate.'

'No worries. Oops, better go, the boss's car has just pulled in.'

He was in the throes of a chopping frenzy when I arrived that evening. His father is a trained chef, so he learned how to do the impressive fast chopping thing at an early age. It never ceases to amaze me how he can expertly shred vegetables with a knife so sharp it scares me, without ever looking at what he's doing.

'It's a kind of a stew,' he informed me, scrutinising the recipe book that lay open on the top of the kitchen scales. 'You're supposed to leave the veg pieces quite big, but you know me once I start – it's julienne or bust!'

314

'Well, it certainly looks impressive.'

'Excellent.' He addressed the book with a mini bow. 'Thank *you*, Gordon.' He beamed at me. 'So I hear your laptop's not a happy chap?'

I glanced down at the offending item I carried under my arm. 'Yup. I think it might be on the way out.'

'We'll see about that. Let's head up to my office and I'll leave this cooking.'

Tom's office is quite possibly the smallest office I have ever seen; it's barely more than a large cupboard. It has a compact, half-size desk (which I have on good authority from Jack and Charlie took a fair bit of sawing in order to 'custom-fit' it into the limited space); an old leather-look office chair that has an unfortunate wobble and a printer he has to counsel, coax or threaten before it will print anything. That his home office is so shabbily attired seems a contradiction when you consider the cutting-edge, millionaire-owned technology firm where he works, with its state-of-the-art terminals, spacious accommodation and swanky office furniture.

I handed him the laptop and he began to inspect it. 'Hmm. Hate to say this, mate, but I think it might be past help.'

This was what I had feared, but having it confirmed – and knowing what cost it might entail to replace it – was not particularly pleasant. 'Oh well. Another thing to add to the wish list.'

He smiled. 'Let me take a look at it for a day or so. I might find some way of patching it up temporarily.' He smiled and motioned for me to sit down on the folding chair he had managed to squeeze in from the bedroom. 'So how's tricks?'

'Oh, you know, same as ever.'

He crossed his arms. 'Liar.'

'Pardon me?'

'How many years have I known you? Haven't you realised by now that I can read you like a book? You've had the weight of the world on you since you arrived – and don't even try to protest otherwise. Now tell Uncle Tom all about it.'

I fidgeted self-consciously on the chair. 'I can't.'

'Why not?'

'Because you know the person involved.'

'Ah.' He rocked back on the chair slightly and nodded. 'So this is about Charlie.'

I stared at him.

'Oh come on, Rom, as conundrums go that wasn't exactly the most cryptic. You two have been skirting round the subject since before Christmas.'

Seeing as he already knew who was at the centre of my quandary, there was no point in being circumspect about the rest. 'He finally admitted how he feels about me and he's asked me to think about us being together.'

His eyes lit up. 'But that's great, isn't it? That's what you've been waiting for all these years.' He raised his eyebrows when I didn't reply. '*Right?*'

'I don't know. It's almost as if the moment I stopped looking his way, he changed his opinion of me. But was that just because I became some kind of unattainable woman or because he's felt that way about me all along? Surely if he likes me he should know, not have to be cajoled into it . . .'

'Rom, Rom, slow down. First of all, Charlie is a *bloke* – we take ages to catch on unless we think it's our idea, and even then we usually go for the wrong women. We've all known that Charlie sees you as more than a friend – it's just that he was the last to realise it. And yes, you taking your eyes off him and pursuing someone else was definitely an effective motivator. He just needed a swift kick up the backside. Face it, dude, we're simple creatures: it's anything for a quiet life. No man – unless he's certifiably insane – is going to willingly stick his neck on the line unless he has a convincing amount of corroborative evidence in favour of it. Look at Jack and Sophie: she had to practically walk round wearing a sandwich board with "I Fancy You" painted on it before he was willing to risk asking her out. But once he'd said it, he was in there for the long innings. Charlie will be the same.'

'But it isn't just about Charlie.'

'No?'

'I said I'd search all year for the guy that kissed me, and I can't get him out of my mind. *He* didn't need convincing: I could tell he had already made up his mind about me when our eyes first met. Shouldn't that be the kind of response I'm looking for? Not someone I have to persuade that I'm worthy of their affections?'

Tom watched me for a while, stroking the day-old stubble that peppered his chin. After some consideration, he sat forward in his chair. 'OK. The best way I can describe it is like this – so bear with me, it will make sense.'

'OK.'

'The way I see it, you have two choices: what's new and what you know. It's a bit like when you're looking for software for your PC or Mac. There will always be the latest program, or app, or gadget that promises all manner of new and shiny things for you. You don't know it because you haven't worked with it before – but that's exciting because you don't know what to expect. Compared to this, anything familiar seems dull. But sometimes what you know is the best option: sure, it might not be as shiny or fancy as the new thing, but you've taken the time to get to know it, you know what to expect from it and you can trust it to do what you need it to. You're frowning. Is this making any sense to you at all?'

I had to be honest. 'Are you giving me relationship advice or selling me software?'

He chuckled. 'Hopefully, both. I have my overheads, you know.'

I rubbed my forehead. 'I'm sorry. What are you trying to say?'

'Your handsome stranger is like the new software. He's exciting and mysterious. He burst into your life and swept you off your feet. He could be the love of your life, and if you find him you could be about to embark on the most fulfilling, amazing relationship you've ever found.'

'Or?'

He leaned closer. 'Or behind all the thrills could lie problems you can't see: glitches and bugs in the system, if you will. He could completely ruin your life, shake everything you thought you knew and leave you with nothing. He could be a destructive virus waiting to happen – causing damage it could take years to repair.'

'So I take it Charlie is like a word processing program?'

He shook his head. 'I've taken this analogy about as far as I can, haven't I? Look, what I'm trying to say here – badly – is that you know Charlie. You know how he operates, what he likes and dislikes, how he sees the world. You know all this because, let's face facts: you've been in love with the guy for three years. Sure, he isn't the fastest car in the garage when it comes to making decisions – I mean, you've seen some of his former girlfriends – but the very fact that it's taken him so long to see you for who you really are means that he's been learning the whole time. He won't forget any of that.' His voice grew very soft. 'But can you say the same thing for the guy you've been chasing all year? Does he even remember who you are?'

It was hard to hear it but he was making sense. 'So I should go for the default setting, not the dodgy app?'

Tom shrugged. 'Only you can work that out. But make it soon: the poor guy will be going crazy waiting for your decision.'

When I left Tom's house later that evening, his words played over and over in my head, like a sequencer sample.

Whoever I chose, he had to be the right one.

CHAPTER NINETEEN

Stuck in the middle

'*Making your Christmas go with a ho-ho-ho – this is Brum FM.*'

'What do you reckon? Cheesy enough?' Mick asked as I battled my way through the studio door carrying two huge coffee shop takeout cups and a bag of pastries to keep us going on what promised to be a long day. 'Are you struggling there?'

'This door hates me.'

'Does it now? Bad door, *naughty* door,' he grinned.

I passed him a coffee. 'Funny. Good jingle, by the way. Lots of cheese going on there.'

He rummaged in the paper bag for a cinnamon swirl. 'Amanda wanted more, apparently. Think she's been passed over for another promotion, so expect her to be the PickMeister today.'

'Great. That's all we need.'

Mick stopped, mid-munch. 'Hey, don't let the woman get to you. If we stick together, she can't do anything. We, my dear, stand in between her and her precious departmental results spreadsheet. She messes with us, her figures are going *down* . . .'

'Ha, that's a cheery thought. I'm not worried about Amanda. I'm just a bit tired, that's all.'

'Well, *that's* what happens when you're out all night gallivanting with musicians . . .'

He had a point. I hadn't planned to come straight to work from Jack and Sophie's this morning, but a late-night conversation with D'Wayne after the band's midweek charity gig had kept me up until the early hours, by which time it made more sense to grab a few precious hours there than try to make it home.

I noticed D'Wayne had been a little subdued when he arrived at the social club on the outskirts of Wolverhampton during our pre-gig sound check. The fundraising event had been organised by his brother in aid of the children's ward at New Cross Hospital, where his young niece had spent six months following reconstructive surgery for a twisted spine. I assumed that his lack of trademark swagger was due to the presence of his family who all possessed incredibly strong characters, but much later I discovered the real cause was a world away from family tensions.

D'Wayne had been quiet when I joined him on the sofa at Jack and Sophie's after the gig. He was known for being quiet sometimes, preferring to observe from the sidelines than leap into the action, but his humour was never very far away and he could usually be easily cajoled by the guys in the band to join in. Tonight, however, I noticed a heaviness in his eyes that I hadn't seen before. Around us, the usual Pinstripes conversations flowed, but our manager remained still.

I nudged him as I sat down. 'Everything OK, boss?'

He smiled hollowly. 'Never better.'

'Hmm. Don't ever take up acting, will you? That was rubbish.'

This elicited a more genuine smile. 'Sorry. Spending too much time in my head at the moment, that's all.'

'Want to talk about it?'

Surprised, he shifted position to look at me. 'Are you sure?'

'Of course I am.'

'Thank you. I can't really explain why, but . . . You saw my family tonight, yeah? I was watching them together and it suddenly struck me how sorted my brothers are. All five of them, settled down with kids and everything. But I'm the eldest and what have I got? I've got the nice house, the top of the range car, I'm making money and I wear expensive clothes – but at the end of the day, what does any of that mean? You know, I looked at them all tonight and for the first time, I was jealous. When I close the door at night it's just me – well, most of the time. But even when there's a lady there, it never lasts . . .' He broke off as Tom claimed the seat next to me.

'All good here?'

D'Wayne made a close inspection of his wine glass. Tom raised his eyebrows at me and, taking the hint, stood again and walked over to Jack and Sophie.

I smiled at D'Wayne. 'Go on.'

'I never thought I'd say this, but I don't want to just date any more. I've a phonebook full of numbers but nobody to talk to when I come home.' He laughed at himself. 'Man, that sounds so lame.'

'I don't think it does. I think you've just realised you're ready to look for something a little more serious.'

'I think I'm lonely, Rom. Just a shock to realise it, you know?'

I assured him that it was a good thing to be able to recognise how he felt, but beyond that I didn't really have any answers. After all, I was secretly still torn between accepting Charlie's advances or sticking it out until the bitter end with my search for PK. When I had finally fallen asleep under a borrowed duvet on Jack's sofa in the early hours, images of both of them swirled together restlessly in my dreams.

Mick raised his eyebrows. 'No closer to making a decision then?'

I shook my head. 'I'm afraid not. It's driving me insane.'

'Why don't you try this?' He grabbed a notepad from a drawer and pulled a pen from his back pocket. In the middle of a page he drew a vertical line with a horizontal line forming a cross at the top, wrote 'Charlie' on one side and 'Kisser' on the other and handed it to me.

'What am I supposed to do with this?'

'Pros and cons, mate. Well, it'll have to be pros actually, seeing as I've only got two columns. You write down all the reasons you should choose Charlie, and then do the same with the other chap. By the end, one of them should emerge as the winner.'

It seemed an extreme and callous measure but, as the confusion raging in my head showed no signs of abating, I decided that anything was worth a try.

Instead of going straight home, I headed into the town centre. I needed space to think. Walking through crowds of homeward bound students, their teenage energies made me smile as I remembered Charlie and I waiting at the bus stop outside our sixth-form college with Tom, Jack and Wren. It seemed a world away now – thirteen years in the past and a million miles from where my teenage self had dreamed I'd be.

One thing that seventeen-year-old Romily Parker never expected was that her twenty-nine-year-old self would be caught in an impossible choice between two men. To be honest, it was a surprise to me. A year ago I wouldn't have been sitting in the corner of the café in the High Street agonising over a growing list on a sheet of crumpled radio station notepaper – I would have been in Charlie's arms feeling I was the luckiest woman alive. What a difference a year made . . .

Sipping a mug of mocha, I stared at Mick's list. By now, Charlie and PK were neck and neck with five pros each. How on earth was I ever going to decide? I couldn't shake the memory of Charlie's expression when he'd told me how he felt. He had looked so vulnerable, his emotions laid bare before me, and when I replayed the scene in my head it was so easy to imagine myself saying yes. But whenever my thoughts entertained the prospect of being with him, PK's face would appear and throw everything into question again.

Of course, PK might never appear – but I didn't want to consider Charlie merely as a default choice. If I was going to be with him it would have to be because he was the right one for me.

As I stepped out on to the darkened street in freezing rain, I promised myself that I would make the right choice, no matter what.

'Romily, it's Tom. You need to come here after work, OK?' He sounded breathless on the phone, next day. 'Can't explain because I've got to make sure I call everyone, but you'll be there, right?'

'Of course I will, but what . . .?'

'Great. Bye!'

Mick laughed when he saw my puzzlement. 'What's happened?'

'I don't know. I guess all will be revealed later.'

I arrived at Tom's house at five thirty and met Charlie walking up the path.

'Evening, you. Any idea what this is about? Tom was very weird earlier.'

'Haven't a clue.'

'Ah well,' he said, 'only one way to find out.' He reached past me to knock the brass knocker on the front door, his face so close to mine that I could feel the warmth from his skin on my cheeks. My heart performed a back flip and a 'pro' was added to Charlie's list.

It was immediately obvious that my bandmates and manager were as eager as Charlie and I to discover the reason for our hastily arranged meeting. We gathered in the living room as Tom stood to address us.

'Right,' he grinned, his eyes twinkling. 'I have a bit of news.'

'You're getting married?' Charlie suggested.

'Not unless you know something I don't, Charlie-boy,' Tom grinned. 'But it's about as much of a surprise.' He took a breath. 'The gig's back on.'

D'Wayne was confused. 'Which gig?'

'The millionaire gig.'

This bombshell reverberated around the room, all eyes wide on Tom.

'When – how?' stammered Wren, voicing the questions we were all considering.

Almost beside himself with excitement, Tom barely paused for breath as he shared the details. The bride, so poorly when the original date for her wedding arrived, had rallied in recent months and two weeks ago had walked again for the first time since her operation. Julian was so delighted that, following his daughter's unguarded comment wishing she could still get married this year, he had called the original venue and managed to arrange a new date, just before Christmas.

'That's the only snag,' he explained, his smile fading a fraction. 'It's Christmas Eve.'

Silence claimed the room as we processed everything.

Wren looked at everyone. 'Well, I don't know about you guys, but I'm well up for it.'

'Count us in,' Jack and Sophie agreed.

'I'm in.' Charlie nodded and looked at me. 'Rom?'

It was a no-brainer as far as I was concerned. Playing at a star-studded event and being able to see the capital in its full festive finery was too exciting for words. 'Definitely.'

D'Wayne clapped his hands. 'Alright! Looks like we're going to London!'

'In that case, we should probably open this,' Jack said, producing a huge bottle of champagne to rapturous applause.

'Did you know about all this?' Charlie asked Jack as Wren went into the kitchen to find glasses.

'Not at all. But I knew it was something big by the way Tom was acting when he phoned. Besides, I was pretty sure nobody would object to champagne.'

Sophie sighed. 'Shame we're so predictable, isn't it?'

'Terrible,' I laughed.

'We should go ice-skating in Hyde Park,' Wren squeaked, 'and walk along Regent Street to see the lights!'

'Er, may I remind you that we're actually there to work?' D'Wayne said. But his grin ruined the impression of a stern manager.

Sophie dismissed this with a wave of her hand. 'We'll fit

326

everything in, don't you worry. We can't go all the way to London at Christmas and not enjoy it a little, surely?'

D'Wayne laughed. 'OK, I give in! I'm sure we can find time to have a bit of fun.' He yelped as Wren and Sophie fell on him in a huge group hug.

Charlie placed his hand lightly on my arm and leant towards my ear. 'Christmas Eve in London, eh? Perhaps me and you will have something to celebrate by then . . .'

I watched him as he walked over to congratulate Tom, my heart racing like a greyhound after a rabbit. *Maybe we will, Charlie*, I said to myself, *Maybe we will.*

After the initial euphoria of the millionaire gig's re-emergence, the reality began to sink in. With barely three weeks until the premier event, time was of the essence and rehearsals became a priority.

To this end we arranged a rehearsal schedule to end them all, squeezing in as many opportunities to work on our performance as possible. Even when we couldn't all make it, small groups of us met to rehearse key components of the music: Wren, Jack and I meeting at his house to practise the harmonies and vocal parts; Charlie and Tom taking an hour during their lunchbreaks to go over stabs and rhythms; and as Sophie was joining us, she, Jack and Tom worked late into the night to perfect solo sax parts for the longer numbers.

A week before the wedding, we gathered for an all-day rehearsal in the shoe factory, arriving at eight in the morning and expecting to stay until at least six that evening. Carrier bags stuffed with supplies were piled up by the kettle and bottles of water were everywhere. The shoe factory was not renowned for its warmth so Tom had placed all manner of heaters around the studio and each band member was attractively attired in several layers of clothes to try to keep out the icy draughts that seemed to permeate through every crack in the building.

Once all the equipment was set up Tom passed out steaming mugs of strong coffee. 'There's about three spoons of coffee in that,' he said. 'If the caffeine doesn't help us, nothing will.'

Charlie screwed his nose up as he received his mug of murky instant. 'Ugh. It's like the Pot Noodle of coffee.'

'You're such a coffee snob,' I giggled. 'Just drink it and be grateful.'

He feigned offence, but his eyes were smiling as they held mine. The chemistry between us had been steadily growing as my weeks of debating Mick's list had passed and Charlie's 'pros' were beginning to edge ahead of PK's for the first time. As I watched him mucking about with Tom and Jack, I sensed that my decision, when it came, might be easier than I was expecting it to be.

D'Wayne arrived with a huge box of doughnuts at eleven, much to the collective joy of all present. When Wren (who, despite her petite frame can put away more food than Tom and Jack combined) sneaked a second doughnut from the box, D'Wayne tutted loudly.

'I'd have thought you'd be watching your weight for the gig, Wren.'

Uh-oh.

There are many things I have learned about my best friend since the day we met in the Wendy house at playgroup, but the most crucial has been to recognise the warning signs when she's angry. Unfortunately for D'Wayne, he had yet to acquire this skill. As he continued to mock her, the rest of the band fell gradually silent as we waited for the inevitable consequences.

Sure enough . . . 'Oh right, so you have the right to make

sexist, offensive comments because *why*, exactly? Because you're such a comedian? Oh, wait, no we can't accuse you of that because you're *not*.'

D'Wayne gave a nervous laugh. 'Whoa, Wren, can't you take a joke?'

Tom and Charlie cringed as Jack and Sophie pulled faces. D'Wayne was *history* . . .

Incensed, Wren punched her hands on to her hips and prepared for war. 'Oh, I can take a joke, D'Wayne. I'm *looking* at one!'

'Now hang on . . .'

'I'm sick of your stupid attitude to *everything* – your cynicism at every wedding, your unreliability. I stick my neck out to defend you time and time again, and for what? So you can throw it all back in my face because you think it makes you look like the big man to be mocking me?'

For the first time, D'Wayne's expression did not defer to Wren's words. Real anger now flashed in his eyes. 'And you're always calling the shots, aren't you? Makes you feel worthy, does it, lording it over the badass manager? You think you're so high and mighty, Miss Ice Maiden, but you ain't all that.'

'Right. Outside. *Now*!'

We watched in shock as Wren grabbed D'Wayne's arm and bundled him out of the door into the shoe factory's dusty corridor.

'Man, he's in for it now,' Tom said, as we all moved to the door to listen. 'It's years since I saw Wren that angry.'

We could hear Wren's indignant tones echoing through the corridor, followed by the deep boom of D'Wayne's. For a full five minutes the battle of wills stormed back and forth, increasing in intensity until, after a final shout from Wren, there was silence.

'She's killed him,' Jack said, concern breaking through his mirth.

We waited. Still nothing. 'Perhaps I should go out there,' I suggested.

Jack opened his mouth to reply, but the door began to open slowly and we all dived back to our places.

The change in Wren was dramatic. Gone was her seething indignation, replaced by a serene smile. As she entered, we realised D'Wayne was walking – unscathed – behind her. And they were *holding hands* . . .

'Well that's sorted,' she smiled, patting D'Wayne's hand, 'isn't it, darling?'

D'Wayne, visibly shaken, nodded dumbly.

As we watched them, open-mouthed, Wren proceeded to pull our manager towards her for a passionate kiss. Tom and Jack whistled as Sophie, Charlie and I applauded.

When she pulled away, Wren flicked her hair back. 'Any questions? No? Let's get back to rehearsing, shall we?'

At nine that night, we waved the happy couple off at the shoe factory and returned to Jack and Sophie's house. We were all still agog at this unexpected development.

'I never saw that coming,' Jack said, passing round an enormous bowl of nachos and cheese.

'I did,' I replied, picking a handful from the plate. 'Didn't you ever wonder why she defended him so often? Wren doesn't give that kind of support out unless she thinks it's deserved.'

'You know, I did wonder,' Sophie agreed. 'But I never thought they'd get it on like that.'

'That's our Wren,' Charlie laughed. 'Never one to do things by halves.' His smile deepened when he caught my eye.

When it was time to leave, Tom left first, catching a taxi

home. Charlie and I helped to wash up and then said our farewells.

'Hope you can sleep after all that excitement,' I said, letting my elbow bump against his as we walked down the garden path together.

'I'll try,' he replied, his breath illuminated by the white light from the streetlamp overhead. 'Rom?'

'Yes?' I turned to face him and my heart picked up pace when I saw the shadows marking out the hollow of his cheekbones, casting his eyes into darkness. I was fast remembering my feelings from a year ago – the way he could steal my breath when I least expected it, simply with a look.

'I know you have a lot to think about and I'm not rushing you, but –' he pushed his hands deeper into the pockets of his jacket, '– it's been three weeks and I just wanted to know what you were thinking. I *need* to know . . .'

I shivered and wrapped my coat tighter around myself. 'I know you do. And I'm sorry it's taking forever. I want to make the right decision – I feel I owe it to both of us, if that makes sense? The quest is nearly over and—'

'So tell me at the gig,' he said suddenly.

I looked up at him and caught a glint of reflected streetlamp light in his eyes. 'What do you mean?'

He took a step closer. 'Your quest ends on Christmas Eve, doesn't it? So to put your mind at rest – and make sure you accomplish what you set out to do – give me your answer at the millionaire gig. There will be a gap of about an hour between the first and second sets. Tell me then.'

A flood of warmth spread through my body. 'And you can wait till then?'

He breathed out. 'This is important to you, and you're important to me. I know you'll make the right decision – so I'd rather wait until it's the right time.'

331

At that moment, I was struck with an overwhelming urge to tell him there and then, gazing up at his lovely face in the freezing night and longing to be in his arms. 'Charlie, I think—'

He shook his head. 'Don't say it until you're sure. Either way. Christmas Eve, OK?'

Mind racing, I agreed. 'Christmas Eve.'

CHAPTER TWENTY

Let there be love

The week before Christmas passed by at breakneck pace, so much so that I hardly had time to think about anything, let alone the decision I would have to make in a matter of days. Business at Brum FM was crazier than ever, Mick and I struggling to clear a raft of adverts and indents ready for the New Year schedules.

The day before Christmas Eve, The Pinstripes gathered at Jack and Sophie's, fired up with anticipation about what lay ahead of us. Sophie and Wren had already compiled an itinerary for our London visit and started chatting animatedly about the shops they wanted to visit and the Christmassy activities we absolutely *had* to indulge in during our brief stay in the capital.

I had been plagued with butterflies for two days, a mixture of childlike excitement at the prospect of the trip and the knowledge that things would never be the same after this, whatever my decision was. Charlie's smile when I arrived revealed his own anxiety and, while the others were engaged in excited discussion, he beckoned me over to the other side of the van.

'How are you doing?' he asked, a gentle blush warming his cheeks.

'Good – I think. How crazy is this?'

'I know.' He held out his arms. 'Give us a hug, will you?'

I gratefully accepted, not minding in the slightest when it lasted longer than usual.

As we travelled down the M40 in a minibus provided by D'Wayne (who had acquired a notably generous side since hooking up with Wren), following Jack and Sophie in the van, my thoughts strayed to the quest. Last night, I had brought out PK's photo and the Christmas bauble and sat on my bed with them in my hands, gazing again into his motionless eyes. I may not have found him, but the dream of rediscovering him still lingered. Days were no longer left for my search – only hours, minutes and seconds that were fast slipping away.

Reaching for my laptop, I had written the last blog post before my quest came to an end:

So tomorrow is D-Day for the quest. And no, I haven't found him. But I might just have found something more important . . .

In a funny way, I feel like I've won. I set out to spend my twenty-ninth year following my heart, and that's exactly what I've done. I've been on a bit of a rollercoaster ride – dodgy dates, national humiliation and becoming a Twitter trending topic, to name but a few highlights – but I've learned so much and had one of the most exciting, positive years of my life.

I'd like to thank you for coming with me on this crazy journey. I'll probably keep blogging next year, if anyone fancies hanging around. I might change the blog's title, though, so there's likely to be less about looking for a man and more about great music (not to mention my auntie's cakes, which have been such a hit this year!).

I haven't given up hope, by the way. But it might just be that I'll find my happy-ever-after somewhere I haven't been looking for it.

Happy Christmas, everyone.

Rom xx

I've loved following you Romily and I don't think it matters that you didn't find PK. The point is that you looked for him in the first place. I'll definitely keep following your blog because it's become something I've looked forward to every week. Have a lovely Christmas and I hope your happy-ever-after is really close! xx **pasha353**

There's still time! Don't stop looking! But seriously, be happy. You deserve it x
MissEmsie

Thanks so much for introducing me to your lovely aunt! I visited Tea and Sympathy last weekend and the cakes are gorgeous. You're so right about them being spookily right for however you're feeling! Happy Christmas xx
cupcakefairy

Romily, you're an inspiration and I would like to thank you for your positivity. I'm entering the New Year with everything I ever wanted and that I'm here at all is down to people like you who have reminded me that life is beautiful. I'm so sorry you didn't find your

335

handsome stranger. All I can say is that life
has a funny way of sorting things out. You'll
find your true love and when you do it will be
like you've known him forever. Much love
xxx **Ysobabe8**

I had been so sure that he was what I was searching for, but this morning, as the hum of conversation, road noise and the set list songs playing through the minibus speakers filled the space around me, I started to wonder if PK had been nothing more than a catalyst for me to stand up for who I was.

Would I have found the confidence to stand up to my parents without that meeting? Could I have dared to dream about the possibility of pursuing songwriting as a career, or worked my way through the challenges of becoming an unwilling celebrity following Cayte-gate?

And what about Charlie? It had been a rocky road from the embarrassment following my declaration of love to him, through the questions and misunderstandings of the spring and summer months, to his own declaration of his affections and the impending decision that lay ahead – but I was still here. I had held my ground and now the decision for us to be together was mine alone in a 360-degree reversal from this time last year. Maybe Ysobabe8 was right – maybe I had known my true love all my life . . .

Yesterday, I had gone to visit Uncle Dudley and Auntie Mags at Tea and Sympathy, where Christmas had well and truly moved in – tinsel and sparkly fairy lights were wrapped around every available surface. When Auntie Mags met me, she immediately prescribed a thick slice of blackberry and apple cake 'to focus your mind, sweetheart' – and proved her uncanny ability yet again.

'The thing is, I honestly couldn't choose,' I explained, as I showed them the almost completed 'pros' list. 'But the only thing I came up with in Charlie's favour over PK was this.' I passed it to them:

Charlie is here. PK isn't.

Auntie Mags sighed when she read it, and for a moment I thought she was going to burst into tears. Uncle Dudley saw it too, and put his arm around her shoulders.

'Bab, you did everything you could. We all did. Us and all them believers out there who've been hoping he'd show up. But nothing's in vain, kid. I reckon you'll look back on this year and be proud of what you've achieved. We're dead proud of you, aren't we, Magsie?'

My aunt nodded. 'You're a wonderful young woman, Romily. And it sounds to me like Charlie's finally realised what we knew all along. If he's the one in your heart – the one you *truly* want – then choose him. We know you aren't going to settle for anything less than the best.'

Watching the world pass by in a blur of merging colour as we sped towards the biggest gig of our lives, I knew they were right. I had followed my heart all year: now I was going to trust it with the biggest decision of my life so far.

Nothing could have prepared us for the sight that met our eyes as we drove through Syon Park's stunning parkland towards the Duke and Duchess of Northumberland's home. It was breathtakingly grand; expansive manicured lawns stretched away as far as the eye could see, with classical follies visible in the far distance and ancient trees standing guard around immaculately tended beds of formal planting.

337

A sharp overnight frost had covered everything in a layer of white, lending a magical air to what was already an amazing setting. It was impossible not to be impressed by the opulent beauty of this place. I don't think any of us had seen anything quite like it. When we reached the large turreted stone palace, glowing almost white in the morning sun, our conversation died away as we took it all in, as if a sudden noise might make it disappear altogether. It was a venue fit for a princess – the ultimate dream location – and I could hardly believe that I was going to sing here tomorrow.

A woman in a smart suit carrying a walkie-talkie and a clipboard approached the minibus as D'Wayne wound the window down. After a brief conversation, she left and D'Wayne turned to us.

'We're going around to where they're setting up,' he explained, as a man wearing a black coat with a yellow hi-vis jacket nipped past us in a golf buggy, beckoning us to follow.

I have to admit that when Tom had uttered the word 'marquee' for the wedding location, my heart had sunk to my boots. A marquee? In *December*? Even the most outlandish weddings we had been booked to play at had always been set in appropriate venues for the time of year. Weren't we going to freeze if the venue was basically a glorified tent?

However, when I saw the structure in question, I finally understood. 'Marquee' didn't quite do it justice: 'temporary Bedouin palace' might have been a more apt moniker. It was enormous, more like a circus tent in proportions, dwarfing the vans, lorries and cars parked around it as caterers, florists, delivery people and venue staff hurried in and out with boxes, bags and trolleys.

Jack blew out a whistle. 'Flippin' Nora, Tom, your boss doesn't do things by halves, does he?'

Tom grinned. 'Nope. Are we going in?'

'Lead the way, mate, this is your booking,' D'Wayne said.

'Great,' he replied as we joined Wren and Sophie and walked towards the venue. 'Does that mean I get your fifteen per cent commission fee?'

Inside, the full spectacle of the venue was revealed. Fibre-optic-studded 'star cloth' curtains were draped from the white muslin-covered central support pillars and eighty tables with silver chairs filled two-thirds of the space. At the far end, a wide stage was being erected, much to Wren's delight.

'That's the biggest stage our band has played on yet,' she said, clapping her hands like an excited cheerleader. 'I already love this gig!'

A tall, broad man with an impressive set of dreadlocks looked up from the vast sound desk and lifted his hand in greeting.

'You're the band, yeah? I'm Sid Heelis, Head of Sound.'

He led us up on to the stage and I could see the thrill on all my friends' faces at our first glimpse of the view we would be enjoying tomorrow evening.

'We run everything from D.I. boxes through the desk and set up monitors for bass, guitar, keys, drums and so on,' Sid said, as he walked us around the stage. 'As for gear, you can set up now and it'll be safe to leave overnight – we've got 24-hour security and we'll be cranking up the heat in here from this afternoon, so there won't be an issue if we get another frost tonight.'

'Do you do many weddings like this?' Charlie asked, looking out across the impressive interior as people buzzed around.

Sid laughed. 'Never done one this big in the winter. But Jules is an old mate from uni and when I heard what he was doing for his daughter, I had to be a part of it, even if it is on Christmas Eve. She's a special lady and it was the least I could do – she deserves it.'

'Can you imagine doing these type of events all year round?' Sophie asked me twenty minutes later as we brought in Charlie's drum cases. 'Talk about fantastic! I just hope that people recommend us after tonight.' She giggled. 'Jack and I are going to need all the money we can save next year.'

I stared at her. 'Why? What do you mean?'

Her smile was brighter than the sun pouring in through the white canvas. 'Don't tell anyone, but I think we might not be too far behind this happy couple down the aisle!'

I whooped, dropped the cases on the ground and threw my arms around her. 'Sophie, that's fantastic news! So when . . .?'

'He was planning to ask me on Christmas Day, but when we were driving down this morning he just blurted it out. So we're kind of unofficially engaged. We'll do the big reveal on Christmas Day, but I had to tell someone – I'm so excited!'

As we were setting up the equipment on stage, it suddenly occurred to me that I was not the only one for whom this year had been important: Jack and Soph with their secret engagement; Tom with his breakup from Anya and his new relationship with the one-woman soap opera known as Cayte; and D'Wayne's recent appointment as Wren's boyfriend. And Charlie? Perhaps he had learned to see me for who I really was and had found the courage to speak out when it mattered most. Would this year be the start of a lifetime together for us?

It's amazing what a difference working with a professional sound company makes. Wren and I exchanged blissful looks as we tested our mics and in-ear monitors. The crystal clear sound, differentiation between instruments and voices, and general all-round polish to the sound were incredible. Looking around the stage, I could see identical expressions of joy on everyone's faces.

After the sound check, Jack left his van and we all piled into the minibus to head to the hotel, giddy with the thrill of it all.

In an unbelievably generous gesture, Julian had booked us a room each in a luxurious Kensington hotel – leading Sophie to exclaim that she had obviously now died and gone straight to heaven.

An hour after we'd checked in, we assembled back in the vast marble lobby of the hotel. Wren, wrapped up in a bright green coat with a long purple scarf and a striped beanie hat, flung her arm around Sophie's shoulder as she addressed us all.

'OK, everyone, now I know we have a big day tomorrow but for the rest of today we're going to enjoy everything that this city has to offer.'

'Now, we've put together a little list of things you might like to do.' Sophie handed us each a piece of paper. 'We realise that not everyone will want to do the same things, so I suggest we split up and meet back here in the hotel bar, about eleven-ish?'

Jack and Charlie wanted food, so they headed out to find a restaurant. Wren was desperate to visit the Winter Wonderland in Hyde Park, so D'Wayne, ever the attentive boyfriend, agreed to go with her. I didn't really mind what I did, just wanting to soak up the festive atmosphere, so I tagged along with Tom and Sophie.

I'd never been in the capital just before Christmas – I'd only ever seen Christmassy London scenes in Richard Curtis films – but there was definitely something magical about the city in the throes of festive celebrations. Music from carol singers and a Salvation Army band floated up from street corners and every shop window glowed with Christmas displays. The pavements were packed with shoppers – Oxford Street and Regent Street barely passable at anything faster than a snail's pace – but it all somehow added to the excitement. And nobody was more excited than Sophie.

'Look at the lights!' she squealed, pointing up at the beautiful Christmas lights spanning the street above our heads. 'Aren't they the most gorgeous decorations you've ever seen?'

Tom rolled his eyes and linked his arm through Sophie's. 'You know, I think they probably put them up just for you, Soph.'

She glared at him. 'Perhaps they *did*.'

I smiled at them both. 'So where to now?'

'I vote we find hot chocolate, something very indulgent to eat and maybe a spot of skating?' Tom suggested, laughing when Sophie's eyes lit up.

We managed to bag a table in the window of a beautiful patisserie on Regent Street overlooking the brightly lit street and settled down to enjoy huge cups of hot chocolate with marshmallows.

'So, how are you feeling about tomorrow?' Tom asked, as the waitress arrived with three enormous slices of multi-layered gateaux – white chocolate for him and dark chocolate for Sophie and me.

'I just hope I remember all the sax parts,' Sophie said. 'I know we've rehearsed them to death but I'm still worried I'll get on that stage and draw a total blank.'

'You'll be fine,' Tom assured her. 'You sounded awesome at the last rehearsal. Just get up there and enjoy it – we've worked so hard for this one. I can't wait. How about you, Rom?'

My stomach did a little flip at the thought of everything tomorrow might hold. 'I'm a bit nervous, but it's going to be amazing.' Silently, I added, *I hope*.

After we finished our cake, Sophie suggested we visit Harrods. I didn't feel like walking round a crowded Christmas store, so Tom agreed to take Sophie.

'Will you be OK?' he asked me.

'I'll be fine,' I assured him. 'I'll just wander round for a while.'

As Sophie dragged Tom out of the door, I smiled at the waiter who had arrived to clear our table. 'It's her first time in London at Christmas. I think she's a little overexcited.'

The waiter laughed. 'You're not joining them?'

'No. I thought I might go for a walk somewhere.'

'I'd recommend the South Bank,' he said, wiping the table. 'Very festive and really beautiful by the Thames.'

He wasn't wrong. When I arrived at the South Bank a truly magical sight met my eyes. Every tree was covered in nets of tiny white lights, making them appear to be encrusted in sparkling diamonds, and multicoloured lights reflected in the dark waters of the river. All along the path were small wooden stalls, identical to those that lined New Street last year for the Christmas Market, and the same Christmas music was playing that I'd heard then.

Walking along with crowds of visitors, I couldn't help but remember the way that Charlie and I had walked along New Street, laughing and happy, before we'd stepped into the coffee shop last year. And then, as I passed a group of revellers dressed in Santa outfits, I saw it: a toy stall,

343

identical to the one I had collided with twelve months ago. The parallels between this scene and the Christmas Market in Birmingham were unavoidable, but rather than confusing, I found I was comforted by the memories flooding back – and excited about what the future held for me.

Later that evening when we all met up in the plush hotel bar, Wren was beaming. 'The ice rink was *amazing*! D'Wayne insisted we go on the Ferris wheel, and I was so excited I went with it – completely forgetting that I'm not good with heights . . .'

'You should have heard her screaming when we reached the top and the wheel stopped to let people on,' D'Wayne chuckled, squeezing Wren's hand. 'Anyone would think she was being murdered or something.'

'Ah, D'Wayne,' Jack said, slapping his back sympathetically. 'This is the kind of fun that lies in store for you now, my friend.'

'Oi!' Wren retorted. 'I'm *fun* to be with, thank you very much.'

'Yes, of course you are, dear.' D'Wayne feigned terror, which made everyone laugh. It was so good to see Wren and D'Wayne so happy and comfortable with each other already.

'We ended up in Trafalgar Square,' Jack said, handing his mobile around so we could see the pictures he'd taken. The tall Norwegian Christmas tree, covered in multicoloured lights, was reflected in the water of the fountain and looked stunning against the darkened December sky. 'The vibe there was incredible. While we were admiring the tree, this group of tourists arrived and just started singing Christmas carols – completely improvised.'

'I hope you joined in?' I asked.

'Of course.' Charlie's eyes were sparklier than all the

lights on the Trafalgar Square tree combined as he looked at me. 'In three-part harmony, too, I'll have you know.'

Jack tapped his wine glass with his mobile. 'Your attention please, ladies and gentlemen! Seeing as we didn't have our annual Pinstripes Christmas soirée tonight because of some random last-minute wedding, I would like to propose a toast. To The Pinstripes – onwards and upwards!'

'Onwards and upwards!' we cheered.

Later that night, snuggled up in the complimentary towelling robe watching television, I fetched PK's photo from my bag and stared at it. This would be the last night I would ask him the question, but it had to be done.

'If you're still looking for me, come and find me. There's still time . . .'

The shrill tone of Stevie Wonder from my mobile interrupted me.

'Hey, you.'

I swallowed hard. 'Hey, Charlie.'

'I just wanted to say – I'm here for you whatever happens tomorrow. You're my best friend and you always will be. I need you to know that.'

I smiled as a shiver of joy wriggled free and made its curly way to my toes. 'Thank you. Ditto from me. Um, Charlie?'

'Yes?'

'Thanks. Even though – well, even though I know this whole quest thing has been difficult for you to understand, I promise you I'll make the right decision – for us. Goodnight.'

His voice was gentle and velvet-soft against my ear. 'Goodnight, beautiful.'

*　　*　　*

The next morning was bright and crisp as I joined the rest of the band in the hotel's sumptuous restaurant for breakfast. Wren and Sophie had sneaked out before the rest of us were awake to do some early morning Christmas shopping, much to the amusement of D'Wayne and Jack, and now an impressive array of shopping bags occupied the floor underneath our table.

'Never let it be said that you two aren't committed when it comes to shopping,' Tom laughed.

I had slept like a baby in the enormous king-sized bed in my elegant room; for the first time in many months, neither PK nor Charlie entered my dreams. With my decision – and the death knell of the quest – fast approaching, my subconscious mind could offer no more supportive evidence. What happened this evening was down to me alone.

'You know how people always nick things from hotel rooms?' Sophie asked, as we tucked into a hearty English breakfast. 'Well, I was wondering if they would miss the entire en suite in my room? That marble is to *die* for!'

'We'd never fit it in the van, petal,' Jack winked, as his secret fiancée made a swipe for him with her linen napkin.

'What time do we need to get over to the venue?' Charlie asked D'Wayne.

'Sid said any time before five. I think we should aim for about four pm. We have dressing rooms, apparently, so we can chill there until it's time for you to go on.'

'I think we should get out and enjoy London some more before we have to work,' Sophie suggested.

'Haven't you and Wren had enough already?' Charlie laughed.

'I think it's a good idea, actually,' D'Wayne said. 'Blow the cobwebs out a little, get in the mood for tonight. But can I suggest that we don't all dash about like lunatics this morning? You guys need to be well rested for tonight.'

Heeding our manager's wise words, we decided to go for a walk together. Leaving the bright lights and bustle of Kensington behind us, we caught the tube to Hyde Park Corner and walked into the frosted park. The whole place felt imbued with Christmas spirit – twinkling lights were draped between the streetlights that lined the paths and framed the small refreshment booths beside the lake, families were enjoying the bright winter's day together and couples snuggled close on park benches. It felt good to be out with my best friends in the crisp air, laughing and fooling around.

Tom found a discarded tennis ball and held it aloft like a prize. 'Game on!'

Charlie, Jack, Sophie and I dashed on to the frozen grass for an impromptu game of catch, the activity made significantly harder by the slippery ground beneath our feet. Several times, we came crashing down, much to our amusement – and D'Wayne's despair.

'Come on, guys,' he protested. 'I said a *gentle* walk, not World War Three!'

Grinning like naughty schoolkids, we dutifully abandoned the game. On our way back into the elegant chaos of Kensington, clutching paper coffee cups to keep our hands warm, we stopped to watch a barbershop choir who were performing a great set of Christmas songs to a crowd of shoppers outside one of the expensive restaurants. It was impossible not to feel a sparkle of Christmas magic hearing tunes like 'Let It Snow', 'White Christmas' and 'The Most Wonderful Time of the Year'. Jack started dancing with Sophie, moving until they were under a bunch of mistletoe tied to the restaurant's awning and sweeping her into a passionate kiss as the onlookers cheered. It was beautiful

– and perfectly set the scene for the romance of the day ahead of us.

We arrived at Syon Park at four thirty and were directed to our dressing rooms by a member of security. Jack laughed when he saw the two blue Portakabins in the backstage area. 'Wow. Normally when an organiser says we have "dressing rooms" they mean more than one cubicle in the loos. How things change!'

Sophie, Wren and I changed into our stage costumes, chosen with great care and attention the week before. Sophie's deep turquoise cocktail dress and matching shoes made her blonde hair shine like spun gold; Wren looked amazing as always in an opulent black velvet mini-dress and impressively high heels, the diamanté choker and matching bracelet she wore sparkling with every move. After much deliberation (and passionate persuasion by Wren), I had blown my Christmas budget on a silver slub-silk strapless dress, that I teamed with matching heels and a long string of amethyst beads. After much twirling and appreciative oohs and aahs, we picked our way over the frozen lawn to the boys' dressing room next door. When we entered, the boys were gathered around Jack's folder of lead sheets for the songs, going over the structure and making sure that everyone knew the nuances of each one.

'. . . Don't forget the double-push after the middle eight when the chorus comes back in – here.'

Tom looked up. '*He-llo*, mommas!'

Jack wolf-whistled as we entered their dressing room. 'Ladies, lovely as ever.'

Charlie winked at me as the others made room for us to sit. 'It's possible they might want us to play background stuff while they rearrange part of the space for the evening gig – D'Wayne's just finding out. Jack suggested we do some of the afternoon set we did for Frankie and Owen and the crooner stuff from the golden wedding gig last month.'

'Sounds good,' I replied.

The door opened and I was secretly thrilled when I noticed Wren's eyes light up as she saw D'Wayne walk in.

'OK, we're on for a background set at five thirty,' he said, checking his watch. 'That gives us an hour before we're due on stage. Sid reckons we can use it as a bit of an elongated sound-check, too. There'll be a monitor desk at the side of the stage, so if you need any changes in your monitors you can ask the technician.'

Half an hour later, I remembered that I had left my earrings in my bag, so left the others to return to our dressing room. I checked my reflection in the large mirror, pleased with the elegant chignon that Wren and Sophie had swept my hair up in and the sparkling amethyst hair pins that shimmered as I turned my head. The effect with the soft silver of my dress was fantastic, and as I looked at my reflection I was thrilled to see the confident woman smiling back at me. Picking up my set list and water bottle, I stepped out into the chilly afternoon. The sun had already set over the park and house, but now a magical transformation had occurred: not only was the house dramatically floodlit behind the glowing marquee, but every tree had been lit from below with a different coloured light. It was so beautiful that I decided to take a detour around the front of the marquee to get the full effect across the immaculately maintained lawns and great lake beyond.

This was the most breathtaking place I had ever seen – a fitting location for the end of an extraordinary year. Over to my right, I spied a bench between the intricate frames of two beech trees, one lit with a golden yellow light, the other an emerald green.

That's where I'll tell Charlie, I decided. It was the perfect place.

Feeling pleased with myself, I turned to head back to the dressing rooms . . . and froze.

Walking in my direction, fifty yards away from where I stood, a dark figure passed the entrance to the marquee, the light from within suddenly illuminating his russet-brown wavy hair and a face I had become so accustomed to seeing in my memories and the blurry photo. I blinked a few times, convinced that my mind was playing tricks again as it had done months ago with look-a-like Mark in George's cosy interior. But there was no mistaking what I saw this time: PK was here, at the millionaire gig in stunning Syon Park, heading towards me. He was dressed in a full, dark grey morning suit with a scarlet embroidered waistcoat, his white cravat slightly loosened at his neck. He was just as I remembered him . . . only better. But a shot of panic seared through me as I suddenly remembered something Sid had told us earlier when Tom had asked how we would spot the groom in the sea of guests.

'Oh that's easy. The florist says that all the groomsmen are wearing buttonholes with two roses – one white, one red. But the groom has two white roses to match the bride's bouquet.'

My eyes moved to PK's chest – and my heart broke into a hundred million shards.

Two white roses.

In a moment I had both found and lost him forever, the earth-shattering revelation almost stealing my legs from under me. Feeling a strong wave of emotion cresting within, I ducked my head and started to move, desperate to return to the sanctuary of my dressing room. Walking quickly, I didn't see the raised tree root barely visible among the grass and my

350

foot caught it, causing me to stumble as I came level with him. Immediately, his head jerked round and we came face to face. I saw his pupils widen as he recognised me. He opened his mouth to speak, but I couldn't face hearing his voice again – not now I knew the truth. I hurried past him as he called 'Wait!' behind me. I could hear his steps quickening on the frozen ground behind me and picked up my pace.

'Will!' A voice called from the entrance to the marquee, causing his footsteps to skid to a halt. 'They want you inside for photos.'

'I'm just . . . OK, fine, I'm coming.' I could hear the battle in his voice as I hurried away.

I reached the steps of the dressing room and turned back to see a groomsman flinging an arm around him. 'You don't want to go upsetting the bride, today of all days. Wouldn't be a good start for married life.'

Crushed, defeated and shaking, I watched him take one last look in my direction before disappearing inside. Gasping gulps of cold air into my lungs, I sank down on to the steps, head in hands.

It was no accident that the wedding had been rescheduled for Christmas Eve. Fate itself was at work here: revealing, in the fading moments of the quest, the truth about the man I had spent all year searching for. And, as a parting gift to remind me of my yearlong search, I now knew his name – Will. It seemed strange to finally have that piece of the puzzle in my possession.

My quest had come to an end: the search was over. How fitting that I should find him in the dying moments, only to discover he had just married someone else! The bittersweet reality hit me full on as tears started to fall, my thoughts shaken into a jumble of nonsensical abstracts, swirling around indeterminably inside my head.

Of course he would have had someone else! Perhaps the person calling his name when he had to leave me last Christmas knew this, and the battle I saw in his eyes was that of a tempted man?

It seemed somehow right that I had met him today – at the very moment I had decided to choose Charlie. Under any other circumstances I would have marvelled at the irony – but not this evening. Scrambling up the steps to the dressing room, I closed the door behind me, my tears falling fast and free.

The hurt I was experiencing, I realised slowly, was painful, but *necessary* – a final chance to mourn the passing of a dream. I stared at my reflection in the mirror and noticed strength in my eyes that I hadn't seen before. Maybe this was what Jack, Tom and Charlie had spoken about. I might have finally laid my dream of being with Will to rest, but I still had dreams and aspirations of my own, and knowing that I had successfully searched for a whole year until I had found him again, I finally believed wholeheartedly that I could do the same next year with anything I put my mind to. My mother had been wrong: I wasn't wasting my life with the quest. It had been the making of me.

As I considered it all, an image of the final line of my 'pros' list flashed into my mind:

Charlie is here. PK isn't.

Through it all, Charlie had been there for me, steadily working out his own feelings and never once taking his friendship – which I valued so much – away from me. All PK was, in reality, was a made-up name for a fleeting glimpse of someone I was a complete stranger to. My choice had been made long before I consciously chose it: and now I knew what to do.

Finally calm, I reapplied my make-up and, after a final check, walked out to join the others.

I didn't see Will as we performed, but then I wasn't looking for him. Not any more. Instead, I focused my attention on giving the brightest, most impressive performance I could, the confidence of my decision strengthening my bones and lighting up my smile.

Filled with guests, the marquee was alive with elegant activity. Everything seemed to sparkle as eight hundred guests chatted, laughed and tapped their feet along to the music. The atmosphere was happy and festive, the combination of Christmas Eve and a romantic wedding clearly having the desired effect on all present.

Meanwhile, the venue's staff worked stealthily, deftly moving tables to open up the large dance floor directly in front of the stage in readiness for the evening's dancing.

Halfway through 'Dream a Little Dream of Me', I caught Charlie's eye and he smiled at me. He looked utterly gorgeous in his black shirt and trousers, his eyes alive with the thrill of performing in this amazing place on this enchanting night.

By the time our background music set came to an end, a crowd of around a hundred people had gathered on the dance floor, applauding appreciatively.

Sid's voice came through our monitors. 'The crowd loves you, guys! If you're good to go, you might as well launch into your first set – that should tie in perfectly with the evening buffet.'

Jack gave the thumbs-up, and Sid spoke into the front-of-house microphone.

'Ladies and gentlemen, you have been enjoying your band

for this evening – the very excellent Pinstripes. Put your hands together please to show your appreciation.'

The smiling guests obliged.

'And now, they will lead us into the evening's festivities proper,' Sid continued. 'Ladies and gentlemen, let's welcome, once more: The Pinstripes!'

Charlie yelled a countdown and Wren slid her hand up the neck of her bass guitar as the opening bars of 'Love Train' rang out into the marquee.

With each song we performed, more guests gathered on the dance floor, gradually filling it with a mass of laughing, dancing bodies under the giant crystal chandeliers suspended from the roof; and my heart rate increased as the moment I had chosen to share with Charlie moved ever closer.

Wren was delighted when her vocally acrobatic rendition of 'Ain't Nobody' drew such tumultuous applause from the guests that we had to wait until it died down before beginning the next song.

'I *love* these people!' she whispered to me, her eyes brimming with emotion at their reaction. 'I want to take them all home with me!'

As we began the intro to the 'Lovely Day/Valerie' medley that would end our first set, I looked back at Charlie. His smile was full of affection, spurring me on to make the decision my heart was now set upon.

Six minutes later the final bars rang out, and Wren thanked the crowd for their response. 'You've been fantastic so far, so thank you. We'll see you back on the dance floor in an hour or so. Enjoy your evening!'

She turned back to us and shrieked. 'How *cool* was that?'

Jack's grin said it all. 'We sound awesome. And that audience – wow!'

Sophie grabbed my arm. 'Did you see Victoria Beckham dancing? And Dizzee Rascal! I'm going to try to take some photos for my mum – she'll never believe it!'

Sid appeared at the edge of the stage and beckoned us over. 'Guys, you're phenomenal. Best event band I've heard in a while – and I don't say that lightly. Listen, my company is doing a big corporate gig in March next year. Don't suppose you'd be up for it? It'll be good money, I promise. Music industry people will be there and it's where we pick up a lot of business each year.'

Jack shook his hand. 'Mate, we'd love to. Have a word with our manager and we'll book it in.'

Sid grinned. 'Excellent. Grab some food and go and relax – I'll send a runner to fetch you for set two.'

Tom needed no further invitation to pursue food, jumping down from the stage and disappearing through the crowd. Wren and Sophie followed suit as Jack joined Charlie and me at the edge of the stage. 'Great gig. You coming for something to eat?'

'In a minute,' Charlie said, his arm involuntarily brushing against mine. 'We just need to sort something out.'

'Cool. Don't be too long. If Tom has his way the buffet tables will be cleared out in five minutes flat!' He jumped down and followed the others.

I smiled at Charlie, my heart thumping wildly. 'Come on. There's something I want to show you.'

Syon Park looked magical when we emerged from the marquee into the frosty night, the floodlights in the trees casting rainbow-coloured sparkles across the iced lawns. Charlie surveyed the scene, his eyes drinking in all the details.

Suddenly self-conscious, I folded my arms as Charlie pushed his hands into his pockets, and I led him to the green ironwork bench, set between the two ancient beech trees. We sat down and I could feel my breathing quicken as the butterflies returned to dance in my stomach.

It was time to say what my heart wanted me to.

'You were right when you said you thought I'd known all along who I wanted to be with. I've just been working everything through – and I feel like I've learned so much along the way.' I paused, suppressing a sudden nervous urge to giggle. 'But I know what I want. I want to be with you, Charlie.'

A huge smile spread across his face as he cradled my hands in his. 'Oh, Rom . . .'

'I want to be with you,' I said again, feeling a rush of emotion as I finally made my decision in the midst of the darkened garden, with Charlie's warm hands caressing mine as our bodies moved closer. He reached up to stroke my cheek – as he had in the forest of the Chase a month ago – and I closed my eyes as our lips met for the first time . . .

And then . . .

. . . then . . .

CHAPTER TWENTY-ONE

It had to be you

. . . NOTHING.

My eyes flew open as our kiss ended – and Charlie was wearing the exact same expression as me.

'Did you feel anything?'

I shook my head, bewildered. 'Nothing. You?'

'No.' He scanned my face for answers. 'I'm so sorry.'

'Me too. But I was *so sure* . . .'

He held up his hands. 'I *know*, me too.'

We sat in silence on the bench, the sounds of the evening reception in full swing floating from the marquee across the floodlit parkland. Charlie gave a long sigh, his breath sparkling in the light of the gold floodlight by the tree beside him.

'I wanted it to be you, Rom. For weeks now – no, months, probably. It all made so much sense: I mean, you saying you loved me last year, the way we always end up organising things together – the "Old Folks" thing. And you're beautiful, Romily, absolutely stunningly beautiful. So why . . .?'

I squeezed his hand. 'I've no idea. I was so sure you were

357

the one for me – even earlier tonight when I saw . . .' I hesitated as I realised what I was about to say.

'Saw what?' His eyes narrowed and a wry smile appeared. 'Come on, we just kissed – I think that qualifies us for sharing deeper things.'

I laughed and shook my head. Tonight was fast becoming the strangest night of my life. Telling Charlie the truth wouldn't make it any worse. 'The guy – from last Christmas – he's at this wedding.'

Charlie's face was a picture. 'You're kidding me! What did he say to you?'

'He didn't. Or rather, I didn't hang around long enough to find out.'

His expression clouded. 'How come?'

I raised my eyes to the canopy of stars high above us. 'Because this is his wedding.'

Charlie winced. 'Ah. Not so good.'

'Nope.'

'Oh, Rom.' He wrapped an arm around my shoulders and I leaned my head against the warmth of his chest. 'Poor you. And then *this* with us – are you OK?'

Surprisingly, I was. I felt as if a crushing weight had been removed from my chest – it was like I could breathe fully for the first time in months. The past few weeks spent debating whether to choose Charlie or PK had been exhausting – and I realised now that for most of that time I had felt dreadful, as if I was somehow a bad person for taking my time to choose. Now I knew that Will was married and Charlie was – well, just a *really* good friend – I could finally focus on moving into the next year of my life with a renewed sense of excitement about the possibilities that lay ahead of me.

'I think I'll be fine. You?'

'Don't take this the wrong way, but I'm kind of relieved. I was so worried I was losing my best friend. You have no idea how much I agonised over everything. I think – no, I know – I was just incredibly jealous that some bloke had stolen your heart when you'd said it was mine. It came down to sheer bloody-mindedness at the end of the day. But I meant what I said: you are beautiful. I'm just so sorry I couldn't be the man you wanted me to be.'

I sat up. 'Charlie, you've always been the man I wanted you to be. I love you to bits and you know I always will. How were we to know the chemistry would be missing?'

'True. So you're OK?'

I nodded. 'I'm fine.'

We hugged – both relieved. And it felt good. Charlie stood. 'Right, I'm going to see if the locusts have left any food. Coming?'

'No, I think I'll stay here a little while. I need to compose myself for our show-stopping second set. Don't want those millionaires losing interest in us, do we?'

'Too right. I'll see you in a bit then.'

I watched him leave, feeling my body relax. Closing my eyes, I inhaled the frosty air and let the maelstrom within me finally subside. *What a year, Romily Parker*, I said to myself. *How are you going to top that one?*

Maybe Integral would commission more songs from Jack and I – the thought of which thrilled me intensely. Maybe I would encourage Auntie Mags to start a website for Tea and Sympathy – Uncle Dudley and I had been joking about it with her for months – to prescribe motherly advice and excellent, spookily appropriate recipes to her charges from my blog. After all, they would need someone to turn to when they discovered the real conclusion of my virtually-famous quest.

And perhaps I might see if Mick and his new lady friend knew any hunky single thirty-somethings. *Onwards and upwards, Romily* . . .

'You ran away.'

I jumped as the voice spoke beside me, opening my eyes to find Will sitting where Charlie had been moments before.

'You ran away before I had a chance to speak to you. You are who I think you are, aren't you?'

'I . . .' Words failed me.

'From the Christmas Market – you crashed into the toy stall. Last year? Only I remember your hair was down and you were wearing a red coat.'

'And now you're at a wedding,' I managed to blurt out, rising to my feet.

He frowned. 'Yes. And so are you. The wedding singer, in fact. Amazing voice, by the way. Stunning.'

'Um – thanks . . . Look, I really have to get back . . .'

'No you don't. Not for half an hour. They're only just serving dessert.'

His eyes never left mine – the same wide wonder I had seen last Christmas. But what was the point in subjecting myself to this when I already knew what he was going to tell me?

'Please – would you sit down? I've been planning what I would say should I ever meet you again and . . . No matter how crazy you think I am, please just let me say it?'

I sank back on to the iron seat. 'Where did you go? Last year, I mean. Why did you have to leave?'

He sighed. 'My brother had just been told about Issie's accident and the doctors were predicting the worst. She's the bride today – so I expect you know about the struggle she's had this year since the accident? I had to be with her – we had no choice. For what it's worth, I'm sorry.'

360

Of course, it made sense now. Anyone in that situation would have done exactly the same.

I looked down at my silver platform heels amid the glistening frosted grass. 'I understand. I'm sorry about your wife. Still, it's great she was well enough to enjoy today.'

'It's—'

'I'm sorry I ran away this evening. It was just a shock, you know, seeing you again after all the search and everything.'

I could feel his eyes boring into me. Looking up, I could see complete confusion scrawled all over his face. 'Sorry? What search?'

I stared at him again, disorientated by the sudden turn of events. 'Erm – I don't – sorry, what was the question?'

'You've been searching – for me?' he asked carefully.

Oh boy. This was going to be embarrassing. 'Er – yes. It started out as just a bit of a challenge, to see if I could spend a year following my heart. The only trouble was, it kind of assumed a life of its own and just grew and grew, into a blog and a viral article that almost everyone read, and then the journalist who wrote the article realised what she'd done and wrote something different which sent more people to my blog and my aunt opened a tea shop where people she met on my blog now hang out . . .'

At that moment, I wasn't sure which was worse: having to admit my quest to the startled subject of it, or seeing the extremely confused expression on his unbelievably handsome face.

'A blog? And a tea shop . . .?' His eyes grew wider still. 'Hang on, you're not the girl from the *It Started With a Kiss* blog, are you?'

Busted. I hung my head. 'Yes. I am.'

He ran a hand through his hair. 'Issie's kept going on

361

about that blog for weeks. She said she'd talked a lot with the girl who wrote it and it really inspired her to be positive when she was going through physio last month, trying to walk again. She kept sending me the link when she was in hospital – she was so adamant that I should read it and I couldn't understand why. I thought it was just one of her passing fads, so I never looked it up.'

Hang on a minute: Issie?

'What's her username?'

'Ysobabe8. It's a bit lame and I'm always making fun of it.'

Oh great. The focus of my quest was receiving links to my site from his wife-to-be, who I had been chatting with for months – and liked immensely. Of all my followers, Ysobabe8 was the one I had felt the most connection with, and her constant encouragement had helped me immensely during the closing months of the quest. This was just getting better and better. 'Probably just as well you didn't follow the link, considering.'

'Considering what? That she'd unwittingly found and befriended the girl I haven't been able to get out of my head all year?'

'No!' This was getting beyond a joke. 'That she was about to *marry* you!'

He shook his head in disbelief – obviously the truth hurt.

It was definitely time to leave now. 'I'm sorry. I really should get going . . .'

'Wait. You think Issie's my wife? That this is *my* wedding?'

'I know it is.'

'I don't see how you can.'

I groaned and pointed at his buttonhole flowers. 'Two white roses for the groom. One white and one red for everyone else.'

'Is it?' He looked down at his buttonhole. 'So *that's* why it looked bigger than everyone else's! Man, I am such a div – Issie's going to cry laughing when she finds out.' He saw my expression. 'Issie's not my wife. She's my *sister*.'

'What? But I thought . . .'

'I know what you thought. But you thought wrong. Issie's just married my best mate, Dan – I'm his best man. He was supposed to be meeting my brother and me in the Christmas Market last year but then he was told about Issie's accident and that's when he called my brother.'

My head was awash with everything that had happened tonight. Tears started to flood into my eyes and I looked away.

'But I'd just bumped into you – and I didn't want to leave,' he added, his voice softer than silk. 'I didn't have time to say anything, or give you my number – I didn't even ask your name.'

I sniffed. 'It's Romily.'

He held out his hand. 'Hi, Romily, I'm Will.'

I placed my hand in his – and instantly I was back to when he had first held it, all the fire and fury of the moment stealing my breath and fuelling my insistent heart. Slowly, he lifted my hand and I closed my eyes as I felt the brush of his lips across my fingers.

'I've played this moment over and over in my head,' he whispered, the waves of his breath passing over my hand as he spoke, 'and I never thought I'd get the chance to say it.'

'So tell me now.' I opened my eyes and looked deep into his, the floodlights from the surrounding trees reflected in them as the Christmas lights had been over a year before.

'I never believed in love at first sight – until then,' Will said. 'But I looked into your eyes and there it was. Like the rest of my life was staring back at me. I just *knew* you, even though . . .'

'Even though you didn't?' I completely understood what he was saying – because I had felt the exact same certainty.

He let my hand go and gently placed his hands on my shoulders. 'This is totally crazy – we know nothing about each other, except what we saw last year and what we've said tonight. But it's like you've been with me, all year, through Issie's recovery and the scare she gave us all in the summer . . . and on towards today. Meeting you that day was the only bright point in what became the most traumatic time of my life. You've been the face in my dreams, the one that got away. I need to know if we have a chance together. Because I don't think it's a coincidence we're both here today. Fate has brought us together twice: do you think maybe we should take the hint?'

It was as if he was saying the very things that had buzzed about my head all through the quest. It was utterly ridiculous – but then, isn't love like that when you first begin? What if the year I'd spent searching for him was preparing me for this step: to take his hand and jump into the unknown?

This was my chance to put into practice everything I had learned – and finally follow my heart.

Reaching out, heart dizzy with emotion, I cradled his face in my hands and kissed him. And it was unlike anything I had ever experienced before, as if everything in the universe had come together at once for one almighty, cataclysmic event that would change everything . . .

In his arms, I felt more alive – more myself – than I thought was possible. Here was where I belonged. And although I knew nothing about him, it was like our hearts had been introduced a long, long time ago.

As the kiss ended, and we gazed at each other in the multi-hued glow of the park, we knew everything we needed to know.

Taking my hand, he stood and pulled me to him.

'We should get back inside.'

'We should.' I stopped and looked at the man I'd searched my whole life to find. 'Are you ready for this?'

He smiled. 'Lead on.'

Hi everyone – guess what?

I FOUND HIM!

Let me introduce you to Will Hammond. He's 30, makes handcrafted furniture for a living and lives in Stratford-upon-Avon. And he just happens to be the man I've been searching all year for. I found him on the last day of my quest – in the final hours of it, to be precise – and it turns out he'd been dreaming about me, too.

Not only that, but I found out that one of my followers knew him all along. So thank you, Ysobabe8, for seeing what neither he or I could see – and for becoming a fantastic friend, too.

I'd just like to thank you all for supporting me so much during last year. You have no idea what your words of encouragement have meant to me, and to my aunt and uncle.

I want to tell you this: that crazy, completely impossible things can happen. I followed my heart and it led me back to the man who stole it when he kissed me.

Who knows where your heart could lead you?

Lots of love,

Romily xxx
p.s. Will says hello ☺
He reckons you should all come to Tea and
Sympathy and try Auntie Mags' triple chocolate marble
cake.

It's perfect for following your heart, apparently.

Cake Therapy by Auntie Mags

Hello sweethearts, how are you doing today? I'm sure I have a little something sweet to help ... Look down the list to find the perfect remedy for how you're feeling. Enjoy! Lots of love, Auntie Mags xx

Anticipation – Raspberry Meringue cake
Calming anxiety – Bakewell tart
Celebrations – Maple and Walnut pancake stacks
Clear focus – Blackberry and Apple cake
Courage – Ginger cake
Determination – Millionaire's Shortbread
Dreams – Fruit bread with real butter
Energy – Triple-layer Chocolate cake
Feeling under the weather – Victoria sponge with real strawberries
First love – White Chocolate and Rose torte
Following your heart – Triple Chocolate Marble cake
Hangover cure – Honey and Almond chewy flapjacks
Happiness – Lemon and Lime Meringue pie
Honesty – White chocolate and Elderflower cake
Hope – Carrot cake
Making decisions – Coffee and Walnut cake
Mending a broken heart – Lemon Drizzle cake
New beginnings – Strawberry and white chocolate cake
Spontaneity – Fruit cake
Tiredness – Apple and cinnamon pie
Uncertainty – St. Clements cake

Here's a sneak peak of the author questionnaire
that will be appearing on Miranda's website:
www.miranda-dickinson.com

Do you spend a lot of time researching your novels?
Yes, I do. It's something I've always done with my writing,
long before I was published. I love stories where I can learn
something, whether it's about the location, the type of job
that a character does, or a central theme of the book – so I
try to bring that into the stories I write.

For this novel, a lot of the band and gig references came
from my own experience, but I wanted to research the bits of
weddings that the band don't generally get to see. So I looked
at a lot of wedding venues, met people who work in the
wedding industry and spent many happy hours wandering
through magazines and excellent wedding blogs like www.
rocknrollbride.com and www.theweddingofmydreams.com.

I also received amazing research help from my fabulous
Twitter followers, who have saved my sanity on many
occasions through the writing and editing process of
my books. This time they've shared their best and worst
wedding stories, told me about amazing wedding venues
and even inspired details about the characters. I love this
side of research – not least because it makes a nice change
from the solitary pursuit of writing!

What is a typical working day like for you?
I don't have one! I work part-time, so writing has to take
place around my day job. I have two days a week to write,
together with evenings and weekends. I don't have a set
working pattern, but actually this works well for me – with

everything else so varied, it helps to be flexible about when, where and how I write. When I have a deadline to meet, I will write at every opportunity and at all hours to get it done!

I generally try to write something every day (although I never beat myself up if I don't) and I always carry notebooks with me for jotting down ideas, snippets of dialogue and character sketches. One of the things that makes writing so exciting is the fact that inspiration is everywhere. For example, Harri, the main character in *Welcome to My World*, was inspired by a really cool-looking young woman I saw in my local coffee shop in Stourbridge. She just looked like the kind of person who could have a fascinating life – and that was my starting point for the character. Love it when that happens!

Have you ever had writer's block? If so, how did you cope with it?
I've definitely had times when I can't resolve a problem in my plot, or not been sure where to take a character next. I think every writer experiences that. But since I became a published writer with a schedule to meet and scary deadlines, I've had to find ways of getting round the problems!

The best remedy I've found is to write ahead of the obstacle. I'll write a scene that comes later in the plot and focus on that rather than feeling helpless about the problem. I believe that writer's block is ninety-nine percent psychological and one percent problem. So if you can trick your mind into thinking you've already resolved the problem, it will often resolve itself.

Do your characters ever surprise you?
All the time! In fact, I would be rather disappointed if they didn't . . .

I know that some writers like to have everything neatly planned before they begin, but I can't work like that. While I believe wholeheartedly in having a good structure for my novels, I always leave room for serendipitous things to appear. More often than not, the little scenes, bits of conversation or cameo characters that appear when I'm not expecting them to are the ones that people who have read my books seem to love the most.

Major characters surprise me, too (which is one of the things I love best about writing). For example, in my first novel, *Fairytale of New York*, Ed Steinmann was initially just meant to be a supporting cast member and a bit of a sidekick for Rosie in her florists' store, Kowalski's. But as soon as I started to write him, he assumed centre-stage and ended up becoming one of the book's major characters. Although I know I'll look like a loon for saying this, I am almost convinced that *he* decided to build up his role . . .

Which five people, living or dead, would you invite to a dinner party?
Awesome question! OK, here goes . . .

1. **Jane Austen** – she would have the inside track on everyone else at the table and would be a fantastic person to sit next to. Imagine the wry observations she'd be whispering all evening . . .

2. **Victoria Wood** – she's my hero and a massive inspiration to me as a writer. I think she would have the best stories to share at the dinner table.

3. **Jim Henson** – just because I'm such a fan. I can imagine him making napkins and cutlery talk to entertain the other guests.

4. **Albert Einstein** – I read a biography about him a couple of years ago and was fascinated by him and his life. It

would be amazing to sit with him and just listen to him speak.

5. **Russell Howard** – because he's such a positive person who clearly loves life. I think his energy would be a great addition to the dinner party – and can you imagine the conversations he would get into with Albert and Jim? Now *that's* a party I'd love to be at!

What's the strangest job you've ever had?

It's a joke among my friends that I end up with the most random jobs and, believe me, I've worked in some odd places. I once had to sing backing vocals for a Nigerian reggae gospel singer in a Nigerian accent so it fitted in with his voice. I also worked in a small industrial bag factory in a converted stable that was allegedly haunted by a ghost horse (I'm not kidding, they brought a medium in and everything). But probably the oddest job I've had (and, strangely, one of the jobs I've enjoyed the most) was a tour guide at a nuclear power station when I lived in Essex. Imagine an air stewardess' uniform with matching hard hat, ear defenders and steel toe-capped shoes – that was my uniform! It was a great job and I met so many interesting people as I took them around the site, including a team of nuclear physicists and a Dambusters pilot!

And what can you tell us about your next novel?

It's going to be fabulous! There will be rivalry, awesome tunes and maybe the odd jazz hand, all set in a gorgeous seaside location. I know you're going to love it!

Loved the book? Want to know more about the characters, read extra scenes and access bonus content to extend your *It Started With a Kiss* experience? Visit Miranda's website!

Miranda explains: 'I love it when you get a bonus features section on a DVD of a film or TV series and I thought, why not do that with a book? I've created my 'Book Extras' – soundtracks, deleted scenes, character notes, random facts about the making of the book, interviews with the lead cast members and more. You can even hear *Last First Kiss* – the song that Romily writes with Jack in Chapter 8! I hope you'll find something on my website that you'll love!'

www.miranda-dickinson.com